TEACH THE SKY 2018 SHORT STORY ANTHOLOGY

Robert V Aldrich

To MAGFest

Book Title Copyright © 2018 by Robert V Aldrich. All Rights Reserved.

All rights reserved. No part of this book may be reproduced in any form or by any electronic or mechanical means including information storage and retrieval systems, without permission in writing from the author. The only exception is by a reviewer, who may quote short excerpts in a review.

Cover designed by Noircomics94

This book is a work of fiction. Names, characters, places, and incidents either are products of the author's imagination or are used fictitiously. Any resemblance to actual persons, living or dead, events, or locales is entirely coincidental.

Robert V Aldrich
Visit my website at www.TeachTheSky.com

Printed in the United States of America

First Printing: December 2017

ISBN-13 000-0-0000000-1-2

Table of Contents

Blackhole Sun 1
Robots: Zeta Danger, part 3 22
Music as Life, part 02: 36
Rhest and the Trip Out East 51
Chip Masters, Ninja: part 4 91
Second-Hand Memories 111
Trial By Numbers 126
Block-Rockin' Beats 151
Robots: Zeta Danger, part 4 166
Carved 185
Rhest and the Long Walk 191
Rise of Team Demon 212
Chip Masters, Ninja: part 5 233
Healing Prowess 259
Inequitable 279
Music as Life, part 03 303

TEACH THE SKY 2018 SHORT STORY ANTHOLOGY

Blackhole Sun

On a Tuesday that no one expected to be important, the world learned the sun was going to turn into a black hole.

The scientific community came together as one to announce that a gravitational anomaly was building within the sun. This would intensify until a cascade of events would lead the star to a total collapse and become a black hole. All matter in the sun would contract into a ball roughly the size of the head of a pin. Long before the rest of the solar system would be drawn in, though, the Earth would freeze completely from the lack of sunlight and energy.

What was worse, the timetable for this event was a matter of days.

The world leaders initially rejected the science, but their unanimous consensus was unprecedented. Even the most ardent deniers could look into the sky and see the first signs of dwindling light. There was no escaping the inevitable, and the inevitable was close at hand.

Faced with the impending doom, world leaders immediately began to distribute 'peace capsules'. Freely available and widely distributed, the capsules offered a painless alternative: suicide. The poison would allow the populace to slip into a peaceful sleep from which they would never wake up.

Not one day after the announcement, two-thirds of the world's population was dead.

--Three Days Until The End Of The World--

"It's a warm morning waiting for all you sleepy heads just waking up," said the broadcaster coming over the hand-cranked radio. "It's supposed to be clear all day, with a possible chance of some showers in the next couple of days. Hopefully it will help cool us down before the big blast."

There was the sound of shuffling papers and the broadcaster continued in a more casual tone. "You know, I was watching an episode of Stargate last night on one of the over-the-air channels. That's all I get now because my cable died and, let's be honest, good luck getting someone to come out and fix it. So, in this episode, they dealt with a black hole. And they were caught in it because of time dilation or something. So, I wonder if we'll experience anything like that. In the episode it was like—"

Sam Young clicked off the radio. It wasn't like he was listening to it anyway.

"Why'd you turn it off?" asked Beverly Easton. Walking next to him, she wasn't protesting so much as simply curious.

Sam shrugged, as much an answer as to adjust the way his backpack fell on his shoulders. "Whenever he talks about the black hole, he gets really depressing." The pair of teens didn't say anything else, only kept walking.

Around them spread the metropolis of downtown Birmingham Alabama. The air was hot, with vapor trails wafting through the distance. Car accidents dotted the city road, with more than a few having taken their toll on the local roads and buildings. A fire was burning itself out behind one storefront window. Confederate flags had been draped and spray-painted everywhere, as had Christian symbols and other doomsayer graffiti. Some windows were smashed but for the most part, downtown of the major southern city looked fairly normal, if unsettlingly still.

"It's nice not having to be in school," said Beverly, her thumbs stuck in her backpack straps. She looked up at the city around her with a bright smile, like an ordinary high school girl out on a field trip. "I always felt like I learned more being outside the classroom than inside."

Sam realized he was staring at the girl and averted his eyes. "Yeah," he agreed out of rote habit. He tugged on the collar of his shirt that had gotten turned over as it often did. The edges and hem were threadbare, which wasn't a recent development.

"Do you like school?" Beverly asked the sophomore.

Sam just shrugged again. "I guess I did." The contrast of tenses wasn't lost on either of them. Beverly turned away, her shoulder-length brown hair falling in front of her face. Sam regretted his answer that took away her eyes and her smile. Deprived of them, he looked ahead as they arrived at an intersection. "Beverly," he gasped. She looked and gasped as well.

Hanging from the traffic lights were five black men, all strung up from nooses. Two bodies showed the signs of weather and decomposition but the other three looked so fresh, they might still be alive. They twisted slowly in the slight urban breeze.

"I can't believe it," Beverly gasped, her hands in front of her mouth. She didn't look afraid but repulsed.

Sam came to a stop. He turned his head and listened. Beverly did the same and heard distant engines. High-pitched and growing louder, the din was soon joined by the clomp of horse hooves. The two teens looked frantically about for a place to hide. They dove into a local restaurant where the lights were off and the windows covered by curtains of southern charm.

Moments later, the Klan rode into town.

Two dozen men in white cloaks and hoods came trotting through the intersection. With big horses and loud motorbikes, they all wore or carried Confederate flags. They ambled through the intersection, not lingering and certainly not hurrying. One slowed as they passed through the intersection, decelerating just enough to reach up and slap the foot of one of the lynched men. He laughed with one of his riding buddies as they kept on.

Sam and Beverly shared relieved sighs that they hadn't been noticed. Their relief was short-lived when they were startled by a noise from the back of the restaurant. Out through the storage area, an old man with a double-barrel shotgun appeared. The instant he saw the kids, though, he lifted the gun barrel and smiled a kindly grin. "Why hello," he told them. He put the gun to the side. "Come on out, Jackie. It's just some kids." Behind the old man appeared a silver-haired woman who looked cautiously into the restaurant. Seeing the two kids, she sighed with relief just as they'd done.

"Don't be afraid," the man said without approaching the two kids, like he was speaking to two fawns. "I'm Fred, this is Jackie. This is our place."

Sam glanced at Beverly, then took the lead. "I'm Sam," he said, moving between his traveling companion and these two. He glanced at the window and saw the bodies in the intersection. "When did that happen?"

Fred couldn't see out the window but knew what he meant. "Don't know," he said remorsefully. "The day of the announcement, I think. I didn't see it happen." He ventured, "I'm not sure they were alive when they got lynched. I think those bastards just lynched corpses out of spite."

"Freddie!" said Jackie, smacking her husband with a Penny Saver.

"What?" he exclaimed back. "These kids have heard worse." Their bickering comforted Beverly and Sam. "Public school kids, aren't you?" he asked, picking up his shotgun like he would a broom.

Sam and Beverly both looked at each other. "No," they collective answered.

"Oh, well, then maybe they haven't heard 'bastard' before," Fred acknowledged. Beverly hit him again, grinning at him like he did her. "You two hungry?" he asked the kids. "We got plenty of food." With giant smiles, Sam and Beverly followed them into the back.

"Seems a shame," said Fred as he sliced some turkey. Using a long knife, he cut through the delectable meat as easily as a conductor might swish a wand through the air. "I feel like I was just getting the hang of being an adult."

Sam and Beverly sat at a small table in the back of what was part kitchen and part storage room. After the southern heat of the morning, they enjoyed their backs being to the freezer. The door was slightly frosted and the air coming off it was invigorating. Jackie explained, "When the news told us the sun was going nova or black hole or whatever it is it's doing…"

"Black hole," Beverly interjected quietly, unable to let an inaccurate statement stand. She averted her eyes immediately afterwards.

"Yeah, that," Jackie smirked at the girl's impulse. "When they announced that, we thought…well, I guess we don't need to open the deli today. But then, after about ten minutes of doing nothing, Fred and me, we just decided this was our life."

She looked at the deli, in all its banality. She smiled with parental pride. "Yeah," she agreed with her husband, a tear in her eye. "Seems a shame."

"You know much about science?" asked Fred as he brought over the overstuffed sandwiches.

"Yeah," said Beverly. "I went to the state science camp two summers in a row." Fred and Jackie both looked at Sam and he just shook his head.

"Well, what's this black hole business?" asked Fred, like he was discussing an odd movie coming out that weekend.

"A black hole is a super-dense astronomical object," Beverly explained between gentle and measured bites of the generous sandwich. "They're incredibly tiny, but they have the mass of, of everything in our solar system. Or the mass of like ten, twenty, a hundred suns. All slammed down into a tiny dot about as big as a sandwich." She held up the artisanal lunch Fred had fixed for her. "The process has already started in our sun. Astronomers have found this tiny black spot on the sun. That's it." She just sort of gestured at the finality of it all. "The rest of the sun is getting sucked into the black hole, and the more of the sun that goes, the faster it will happen."

"Wouldn't we go spinning into space or something?" asked Jackie, her wrinkled face on her hand as she listened intently.

"No, because the mass has stayed the same," Beverly told her. "So the gravity will stay the same...sort of," she allowed, knowing the details were too complicated to bother with. "But whether we go spinning into space or not, the sun's light is what will go first and once it goes..." She let it linger.

"What about, like, the earth's core or something?" asked Fred.

"Geo-thermal," Sam piped up, excited he could contribute something to the discussion.

"Yeah, geo-thermometer," Fred said. "Why can't we live on that?"

"It won't last," Beverly said. "And we don't have the infrastructure to access it, either wide-spread or really even at all. It would take weeks at least to construct a single power station with the adequate insulation and life-support." Her hands in her lap and her appetite dampened, Beverly smiled sadly. "There just isn't time."

A pessimistic cloud fell over the lunch. The rattle of the air conditioning vents overhead filled in the space as the four ate and chewed.

"Do you guys listen to Raymond Silver?" asked Sam. Fred and Jackie looked at each other, then shook their heads. "He's the meteorologist for Channel 9? He's on the radio now, and online. He's still broadcasting."

"We were listening to him as we came into town," said Beverly.

"Came into town?" asked Fred. "You're not from here?"

"Tuscaloosa," said Sam with a grin. He added a little weakly, "Roll Tide."

Fred smiled, proudly. "War eagles."

Sam grinned. "Oh so that's how it's going to be?" Fred smiled as well.

"What brings you two to Birmingham?" asked Jackie. "Why are you both away from your families?"

The children fell silent. Beverly looked down at her sandwich and said nothing. She turned over her pickle spear with her fingers. "We wanted to see Vulcan," Sam chimed up, trying to give a convincing smile. "I remember coming to see it as a kid, you know?" He shrugged. "I just, just wanted to go see it again." He shrugged yet again. "Seemed like as good a time as any."

"Yeah, but what about—" Jackie pushed but Fred put his hand on her knee, subtly silencing her. Both kids kept eating in silence, neither wanting to discuss the matter further.

"Well, I'm honestly relieved," Fred said after some time. "I liked this place, but...it's not like it had turned a profit. The bank seized it last month. Some kind of imminent domain or something."

"That's not..." Beverly started to argue but it was Sam's turn to silence her with a look that reminded her it didn't matter.

"The city did it, or the bank did it on behalf of the city, I don't remember. I didn't understand it," Fred said. He laughed a stoic, melancholy rattle. "I was honestly relieved when the news announced the whole sun thing." He looked at the ceiling as the air conditioning rattled on. "I had no idea how to spend retirement." His eyes glazed over. "I spent my adulthood thinking I was still a teenager. I finally get to retirement and I feel like I'm finally an adult. I been a step behind my whole life."

Jackie took his hand and squeezed it lovingly. Sam and Beverly both stared at their held hands. Sam put his hand on the table, right between them. Beverly looked at it and smiled lightly. She looked at him and he at her. She smiled, apologetically, and didn't take his hand.

"I think we're going to take the pills soon," Fred remarked distantly. He was still facing up, like he was seeing passed the ceiling. He stroked Jackie's hand as she held his. "I don't feel like I'm in a hurry. I don't think either of us do, but I don't want to be here right at the end, you know?" Jackie nodded at her husband, proud of his acceptance. "We've got plenty if you want some." Only polite, quiet refusals followed.

A bird flew overhead, shaking the phone line from which it took flight. A single whistle followed it as it soared through the urban air. Down the empty street, the two kids walked with unhurried, meandering steps. Beverly slowed, falling behind Sam. He turned back to her. "What is it?"

She smiled and nodded ahead. Sam turned and looked. On the horizon, raising up behind the trees, was the first glimpse of Vulcan: the great iron statue of the Roman god that overlooked Birmingham. "There he is," Beverly smiled. Sam looked and nodded, not smiling but not unpleased either. Beverly resumed walking. "Why'd you tell that old couple that you wanted to go see Vulcan?" she asked the sophomore next to her. "This was my idea."

Sam shrugged, his backpack jangling when he did. "I don't know. It seemed the thing to do."

Beverly exhaled heavily as the road began to rise just slightly. Their reflection in street windows of empty sidewalk shops kept them company. "Why didn't you take the pill?" she asked randomly.

"Why didn't you?" Sam countered. Beverly fell silent, and Sam remained silent. A crack in the sky startled both kids. They looked up and saw heavy clouds swirling in. "Holy crap, I didn't even notice!" Sam exclaimed as a torrent of hot rain began to fall. The two looked around for shelter, seeing only a few distant awnings. Sam started to run for one, but Beverly caught his hand. She tugged him in the opposite direction and threw open a car door. The two kids dove into the backseat together, hiding from the pounding rain that had come seemingly out of nowhere.

"Cripes, that hurt," Sam remarked, touching the back of his neck. It stung and he looked at his clothes, seeing wafting trails of gray coming off his overshirt and jeans. Terrified, both kids looked onto the street and saw vapor billowing up.

"That's not steam," Beverly realized. "It's acid rain."

"It's what?" Sam exclaimed. He turned to Beverly, only to realize how close she was, peering out the window with him. He swallowed and focused on the world outside, against his will. "That's real?" he stammered.

"Of course it's real," Beverly said. She sat down with a sigh. "I guess a nuclear reactor went meltdown in Japan or something. Maybe a coal facility in Virginia blew up." She waved at the sky. "This is environmental damage on a catastrophic scale. Alabama saw this kind of thing in the 1950s and 1960s when the steel mills were unregulated."

"A nuclear reactor," muttered Sam in fear, staring out the window, in awe of the smoke.

"Yeah," said Beverly. "Nobody's going to work. The big, giant power factories are going to start falling apart. Probably started already. If the world wasn't going to end in two or three days, it would be a big deal." A somber moment followed.

Stoicism gave way to boredom and Sam fished out his hand-cranked radio. He wound the handle a bit while Beverly watched the rain fall. With a click, Sam gave the car life. "It's a warm morning waiting for all the listeners out there," said the announcer. "It's supposed to be clear all day, with a possible chance of some showers in the next—"

Sam shut off the radio and griped, "It's a rerun."

"Why do you keep playing that thing?" Beverly asked. Realizing how that sounded, she recanted quickly. "I mean, it's fine. It doesn't bother me or anything. I just...I was curious."

Sam put the radio away. "I think it's cool. Dude knows he's going to die, but he's still going to work. He's doing more than his share. He's broadcasting all the time, just keeping the few of us still around in the know." Beverly looked smug. "Okay, maybe not ALL the time, but you know what I mean." Her amused smile made his heart skip a beat. He turned and looked out at the fierce torrent of rain slamming on the back window. "He's probably trying to figure out this rain, see what happened to cause it. Like what nuclear reactor went up or whatever."

"I guess," was all Beverly said. She stared distantly, then glanced into the rain. Something about the poison water gushing down the window made her feel introspective. "My parents gave me the pill to take." Sam was taken by surprise by the statement, the confession. Looking at her fingers as she touched different tips together, Beverly shared, "We got everybody together the day the announcement was made. Aunts, uncles, cousins. Big family reunion." A streak of a tear came out. More than just sadness; relief to finally speak.

Beverly's chin quaked, but not from mere sadness. A complicated cocktail of emotions swirled inside her, feelings like she didn't know and had no vocabulary to express. "I was going to be a senator," she whispered. "Mom told me that since I was a baby. Senator. Maybe even governor. Maybe even preside—" She choked on the word. She grabbed her hands together, her knuckles whitening as she clinched her fists in a ball. "We'd been in the state government since, since before there was an Alabama. All the way back, and before. Mom said I would be the first to go federal."

Sam very carefully and quietly slipped his backpack off. He moved like he was afraid to make sound, afraid to disturb her. He laid the backpack on the floorboard, letting her have all the room to speak. "We all got together, like it was Christmas," Beverly remembered, relieved. "Dad tapped the glass - the good crystal – and told everyone that God had made his decision. He told everyone that..." Beverly closed her eyes tight rather than succumb. "I knew something was up when I first sat down and I saw that everybody had a butter dish in front of them, just past the plate. Dad told us to remove the lid and take the, uh, take the vitamin." Her chin quaked and her voice stammered. "He didn't want to scare the kids."

"I took the pill," Beverly sobbed. She looked at Sam. "I kept it under my tongue until..." Her face fell into her hands. "Oh god, I saw them. I just sat there while they all...while they all..." Her shoulders shook as she was bent over, crying.

Sam felt bad for noticing the back of her neck, the slight tender skin between her fallen hair and her collar. While she was crying, having bared her soul, all he could think about was her soft, vulnerable skin. Feeling like a cad, he faced away from Beverly. At a loss, he matched confession with confession. "Dad went to get my sister," he said quietly, staring into the rain. Beverly looked up, her cheeks red from her tears. "She's going to UNC. Dad took the car and told mom and me to stay put, that he'd be back." Sam looked at the floorboard. "I called him, but he...there hasn't been answer. Called Candace too but she hasn't..." He shook his head, his face a placid mask.

Beverly realized she had no monopoly on sorrow and sat up. Sniffling, she brushed her hair back and tried to make herself presentable. "What about your mom?"

Sam fixated on the floorboard. "She woke me up screaming. Throwing up. She'd taken the pill. She said she didn't mean to. She said it was just a momentary thing. She had vomit all over her fingers. She'd tried to throw it up but..." Sam shrugged defensively. "She apologized herself to sleep." He whispered with finality, "Didn't wake up."

Beverly stared at him, her heart breaking. She reached for the seat buckle, only to realize she'd never put her seatbelt on. She laughed sickly. "I've never been in a car without putting my belt on. It's always just an automatic thing."

"Yeah, me too," Sam agreed sadly.

Beverly slid across the backseat, sliding next to Sam. His heart stopped as she neared him, her face looming above his. She put an arm around his shoulders and he tilted his head up towards her, his lips moving to meet hers. Without acknowledgement or awareness, Sam didn't know which, Beverly guided his head onto her shoulder. She cradled him against her. Sam's disappointment lasted only a moment when he realized how soothing the affection was. Under the torrent of rain, they stayed close together into the night.

--Two Days Until The End Of The World--

Sam awoke atop Beverly.

His eyes went wide at the morning surprise, both that they'd shifted in their sleep and that they'd slept at all. Beverly lay on the backseat of the car, and Sam had ended up somehow mostly atop her, one leg thrown over her. He looked down at her, still asleep, and found his mind racing. He swallowed and felt compelled to lean down to her lips, needing to lean down to her. A kiss, however slight, was everything in his mind, but he stopped himself. He instead shifted off her as best he could in the cramped space.

"You know how to be quiet," Beverly said with her eyes still closed. She opened them, her lashes draping wide, and she smiled at Sam. She slid back against the door and stretched her arms. "Oh!" she groaned. Her stomach made a loud noise and she just patted it.

Sam fished out his radio and cranked it again. "I think we can find a grocery store on our way to the statue," he said. He clicked on the radio and let the announcer come through.

"—storm is clearing out, thankfully," Raymond Silver was saying. "Good thing too. As most of you probably noticed, it was acid rain. As near as I can tell, it was the result of a coal mine explosion in east Texas. Some of you on the western edge of our viewing radius may have even heard it. Details are sparse. As most of you know, the internet is largely down, but I'm trying to get what information I can. I'll certainly keep you posted. For now, though, I wanted to give you an update on the flooding in—"

"You were right," said Sam, clicking off the radio. "It was due to pollution, or whatever." He took out his cell phone and activated it. Beverly watched him hold the phone up and turn this way and that. He got enough connectivity to say, "It's 6:49." He shut off the screen. "We've got two days left."

Sam sat back down in the backseat of the car. He looked out the windows at the town outside. A morning moroseness came over him and he asked, mostly of himself, "Why are we doing this?" Confronted with the question, Beverly drew her knees to her chest and looked into the distance. "The sun's going to turn into a black hole in, like, sixty hours or something." His eyes glazed over sadly. "We're all going to die."

Beverly sniffed a tear. She wiped her cheeks with her palm and refused to give in. "We were going to die anyway," she said with shaky stoicism. She shifted and sat properly on the wide seat of the car. She faced forward, opposite Sam, like the two were on their way to the saddest school dance ever. "If we're going to die, why do anything?" What Sam mistook for a nihilistic dismissal was actually a prompt. "Just because something is inevitable doesn't mean it should be sped along." Beverly spoke in disjointed words, like her reasoning was as revelatory to herself as to Sam. "And just because something won't last doesn't mean it isn't important."

Sam looked across the spacious car at Beverly, surprised at her stance on the matter. She seemed equally surprised. "The immortality of a thing, of an event, isn't the ultimate qualifier of something's importance. And impermanency doesn't automatically render a thing unimportant." Sam faced forward again, unsure about what she'd said and feeling guilty for his own questioning. "Just because nobody will exist in three days, just because everything and everyone will be smashed into a single atom or whatever, doesn't mean that the time before that happens isn't important."

Sam asked in a quiet, humbled voice, "So what makes something important? If it isn't the lasting legacy or whatever, if it isn't...if it isn't the, the permanency of it, then what is it?"

Beverly smiled and shrugged. "I don't know. I just know this is important to me." She hedged, swallowing nervously. "To us." Sam looked at her, their eyes meeting. Tension and nervousness swelled. But so did music.

With the same befuddled look, Sam and Beverly both sat up straight and looked out the windows. They turned simultaneously to each other, confirming the other heard the organ music. "What is that?" asked Sam as they both got out. Stiff legs stretched out onto the pavement, the street steaming. Not from the pollution but the moisture burning off the hot pavement as the day's heat built rapidly. The pair began to sweat almost immediately.

Following the enigmatic religious revival music, Sam and Beverly headed down the street, shouldering their backpacks as they went. The music that was distant at first, slowly grew as they followed it with bewildered looks. The road began to curve upwards, starting the ascent up towards Red Mountain.

As they reached the end of the line of buildings, the music of hymnals became louder. Sam peaked around the brick corner, Beverly above him. They saw a crowd behind a nearby building and could hear the organ music leaking into the air. They heard a man speaking but his words were lost into the music and the distance. Sam looked at Beverly and conveyed their mutual uncertainty but also their curiosity. They stepped out into the street, approaching cautiously.

A congregation had gathered on the outside of a church. Banners and streamers and signs dotted the few hundred people. 'Repent'. 'The end is here'. 'God's judgment is upon us'. Babies to the elderly made up the group. On a car, an older man spoke to the crowd. So skinny, he looked more like a skeleton with skin except for a pronounced gut that proceeded him. Circular glasses reflected the early morning light, hiding his eyes as he spoke in an accent thick even for natives.

"Our SINS have led the lord GOD to seal off the world!" screamed the evangelist into a cheap, static-crackling bullhorn. "It is because of our UNWORTHINESS that we must all be CLEANED in the FIRES of his glorious wrath!"

A splatter hit Beverly and she jerked away. She patted her face, thinking it was sweat, only to discover she'd been splattered with blood. She looked terrified at Sam and they both checked to see where it had come from. A shirtless man ahead of them held a flail with gore lodged deep. He periodically struck himself on the back, flaying skin and muscle, sprinkling blood and matter everywhere. In fearful silence, Sam guided the terrified Beverly away.

The pair watched the crowd as they would a pit of vipers, all while moving away. They saw similar sights of self-mutilation dotting the fanatics. Cutting on the forearms. Bruises and black eyes. Bloodied knuckles. The crowd of the faithful were living on violence, subsisting on it.

Sam and Beverly began to back out. Staying quiet, they slowly departed, trying not to draw attention. They hugged a line of recently-planted trees, hoping to go unseen by the evangelist and his flock. They paused, however, when the din shifted and the cheering began.

Atop a car next to the evangelist's were two young men. Barely older than Beverly, they were shackled, tied with ropes, stripped nude, and badly beaten. Black eyes were swollen shut. Blood poured from their noses, mouths, and wounds. Amid the inane howling of their accuser, 'sodomites' came spitting out. Howls of brimstone and hate followed as the evangelist charged the two men with every crime imaginable, most of which were only imaginable. In the crowd, the people readied stones, rocks, bricks, and other implements of mob death.

Beverly gasped and covered her mouth. Sam turned her, against her will but not against her strength. He guided her on, the two walking until out of sight, and then running when they heard the bombardment begin.

Holding a spear head aloft, Vulcan stood atop a pedestal overlooking the city of Birmingham. Sam and Beverly stared up at the giant statue, taking in the majesty of it, until Beverly remarked, "I always liked his butt." Sam suddenly erupted in giggles. "What?!" she laughed. "It's, it's like, all muscle, you know." She flexed her fingers like she wanted to grab the statue's rear. "He's got a great butt." Sam was nearly convulsing, trying to keep his laughter in. "I'm just saying," she insisted. "And he's not wearing pants, just that apron thing."

"Yeah, that's some Porn Hub business happening," Sam agreed as he regained some composure.

"Like, when I was a little girl, I thought it was funny," Beverly insisted. "Now, I'm all...Uh!" She again mimed grabbing the statue of the god's behind.

Giggling again, Sam wondered into the museum, saying, "I'm getting a Coke."

The automatic sliding doors still opened, allowing Sam into the air-conditioned lobby. The air felt stagnant in the room, and hot, although noticeably cooler than the air outside. Glass shelves of memorabilia and trinkets dotted the store, as did a reception area for tours. Sam picked out a tube of caramel-covered peanuts and tore it open. He spotted a security camera and toasted it with the tube.

Beverly entered a moment later, surveying the place. "Hello?" she called pointlessly. She looked around, asking herself, "Where's the bathroom?" Sam pointed towards the far back, secluded but not hidden.

Rather than go for it, Beverly's eyes went open. "Holy crap!" She rushed to a set of statues. Replicas of Vulcan in half a dozen assorted sizes covered reinforced glass shelves. "I always wanted one of these." Sam wondered over and picked up one of the smaller ones and balked at the price. "When we were here, my family, my parents wouldn't let me get one." Beverly selected a mid-sized statue and carried it to the counter.

"You're paying?" Sam asked in surprise. "Why?"

"Because I wanted to buy one," she said, fishing out her wallet from her backpack.

"We've been stealing food this whole time," he argued.

"Food we need," she said, laying down bills. "This is a want."

Sam didn't get it but let it drop. Instead he asked, "Why didn't you parents want you to have one? Because they knew you liked his butt?"

"Things have value because they are useful," she practically quoted to him as she set the statue down on the floor. It came up to her knee. "If it isn't useful, it isn't valuable."

"Yeah, that doesn't exactly jibe with the whole 'permanency doesn't dictate something's importance'," he half-quoted to her.

"When you're being groomed for a career in politics, it's important to understand from an early age when and what to let go," she laid out for him as she pulled cash from her wallet. "The more things you have that are important to you, the more they have control over you. He who can walk away from the deal controls the deal, and things being important keeps you from being able to walk away from deals."

"He?" remarked Sam.

"He," Beverly confirmed, underscoring the nature of her parents' expectations. "Being a girl didn't absolve me of their expectations. It was just a handicap that I was expected to overcome."

"Geez," Sam said, not sure how else to respond.

After a sad silence, Beverly asked, "Watch this for me. Make sure nobody takes it," she teased as she headed for the bathroom.

While she was gone, Sam looked at the statues and then around the museum lobby in general. For some reason, his eye turned to the register. Ignoring the money Beverly had put down on the counter, he hit the release and the draw came out. A fresh drawer was waiting inside, including stacks of ones and fives as well as unopen rolls of coins. He picked up the stack of fives and looked them over. What had once been valuable was now merely a trinket, a curiosity. He turned the bills over, then returned them to the register.

He glanced again towards the camera and watched it watching him. For some reason, he found it creepier to know the camera was watching him, but with no one watching its feed.

Hot wind blew in Beverly's hair as they stood atop the statue's walkway. Staring out into the daytime, the high school junior smiled, leaning forward just a bit on the railing. She lifted her toes off the walkway and stayed elevated on her palms. Her eyes closed, she smiled, her hair blowing behind her.

Sam watched her stand, unable to keep from smiling as well. The sight of her joy, her exuberance, was more than he could handle, though. He averted his eyes. His gaze slid down from her face, down her back, to her hips. His eyes lingered there for only an instant, but long enough for Beverly to notice. She looked at him, aware of where he'd been staring. Sam swallowed and looked away from her entirely.

Night had come.

Under heavy clouds, the stars had been stolen from the pair. The car they had selected was parked under a bridge, beneath which was a sewage outlet. Water pumped by, the smell of waste and acid from the rain storm, creating a strangely sweet odor. Crickets chirped in a constant background din. Fireflies floated in the wooded distance, lighting up the night like a haunting party.

"Did you just come with me to have sex?" Beverly asked out of the blue. Sam was taken by surprise, more by a question than the question itself. In the silence of the night, her voice was quiet yet carried in the stillness like an evening breeze. Beverly tilted her head a little to see Sam's half-hidden expression, and asked further, "Are you just here hoping that I'll change my mind and sleep with you?" Sam shook his head but didn't expound. "I'm not going to have sex with you."

"I know," he nodded with a guarded expression as he fiddled with his radio. "You told me."

"And you're okay with that?" she asked, a little incredulously. He seemed surprised. She shrugged harmlessly, trying to disarm any offense her question might have caused. "You clearly want to have sex."

"Is there a reason you want to die a virgin?" he countered at her. Her eyebrow raised, challenging his assumption but he wasn't sure which one.

Rather than answer his question, she pondered her own, as if Sam was a puzzle she hadn't yet figured out. "It's just, if you want to have sex, I'm sure there are girls who would do it," she said, facing into the stream again. "Why not go find them?"

Sam faced the stream as well, listening for a moment to the coursing water and the chirp of nighttime insects. "I want to have sex," he said aloud, as if to himself. "But not just with anyone." He had to will himself to keep from looking at her. "With you."

"Why me?" she asked. He only shrugged. "Oh, gee, thanks," she teased. The second of levity made them both smile. "But I mean, really, why? Do you think I'm good at it? I know I'm pretty but there are hotter girls." Again, Sam only shrugged. "You don't know me that well, so don't tell me its love." He shrugged again, but differently, not so certain he agreed with her.

"Do I need a reason?" he asked, looking at her now. "I like you. I want to have sex with you. Does it really need to be more complicated than that?" He faced into the stream once again. Fireflies danced over the water, their flashes mirrored in the stream's surface, doubling their glow.

Beverly broached the scariest topic. "Why haven't you tried?" Her voice was lower, and courser. Fearful.

"I mean, I've asked," Sam admitted.

"You know what I mean," she ventured in a tense whisper. "While we were asleep together...or just..." She didn't move when she asked. Sam only shook his head and stayed silent. "Why not?" she asked, her voice a rasp, afraid of what his reasoning would be.

"Because that isn't sex," he told her certainly. "I mean, yeah, maybe I could cop a feel while we were asleep, but..." He again just shrugged. "I'm not sure I could take you," he told her with a complimenting smile. Even in the dark, she saw it and smiled in response. "But even if I could, that's not sex. That's rape." Saying the word felt wrong all on its own. "Even if that wasn't the worst – maybe worse than that church stoning those guys – it's still not what I want."

Silence behind a mask of flowing water and the night.

Sam's mouth curled into a smile. "Are you saying you want me to be all forceful—" Beverly smacked him on the arm, laughing at the suggestion. Sam chuckled as well.

"Shut up, perv," she teased. "No, I don't," she clarified, just for posterity's sake. With a tremble to her lip, she looked up rather than down. Despite the darkness, she could make out some texture of the sky. "Tomorrow's the day," she breathed. "I guess...I guess it's getting to me is all." Her eyes fell, as did her hope. "I don't want to die."

Sam took her hand and held it, offering all the comfort he had to give. Within the curtain of night, they fell into sleep together.

--THE FINAL DAY--

"Move, move, move!"

Beverly and Sam awoke with a start in the backseat of the sedan. They both sat up from where they'd slept to look out the rear windshield. On the street behind the small park, separating it from the low-rent neighborhood beyond, they saw three men running. Younger men, one not much older than they, they were running for their lives. Their frantic pace carried them out of insight through the tree line beyond.

"What's going on?" asked Beverly. Sam only cringed as a white-hooded figure on horseback came charging down the street. Carrying a torch and a machinegun strapped to his back, he led the charge as dozens of men ran after him. A few others on horseback, they chased after the black men, heading into the trees as well. All but one.

A solitary figure slowed and turned his horse around. The brown and white spotted horse reared its head and stomped its feet while the ghostly figure atop its saddle surveyed the parking lot. Sam knelt low, Beverly following his lead. They disappeared behind the headrests of the backseat and waited. Sam noticed the window nearest him fogging up and he covered his mouth, though it did no good.

Beverly peaked over the headrest, exposing as little as she could, and saw the rider gone. She let out a short exhale and whispered, "Let's go."

Sam checked as well and, seeing no one, grabbed up his backpack. Beverly did the same as Sam slipped out the far side of the car. Together, they rushed in the opposite direction.

The specter of inaction hung over the two kids as they walked. Periodically, Sam glanced behind them, his thumbs stuck in his backpack straps. Seeing only a lonely road, trees of a gentle neighborhood swaying in the morning breeze, he felt a sense of peace. But also unease. The movement and the noise of rustling leaves kept him on edge.

"I feel bad for not helping," Beverly regretted rhetorically.

Sam didn't engage the topic. He took out his phone and powered it on. Keeping an eye out on their surroundings, he checked the time. "We've got about eleven hours." He did some math in his head. "Last prediction I saw was that the effects would hit at, like, right at 6pm."

"The sun's turning into a black hole," said Beverly. "Why is there supposed to be this sharp end of it all? Wouldn't it take at least a minute or something? It seems like it'd take days. There'd be a lead-up. You know, the sun getting darker." As she spoke, she spotted the sun in the sky through the trees and could see the tiny black spot. "Well, I guess..."

"I don't think anybody knew-knew," Sam said as he put his phone away. "It's like Raymond Silver was saying. Maybe we won't notice. Maybe as we're pulled into the event horizon, time will slow and stuff until it's stopped entirely. We wouldn't even be aware of it. Not sure how that would work. I mean, I guess technically we could already be inside the black hole and we don't know it? And maybe never will? I don't know. That's some super-physics stuff."

"But I mean, wouldn't the sun start to get cold at a point?" Beverly reasoned as they walked, looking at the neighborhood as it gentrified around them. "I thought if the sun lost some of its mass or, not lose its mass, but..." She let the specific details take care of themselves. "It just, it wouldn't burn as hot and that would affect how much heat we got or something."

"Yeah, but you said it's not losing any mass, the mass is just changing form," said Sam. "But yeah, the amount of heat it gives off should...I don't know, change. Maybe that's what's happening at 6pm. That's when the black hole will take noticeable effect."

Beverly again struggled with her intellectual frustration. "But it's not going to be, like, boom, end of the world. It'll get super-cold and dark and stuff."

"I don't know," Sam said with a shrug and an indistinct hand gesture. "I don't think anybody does."

"We will," Beverly lamented with pride. She started to reach towards Sam's hand, to once again feel what little reassurance there was in the world, but a thought hit her. She stopped in the middle of the street and stood stock still. She began to look around with confused scrutiny.

"What's up?" asked her companion.

"I know this place," she reasoned, her thumbs stuck in her backpack straps. "What street are we on?" She walked briskly towards the nearest intersection. "Yeah," she connected. "We're near the Elders Estate." The significance of that was clearly lost on Sam. "The Elders are, like, the first family of Birmingham." Beverly smirked cynically. "At least as far as political donations go."

"Think they're ali...still home?" asked Sam as he joined her at the intersection.

"I don't know," Beverly guessed. A mischievous smile appeared. "My dad said they had really good, really expensive wine."

"Ah, one of those families," Sam realized.

"Yeah," Beverly grinned. "You ever see Zombieland?"

It made sense to him immediately. "Bill Murray's house?" Beverly smiled wider.

"Come on," Sam groaned as he held Beverly's foot. "Got it?"

"Almost," she said as she tried to pull herself over the gate. With a kick, she knocked Sam down but managed to get a secure hold on the top of the rolling gate. With surprising acrobatic flare, she pulled herself over the side of the gate and to the other side. "Beverly!" Sam exclaimed as he scrambled up. "Are you okay?"

"Yeah," she answered from the other side, a bit breathless. "I actually stuck the landing!" she relayed with a laugh. He heard steps and her voice growing distant. "Just hang on."

"Yeah," Sam said, checking his surroundings. In the nicest neighborhood he'd ever seen, he looked about. Worries of white-hooded men danced in his mind as he stood there. Fortunately, he wasn't standing there for long.

The gate began to hum and slid smoothly along the wall. Inside was a multi-acre estate with manicured grass, enough trees to constitute a grove, and a palatial three-story mansion. Beverly was walking away from the nearest of several extremely wealthy-looking cars, the gate remote in hand. "The Elders were oil barons for a while, and then kept with the times. Now they own the factories that make probably half the components on your phone." Sam inside, Beverly set the gate to closing.

"Cool," said Sam. Once the gate fell quiet, he felt a sense of safety but still more unease. He was less worried about hooded figures and more what awaited them at the end of the day. As they began towards the mansion, he asked, "Think the Elders are home?"

"I doubt it," said Beverly. "Their helicopter's gone."

Sam scoffed. "Helicopter. Geez."

"Yeah," agreed Beverly. "I thought my family was rich—"

"Your family IS rich," Sam corrected her.

"But the Elders are wealthy. Own-their-own-island wealthy. Probably where they are." She stopped before the mansion and looked up at it with growing disdain. "I never liked Mrs. Elder. I always thought she was kind of creepy." She looked at Sam with a sour expression. "She liked to buy me dresses and stuff, but always insisted I change in the room with her." Sam sneered as well. "Yeah," Beverly confirmed. "That was it, but that was enough."

"Pssh," Sam scoffed again. "Then let's go find her favorite thing and break it."

"Deal," concurred Beverly with total commitment.

The mansion was everything Sam expected a mansion to be. Polished, shiny floors. Grand stairwells. Rooms with solitary purposes that likely had been used a dozen times total. Signs of abject wealth everywhere, more reminders to the insecure than to provide the possessors any delight or even benefit.

As the pair of teens scoured the house like they were on a treasure hunt, Beverly led them into the kitchen. Here, she came to a stop as her eyes lit up. On the counter was an array of cakes, pastries, and muffins. Her eyes wide and her mouth open, she looked more pleased than she'd ever known. "I guess we're starting out looting here," Sam accepted.

"Oh my god," Beverly squealed. She grabbed a muffin off the rack and practically shoved the entire thing in her mouth. Before she'd even finished chewing it, she grabbed another and stuffed it into her mouth, moaning. "Oh my god," she groaned with delight. "This, right here," she said, pointing at her cheeks swollen with muffin. "This is probably more calories than I've ever eaten in a single day." She swallowed dryly and grabbed another muffin. She tossed it aside when she saw the apple turnovers. "Oh my god," she delighted again, eating one turnover in as few bites as humanly possible. "My mom," she told Sam who approached the food a bit more casually, "she was always worried about her little girl turning into a fattie. 'Won't look good to voters', she'd say to my dad when they thought I wasn't listening. Of course, I couldn't be too skinny. Or too muscular. I had to look like a really fit mom. That's what voters want." Another pastry disappeared down her mouth. "God, this is amazing."

Sam sliced a crude piece of cake and carried it in his hand as he headed on through the kitchen. "I think we've checked the whole house."

"We even checked the safe room," said Beverly with a full mouth and cream on her nose and lips.

"Yeah, I guess this is it," Sam realized. He checked the time on his phone and confirmed it was noon. "Six hours, give or take," he said to himself. He turned back to Beverly as she kept eating. "What do you want to do now?"

"This," she said with another turnover disappearing. "I'm good. You go..." She waved at the house. "This is me."

Sam was beyond amused when a thought came to him. "You know what I've always wanted to do?"

"Besides me?" Beverly teased.

"Well, yeah," he felt no hesitation in admitting.

Her curiosity grew genuine. "What?"

Sam punched the computer monitor.

The glass cracked and the plastic warped as Sam drew back his fist, his knuckles wrapped in a towel. He leaned into the next punch, knocking out a giant hole in the screen. With a scream, he punched it again, this time so hard that it broke the entire screen. "UGH!" he yelled at it before throwing an array of obscene gestures at it. Panting, he took a second.

"Feel better?" asked Beverly as she continued to eat a cake she carried on its platter. She hadn't even sliced it. She ate directly from the platter with a fork.

"My computer at home is SUCH crap!" he groaned with cathartic relief. "Just running Word, nothing else. New document, nothing else, and it takes three minutes just to change the font. It took five minutes just to turn on Word. You want to surf the web? Forget about it." There was a hop in his soccer-kick to the tower.

"Hold on," said Beverly. She handed her cake to Sam and rushed out. Confused, Sam stood where he'd been told. He looked at the cake and, realizing it was probably the richest red velvet cake he'd ever seen, helped himself to a bite. He nodded in impressed approval.

Beverly returned, trading the cake for a ball peen hammer. "Get to it, John Henry," she told him as she stepped back. Sam grinned and worked out a decade of computer frustrations with berserker fury.

With a pop, Sam let the bottle of champagne fizz over, spilling into the kitchen sink. "Here we go," he said, pouring the bubbling crystal liquid into a pair of genuine German beer steins. Beverly entered the kitchen with an amused look, wearing sweat pants and a tank top. Sam saw her and looked astonished. "What's this?"

"Fat pants," she said. "The most casual thing I was allowed to wear was yoga pants," she said, accepting a stein from Sam. "You know this is supposed to go in flutes, right?"

"I don't play," he quipped as the toasted. The pair sipped the champagne. Beverly immediately convulsed, barely keeping from spraying it out. Sam didn't have the control and spewed the alcohol all over the kitchen sink. "Geez, adults like this stuff?"

"Ugh," groaned Beverly, pouring it down the drain. "That's crap. Do they have any orange juice?" She went looking for some. In the refrigerator, she found an array of drinks and selected an unopened bottle of orange juice. "Don't drink your calories," she quoted. "Go to hell," she told somebody in her past.

Sam came and snagged a soda. "This stuff is bad for you," he said, popping the top. "Mom never let me have any." He took a sip and nearly threw up. "Geez, man, everything adults drink is crap."

"I think a lot of being an adult is crap," said Beverly, walking away to get more cake.

As the afternoon wore on, the first signs of dusk appearing at the edge of the sky, Sam and Beverly sat together on the couch. They looked out through the floor-to-ceiling windows of the den at the wide orchard of trees on the back of the property. The wind swayed through the leaves, causing them to bend and dance in happy serenity.

"Think the trees know what's going on?" Sam asked. He discreetly checked the time. They were down to minutes.

"I doubt it," Beverly said sadly as she opened a bottle of water. She popped a pill and drowned it. After swallowing, she settled in. "Makes me sad. All the dogs and cats, all the lemurs and horses, all the animals, everything that isn't human. They're going to die and they don't know it." She had grown emotional over the last hour but now she was tearing up. "They don't have the chance to have one last meal, to do whatever they want." She was crying now. Not an ugly, blubbering cry. Merely a stream of tears going down her placid face. "It's like, humans kind of deserve it. To be crushed in a cosmic anomaly, you know? But mice don't. Cats don't."

Desperate to change the subject, both for her sake and his own, Sam asked, "What'd you take just now? One of the suicide pills?"

"No," she said. "Some opioid my dad had at the party. I don't know what. I assume it was to help people calm down before they took the real pill." She looked at Sam and smiled. The way her eyes began to blink and her smile widened, he could tell the effects were already beginning to take effect. "You want one?" Sam only shook his head.

Beverly grew more quiet. "My tummy hurts," she whispered. Without any warning, she shifted and laid down, laying her head in Sam's lap. "I want to go to bed," she whispered. With tears, she added, "I don't want to wake up."

"I'll let you sleep," Sam promised her, stroking her hair from her face.

"Thank you," she whispered, already drifting off to sleep.

Sam was alone in the world. He looked out at the trees swaying and felt a kinship with them, just going with whatever was happening around them. No choice in the matter, and not sure they'd do something different if they had one. "Blackhole sun," he sang very quietly. "Won't you come...and wash away the rain. Blackhole sun...won't you come...won't you come..."

He laid his head back and accepted the end of the world.

His eyes closed, he waited until he heard the beep of his alarm. The time had come. The world was ended. It was all over.

Except after a moment, the alarm grew annoying.

Growing irritated that the moment of peaceful death was being ruined by the electronic din, Sam picked up his phone and hit the switch. The alarm went silent and he tossed the phone away. He leaned back and waited. Eyes closed, he waited.

And waited.

And waited.

After another few moments, he sat his head up and looked around. Everything looked the same. He looked at his hand and waved it in the air. He was surprised there were no strange effects caused by time dilation or gravity wells or some other scientific machination. He looked out at the sky beyond the mansion and it looked the same as ever. Maybe even a bit clearer. The trees were still swaying. The breeze was still blowing.

Shifting ever so carefully, Sam let Beverly sleep. He rose from the couch and walked to the window looking into the west. He saw the sun far in the sky, looking as normal as ever. No black spot. No unexplained change. It looked perfectly normal, as it had for millennia on end.

"Nothing happened," Sam realized. He glanced away. "Huh."

Robots: Zeta Danger, part 3

Sunsetter rose from behind the boulder and fired three shots. The blue blasts sliced through the air, pelting the rock face of the canyon. The blasts scorched the rocks and tore deep holes through the matter. Setter ducked down behind the rock to avoid the return fire.

Deadon stood from the small ravine he was hiding within and held out his hand. His boxy, camouflaged forearm opened on all four sides and missile compartments popped out. An entire battery of missiles shot forth in a counter-clockwise sequence. Like a swarm of angry hornets, they spun with geometric perfection at the boulder. Staying crouched, Setter dashed out from behind the rock just as the missiles reduce it to vapor. She ran sideways, her blue frame reflecting the midday sun overhead. She fired wildly with her blaster, pelting the canyon wall and Deadon alike.

Taking a hit, the Warbot screamed in pain and dropped to one knee. He covered a gaping wound in his chest, the most significant hit Setter had scored. His armored chassis had been burned away by her blaster, his inner servos and mechanics exposed. He gasped in agony at the sight of his inner workings. He looked towards Setter as she ran towards him.

Forgoing her blaster, Setter sliced at Deadon with a sword. The blade slashed easily through the air. Thanks to a terrified dodge, the slash took off only a piece of the antennae on the left side of Deadon's head. He fell back into the ravine and kicked Setter's feet. His massive, blocky leg slammed hard into her nimble shin and she fell straight down. Deadon rolled at Setter, elbowing her in the back of the head with a loud clang of metal hitting metal. Driving Setter's face into the dusty ground of the canyon, Deadon leapt to his feet.

Hobbling away, Deadon tried to get through the narrow pass of the canyon. He stumbled through the tiny gap, only to get caught when his chest proved too wide to get through. The Warbot checked on Setter, seeing her shaking off the disorientation of his elbow. Deadon gasped in hysterical fear and pushed harder. "Come on, come on!" he yelled at his body. Seeing Setter getting to her feet, Deadon held up his left arm. His hand retracted inside his forearm and a short blade of pure energy formed. Deadon clamped his eyes shut and lobbed off the very front of his chest, affording him just enough room to slide through.

The Warbot fell onto the far side of the canyon and screamed in pain. He rolled onto his back, howling as his inner workings sputtered and sparked at the loss of still more of the forward chassis. Deadon gasped frantically for a moment, then willed himself up. Through the rocky gap, he could see no sign of his pursuer. He gasped again and scrambled to his feet. He started to run, only to hear rotors. He looked up and saw Setter in flier mode passing over the canyon. Deadon stared for only a second, then the violent instincts of the Warbot took over. He leapt forward and reconfigured into his vehicle mode. A small, mobile tank with a giant gun and a missile emplacement on the left side, Deadon lifted his barrel into the sky. "Die!" he screamed before pulling off a shot. The powerful blast blew away dust and rocked the whole canyon. The red energy shell passed just beneath Setter and she reconfigured into robot mode.

Setter dropped out of the air and fired two blasts. The first hit the ground before Deadon but the second struck him right beneath the barrel. The pain shocked him and he reconfigured abruptly with a shout, returning to robot mode. In the instant he was reconfiguring, Setter did the same. She dropped forward into vehicle mode, this time her third form, that of a car. With the squeal of her wheels, she shot forward at Deadon. The Warbot only realized he was being charged in time to spew profanity.

Setter reconfigured at full speed and leapt at Deadon. Punching him at sixty kilometers an hour, she knocked him back against the gap he'd just pierced his way through. She slammed into the wall of stone as well and was momentarily disoriented.

Deadon recovered first and punched Setter in the back, then kicked her in the same spot. Slamming her head into the rock, he tried to elbow her in the neck but she struck him first in the exposed chest. Deadon screamed in pain and fell to the ground, clutching his chest.

Setter turned to the Warbot and lowered her blaster at his face. "Surrender, Rebel," she told him, panting through grinding teeth. In too much pain to speak, he shook his head. He tried to raise his right hand, the missile ports opening but Setter stepped on his elbow to pin his arm to the ground. She put the barrel of her blaster to his temple. "Surrender," she repeated, adding, "This is your last chance."

Terror filled Deadon's eyes and terror fueled strength. With a sudden roll, he threw Setter off his arm. She stumbled and as he rose, he kicked straight back and caught her in the stomach. The mighty kick knocked her into the canyon wall. Not waiting to see how successful he'd been, Deadon reconfigured again into tank mode. He didn't turn but raced forward at the highest speed he could manage.

Knowing his tank mode was no match for either of her vehicle modes, Deadon drove on. He turned his turret back around and began to fire madly into the canyon he was now escaping. Aim sacrificed for fury, he unloaded everything he had. As his treads kicked up dirt and dust, red blasts from his turret tore into the canyon wall. Whole sections of stone and rock collapsed, sending up a cloud of dust that enveloped his own trail.

Deadon turned around just in time to see a thick ravine approaching. Deep but not too narrow, he kept pushing towards it. Just before reaching the deep chasm, he engaged his hover jets. The tank lifted off the ground only a few centimeters but flew at equal height right over the crack in the world. Halfway across, he turned his turret again.

Out from the cloud came racing Setter. In her vehicle mode, her wheels spun with dust still clinging to them like four vertical tornados. The roar of her engine echoed in the mouth of the canyon as she shot like a bullet right for Deadon. The instant Deadon finished crossing the ravine, he fired.

The timing was perfect. Setter was only beginning to reconfigure, shifting from land vehicle to flier when Deadon's shot hit. Striking the inner side of the ravine, Deadon's blast took out a huge chunk of rock. The ground beneath Setter's wheels crumbled beneath her and the dual-rotored flier succumbed to gravity.

Deadon reconfigured and rushed back to the edge of the ravine. He checked down into the darkness, able to see the rocks falling into darkness. He gasped frantically, still in pain, as he looked around for options. Seeing nothing nearby, and only the canyon mouth so far away, he panicked. At a loss for any other ideas, he opened his missile compartments again and fired more shots. The missile swarm spread across the ravine, taking out more and more chunks of rock, falling until they plugged a whole section of the ravine.

Deadon panted for a second, then wiped dust from his face. He looked about, knowing in his robotic soul Setter wasn't gone. He glanced at the sun, then turned and faced deeper into the Western Expanse. Clutching his exposed chest, he staggered into a jog, heading into the desert.

Through heat trails on the shifting horizon, Deadon saw a mirage. He stumbled to a halt, instinctively clutching his exposed chest. He teetered under the burning heat of the sun and stared. Edging out of sight as the far distance churned and rolled like a snake boiling from inside, Deadon saw something. He wasn't sure what, but it was better than the pale, beige nothing in every other direction.

He began to stagger towards the shifting shape, unsure what he was seeing or even if he was seeing. Afraid the heat was shorting out his optic sensors, he surrendered to the delusion of finding anything and stumbled forward.

The flickering shape gained consistency. Then length. Then size. Then it's true form revealed itself.

Deadon stumbled into a small town.

Built beneath a giant dome, the town was half-submerged and entirely covered by the dome. Shaped and colored to look like the desert all around it, the entire complex was almost hidden from scrutiny. Once he realized there was civilization, Deadon raced towards the shade. He was desperate, to escape the heat if nothing else.

The Warbot reached the edge of the town and fell inside. Through the narrow gap between the overhead cover and the surface of the desert, Deadon tumbled down. He landed on caked sand that had been blown inside by the desert winds. On his back, he laughed deliriously as his metal body groaned and ached, the heat dissipating painfully. Deadon laughed for a long time at his good fortune, even as he was pained into immobility.

When his body cooled enough that his joints ceased groaning, he finally sat up. Around him had gathered an entire community of strange-looking bots. Slender, narrow bots like he'd never seen stared cautiously. Gathered in a semi-circle around him, they watched the stranger. Narrow eyes of desert dwellers fixed down on him with distrust and caution, but not aggression.

Deadon sat up, causing some of the locals to back away from him with a murmur of accented whispers. "Where am I?" he asked. Some of the bots looked at one another but they said nothing, the majority still staring. "Do you speak Common?" he asked, a little breathless, his body still scalding hot. He repeated his question in several different languages.

"We speak Common," came an answer from behind the crowd. The bots parted for another bot not unlike Deadon to approach. He was a broad bot, built like a tank or a cargo hauler. He had small wings on his shoulders and a heavy helmet of a head that showed the carbon scarring of battle. Massive arms and a body thicker than some ship armor came over Deadon, dwarfing him in almost every manner. "Who are you?" asked the massive, powerful bot.

Deadon knew a battle veteran when he saw one. "My name's Deadon." He decided against standing.

"The Warbot," said the warrior. He sniffed in disapproval. Deadon said and did nothing. "You're a Rebel."

Deadon looked to the worried crowd. "I'm a Rebel," he confirmed cautiously. In his HUD, he began cycling through his weapons, ready to fight if it came to it. It looked about to come to it.

"We've withdrawn from the fighting, and the Central Authority," said the broad-shouldered bot standing over him and looking down on him.

"Who's we?" Deadon asked with a careful glance at the crowd. Returning war-weary eyes to the big bot before him, he smirked. "And who are you?"

"Obelisk," said the thick bot.

The name clicked in Deadon's head and he chuckled. "I heard of you." He began to sit up, unafraid now that he had a name and an identity to put to the bot. "The CenA escort bot." When Deadon stood, he was still a head shorter than Obelisk. "I heard you went down with the Vimana."

"I did. I died that day," Obelisk confirmed without hesitation. "I decided to stay dead."

Deadon smiled, more in stunned shock than humor. He looked at the skinny bots that still watched the pair. "What is this, some kind of...of peace commune?"

"More or less," nodded Obelisk. "And we don't allow the Rebels or the Central Authority."

Deadon looked challengingly at Obelisk. "Well, I'd say that makes your list of friends real short."

"Longer than you'd think," Obelisk warned him. "And we haven't had to call in any favors in a long time. We keep to ourselves and let others handle their business. We don't bother and we expect not to be bothered."

Deadon nodded sourly. He looked at the timid faces of the narrow bots. "And I'm bothering you."

Obelisk nodded. "And you're bothering us."

Deadon's bravado waned some. "Look, I don't want any trouble," he said in a hushed tone, barely even audible to Obelisk. "And I don't want to bring any trouble. I don't know what you've heard about the Warbots, but..." He considered his comrades and decided it wasn't worth talking further. "I'm fine with what you people are doing here. Like you said, you don't bother anybody. But I got a hunter on me."

"We figured," said Obelisk, glancing down at Deadon's chest.

"Just let me stay long enough to fix my wounds," Deadon nearly pled. "Just give me two days. Let me cool off, get this fixed, and I'm gone." He added, "I'm gone and I've forgotten everything I saw. When I return to my team, when I return to the Rebels, and they want a report, this town doesn't exist." Obelisk hedged. He considered the bad shape of the bot. Deadon mouthed pathetically, 'please'.

The town's defender took a slow, deep breath. He finally said, "You got a day. But we'll help repair you, then you get on your way. No matter your state, though, you leave tomorrow at sundown. Got it?"

Deadon gasped in relief. "Oh geez, yeah, thank you. Thank you!"

Obelisk turned like he already regretted his mercy. "Let's get him a room and some materials." He began to walk away, taking a slow glance behind at Deadon, reminding the Warbot that he was being watched. Deadon's relief was tempered with worry.

With a loud crash, a pile of scrap was dropped onto the ground.

In the small hut no bigger than a single room, Deadon began to immediately sift through the materials. "This is all we could find," said the slender bot that had dropped off the hodgepodge of materials. "Everything else is made of ceramic."

Deadon looked up from where he sat on the floor. "You guys are ceramic?" he asked the bot. The young male bot was white with gray highlights. He had a narrow abdomen and a slender but sturdy thorax. He was all curves and smooth edges, totally opposite Deadon's boxy frame. "What do you reconfigure into?"

Answering his second question first, the bot bent backwards and shifted forms. His arms opened, becoming closer in size to his legs. His abdomen folded open, revealing solar plates. "You're a collector," gawked Deadon. "That's...that's...cool," he laughed.

"It makes us fairly self-sufficient," the bot told him before shifting back into bipedal mode. "What other energy we need we either supply communally or we get from the solar and wind collectors of the shield."

Deadon looked at the ceiling of the hut, as if he could see beyond it at the slightly concave ceiling that covered, sheltered, and protected the town. "That thing's a collector too?" He laughed again at the ingenuity of the place, equally impressed and delighted.

"And yeah, we're ceramic," said the young bot. "Most of us. Some, like Obelisk, are metal."

"You got other strays you took in?" Deadon asked, going back to the scrap. He gave up for a second. "What's your name, anyway?"

"I'm called Solaris," he said.

Deadon snickered. "Of course you are," he said under his breath.

"What?" asked Solaris defensively.

"Just...the bot tradition of really obvious names," Deadon told him. "I think it's kind of classist, myself." On his soapbox, he couldn't stop. "I'm named Deadon. You think I can be a mechanic? You think I can be a governor or something? No. I'm a soldier." He scoffed. "I think half the reason we have these wars is because most of us are made for war. Made, named, and disposed to it."

Solaris lingered. "You don't sound like a Warbot," he said, squatting down to sit across the scrap pile.

"How many of us have you known?" Deadon asked him. The boy drew back self-consciously. Deadon nodded, used to such assumptions. He resumed searching through the junk. "Eastbound's like me. Well, not like me, but he's...he's not as bad as Parker or Skyfall. Or Warhorse." He said that last name with exclamation. He picked up a piece of metal and held it to his chest. He winced at the contact, then decided, "I think that'll do." He tossed the metal piece to the side for later. "It ain't got to be pretty. Just get me to civilization."

"We are civilization," asserted Solaris. "We don't fight."

"Refusal to fight isn't the same thing as being civilized, kid," said Deadon as he kept looking through the scrap. "Nonviolence and wisdom aren't the same thing." A tube in his hand, he slowed. "However related they may often be," he said to himself.

Solaris cut right to the intellectual chase. "Do you want to fight?"

"No," answered Deadon simply and without hesitation. "Regrettably, I'm very good at it. And I enjoy it a lot."

"You don't want to do a thing that you're good at, that you enjoy?" Solaris asked him.

Deadon put down the tubing. "When it's one-on-one, kid? Sure. When I'm there and they're there, and we know why we're there, and it's on the up-and-up and we're both ready for it and we're both in for it? Absolutely. Best thing in the world." His eyes grew distant. "But when they don't expect it..." His tone drifted a little. "When they aren't fighters?"

He recovered himself mentally. "The CenA didn't listen to us," he told the veritable child. "We said things had to change. They said committee. They said review. They said..." He snickered, as if at himself for some gullibility. "They said patience." He looked right at Solaris. "Change shouldn't require patience. Not if it NEEDS to happen."

Solaris was quiet. His slender arms wrapped around his legs as he listened, he too stared off. "I guess I never thought about it like that. I always assumed that people who fought did it for bad reasons. Violence always comes from bad things, because violence is bad."

"Violence is bad, kid," Deadon agreed. "But violence can come from very good things." He regretted aloud, "I don't think there's anything that can't come to violence."

"But violence doesn't solve anything," Solaris said.

Deadon only said, "You'd be surprised." He decided the tube was worthwhile. "Thanks for the stuff, kid. You guys got a mechanic?" he asked of the town.

"Just a sculptor," he apologized. "We might be able to get you some ceramic parts. I wonder if they'd fit?"

"This metal'll be fine," Deadon assured him. He picked up the piece he'd selected and held it over his chest wound. He began to model it sarcastically, the flat gray contrasting with his camouflage body. "What do you think?"

"Very stylish," Solaris said with equal sarcasm. Deadon laughed, as did Solaris.

With the dawn came hot winds through the gap running the circumference of the town. Deadon stepped out from his hut, the drape of cloth barely a door on the clay hut. His chest itched terribly where he'd welded the piece of metal over his armor. The patch job was ugly but it protected his inner workings. As he exited, he saw Obelisk walking by. "Hey, big man," Deadon said, rushing to keep in step with the bot. "Is there any way to get some energy? I'm starving."

Obelisk looked back in annoyance at Deadon but reconciled it was a reasonable request. "Yeah, we've got a communal account. I'll get you some charges in a bit, but I'm busy right now." He kept walking. Urgency to go the other way crept into Deadon's mind but instead he followed Obelisk, reaching the edge of a crowd of the locals.

Deadon felt a rush of déjà vu as well as disorientation, being on the opposite side of the on-looking crowd as he had been the day before. Paranoia struck him as he asked, "What's going on?" Obelisk didn't offer any response. He walked right into the crowd, the fragile-by-comparison bots moving out of his way. Deadon spotted Solaris. The boy glanced at him and the two shared worried looks. "What's going on?" Deadon whispered, coming over to Solaris.

Solaris whispered back, not to be heard over the murmurs of others. "You aren't the only stranger that rolled into town."

Deadon came to an abrupt stop. His optics turned and he looked through the crowd. Obelisk shifted as he spoke to the stranger and Deadon saw who it was. Solaris turned to him, worried. "What's wrong?"

Deadon looked terrified. "That's the hunter that was after me."

The nervous bots stood around Sunsetter.

She was collapsed on the ground just as Deadon had been the previous day. Banged up and passed out, she showed the wear of her fall and well as the abuse of the fights leading to it. The heat damage had affected her worse than it had Deadon; the blue of her chassis faded and the silver highlights darkened by exposure. She looked like total system failure wasn't out of the question.

Obelisk clicked his mouth and sighed at this unprecedented yet familiar development. He turned around and found Deadon. The Warbot returned the look, confirming who this was laying before Obelisk. "She's Central Authority," Obelisk said aloud to no one but so everyone could hear. He said with regret, "We have to help her."

"Do we?" Deadon asked with a scoff.

Obelisk turned away. "We helped you."

"She's metal and she's hurt badly," said one bot, touching Setter's shoulder. He withdrew his hand quickly from the scalding heat. The unconscious bot shifted protectively at the mere touch.

"We can't help her," said Solaris. "We don't have this kind of engineering. I'm not sure we even have the parts."

Deadon looked down on Setter, her eyes closed. "You've got the parts." He was whispering, speaking unwillingly. Obelisk turned back to him once again. "And you've got the engineering."

The big bot looked surprised by the insinuation. "I don't," he insisted.

"Not you," Deadon clarified, unable to look away from Setter. He circled a finger at the town. "We."

Setter exhaled slowly and her eyes opened. Robotic sensor pegs like lashes fluttered with the movement and she saw the hut's ceiling above her. The ceiling and Deadon. She immediately began to move but found herself immobilized.

"Uh-huh," Deadon said with a wry, angry smirk. "Yeah, I knew the first thing you'd do is go for that blaster." He wiped his hands with a buffing cloth, removing thick, caked grease. "Don't bother. I've paralyzed you for the moment." The Warbot rose from the seat next to the table upon which Setter rested.

Nearby, Solaris looked on, surprised at Deadon's admission. "You paralyzed her?!" he exclaimed.

The ceramic bot's presence surprised Setter but his protest didn't bother Deadon. "I just impinged the signals to the limbs. It's little more than a snip. Her internal repairs will fix it in an hour and I can fix it in thirty seconds." He tossed the rag away spitefully – spiteful at himself – and returned to Setter's side, looking down angrily at her. "And I'm inclined to fix it."

Despite his words clashing with his tone, Setter realized the situation was less dangerous and more dire than she realized. She began to quickly look around at her surroundings. "Where am I?"

"That's...that's not important right now," Deadon told her.

"We should get Obelisk," Solaris said.

"Not yet," Deadon told the boy as he focused on Setter. He advised Solaris, "Sit down."

"But he should be here."

"Sit down."

"But he should be—"

"Sit. Down." Deadon's tone left no room for discussion. Solaris swallowed fearfully and lowered to the seat.

Deadon returned a hateful gaze down on Setter, his stare bordering on murderous. "Intimidating the young, I see," Setter sarcastically praised the Warbot, wiggling to try and will her paralysis to end.

"Why are you after me?" Deadon asked. His words were less of an interrogation and more a plea. "Why does the Authority...why hire a hunter to come after me?"

"I'm after all the Warbots," Setter told him. "You were just next on my list."

"But why come after us?" Deadon queried, like the act made no sense.

"Because you're Rebels," she told him clearly and defiantly. "Because you're the Warbots. Because you're terrorists. Because you're seditionists. Because you're traitors."

Deadon backed away from Setter. "We're not traitors," he insisted weakly, knowing it would do no good. For his own peace of mind, he defended, "We're patriots." He looked at Solaris. "We believe in a better world." His gaze was apologetic but Solaris clearly didn't know what to think.

Deadon looked down at Setter again, a conflicted look in his eyes. "You can have a meritocracy, or you can have uniformity. Those who want uniformity are simply those without merit." He paced away from Setter, even turning his back to her. Setter tried to shift her arm at all but found her limbs still immovable. "But then I guess who decides merit, or who gets the chance to show merit, that's complicated." Deadon went and sat in a seat like Solaris', only for it to break beneath him. He hit the ground hard and scrambled up. "Um, I'll...crap, I'm sorry. I'll...I'll fix that," he told the boy.

Setter returned his attention to her, saying, "I'm not going to debate politics with you. I don't care. I'm hired to find you and bring you in. That's what I'm going to do." Deadon sighed and turned away again, conflicted. He ran his hands over his blocky head. "I want to do it peaceably," she told him from behind. "But I don't have a problem fighting you. And I'll go through you if needs be. I get paid less if I just return your body but I still get paid." Deadon looked over his boxy, giant shoulder at her. "I'll also go through anyone else I have to."

Deadon turned slowly, a grave look on his face. "That was unnecessary. Don't threaten this place."

"It wasn't a threat," she claimed. "But the truth – the ugly truth – is that so long as you are here, this place will be in danger, as will those who reside within it. Kill me," she all but challenged, "and the Authority will send another hunter. But if I die, they'll know they need to send someone considerably more remorseless than me. And remorseless and cruel are very closely aligned."

Deadon weighed her comments with a despondent, hopeless look. He looked at Solaris and his dread. He gestured to the exit, telling the young bot, "Let's find Obelisk."

Beneath the shadow of the town's cover worked the ceramic bots. The non-metallic types built and maintained an array of communal projects. Condensers free-standing solar collectors, wind turbines, they were all readied for use. Among the worlıday going on around them, Deadon and Solaris spoke in quiet tones with Obelisk. The giant bot stood with his thick arms crossed, not liking what he was hearing. "She said more bots will come after her," Solaris reported. "She said they'll be crueler."

Obelisk only turned his gaze to Deadon for confirmation, getting it with a curt nod. "Not in so many words, but that's not wrong. Nor is she exaggerating," said the Warbot. "My dislike for the CenA, all politics aside, they are thorough. They will send more."

Obelisk stared, unmoving. "You knew this was coming." Neither accusation or statement, it was a supposition.

"I think I did," Deadon nodded with cynical confidence. His eyes trailed off, as did his tone. "I guess maybe I just hoped it wouldn't."

"What should we do with her?" Obelisk asked the rebel, like it was a quiz.

Deadon's eyes slid into the middle distance and he sighed. "There's only one thing to do."

In the hut, Setter tried to get her arm moving. Her legs had some responsiveness but her control was unreliable. Her thick limbs more spasmed and jerked than moved with their normal agility. Her left arm, too, would twitch and jerk but not exactly obey her commands. Her right arm, sitting next to her blaster, was still frustratingly motionless.

Deadon returned to the hut. He walked right inside, right beside the table, and put his fist right against Setter's face. The missile placements on his forearm popped opened and the small explosives aimed right into her eyes. "I want you to remember this," Deadon whispered with deadly earnest. Setter stared defiantly and unflinchingly passed her death and up at him. "I want you to remember how this looks, how this feels." Setter's eyes slid to the missiles and was aware of the absolute certainty of death just a single command away. "With everything that I am, I want to kill you right here, right now."

The missile pods retracted.

Deadon dropped his arm. He backed away from Setter, who was more confused than anything else. He shook his head and metallic tears grew in his eyes. He backed away to the wall and glared at her. "This place..." he whispered with soggy words. "You never saw it," he insisted. "You didn't see it, you don't know that it exists. You found me in a canyon in the middle of the desert and I surrendered. Deal?" His voice cracked when he asked.

Setter hesitated. She twitched her right hand, wondering if she could grab her blaster. Her thumb moved but not easily.

"DEAL?!" Deadon screamed suddenly. The missile compartments sprouted from his arm as he nearly punched Setter with his rage.

She slowly, calmly, turned her eyes up at him. He stood over her, ready to shoot sixteen missiles into her face. She countered by patiently tapping her gun against his inner thigh, poised to blow his leg clean off. He glanced down at the weapon but didn't backdown from his demand. His hand at her head, he tightened his fist.

She told him, "Deal."

Deadon sat on the rock in the middle of the desert, fixated at nothing. His elbows on his knees, his hands hanging loosely together, he just gazed in defeat. The sun overhead beat down on him and his temperature was raising but he didn't seem to care, or even notice.

Setter approached him, keeping a careful eye on her quarry. She checked back the way they'd come, where the commune's dome was little more than an unremarkable rise in the horizon. Setter saw movement approach from the distance. Slowly, the ceramic form of Solaris appeared, but he kept his distance, remaining little more than a discoloration in the heat trails. Setter neither acknowledged him or revealed him.

"It's been a long time since a place felt like home," Deadon said quietly, staring into the gaping desert ahead. "I'm so sick of fighting. I believe in the cause but..." He shook his head. "The other Warbots hate me because I want out." He absently thumbed back to the tank barrel that extended off his back. "I'd get rid of that thing if I could. Become a tractor."

"You really think you could do that?" Setter asked.

Deadon shook his head subtly. "I'd like to see if I could." He and Setter both turned when the long silver train appeared in the distance.

Iron Horse slid along the hot desert ground, shimmying under the dust as he arrived before the two. "Hey there," his deep voice called from within the long train. "How you doing, Sunsetter?"

Deadon smirked with much-welcome levity. He turned and looked slyly at the hunter. "Sun...Sunsetter? That's your full name?"

"Shut up," she jabbed at him. She removed her blaster. "Time to go."

Deadon stayed seated. He shook his head, his hands still hanging loosely off his knees. "No."

Setter put the barrel to his head. "We had a deal."

"We did," he acknowledged, unafraid of her or her weapon. "We do," he assured her with all the honesty he knew. "But I'm not going willingly. You want me on that train, you're going to have to make me."

Setter's hand hesitated. She glanced into the far distance, just barely able to see Solaris watching. She looked down at Deadon as he sat on the rock, unmoving and unwilling but also unresisting. Setter put away the blaster. She grabbed Deadon's arm and pulled. He remained seated, even as she tugged him. With his arm out, she was able to get a better hold and, with improving leverage, she forced him up. He didn't do anything but fight to stay seated. Setter practically scooped under his arm and had to hip-toss him into range of the train.

As Deadon stumbled forward at the train, its side door opened and a spray of tentacles came out. Restraints slapped around Deadon's wrists and ankles, his neck and waist. Powerful actuators and movers within his metal body flexed and Deadon resisted. He stared over his shoulder right at Setter, his mouth twisting in hate. Then his eyes slipped off and he spotted Solaris in the far distance. Setter looked back as well, regretting Deadon noticing. The Warbot surrendered entirely. He went limp and Iron Horse yanked himself without further struggle.

Once the heavy door shut, Iron Horse whistled. "Shoo-wee, he's a fighter. How'd you get him to surrender?"

Setter watched Solaris slowly turn and, his head hung low, walk back to the commune. It wasn't but a moment before he disappeared into the heat trails. Setter's head hung low when she answered, with shame, "By being the bad guy."

Music as Life, part 02:
I Want to Be Sedated

Jie Wong flipped through the records. His fingers danced over the aged cardboard sleeves as he glanced down at the pastel, artistic covers beneath him. Kneeling on the far side of the attic full of music, Jie blinked to see through the dusty, mote-filled air. The records were only part of a wide collection that included CDs, cassettes, 8-tracks, mini-discs, and sheet music.

"Find something?" asked Morgan Brandywyne as he ascended the narrow stairs into the attic. He carried a pair of frosty water bottles, the stubby necks between his fingers.

"I believe so," said Jie in a moderate Mandarin accent. The small Asian man pulled from a blue milk crate a record of 'Pictures at an Exhibition'. "I'm surprised to find such a copy."

"Yeah, it's pretty rare," Morgan observed, trading the record for a bottle of water. The taller white man took the sleeve over to the elaborate stereo system. Set into the shelves next to the stairs that led down to his home, the system held a player for virtually every form of music media. Tall but not huge, Morgan was physical imposing which contrasted with the delicate care he took removing the record from the sleeve. Opposite him, the slight Jie sat in the nearer of the two padded seats, opening the bottle of water. "It's just refilled tap water," Morgan told him as he started the record.

Leaving the sleeve atop the stereo case, Morgan sat in the opposite chair and let the music begin. He had some water himself, the attic a bit stuffy from the heat of the late spring day. "Is it good to have records in this heat?" asked Jie.

Morgan shrugged. "I don't have the A/C on right now. Once it's on, this place can actually get kind of chilly." He looked at the sloped roof over his head. "It's pretty well insulated. Me and a friend took care of that as soon as I bought the place." Jie nodded inconsequentially, appraising the mostly finished but still raw-looking attic. Morgan listened to the horn section at the opening of the record and glanced across at Jie. The academic man sat in the chair, listening placidly to the music, his fingers dancing a bit to the melody. He glanced out of the corner of his eye at Morgan and saw him watching.

"I've always loved classical," Jie told him, as if preempting the coming question. Morgan just nodded. "In China, my family, we lived in the far west when I was young. I listen to classical music all day. Walk to school. Come home. After my homework is done, I play on the piano." He closed his eyes and danced with his hand to the music.

"Interesting that you'd choose a Russian composer like Mussorgsky," Morgan remarked as he studied Jie, specifically his hand movement.

"China borders Russia," Jie told him. "I grew up in Urumqi, which is not far from the Russian border. Much of Russia influenced our land historically." Morgan only nodded, watching Jie and listening to him more than he heard him. "This is the music of my people," Jie said, his fingers drifting through the air.

Morgan nodded and then asked, "What's your music?" Jie's hand stopped as he looked at Morgan, confused. "This is your people's music," Morgan said, nodding at the record, at the music in the air. "What's YOUR music?"

Jie shook his head. "I don't understand."

"This class," Morgan told Jie, gesturing at the two of them in their seats, "is about discovering yourself through music. It's about figuring out where music fits into your life." Jie nodded, still not quite following. "I appreciate that this is culturally significant to you," said Morgan, again acknowledging the music that played on the stereo, "but I want to know about what music is personally significant to you."

"I play classical music since I'm a child," Jie tried to explain.

"But I'm betting you didn't just listen to classical," Morgan countered. "You say you listened to this going to school, coming home from school, after school," he recounted, getting a confirming nod from Jie. Morgan began to smile a bit as he shook his head. "I bet by the time you were a teenager, you hated it."

"When I was a teenager, I fled China," Jie told him, his tone not changing but his accent intensifying. "Tiananmen Square." He stated the name and needed to say no more. "My father, he's terrified that revolution has come. He's afraid that Russia will invade. With the loss of the Berlin Wall, he's afraid Russia is going to look east instead of west. Unrest is everywhere, or it seems that way. My father sneaks us into Tajikistan and we get to Pakistan, and then into India. From there, we go to Great Britain, and then we come to America. I spent half a year fleeing."

"When we get here," Jie continued, "my father – a doctor – becomes taxi driver for a year. Nurse after that. It takes him a decade to get his medical license in America. My mother, a pianist, can get no work except as tutor for local children." Morgan just listened. "I cling to this," he told Morgan, gesturing at the music. "This is home."

Morgan let the topic drop. He didn't push the matter and, instead, they talked about the melodies and pacing of the pianist prodigy's favorite piece. But all the while, he watched Jie with suspicion.

Jie Wong parked his tiny, two-door car on the street outside his townhouse. He ignored the garage on the first level where his wife's car was parked. He headed up through the front door that was double-locked. Inside, he was greeted with the scent of baked chicken and vegetables. The white house with sparse decorations felt more than clean. It felt sterile.

"Mei?" he called as he took off his suit jacket. He went towards the back of the narrow, two-story townhome where his wife was in the modest kitchen. "It smells nice," he told her.

"<Thank you,>" she remarked absently in Mandarin, stirring the boiled vegetables. She undid her apron and said, "<It'll be ready in a minute,>" as she set about checking the chicken in the stove.

Jie left her in the kitchen and headed upstairs to their bedroom. It was every bit as spacious and sterile as the rest of the house. Clear of distractions and only the most basic and fashionable of decorations, it was pristine as a photograph. Jie looked at the heavy comforter on the bed and felt strangely troubled by its dark purple color. He turned to the sliding closet doors with their mirror surface. He looked at his reflection as he undid his shirt and tugged off the tank top underneath.

Over his right chest was an anarchist symbol sloppily tattooed into his skin.

Jie pulled on a heavy cream-colored T-shirt, covering the antiquated tattoo. He changed into jeans and pulled on slippers before returning downstairs for their sensible dinner.

***

As the class bell rang, Jie looked back at the wall clock, surprised the class had passed so quickly. "Test tomorrow," he announced to his class that was already packing up their bags. Forty students filed out of his classroom meant for twenty-five and pushed into the already choked hall beyond. Jie put his papers into his briefcase and buttoned the top two buttons on his suit as Mrs. Caker pushed her cart in through the door. "Crazy day today," said the old woman as she rumbled her projector towards the front of Jie's classroom.

"It always is," he told her with a smile and a polite laugh. He didn't even look her in the eye as he headed for the door.

He reached the hallway as students rushed by. Jie checked his watch and contemplated his hunger at the start of his lunch break. He began to push out into the crowd until a familiar sight caught the corner of his eye. He turned and looked but couldn't see what had grabbed his attention.

Turning to the left instead of the usual right towards the teachers' lounge, Jie chased vaguely after what he was sure he'd seen. He darted ahead of several students. Amid the clatter of steps and the din of conversations, he finally reached the far end of the school's main building. Not sure what he'd seen, he turned around, troubled.

As he turned, he spotted a student just a few steps back. A young black boy with headphones in his ears, he wore a cut-up Ramones T-shirt with the sleeves missing. He glanced at Jie as he kept walking by, leaving the teacher haunted.

Jie Wong parked his tiny, two-door car on the street outside his townhouse. He ignored the garage on the first level where his wife's car was parked. He headed up through the front door that was double-locked. Inside, he was met with the smell of grilled chicken and vegetables. The sterile house was unchanged, as white and calming as ever.

"Mei?" he called as he took off his suit jacket. He headed to the back of his home, where his wife was cooking dinner. "<How was your day?>" he asked her.

"<Good,>" she remarked absently in Mandarin as she turned the vegetables on the indoor grill. "<Dinner will be ready in just a bit,>" as she set about checking the kitchen.

Jie went upstairs, as was his routine. He changed clothes, as was his routine. He watched himself in the mirror of the bedroom closet, as was his routine. As he routinely removed his tank top, he saw the anarchy symbol on his chest. Without warning, his mind returned to the Ramones' t-shirt. His vision centered on the anarchist symbol, the jagged A within a circle. The smell of a dingy alleyway and sharp pain touched the back of his thoughts.

Jie turned away from the memories. He pulled on a dark blue t-shirt and jeans and headed downstairs for his wife's healthy cooking.

***

The perfect silence of students testing was like a comforting pain for Jie.

He watched the kids in his class as they took the test. Forty students were a lot to keep track of, so Jie paced among the tightly-packed desks. The space between the students was barely wide enough for his steps. Bookbags and purses were stuffed under the metal desks as students flipped through the math test. All around were sighs of frustration and the occasional muttering of confusion. Jie glanced at students' pages as he walked, spotting wrong answer after wrong answer. Anger welled up in him at the students for not doing better. He stayed quiet and kept walking among the kids, already drawing up new assignments in his mind to better ingrain the lessons.

As he passed Charles Ramirez, a student right on the cusp of being a problem, he heard the strangest sound. Jie slowed but didn't stop, not wanting to let on that he'd heard. He glanced to the boy's desk and saw a tiny spot of water just beneath the test. Ready to chastise him for drinking in class, Jie kept walking, watching the boy out of the corner of his eye. A second drop fell of Charles' chin.

Jie realized his student was crying.

A bench warmer for the school's mediocre baseball team, Charles' face was still. He looked totally placid except for the subtle wet streaks down his face. He wiped his chin and cheek, playing it off as nothing, but the frustration was clear. The alien language of the math was beating him. Beating him down, beating him up, beating him.

Continuing his patrol, Jie felt a deep-seated empathy he had forgotten he had.

Jie left his car on the street and entered his house. White, sterile, bland. He crossed to the back of his house as he smelled baked fish and a vegetable stew. "<Was it a good day?>" Jie asked his wife.

"<Yep, good,>" she said absently as she stirred the stew. "<Dinner's almost ready.>"

Jie went upstairs and changed clothes, then came back downstairs to finish his evening with his wife's dinner.

***

Wagner played on Morgan's stereo.

Jie listened to the music, shaking his hand through the air, like he was dotting the notes of the piece. He hummed a little and glanced at Morgan who was watching him. "I'm not much of a Wagner fan," Jie told his musical counterpart. "I think his polemic viewpoints were questionable and his music a little sensational, but it's a fun, light fare."

Morgan smirked, almost laughing. "Most people don't call Wagner 'light', but okay." His expression was always tinged with cynicism, as usual.

"People think this is complex?" Jie asked derisively.

"I wouldn't argue complex necessarily, but I've heard Wagner described as the birth of heavy metal, if you can believe that," Morgan remarked. Jie shook his head and turned back to the music. "What do you listen to besides classical?" Morgan asked, for the first time that session but far from the first time ever.

Jie just shrugged. "I'm not sure. Opera, I suppose. I listen to—"

"Opera is just classical with lyrics," Morgan stopped him. "You listen to more than classical. In fact, I don't think you even like classical."

"Why do you say that?" Jie asked, like he'd been insulted.

Morgan bore a hole through Jie with an unblinking stare. "Because you're swaying your hand exactly like you did last week, during Muggorgsky's Pictures at an Exhibition. Pictures has an 11/4 time signature. Gotterdammerung has 6/4 time." He tossed his point at Jie's hand. "You're off." Jie looked angry. "You're not listening to the music," Morgan all but accused him. He smiled cynically, almost defiantly. "Not really." It was a stinging accusation, one Jie wasn't prepared to refute. "That tells me you're not emotionally invested in this," he explained. "That means you're either deliberately wasting my time...or you're hiding something."

Jie felt an anger well up inside of him, but Morgan didn't relent. "Buddy, you are not the first person to be ashamed of your musical tastes," he assured his client. "You're not the first person to say they like what is popular or what they think they're supposed to like, when in fact they can't stand it. People can go their whole lives listening to music they think is boring just because they think they're supposed to. They listen to music because they think they have to grow out of earlier tastes." Morgan paused a beat, just to let that register. "But the thing is, music is more important than some fashion ascribed to people by their age, by their station, by their class. Music is more than entertainment. It's an expression of our identity and some people are in denial about who they are."

Eyes still on Jie, Morgan held up the stereo's remote. With the press of a single button, the attic fell to silence. A billowing tuft of cool air from the vents filled the vacancy of noise. The smell of dusty, stale air and generations of forgotten music grew more poignant in the absence of sound. "So," Morgan challenged, "what do you want to listen to?"

Jie stood up from the chair and made a bit of a show of looking down at the seated Morgan, buttoning his suit jacket. He started to turn away, ready to walk out on the counselor, but something stopped. His heart was racing and he didn't know why. Not from the insult, but from some long-forgotten moment of which it reminded him. He recalled a circle of people, faces he couldn't remember, chanting 'fight'.

A teenage stubbornness filled his lungs and Jie unbuttoned his suit jacket. Despite his back being to Morgan, he sneered in anger. He went to the far side of the attic and reappraised the music collection. Looking through the vast sea of media, Jie's anger was quickly dissolved. He stared at the array, unsure what he was looking for. He wasn't staring at opera or classical, but genres he knew existed by reputation only.

Reputation, and recollection.

The fingertips of the mind began to thumb through the milk crates of records. Drag along the racks of cassettes and CDs. The music, like the genres, ranged across the ages and across the world. Arabic. English. American. Brazilian. Japanese. Genres from across time. Pop. Dance. Swing. Jazz. Big band. Rock. Metal.

Punk.

Jie's hand reached eagerly for what his mind didn't recall. Couldn't recall. Wouldn't recall. He flipped through a crate of punk records, haunted by what he saw. Before him were covers he'd seen but never knew. Until he reached Rocket to Russia. Joey, Johnny, Dee Dee, and Tommy, were looking right at him. Through him. More than forty years removed, they were seeing him and seeing him with disdain.

"Punk?"

Jie jumped with a start, like he had stepped out of time. Fear clutched his throat and he shivered in terror that he'd been found. Morgan had stood rom his chair and was watching Jie as he crouched on the floor before the milk crate. "You like punk music?" Morgan was both surprised and strangely delighted.

Jie let go of the records, letting them slump back into the plastic milk crate. He withdrew his hand, but the sudden absence of the four Ramones was like a gut punch. Suddenly, he wanted nothing more than to see them again. "When I live in China," said the high school teacher very slowly, "I'm...I'm delinquent." He spoke with pauses and distance, like the revelation was as much his own. He returned to his seat in front of Morgan. The air was silent and thick as the student and therapist took their seats. They sat in the absence of distraction, in the pregnant silence of illumination.

Jie stared for a long time into the middle distance, seeing the silence and his life as well. "Some boys, in my village, they're delinquents. Punks." His voice was ghostly. "My parents tell me to stay away from them. I cut my arm with a beer bottle to prove to them I'm...to prove to them...to prove to them." Jie realized that his eyes held tears, tears of frustration. He remembered the condescending looks of the older boys, their language of rebellion so foreign to him.

"Cultural Revolution ended in 1969, so they say," Jie told Morgan with a voice soft with emotion. He wiped his eyes, returning to some decorum. "But, it wasn't over. Not in the west. The young, we hated it. So backwards. So ridiculous. Mao, he..." Jie shook his head. He suddenly laughed tearfully. "I remember walking along the streets, when I should be in school. I'm looking for coins. Walking the curb, I look into the gutter for anything that shines." His smile turned bittersweet. "I know a guy who can get bootlegs from India. He sells me a cassette of the Ramones."

"Which album?" Morgan asked cautiously, afraid the question would break the memorial trance. He watched the recollection in awe.

"No album, just songs," recalled Jie, like his memories were the real now. "All mixed together." He laughed. "Such poor quality. The feedback, the reverb..." He smiled.

"Sounds terrible," Morgan said, the left side of his mouth curling into a smile.

"Awful," Jie recalled with distant delight. "I could barely tell one song from another." His eyes spaced out with the memory of a piece of heaven. "I had to listen so closely." He drifted into a hazy cloud of remembrance, saying very little after that. Morgan joined him in the silence, pushing him no more for the day.

***

"The tests were not awful," Jie lied as he handed them back, one by one, laying them before each student. Red Xs denoted missed answers and giant red numbers at the top of the page conveyed the bad news. "I want to make sure," he continued as he handed out the results to the despondent class, "that going forward, we are able to confirm what we have learned while still preparing for the next test."

When Jie reached Charles Ramirez's desk, he laid down the failing test. Beneath the ugly numbers, however was written, 'See me after class, I know you worked hard'. Charles looked at the page and up at Jie as the teacher returned to the front of the class. The instructor began to explain the next chapter, even as his eyes checked back with Charles. To Jie's surprise, he didn't see gratitude or curiosity, but anger.

"I didn't understand," Jie recalled to Morgan as they sat together, listening to Blitzkrieg Bop. "I wanted to help him. I was offering to help him."

"Maybe he didn't see it that way," suggested Morgan, his head propped on one hand as he listened.

"He's going to fail the class," Jie lamented.

"Do you think he cares?" asked Morgan, almost rhetorically. "Best case scenario, he cares about being able to play baseball. And learning math isn't an incentive, just a hurdle to not lose baseball. He's not learning; he's avoiding punishment." Jie was lost in that perspective. "Think about who you were," Morgan suggested, pointing to the stereo as punk music thrashed about in the attic air, "when you first heard this song? How would you have responded to a note like that?"

"Gone to the teacher after class," Jie said certainly. Morgan waited for the complete answer. Then Jie admitted to himself, "and hated him every minute after."

"So did he come see you?" asked Morgan.

Jie hedged. "I don't think so."

"You don't think so?" asked the counselor, confused. "What happened?"

"Read the chapter and do the questions at the end," Jie told his students as they funneled out. Charles was the last to leave. His head hung low, not in defeat but in a street-worn tactic of deception. His hand was in his pocket and his thumb in his one bookbag strap, looking like an unassuming nobody right before the punches started swinging. He approached Jie as the teacher moved to meet him. Neither got the chance to speak however.

"Mr. Wong?" said an older voice. Jie and Charles were both surprised as Dr. Match, the school principal, let himself into the classroom. He carried with him a manila folder of pages that matched his plaid suit with brown elbow patches. The principal smiled on to the young boy he had no idea the name of and let him find his way out of sight. Charles was happy to take the out.

Once alone, Dr. Match said,"Mr. Wong, it's time for the annual review." The principal produced from the folder a stapled pair of pages and handed them to Jie. "Please fill this out at your earliest convenience and have this back to me tomorrow morning before the first bell." The principal didn't wait for a response. With a smile, he headed off, leaving Jie to look over the page.

"I hate performance reviews," Morgan lamented sympathetically. "We did them all the time back when I was a teacher."

"We do them quarterly, but each one is for a different oversight," Jie concurred. "The union says only annual reviews, but since each is different…" He shook his head. I Wanna Be Your Boyfriend played on the stereo. "It's so pointless," Jie remarked. "I don't mind doing it exactly, but it's…it's just pointless. There are no raises. I can't be fired for anything that goes on these forms. All it is for is for some bureaucrat to, to…" His anger turned into an exhausted confusion.

Jie parked his car out front of his house. He readied to walk up the driveway but paused. He looked down the street, at all the cars parked facing one way. Across the street, the same line of monotony. SUVs. Compacts. Sedans. All in line, all in order. He heard a sprinkler going in the dusk light. A few birds chirped, but nowhere nearby due to the lack of meaningful trees. Pet plants were the closest the neighborhood had, token reminders of what wild vegetation looked like.

Jie backed up from his car, stepping a few steps into the street. He looked down the road again, then the other way. He was standing in the middle of the street. He looked down at his aged, sensible shoes. He looked again down the street, seeing no traffic at all. Troubled and not sure why, he returned to his property.

Through the front door, he smelled baked fish and soup. He approached the kitchen and saw his wife stirring the soup. "<Good afternoon, Mei,>" said Jie in Mandarin.

"<Dinner will be ready shortly,>" said his wife. Jie smelled olive oil and felt less than enthused.

He headed upstairs and changed his shirt. Rather than change into his afterwork shirt, he sat down on the foot of his bed, topless. The ugly anarchy tattoo on his chest caught his eye. Somehow, that led him to think about the performance evaluation waiting downstairs in his briefcase. Pointless words on a meaningless page for an empty gesture.

Jie looked at his reflection in the bedroom mirror. A man older than he remembered stared back. He saw fragments of his own face, but they were lost within a mask of a middle-aged teacher who drove a sensible car, wore sensible shoes, lived in a sensible house, worked a sensible job, ate a sensible dinner, and lived a sensible life.

With an anarchist tattoo on his chest.

Jie studied his reflection for a long time, seeing not his face but a collection of shapes he'd forgotten weren't him.

***

"None of it matters," Jie pondered from far away. The stereo was off. The record was over and Jie didn't want to hear anymore. "I love my wife," he whispered sadly, a heavy gaze staring at nothing but his own thoughts and the anguish behind them. "I don't regret our life together, but...but it's...it's so...meaningless?" He looked at Morgan, either to confirm that was the correct word or that was a fair emotion. His counselor only listened and heard. "It isn't a bad life. I don't hate it," said Jie. "It's just so...so sensible." Emotional momentum carried Jie. "I began to do things because it was the best option. It made the most sense. It was sensible."

"There's nothing wrong with that," Morgan assured him. "There's nothing – at all – wrong with driving a sensible car, living in a sensible house, working a sensible job. Making sensible decisions isn't bad."

"Making sensible decisions used to be what I did when my parents watched me," realized Jie. "It was what adults did. It was what responsible people did. But there was a time when what mattered was being irresponsible. Nothing mattered and that was important. That mattered. Now my life is all things that matter and that doesn't matter that they matter." His mental and verbal gymnastics confused him.

After a long silence, stained hot by the sunlight coming in through the slanted windows of the rooftop, Jie recalled, "You know, I don't remember what happened to my bootleg Ramones cassette?" He shook his head at the thought of it all. "I don't remember if I lost it, if my parents found it. Just one day I didn't look for it. I didn't notice it was gone. I don't think I gave it any thought until I started coming to you." He laughed at himself. "It was so important to me. I skipped school to search for money to buy it. I listened to it every single day...and I don't remember when I last saw it. I don't remember what happened to it."

"We change," Morgan said, almost as a consolation.

"If it was important then, and it's not important now, it was never important," said Jie.

"That's not true," Morgan said with unusual and rare certainty. "Just because something doesn't matter now, but did once, doesn't mean it wasn't important then. Or now." He made clear, "Something doesn't have to matter to be important."

Park the car. Up the driveway. Enter the house. Roasted chicken and vegetables.

Jie stopped as he entered the kitchen. He took a moment to take a deep breath, drinking the aroma. Or lack thereof. "Honey?" he asked in English. His wife turned around to him, surprised by the words and his tone. Jie felt possessed. Haunted. In a fog. "Why don't we go out to eat?"

Mei looked confused. Not insulted that he was declining the dinner but like the notion of eating out was even possible. "What?" she asked with a laugh. She turned back to the vegetables. "Don't be silly. Eating out is expensive and we're saving up for a new sofa, remember?"

Jie looked in the direction of the pristine living room. "What's wrong with the one we have?"

"Don't you remember? The spring on the right side pokes through the cushion sometimes," she said.

Jie looked again. "So?" Stunned, his wife turned around to him. "We never sit on it," said Jie with a shrug. "Who cares about replacing it? Besides, eating out doesn't have to be expensive." He walked towards her. "Let's go get some hotdogs." He smiled, not aware of how much he needed those in his life until he said the word.

Wong turned back around to the dinner and resumed preparing it. "<I've got dinner almost ready now,>" she told him in Mandarin.

Dejected, Jie turned to go upstairs and resume his routine. He stopped at the door to the kitchen. "Wong?" he asked. He looked halfway back at her. "What's the difference between things being important, and mattering?"

She looked at him again, thinking over his question. "I don't know. I guess they're the same thing."

More troubled than he had been, Jie excused himself upstairs.

***

"We've only got a few more minutes," Jie said to his Friday class of bored students. His words passed inattentive students and echoed off the white cement walls at the back of his classroom. "I want to talk about the homework." He picked up the printed page he was about to distribute. "I think the questions on here will really help drive home the purpose of the..." Words and thoughts dribbled to a standstill.

Jie stopped entirely. Halfway around his desk, he stopped and looked at the page. Numbers and symbols, all without any context. Looking at the page, Jie could see the answer but could barely remember how to do the math. He certainly couldn't remember why. So many questions and none of them providing any answers. Not exercise; merely work. His students perked up, his silence garnering more attention than his words ever had.

Jie looked out the narrow slit of a window by his desk. He couldn't see a tree or the sky but he saw the bright afternoon sun on the wall across the courtyard. It was a lovely Spring day. Jie looked again at the homework he was about to hand out. Staring down at it, he remembered walking along the streets of his hometown, checking the gutter for change to buy a bootleg Ramones tape.

Jie released the pages.

Forty worksheets feel from his grasp and went falling into the floor, flying out from his feet. As his students were afraid of this sudden deviation from the norm, Jie felt his heart rush. He looked up like he'd come out of a decades-long trance. He turned and stepped up onto his chair and then onto his desk. He looked over his class from the new vantage, seeing nothing new but seeing everything in a new way. "This doesn't matter," he whispered, looking at the pages distributed all over the floor by chaotic gravity. "This doesn't matter," he repeated to the class.

"You're ripping off Dead Poets' Society," called somebody from the back.

Jie was momentarily stunned. "I'm what?" he asked.

"Dead Poets' Society," answered a girl in the front row. "It's a movie."

"Oh," he said. "I didn't see it."

"The teacher - Robin Williams – stands up like that to show the students how to see the world or something," she explained.

Jie nodded, then blew her mind. "I'm not standing up here for you." Like her peers, she was stunned. "I'm standing up here for me." He looked into the back, not sure who had spoken up originally and not caring. "And if I'm ripping it off, so what?" Nothing he had said all year made an impact on the class quite like that one statement.

Jie shook his head. "It's amazing," he told his students from atop his desk, scoffing cynically. "This doesn't matter," he said, gesturing to the homework on the floor. "It's important," he emphasized with total certainty. "But it doesn't matter. I've just—" The desk began to wobble as his weight shifted. "Yeah, okay," he said, getting down. There were some chuckles from his class.

"I've...I've been giving the distinction some thought. What matters and what's important," he told his students. He looked distantly at his thoughts in order to gain perspective, like stepping back from an optical illusion to gain insight.

"What's important doesn't change. What matters does." It hit him so hard to say it aloud. "What matters is important, even when it stops mattering."

"Did you have a stroke?" asked somebody in the class.

Jie smiled. "Everything you're doing right now isn't important," he told the kids. "Who you're dating, what you're into, what sports you're playing," he said with a glance at Charles Ramirez. "These things matter, but they aren't important. And they'll stop mattering when you graduate. In four years, nothing that matters now will matter then. But that doesn't make them matter any less right..." He froze mid-thought, realizing in real-time. "A thing doesn't have to matter to be important, nor does something that does matter have to be important. But by virtue of it mattering is a thing made important." He looked at his students, his intellectual sounding board. "Just because something will matter in twenty years, but not now, doesn't make it less important."

He walked to the front of his students' desks, speaking almost in a trance. "Nothing will ever matter more, or less, than what matters now. But it will change." His students all stared, not quite following but most recognizing that he was on to something.

Jie realized he wasn't making complete sense and felt compelled to not care. "Your homework this weekend isn't that," he said, gesturing to the scattered pages on the floor. "It's going to be...I want to know what you really want to know. What do you really want, whether it's from math or not."

"What does that have to do with math?" asked a girl in the second row.

"Nothing," Jie said. He then laughed. "Everything?" He chuckled to himself, as if it was all some private joke. "Nothing in high school is important, but it's no more or less important than the future." He saw the confusion on everyone's face. He only smiled wider. "You'll see what I mean," he promised them with an honesty they were unprepared to handle. The bell rang and he looked defiantly at them, challenging them to bring their best questions on Monday.

As the students filed out, talking in hushed and awed tones, unsure what to think, Jie fished his cell phone from his pocket and texted his wife. "Let's get hotdogs tonight." He put away his phone, his mouth watering at the very thought.

Jie pulled halfway into the driveway, the rear of his car hanging out on the street. He hoped out, knowing he wouldn't be long and not caring if he was. He headed inside and called, "Mei?"

His wife appeared from the kitchen, as if unsure what to do with her afternoon without having dinner to cook. "What's going on?" she asked her husband.

"Nothing," he told her. He took off his jacket and hung it from the door handle of the coat closet. He began to unbutton his shirt. His wife watched him with growing confusion. He stripped off his shirt and, in just his undershirt, with his tattoo easily noticeable, he took her hand. "Let's go." He added with a grin, "Hey ho."

His wife, laughing, tore her hand from his. "You can't go out like that!" She laughed as she backed away from him. "You look like a...a..."

"A what?" asked Jie.

"An old man," his wife said before giggling at her own candor. "Like those lazy old men who play mahjong all day."

"I am an old man," Jie accepted without fear. He reached again for her hand.

"What will people think?" his wife laughed as she let him pull her to the door.

"Who cares what people think," Jie dismissed. They got halfway to the door and Mei stopped him. "Honey, if you don't want to—" He was stopped when he saw his wife pull off her blouse. She beamed with the sudden rush of teenage exuberance. In her undershirt, she grabbed his hand and, together, they rushed out for hotdogs.

***

"I traded fun for accomplishment," Jie told Morgan, thinking aloud with a proud smile. "I had given away what I wanted in the moment for what I wanted long-term. I don't dislike who I am, but I only ever thought about who I am over time, in the long run. I had forgotten who I am today. I forgotten how to be a person, and instead was a person."

"What's the difference?" Morgan asked, like he was quizzing his client.

"To be is present tense. Maybe even future tense, I don't know," he shrugged it off, clearly not caring. "Was is past tense. Constant tense if there is such a thing. This is who I was, me from here to here," he said, holding his hands wide. "I had forgotten how to be me here, right here." he held two fingers together. "This is what I needed to remember. This is what punk made me feel. This is what the Ramones gave me. Me, right here." He sat back in his chair and smiled, an unguarded, unprotected smile.

Robert V Aldrich

Rhest and the Trip Out East

I don't usually take away trips. Oh sure, occasionally I'll do some work down in Los Angeles or one of the other metropolises (metropoles? metropoleis?), but for the most part, I don't like to leave Sacramento if I can help it. And I never leave California unless I absolutely have to. Or it's really, really lucrative. I know there's plenty of work beyond the Golden State, but you have to stay close to home base. If you do, you risk coming home to a town you don't recognize because the balance of power has changed between local street gangs, political groups, or even monolithic corporations. Believe me, I've seen what can happen during a long weekend. My name's Rhest. I'm a mercenary.

This job I'm looking into is different. It doesn't come from a corporate office (of which Sacramento has a metric buttload) or some local entrepreneur. Businesses are the driving employer of mercenaries, street mercs, street samurai, and hired goons. So when something comes down the pipe that's anything else, it always catches quite a few people's interest, myself included.

I actually bid on this case. Been a while since I've done that. With my success rate and satisfaction rating at the agency – along with my sterling-ish reputation – I tend to either be contacted directly or requested specifically. Or if I express interest in a job, it tends to go to me immediately. That gets into the politics of assigning...assignments at the agency and that's neither here nor there. And besides, the bid I put in was simply to hear out the proposal. It's a big commitment to come all the way out here, to hear a proposal for a trip that will take me to another state.

Where's 'way out here'? Lincoln California, just west of the Endurance Capital of the World, Auburn California. I worked a race in Auburn. You'd think marathons are boring, and they are, until you add snipers. You ever run a 26-mile escort mission? No, of course you haven't because it's stupid and nobody in their right mind would do that. Nobody. That said, it did pay well and I got a participation trophy so that's nice.

Anyway, Lincoln California. Lincoln has become one giant retirement home for the pseudo-wealthy. I say pseudo-wealthy because we're probably talking people worth middle to upper eight digits. Considering I know at least two execs who make eight digits annually and they're upper-middle tier in the corporate hierarchy, it's hard to consider these people truly 'wealthy'. More money than me, though. By a mile.

I arrive at a very nice development property that I think takes up an entire set of hills. There are a lot of houses in this walled-off area but they're very far apart. Plenty of space with lots of exceptionally green grass. The roads are super-nice, without the usual curb or anything. The air is strangely silent, devoid of the buzz of electricity, processed air, and wi-fi signals that I'm used to in the city. I hear a bird chirping, which honestly kind of unnerves me.

I approach the security monitor at the gate. He's an older gent, though he's clearly still got himself together. He's sitting in a wooden chair, his feet up on the counter of his little checkpoint hut. He's reading a medical thriller novel, chuckling to himself as he licks his finger to turn a page. I approach and he looks up at me. He's got some swagger and gives me a look of confidence like he not only knew I was there the whole time, but he's probably got a gun ready to use if it's necessary. He's also got a smile that tells me he'll feel real bad if he has to shoot me. I like him.

"Hey, what's up?" I call ahead of my approach. "I'm here to see..." I have to find the email thread I exchanged with this guy's valet. My Heads-Up Display superimposes over my vision in a transparent blue box. "Charles Eubanks."

The guard sits forward and picks up a clipboard with some pages on it. "You got any documentation?" He begins to consult the pages.

Further consulting the email thread in my HUD. "I got an admission barcode?" I offer, not sure if that's how things work around her or not.

"Rhest?" he asks, pronouncing it 're-est'.

"Rhest, like to take a nap," I correct him casually. I see an email address on a placard. "Want me to send the barcode?"

"Please," said the guard, reading something of note on the pages.

Using my HUD, I go through the menus and forward one of the messages to the email address on the placard. The guard turns his head suddenly, the telltale sign of him accessing an email system in his HUD as well. He nods with increasing approval. On the road between us, an SUV begins to approach. It's a newer model and has the silence of a solar engine. A pair of kids have their faces pressed against the tinted windows, staring at me in awe as they drive into the estate. As they pass, the guy points through the still-open security gate. "Head down to the intersection. First right, first left, first right. House 113."

"Cool, thanks," I tell him. We fist-bump and I start the minor hike. There's probably two or three city blocks of distance between each house so it takes me about fifteen minutes to finally arrive at a relatively simple but very nice house on the side of a Rockwellian hill. Sprinklers are wetting the lawn and the trunk of the single tree before the house disrupts the anime-like front lawn. There's a semi-circle driveway that leads to the main door at its zenith.

As I near, the door opens and a white guy in a butler's uniform comes out. Dude's got spats and white gloves and everything. It's strange because the left side of his head is shaved and the right side is a cascade of blonde hair down to his ear. He's wearing earrings too, but otherwise looks every bit the part of a butler from the silver screen. "Mr. Rhest?" he inquires as I start up the driveway. "Had I known you were arriving on foot, I would have sent a car around."

"Don't sweat it," I tell him as we shake hands. "I don't get to take walks that much, especially in air this clean."

"This way, sir," he says. I enter the incredibly processed air, cooled to clearly a very specific temperature. "May I take your..." The butler pauses when he realizes I'm not wearing a jacket but a combat harness, mid-grade body armor, and six pistols. "...guns, sir?"

"I'm good," I tell him.

I expect him to insist, so I'm surprised when he says, "Very good, sir." He's a young dude. Not high school young but like he should be just starting his career in a corporate office. His old-style demeanor and flawless attire perfectly match his role, which is surprising. Like a parody so well done you can't tell if maybe its genuine. Is this dude going the extra mile for a role, or is he one of those rare people that's committed to his job? I can't decide, nor can I decide if it's cool or weird. Maybe both. He gestures for me to follow him.

The butler leads me through a silent house of smooth floors polished to a shine, chandeliers of a bygone era, and extremely nice paintings. I spot one or two I recognize and it occurs to me only as I pass that they might not be reproductions. We pass through a kitchen that's better than some high-end restaurants. "A refreshment, sir?" asks the butler, looking back at me but not stopping. I just shake my head.

He guides me to two glass doors that are frosted. He opens them and a wall of moist heat hits me like a thunderclap. I start sweating instantly. "Mr. Eubanks is waiting for you, sir." The way he stands at the door suggests he expects me to go first. That gives me some pause but inside I go.

I step into a conservatory, my hands hanging loose, each ready to go for a gun. Equal parts sunroom and green house, the air is absolutely saturated with humidity. It's shockingly rich with the scent of soil that clings to me. My armor, designed to whisk away sweat, gives up and I can feel the swamp ass developing already.

Charles Eubanks has his back to me. He's in a wheelchair and facing out, looking into his yard. I near, about to cough politely, when the butler announces me. "Mr. Rhest, from the agency, sir."

Eubanks half-jumps in surprise and looks back at me. He's an ancient black man with some white stubble where hair used to be. One eye is glassed over, so I'm guessing cataracts. Not sure why he wouldn't get that fixed. "Hello, sir," he says in that tone only generous old man can speak. He wheels around, using a manual chair, not one with machinery. I guess maybe the humidity would be bad for the machinery. It sure isn't doing my cybernetics any favors, that's for damn sure. "Want a drink?"

"No, I'm good," I tell him.

"Nonsense, son, have some water at least," says Eubanks. He turns to the butler. "Bring him a pitcher of—"

"No," I say politely but emphatically. "Thank you," I add. I look at the old man with a very sincere smile, that I'm not being rude but professional.

He develops a shrewd, proud look. "You'll forgive me. That was a test." I don't follow. "People tend not to say no to rich old men." He has a slight southern accent. He folds long fingers with knobby joints in his lap. "I'm glad to find someone who still knows how."

"I'm very good at saying no," I assure him. Water is now dripping off my brow. Holy hell, how high is the humidity? And this old dude's under a blanket. How can he stand it?!

"Well I won't waste your time, Mr. Rhest," says Eubanks as the butler leaves us. "So I'll get right down to it. I want you to travel to Alabama and find an object of some value to me. Me, and no one else." I suddenly have more questions than I know how to count. "I want you to go to Birmingham specifically. There, I want you to find a CD and bring it to me."

My brow furrows (which causes more water to stream down my face). "A Certificate of Deposit."

He shakes his head. "Compact Disc."

I do a double-take. "You want me to go across the country for a computer disc?"

"A music disc," he specifies. I see his one eye glaze over a bit. I'm about to get a doozy of a story. "When I was a boy, growing up in Birmingham, I purchased a CD at a music store from a mall. It was a toss-away CD, barely three or four bucks. Back then, most CDs cost eighteen or twenty dollars. It was the first CD I ever bought with my own money. That should tell you how old I was." He smiles and nods his head, remembering days when life was defined by school and conquering the night meant staying up after 1am. I can't imagine how many memories – good and bad – roll through his mind. His smile tells me it's more good than bad.

"This CD," he tells me, "was rain. It was a recording of rain falling. There was this..." His eyes close as he remembers it vividly. "This slight instrumentation added. Some strings, I think. Maybe a flute? I'm not much of a musician. Piano mostly, and not very good." He wrings his calloused hands. It's been awhile since those long fingers have touched ivory, I'm guessing. "I'd fall asleep listening to that CD," he continues to recall, unable to keep from smiling at the serenity he remembers. "I'd gotten a CD player for Christmas. I was so excited. It was such new, exciting technology. A boombox with a CD player. Curved sides, and a tape deck too." He laughs. "So exciting." He opens his eyes and his trance is broken. He looks at me. "I don't know what happened to that CD. And the memory of it has haunted me. Before I die, I want to hear it again."

I'd be lying if I said I wasn't touched. Sadly, a touching story doesn't pay the bills.

"What you're asking..." I begin to say.

"Travel expenses won't be a problem," he tells me straight up front. "Of course I'll pay for the travel to and from. Business expenses too."

I nod. That's not a bad start. "Yeah, okay, but even at my base hourly rate, you're still talking about a considerable amount of money." Eubanks just looks at me, his old mouth melting into a smile. "Which I'm guessing isn't an issue for you." The smile widens, sympathetically. He looks like he both appreciates and feels bad for my tact.

"What would you like?" he asks. I hate when they just come out and ask. I wish he'd given me a number and we could go from there.

"I don't want to gouge you, but what you're asking...that's a serious operation." I start doing numbers in my head.

In the intervening silence, as plants respire around us, his gaze drifts down to my guns. They settle specifically on Affinity and Alternative, my backup pistols that hang under my armpits. He starts to reach towards Affinity, then asks, "May I?"

I remove the gun without hesitation and hand it over. Barely bigger than my hand and made entirely out of plastic, Affinity is a stealth weapon. Most scanners won't notice it but it still packs a punch. He takes the gun and seems surprised by its slight weight. It's sturdy but light. He pulls back the slide with more experience than training and looks down the barrel with his one good eye. He discharges the magazine, again like someone who wishes he didn't know what he was doing. He hands the gun back to me and says nothing. He looks at the other guns, Reason and Respect, Vicious and Victory. A new smile creeps onto his kindly face.

"How about instead of money," he offers, "I give you a supply account at one of my companies. I own two companies that make bullets. Say, a year's access?"

I swallow tightly. Old man, don't be playing with my heart. That's not a king's ransom. That makes a king's ransom look like a middle school allowance. A merc with an unlimited ammo account? Even for one year, that's...insane. My jaw just dangles.

Eubanks smiles, big white teeth. "I guess we have a deal then?" He extends a hand.

I shake it gently but enthusiastically. "Yeah, we got a deal."

I'm going to Alabama.

Whenever you embark on an operation like this, you need to confirm as many details as possible. Even in the age of anti-Alzheimer's treatments and memory reinforcement, you'd be surprised what details an old survivor can forget or transpose. A CD Eubanks may remember purchasing at a mall music store may have actually happened at a flea market. Or he may have bought a different CD from the counter. Little details can make all the difference. But first, I have to confirm that stuff like this even happened.

First step in a long trip is research. Lots and lots of research. In the old days, this meant hitting up the library or going to the local university to get some first-hand knowledge. Then came the Internet and search engines replaced a lot of that effort. A fool, however, would think everything there is to be found is on the web.

The apartment door opens in front of me. Gladys Offerman is staring at me. A wiry woman, she's still got the slight bulge of her most recent baby. She's also got the diesel arms of a street merc who, in her off time, competes in every athletic competition she can find. No cybernetics but 'roided out her eyeballs, she's might be the most intense person I know. And boy, is that saying something.

"Yeah?" she barks at me. Before I can answer, she turns back into the apartment and yells, "Boy, don't make me tell you again to turn off that music and get your homework done!" What music? "Yeah?" she asks me again, like I better have a damn good reason for disturbing her.

"Can I talk to your grandmother?"

"The hell you want with her?" Gladys says, letting me into the apartment. It's not messy per say but it's got stains everywhere. There's plenty of clutter, but it's stacked well enough. The wrap-around kitchen is to my right and the first bedroom's wall is to the left. Gladys leads the way into the living room where two kids, one baby and one infant, are somehow asleep in a playpen.

"I've got a job in her neck of the woods," I tell Gladys as I check out some of the bodybuilding and endurance running magazines on her kitchen island.

Gladys is suddenly very interested. Street mercs are like sharks, only instead of blood, once we catch a whiff of money, we're there. "The money's not great," I mention casually. "Hour for hour, it's...he's barely paying more than travel."

Yeah, like she's gonna buy that. She asks, "Then why do it?"

I shrug, trying to play up some professional boredom. "I don't have too many interesting gigs lined up. Macee's trying to get some people to take up that highway case." Gladys rolls her eyes, agreeing that job's a hard sale. "There's the usual bodyguard stuff. There's that one hit, but come on."

"Yeah," she agrees.

"This sounds interesting, even if it's not lucrative. And it sure sounds easy." I hope she buys that.

Based off the way she nods, I think she did. "Grandma!" she yells suddenly towards the back of apartment. Geez, the two kids sleep right through it. I guess it doesn't take long to get used to shouting.

"Yes?" yells another woman.

"One of my work friends wants to talk to you!"

I look at Gladys. "Work friends?" I smirk.

"What? We work together."

"Yeah, but you make it sound like we work an office job," I chuckle. "Last job we did together was that school one. Remember? We were raiding a school for evidence that lunch ladies were stealing food and replacing it with rabbit kibble. Dave fell into that den of brown recluse spiders." She nods, remembering with sadistic fondness. "He really likes his new face," I share off-handedly. "His lungs aren't quite calibrated yet, but they work and they play music."

"That's a plus," agrees Gladys.

From down the hall comes Grandma Offerman. An ancient Korean woman, she's wearing sweats and a bandana. Her legs hiss slightly, the telltale noise of old and cheap cybernetics. I don't know if she can't afford to get them replaced or doesn't want to, but it's an irritating sound. "Hello there," says the kindly old woman.

"Hey there," I tell her. We're suddenly hit with an awful smell. I glance at the babies and hope it's one of them. Gladys scoops up the infant and takes him to the kitchen to start the necessary proceedings. I focus my attention on Grandma Offerman. "Um, Gladys told me a while back that you lived in Alabama as a kid."

"Oh, that was a long time ago," says an accent that is strangely Asian and southern at the same time. She shuffles to the couch and sits. Both she and her cheap hydraulics groan. She pats the adjacent recliner. "What about it?"

"I've got a job down there," I say as I sit. The recliner groans loudly. Guess it's not meant for somebody with as much cybernetic weight as me. "Just trying to get the lay of the land."

Grandman Offerman shakes her head. "I moved away from there when I was a teen. My dad ran from my mom. She was a devil woman, to be sure. Beat him and me." Domestic violence against the guy. Don't hear it every day but you do hear it. "Before that, I tried to avoid going home as much as possible. That's how I got addicted to tobacco. Lung cancer's what took my legs." She rolls up her sweats to show the mechanical ankles inside her sneakers.

"What did you do?" I ask the old woman.

"We had to have them amputated," she begins.

"No, when you were avoiding going home, in Alabama," I clarify. I deliberately avoid looking at Gladys. The smell's gotten worse. I'm not afraid of babies or diapers or anything, but this smell is so bad, it could be weaponized (and I've seen that done!).

"Well, malls were still around back then," she says. "Me and my girlfriends – we had a little click, us and some Mexican girls – we'd go hang out at the mall. We had to stick together. Mostly there were white girls and a few black girls. Latinas and Yobos, we had to stick together. Because we got lumped in together a lot of the time." That doesn't make sense to me, but it doesn't matter if it does.

"Was this...did you ever have any CDs? Compact Discs? They were a music medium."

"Oh no," she says. "That was before my time. They still were around, sure, but music players were the big thing. MP3 players. I had some friends, one girl Maria, she had a mini-disc player. But CDs were on their way out."

"But they were still around," I reason.

"There were still music stores," she nods. "There were even video rental stores, if you can believe that. Streaming hadn't taken off yet, so you had to go to places and actually borrow videos and bring them back."

"That's been making a comeback," I tangent on her. "We've got some of those here in Sacramento."

Grandma Offerman looks surprised and a little impressed. "Hear that Gladys? We should make a run to Blockbuster." Gladys scowls at me, like she blames me for giving her grandmother ideas.

"Where were the music stores?" I ask her, getting back on the task.

"Mostly inside the malls themselves," she tells me. "I don't think I ever saw one that wasn't in a mall. As malls declined, you started seeing more CDs in big retailers but that didn't last long either."

"How many music stores were there in a mall?" I ask.

She shrugs. "Two or three? They were like shoe shops. You might have a specialty shop, that just had women's shoes or just had sneakers. But otherwise you had maybe two or so generic shoe places."

"You may not know, or remember, but did you ever see CDs for sale at the counter? Like when you went to checkout, they'd have cheap CDs for sale? Like instrumental music?"

Grandma Offerman strains for a second. "Yeah," she decides. "Yeah, I think so. I never bought any of them, but I remember seeing them once or twice."

Not exactly a solid confirmation, but it's good enough for me.

I'm interested to see the mall in question. Malls were a fascinating phenomena. Gigantic enclosed shopping centers with a vast array of often-niche specialty shops. They were a staple of the United States for just under half a century, thanks to some dodgy tax loopholes. Nowadays, they're giant wastelands of rot and abandonment. We have shopping centers not unlike malls, but they're more small cloisters of shops, nestled into the empty spaces in and around corporate megaliths. The first two floors of a biodome might be shopping, which could debatably be considered a mall, but the idea of a free-standing structure of nothing but small shops is a thing of the past.

It takes me another day to get a connection with the Alabama state government. Alabama doesn't like California and, to be honest, California doesn't like Alabama. But pay some fees, and overpay one or two of them, and you get the cooperation you need. It's a game of trial and error, all done via email and requests submitted through decade-old websites. Get the names of all the malls in Birmingham Alabama (and surrounding areas, just in case). Maybe whittle that list down to malls that would have been open during Eubanks' time there. Get a list of all the music shops. Again, narrow that list some with music shops that would have come later or be gone by his time.

This leaves me with a list of fourteen different stores and chains, spread across fifty-six possible locations. Getting a list of every promotional or discount CD sold at the register isn't something that can be done online. That, I'll have to suss out on-site. Not a hundred percent sure how, either.

I push through the door of the staffing agency to find Psychic Steve and Antonio the Great playing chess with their minds. There's a small crowd and money in two stacks on the table, which is about par for the course with street mercs.

I bypass the telekinetic spectacle and head to the counter. Macee is back there, an older white (I think?) woman built like a burnt-out refrigerator and with the manners to match. She's flipping through a men's fashion magazine to ogle the guys. "Hey, what's up?" I begin. "Look, I'm taking the Eubanks job." Macee just nods, not looking up from a rather dapper-looking trench coat and suit. "I'm probably going to be out of town for a week or two." Now she looks up. "Yeah," I confirm.

"What's the job?" Macee asks me.

"It's..." I glance back at the chess game. Everybody, including Steve and Antonio, are staring at me. "I signed an NDA," I lie. "I need to arrange somebody to check on my apartment twice a day."

"Patrol duty? Really, Rhest?" chides Domink from Antonio's side of the folding table somebody got out of a dumpster two decades ago. A street samurai, she's got cutting edge ninja armor and two vibroblades that look cool and are about as useful in a fight as harsh language. So is she.

"Half rate for ten minutes work total," I offer to anybody in the room. I start to lean on the counter and it groans, nixing that idea. "Just swing by morning and again at night to make sure nobody in the building has broken in. Maybe give some of the strays some tuna. Except the tabby. That ass can go hungry." I turn back to Macee. "Bastard bit me yesterday."

"Maybe he thought you tasted yummy," Macee teases. I hold up my finger that's got two puncture marks through the nail. "Damn."

"Yeah, he doesn't get fed again until he apologizes. I don't need him to bring me a rat but it'd go a long way to making me feel appreciated," I tell her. Back to the task, I say, "I don't care who does the job. Adelphus? Somebody who's got some subtly." I almost hear Psychic Steve and Antonio's hands going up. "None of the psychics, though. They'll eat everything in the kitchen." I hear both hands going back down.

"I'll take care of it," Macee tells me. "You just be safe."

"If I was safe, I wouldn't be doing my job," I quip to her as I start to leave. I tap the counter twice before departing. I've got a plane to catch.

I'm dozing at the front of the commercial plane. Facing into the crowd, it's obvious who I am (aside from the guy with the guns). Because air traffic has gotten increasingly dangerous (and expensive), air marshals are needed to police the skies. Only problem is there's, like, eleven of them in the whole nation and sixty-three gazillion planes. So how to airlines handle the gap? Why, they do what everybody else does: they hire mercenaries.

I got my airfare comped by playing air marshal. Well, half-comped if there's no incident, but fully comped if somebody gets uppity. This would lead many mercs to make sure there's an incident. I'm not planning to do that, but it's a long flight. Let's see if anybody pisses me off.

We're somewhere over Texas, which is not a place anybody wants to be. Fortunately, we haven't had any 'turbulence' yet, so maybe we'll get lucky. We're in a larger plane, with three seats down the middle, and two sets on either side. It's a double-winged plane, so there's a bit more stability than usual. It's kind of ugly on the inside, like the taupe-colored cabin is to remind the passengers they paid for a flight, not a stylish flight. Since the cabin is awash with the glow of the screens of digital devices, it doesn't seem to matter.

From my vantage, I see mostly dim faces lit brightly from behind the headrests. It'd be creepy if I was paying attention, but I'm barely aware of anything. An insulated, contained space with giant motors just outside makes for a lot of white noise and very little stimulation. As such, it's easy for me to hear the spritz of somebody opening a soda can. Oh boy. That's a no-no on a flight. You aren't allowed to bring any food or drinks. You have to buy a soda from the airline for 1000% markup.

One of the attendants practically sprints down the aisle passed me (they get paid on commission). I'm not sure how she moves so fast in the knee-length skirt but she moves like a cheetah. "Sir," the woman snaps, harsh but still professional, "I'm afraid I must confiscate your illegal beverage."

Dude looks like an orthodontist on his way to visit his mom at Disney World (if Disney World was still around). "But it's just a soda," he practically whimpers.

"The airline will be happy to provide you a soda," she insists, reaching for his drink. He yanks it out of reach, across the lap of the guy sitting next to him.

"Yeah, but they cost ten dollars for a six-ounce can," he argues.

"Sir, I must insist, give me the—" She lunges and the drink gets dropped. Soda goes dribbling all over the floor, immediately soaked up by the same ugly-ass, super-absorbent carpeting all planes use. The attendant scowls down at the man like mother-superior at a sinful child. "I'm going to have to write up a report on this. Authorities will be waiting at the gate."

The guy stands up. His knees are shaking. "Y-you can't be serious."

"Sir, stand down or I will defend myself!" the woman shrieks, escalating this way too quickly. People are watching. Cell phones are out, recording this.

"You'll what?!" the guy panics. The woman draws back a fist and the guy starts to cover up.

"Sit down!" I bellow like a hibernating bear. They both look up at me, both knowing they done messed up.

The guy starts to meekly protest. "But she—"

"Not you," I assure him caustically. I stare at the attendant to almost challenge her to defy me. She looks irritated that I either cost her a sale or cost her the chance to punch a passenger. I just look at her indifferently, daring her to have security waiting at the gate. I don't know what kind of mercs they've got in Alabama, but I know what airline security is. Unless everybody at the airport is going to back them up, they ain't gonna mess with me. Not if they're smart.

The flight continues uneventfully.

Disembarking from a plane is always a hopeful experience. That moment of walking up the gangway and exiting into the terminal is almost like being born. You've been cooped up for hours and then to finally have the world open up before you is incredible. Recycled air can't compare to fresh air (or even semi-fresh air). Florescent lights can't compare to daylight streaming in through windows (even filthy windows). A metal tube flying through the air can't compare to a new city. No matter how cynical or how jaded I may become, I don't think disembarking from a plane ride will ever cease to give me at least a single moment of hope.

So. Birmingham Alabama. Birmingham is the largest city in the state of Alabama, one of the southern-most states behind Texas and what used to be Florida. This is of course not including Puerto Rico and the Caribbean states. They're south of the equator (I think?), so they don't count. Sort of like how California is the western-most state because Alaska and Hawaii are cheaters. But I digress.

Alabama is famous for industry, college sports, and overt racism. A state proud of its seditious heritage, little in the last hundred years has done anything to change the locals' minds that the Union started it. These days, Alabama is mostly known for their two-tiered social strata. You have the impoverished lower- and middle-class people who make up the majority of the state. Aggressively proud of their ignorance and lack of education, they cling to their poverty like it's a badge of honor. They consider their often-self-made struggle to be a sign that they're real, genuine people. Which, by default suggests that the rest of the country is made up of fake people...which, having been to Los Angeles, I can't 100% argue with.

Atop them, you have the educated elite. While most of Alabama is dirt poor, racist, and proud of it, it also boasts some of the best colleges and thinktanks in the country. Maybe the world. California loves to brag about all its corporate technological innovations, but lots of cutting-edge work is done at the University of Alabama-Birmingham and other colleges. Unlike most other places in the country (and the world), where the polarized social strata is caused by money, in Alabama, it's caused by education.

All of this, I reflect on as I ride the cab into town. Rundown shopping centers dot the landscape. Buildings are overgrown and falling in, some of which are still open for business. The road is in terrible disrepair and more than one stoplight we pass through doesn't work. The car is a gasoline engine with electric emergency chargers. The windows are armored and there's glass between me and the driver (I'm betting it's armored as well). I have no contact with the driver (his door doesn't even have a handle, neither does the passenger-side door). I had to input my destination on a keypad when I got in. There's a monitor showing my route, as well as local authorities nearby. Is that to let me know where to run for safety, or from what direction danger will come?

The taxi comes to a stop before a four-story hotel. The car door swings open after I pay and I disembark with little more than a 'thanks' back to the driver. The trunk is opening as I get out. I grab my backpack and two bags and the car takes off before I've even stepped away. Is he in a rush? Given the unsavory fellows I spot out of the corner of my eye as I head into the hotel, I'm guessing he wants to avoid the mugging about to take place.

I spot two guys at the far end of the hotel, one near the door, and one guy across the street (at least one guy, I didn't get a good look). At the far end are two good ol' boys who look like they could audition for a country music video. Cowboy hats and boots and belt buckles bit enough to be pro-wrestling championships. Across the street is a dude wearing a UAB jersey and jeans so paint-stained, I could have mistaken them for camo pants. By the door is the most stylish of the guys, in jeans and cowboy boots, a blazer paired (sort of) with a bolo tie. He's got a mullet and a mustache so porno, it probably has an STD named after it. I chuckle as pass them all, well aware they're watching me.

Through a revolving door and inside the hotel lobby, I'm greeted by a giant chandelier over an imitation marble floor. There are rich wooden counters on either side with well-dressed and well-groomed attendants at the terminals. A grand staircase is opposite the entrance, leading to the second floor. There's a steak house to the left and a hallway to the modest convention center to the right. Given the flickering light I spot down the hall, I'm guessing it doesn't see too much use.

I approach the desk to my left to see a young man with a cybernetic eye and an artificial hand. He smiles at me and asks, "How was your trip?"

"Good," I tell him, handing over two forms of ID. I glance out the window of the lobby to see a guy walking passed. He's looking right at me, his hands hanging into his jacket pockets. I make eye-contact, which sends him on by all the quicker. I glance at the security cameras in the corners of the lobby. I'm not entirely confident that they're working.

"And how will we be paying?" asks the attendant. He accepts my credit stick with a white hand that harshly contrasts his black skin. Man, even the cyber-docs are racist down here. That said, the fingers move with agility comparable to his real hand, so maybe he chose quality over aesthetics.

"Room three-sixteen," he says, handing me my keycard.

"Thanks," I tell him and I start up the grand staircase. I don't bother going to the third floor. On the second, I walk all the way to the far end of the hotel and take the auxiliary stairs down to the first floor and slip out the side.

The two cowboy cosplayers I spotted before are still there at the corner of the building, watching the front. They are completely oblivious to the worker's door opening behind them. I contemplate drawing a gun on them but decide against it. If they're focused on this hotel, maybe they'll leave me alone. I just walk off, leaving them to figure out how they're going to mug the new arrival.

Stuff like this used to worry me. The first few times I encountered these types of muggers or kidnappers or whatever the modern term is for highwaymen, I thought 'oh crap, what have I gotten into'. If dudes were waiting for me at the hotel, then that meant whatever job I was on was bigger than I thought. I had stumbled into something BIG! What hubris.

These are hoods. This is what they do. They jump ANY traveler. Either to get their belongings or hold them for ransom, whichever looks more lucrative (or easier). It's just a business. It's just a job in a place where jobs are scarce. They've got about as much to do with why I'm here as the cloudy sky overhead.

I hoof it about half a mile down the road. Alabama is surprisingly hilly, or at least Birmingham is. I'm not sure if that's due to the natural topography or the mining history. Birmingham was SERIOUS in the iron and steel industry. Still is, judging by the pollution in the sky.

I decide to go sliding down the side of the hill I'm walking along. Given how rocky the broken sidewalk is, I don't expect it could be much worse. Combat boots kick up serious dirt and a cybernetic body made for battle knocks free still more. I almost lose my balance a couple of times, but I finally come trotting down into somebody's backyard. A boy and a girl are playing on a swing set that's more rust than metal. They stare at me with hollow, vacant expressions of people who have seen their government-assisted home invaded so many times, it barely registers as a big deal anymore. "Sup," I toss them as I walk right by. The boy just nods back at me.

I'm in a small cul de sac neighborhood of tiny brick houses that all look the same except for the graffiti. A street light flickers as I walk underneath it. There's a smell of smog even though it's not immediately visible. There's also a smell of mold and it's hard to tell what's mold, what's stain, and what's just dead dirt. Two guys sit on a stoop up ahead. One's got a pistol sticking out of his waistband. It's a modified machine pistol, old and probably a good chance it will blow up in his hand. But I'll wager until it does, it can probably throw lead like a politician can throw lies.

As I stride passed their house, the two stand up like I'm prey. I draw Respect without even slowing a step. I don't want to shoot him with both bags slung over my shoulder but I don't let on. Dude grabs his gun even after I've drawn and he returns the favor. We've both got guns for killing aimed at each other, but I'm walking and he isn't. When he saw me just strolling through his neighborhood, he thought I was an easy mark. My gun showed otherwise. I think he's content to leave it be. His second friend isn't.

The slap of bargain basement sneakers gives away the steps of the third guy coming up behind me. I keep watching boss man and his buddy on the stoop that I'm passing and whip Respect under my arm. Activating the laser sight as I do, I point the giant pistol in my right hand at the blind-sider trying to come up on my five o'clock. His steps stop cold as he realizes the element of surprise isn't his.

All three are still, watching me as I walk right out of their neighborhood.

It takes me about four hours, but I finally find a motel to crash in. I don't like nice hotels, but I also don't like dive motels that have more roaches than beds.

The motel I find is okay. It's not bad but I sure as hell am not using that shower. I pay an extra bit for them to check me in as Bear Bryant, which makes the dude behind the counter chuckle.

Once I'm in my room, I set about my chores. First up, scan for surveillance devices. This is a dive so I don't expect much and I find nothing. Not even a mic or a hidden web cam. Sweet. This place just got an additional star for their online review.

Secondly, security. I secure the door with a standard doorjamb/crossbar rig, and make sure the window is secured as well. I have this nifty little suction-cup doohickey that I put in the corner of the window. It uses electrical pulses to magnetize the glass. It won't make it unbreakable but it turns ordinary glass in security glass. Unless they're shooting a cannon, it'll hold for a minute. Lastly, I check the drywall situation itself. The walls are made of shoddy wood but it's in a grid formation without any holes too wide. This is important if you're dealing with cyborgs as street mercs have a tendency to be, because they might just burst through the drywall. Hell, I've done it once or twice and I'm not even built for strength.

Third, time to make contact.

I get out my laptop and start searching for the local mercenary groups. Merc agencies are a dime a dozen in every town, but the poorer the population, the more agencies there are. Mercs are a way for street toughs to get paid while still having some air of legitimacy. Most groups in California evolved out of old staffing and placement agencies. Once the economy starts to tank, hiring temps for clerical work and construction slides into assassination and high-conflict theft quicker than you'd think. In other towns, the mercenary groups form differently. Sometimes they're just gangs that increasingly formalized their rates and procedures. Sometimes it's unions for a totally unrelated industry that just found themselves lending out their muscle. I heard of one union in Wisconsin I think that was made up of teachers, and they got into mercenary work. Those have got to be some hardcore teachers.

It doesn't take long to find a dozen agencies – groups, teams, whatever they call themselves in Birmingham – within the city limits. They've got decent websites, so I put in a few bids. The way most mercenary groups work is you submit a job and a proposed bid (how much you'll pay for the job). Either the group's main person will assign somebody to the job, or the local workers will bid on it. They'll offer to do it for less money, or with more skill, or other reasons; Teresa and Dale both get work all the time just by doing the jobs while wearing thongs. If the merc accepts the bid, you come in and handle the details, or just confirm acceptance. I'm posting about wanting an escort to and from a local mall. I'm contracting out for two reasons: one) they know the area and I don't and two) it's a professional courtesy.

Professional courtesy or no, I still spend the rest of the night hacking into their websites. The code is pretty good but it's still commercial-grade security. It's not hard to get into; it just takes some time. I review their staff listings to get an idea of who might work great, who might be great to work with, and who is going to jump me if they decide to revoke all professional courtesy. Ours is not a profession of rules in the truest sense.

I also hack into Birmingham's municipal system. They've got an amazing encryption system, but unfortunately, they let their employees set their own password. Any town with a decent college team is going to have at least one idiot who uses their version of 'RollTide' as their password. I embed some programs in the local municipal code, just in case. If I don't need a Hail Mary, the codes will self-terminate at the end of the next pay cycle. If push comes to shove, though, I have more than one ace up my sleeve.

Nighttime in Birmingham is surprisingly lovely. The college and the downtown areas illuminate the sky. Expanses of learned campuses glow with hopeful light. Monolithic corporate towers rise into the smoky heavens, the tops disappearing into the celestial darkness. Beyond the sky, the stars must be imagined because they can't be seen. On the ground, among the mundane, there are two drive-bys that wake me up during the night. Modern society is nothing but dichotomy.

Chesterfield Security is run out of what used to be a fast food joint in the middle of a shopping center that's more empty than full. I have to step around a pothole so deep, it's gone down to the soil. The security firm has a big neon yellow sign with hand-written letters in the window. '20% off through the end of the month'. Twenty-percent off what? Anything?

Inside is a positively intense bout of air conditioning that chills even me. I look up at the vents over the door that are blasting arctic wind on my head. Sheesh, my eyebrows are going to start frosting over! There's a wooden desk that is way too nice for an otherwise empty room and its academic style clashes with the 'out of business' décor. There's a water cooler at the back of the room, next to a door leading into I guess the storage. The whole thing looks like the world's least capable tax office.

A man with a shaved head and a gray suit is behind the desk, scribbling a notepad. Dude doesn't even have a computer, just a legal pad and an HB pencil. Where the hell am I? "Hey, what's up?" I say as I approach the desk. "I'm Rhest. I posted a bid for an escort job last night."

"Yeah, hey there," says the guy with the most intense southern accent I've ever heard. Geez, that might legitimately be another language. "I'm Matt. This here's my place." He shakes my hand, a grip that feels devoid of any cybernetics. "I've put together a list of guys who will be happy to escort you." He walks back from the desk, heading for the door. "You said you aren't expecting any kind of action or difficulties?"

"Yeah, this should be an extremely boring job," I tell him. "Boy do I hope it is, too."

Matt looks at my guns as he reaches one arm inside the door, pulling out a clipboard. "Well, I think Mel may be your best option then." He brings the clipboard to me and hands over a dossier. Mel's face – and that's got to be a mug shot – is in the left-hand corner while his vitals and credentials are listed below.

"Huh, right tackle," I confirm with some minor approval. Yeah, most of his accolades are connected to high school sports. Everybody pads their resume. You think I leave my high school D&D nights off my resume? Those were some intense, late-night strategy meetings with a creative and diverse set of problem-solvers.

I checked out Mel's record last night. He's a lower-tier threat. He's got more than a few arrests, but only one case that was documented of him flipping on his client. It didn't say what for, but most mercs have at least a couple of black marks where they switched sides. Mel's mostly a bruiser, but he's got some speed. He usually carries a sawed-off shotgun because this is the south. It's practically standard issue. He also packs some kind of high-end fistloads; that usually means brass knuckles mixed with a taser.

"Looks good," I say, handing the clipboard back to Mel. "When can we leave?"

"I'll give Mel a call. Unless he's got something happening, he should be able to be here in a few minutes."

A few minutes means different things in different parts of the world. In the south, a few minutes means roughly half an hour. Any vague amount of time is rounded up to the next half hour. Specific expressions of time like 'forty-five minutes', '12:30', and the like are given a nine-minute standard deviation. If somebody says 'I'll be there in forty-five minutes', you can expect them to arrive anywhere between thirty-six and fifty-four minutes. So yeah, a few minutes.

Mel is a big dude. He's got beefy arms and a neck so thick, it's basically just traps that meet his chin. He's got thick tufts of blonde hair on his shoulders as he walks in wearing a sleeveless armor vest and black-and-white camouflage military pants. Not sure what environment that kind of camo is for, but whatever. He's got a tactical belt and that shotgun draped over his back in a nice-ish harness. He gives me an upward tip of the head, then asks Matt, "Yeah?"

"Mel, this is Rhest," Matt introduces me as I lean on the front lip of his desk. "He put in a bid for a simple escort mission." Did Matt not tell Mel about the job?

"Sure, whatchyu need?" Mel asks a little condescendingly, like he's doing me a favor.

I tell him, "I need to do some local investigating. I'm trying to find a pretty obscure antique that was sold at a mall quite a few years ago." Yes, I'm being vague.

"Whatchyu looking for?" Mel asks.

"A CD," I say. "A compact disc. Music. It's not valuable at all; only to my client."

Mel puckers his lips and nods in growing approval, an act that makes his chin look like a walnut. "Okay, when you wanna go?"

I stand up right then and there. "Let's do it."

Mel's got a supped-up nightmare of a car. It's a red Firebird-looking thing with a huge engine sticking out the front of the hood and giant off-roading tires. Not quite monster truck giant, but they come up to my waist. The thing has two exhaust pipes that run along the chassis, just behind the doors. The rear window is covered in a sunshade colored to look like the Confederate Flag. Like I said, Alabama loves their seditious past. We hop in and I expect the stereo to be blasting country but I'm greeted to 1990s gangsta rap. Huh.

"Where to first, boss?" Mel asks me as he fires up an engine that's way too loud.

"You got a vinyl or record store nearby?" I ask him.

"Dave 'n Berry," he suggests, like that means anything to me. It doesn't but I point forward all the same. This going to be fun or a disaster. Not that the two are mutually exclusive.

***

Dave 'n Berry is not a store. It's two guys who run a stall at a flea market. They've got a folding table and two collapsible chairs and a dog that looks like the brains of the operation. They've got milk crates, liquor boxes, all sorts of containers that are meant for anything but music. But they've got music. Records. Cassettes. CDs. It's all stacked and packed tight, organized very loosely by genre.

As I approach, I'm guessing Dave (simply because he speaks first) says, "Well hello there, Mr Mel. Who's your friend?" 'Mr' Mel? What is this fascination to call people by an honorific, and then their first name?

"This here's Rhest," Mel tells the two men in plaid shirts and jeans so old, I'm not sure they even make that cut anymore. "He's looking for a CD." Berry spits in a soda can and gestures a touch sarcastically at the collection before them.

"It's a specific CD," I tell the prunes. They both smirk at my lack of a southern accent. I half expect dust to fall off them when they do. "It was sold at the counter in one of the malls near here."

"What was it called?" asks Dave, the one not wearing glasses. I have to just shake my head. "Who did it?"

"It was an instrumental CD," I explain, with hand gestures, though I'm not sure why or what the gestures are meant to convey. "Mostly it was rain with some instrumentation added."

"Well boy, if you don't got a title, that's a problem," Berry says in a voice too high for a body with a gut that pronounced.

"Do you know of anywhere I can get a list of all the CDs sold?" I ask them. "I've got a range of years to work with."

"Son, there ain't no way," Dave laughs.

Berry, however, has a thought. Given the pained expression, I'm worried it's the first one he's had in quite a while. "Well, what about that colored fella?"

'Colored fella'?

"Oh!" Dave says with partial recognition. "Uh...yeah." He strains to think. "Jimmy?"

"Timmy!" Berry corrects.

"Timmy!" Dave agrees. "Yeah, you need to go see Timmy. He was a manager or something at one of them music stores. Took it real serious, too. Tried to make it a career. Thought he was gonna go places if he managed a music store." They laugh at his foolishness from behind their flea market stall. "But he got a good memory for the little stuff. He knew every last thing he sold. Knew what the competition sold too." He pronounces it 'com-po-teh-sun'. "Without a title, he's your only hope."

I check with Mel. "You know Timmy?" He shakes his head. "Where can I find Timmy?"

"Down at the old folks' home," say the two octogenarians. Their confidence seems to chiefly come from their mutual recollection.

I check again with Mel to see if he knows where that is. To my relief, he nods and says, "Come on."

Sarah Lee Nichols Sunset Community is the kind of place most people have nightmares about when they contemplate their mortality. It's less a retirement home and more a vast array of death wards. A pre-casket waiting room. I don't look forward to dying – which in my line of work is a statistical certainty to happen sooner rather than later – but I'm grateful that whenever or however it happens, it won't be in one of these places.

It clearly used to be a school or a daycare, based off the once-bright exterior and the once-vibrant rooftop. Now it looks abandoned. The paint on the exterior isn't just peeling; it's taking some of the exterior with it. Spots are cracked, in some places so much that the insulation can be seen sticking out. A few windows are patched with plywood and I see spider-webs between the tiny air conditioning units and the building itself. The grass is mostly dead, but it's mowed short, so hey, that's something.

Me and Mel pass right by two guys in scrubs who are smoking. One guy has a joint, the other guy has an e-cigarette. I guess they work here, but hell if I know what they do. Given the way they are indifferent to me and Mel, I'm not sure they know. Through the vapor and weak smell of pine cones, the smell of death is obvious before the sliding doors even open. The floor tiles are faded and warped, a few even missing. Gurneys that smell like urine are stashed right by the entrance.

I see a nurse's station on the other side of the main intersection. It's unattended. I approach and glance around the chipped light blue counter, not quite sure what to do. Mel just reaches right over and gets a medical chart. The way he tosses it back, it clearly wasn't of any use. He starts for another.

I spot an old geezer on a bench beyond the station. I pat Mel's shoulder and start towards the guy, only for something to upset me. I slow, Mel does as well. It takes us a moment to realize the guy's dead. He's leaned back against the wall and has passed. I touch his neck and feel nothing. Hand to his nose and feel nothing. I switch my vision to thermograph and can see the body heat has long since passed.

"Boss?" asks Mel, like he's reminding me of why we're here. Like I'm distracted.

I don't know if he's callous because he's young or because he's a street merc. A lot of mercs don't have high regard for life. Once you've killed more people than you are years old, you tend not to be phased by death. And to be fair, most deaths don't get to me, but I'm not so callous as to not occasionally be affected. I hope I never get that callous.

I don't argue or protest or anything. I only nod and turn, Mel and I departing from this man. We leave him to find his way to whatever afterlife he wants.

We're just turning when a nurse appears at the nursing station. Given the way the older Asian lady is glaring, I'm guessing she actually cares about her job and the people she's in charge of. Given the way other nurses are walking very slowly about, I'm also guessing she's one of the only nurses here who does. "What are you two doing here?" she snaps at us. Before I can answer, she snaps at Mel, "I told your boss that he can't send thugs to just hire themselves out to our residents."

"These people got rights and they got money," Mel asserts.

"These people are on hospice care!" she argues. Wow, a southern accent is terrifying at high volumes.

I slip between the two. I don't have the patience, the interest, or the time for this. Mostly the interest. "Hi, my name's Rhest and I'm looking for a guy named

Timothy?" I say it like I expect her to automatically know who I mean. She leans in a bit with a sway of her black bob cut and a sarcastic look, like she knows I'm an idiot for just such an assumption. "Timmy?" I clarify. The look in her eyes suggests she has an idea who I mean. "Used to run a music store at the mall?"

The woman straightens up. "Yeah, I know him."

"He ain't dead yet, is he?" Mel asks.

The nurse glares at him. "What do you want with him?" It's not a question, it's an accusation.

"He's got some intelligence I need for an operation," I tell her. People like it when you get all military-like. "Just a couple of questions. You're welcome to join us. Supervise." Mel scoffs.

Something is announced over the intercom overhead, but hell if I can make out what the garbled speech conveyed. The nurse could, however, because she takes her stethoscope off her neck. "Straight down, then left at the T-intersection," she tells me and Mel, gesturing with her hand. She's already turning to go the opposite direction. "He should be all the way at the end." She doesn't run but she walks as briskly as a person can. I can tell it's a life-or-death emergency; just not the first one of her shift. Nor will it be the last one.

Timothy 'Timmy' Halston is sitting on a bench in a medical gown, holding his cane as he watches people (nurses) go by. He's just people watching (checking out their butts) and nothing else. He sees me and Mel approach and he snickers. He's an ancient man, so old it's almost stunning. We get near and he says angrily, "What you want?" His voice is a rasp. It exhausted him just to shout.

"Mr Halston, I—"

"Don't you come no closer!" he tries and fails to bellow. He points his convenience store cane at us like it's a gun.

"Don't you talk like that, boy," Mel tells him.

I hold out a hand to subtlety remind Mel that I'll take the lead. "Mr Halston," I repeat a little slower and slightly less racist than Mel's 'boy'. I approach very slowly. "My name's Rhest." I speak loudly. Not slowly, but clearly and deliberately. "I was hoping you could help me."

"Help you?" The old man laughs. It's a pained laugh. He might just keel over right now, this is so taxing on him. He's smiling, too, so at least it's entertaining him. "Help you what, son? I ain't got nothing. My grandson stuck me in here a hundred years ago. I ain't seen nobody or nothing since then. Ain't nobody know I exist no more, I don't know nothing and nobody."

"I just need some information," I ask. Several nurses walk by us, clearly indifferent to the heavily armed men in the nursing home. I see Timmy's eyes follow the nurses' behinds and I smirk. "Help me out and I'll buy you a nudey mag."

"You trying to give an old man a heart attack?" Halston coughs. "Cause I had three already. Stroke too." He pauses for only a second. "You get me something with some Asian girls?"

I am extremely uncomfortable right now. "No problem," I tell him with faux certainty. "You want full figure?"

"Of course," he shouts, I'm not sure why.

"I'm going to go get your magazine," I promise him. "First, I need to know about when you worked at the music store."

There's a twinkle in his eye when he hears that. He looks up at me and his brow furrows. He looks confused. "The music store? Hollys?" He speaks just a touch more clearly. He laughs and a tear rolls down his cheek. "Son, that was forever ago."

I nod. "Maybe, but you managed it. I need your knowledge. I need your help."

As long as I live, I will never forget his expression. He hasn't been of any help or any use to anyone in years. Decades. Hell, he's so old, maybe that crack about a hundred years ago wasn't a joke, you never know. To be asked to help, to be asked for knowledge that he has, to be needed, is more than he thought he'd ever experience again. "How can I help you?" he asks me with long-forgotten but deeply ingrained confidence. It's like he's at the front of the store, greeting a walk-in.

As nursing codes are called over the intercomm, I kneel down before him. His eyes are distant and he looks passed me. It's like he's in a trance. "There was a CD," I say slowly and clearly. "It played rain with just a little bit of music. It was sold at the counter of one of the music stores here in town." I see the wheels turn in his mind. He nods slowly. "I am looking for one of those CDs."

His eyes turn to me and I'm not speaking to an old man in a nursing home, running out the clock until he dies. I'm speaking with a young man with his whole life in front of him, who is going to make his fortune running the best music store in the county, in the state, in the world. "We don't carry that here, I'm afraid," he says with a young man's manners and an old man's voice. "You want to check out ELP. They carry CDs like that."

"ELP?" I whisper back at Mel. He's at a loss.

"Yessir," he says, the trance fading. He taps his cane twice. "ELP was one of them other stores. Don't know too much, but I know they were the only ones that had them CDs at the register. At least that kind." I stand and thank him. We head out for the nearest gas station where I can get him his magazine.

"ELP was a store, a smaller chain," I review off my HUD of my pre-mission notes as Mel revs the engine. I don't know if that's needed when he cranks it, or if he just likes doing it. To be fair, if I had a car with this kind of muscle, I'd want to let the neighbors know. "They only had a few stores. They didn't operate for long before they got absorbed." Mel waits patiently as I think. "We need to find a shipping manifest," I realize.

I run a quick search and find there's wi-fi at this retirement home. Its password protected, which means it takes me less time to hack then for me to tell Mel, "Hold on a second." I bring up my HUD's browser and start an internet search, checking sites. "I can't figure out what happened to them, if they were bought out or..." I report, more speaking aloud than sharing pertinent information. "If their office is still there..." I look through my HUD at Mel. "You know where Rosemary street is?"

ELP's main office was on the second floor of an office building downtown. Judging by the cardboard over the first floor's windows and the broken neon light outside the tailor's office just below it, nobody has legally been here in a while.

I ascend the cement steps to the front door. Heavy chains are wrapped over the handles. I'm about to break out my trusty-ish lock pick set but just touching the door causes the hinges give. The heavy door leans forward, the chains all that keeps it from falling on me. I check with Mel if this sort of thing happens regularly. He seems unimpressed so I guess so. We head inside.

The smell of urine and mold greets us for a second time today. The office space has been turned into a shanty town by the homeless. I smell fire and see burn marks on the roof. Trash is everywhere. Little forts and other structures have been erected in corners. The place is clogged with cheap tents and other housing options that should have been temporary years ago.

There are stairs to immediately greet us, the third stair rotted out. When I step on the first stair, the whole structure groans angrily. I check back with Mel who seems amazed at my weight. I guess it didn't occur to me, or maybe he doesn't even realize, how cybered I am. Funny, I tend to assume that's a job requirement. Maybe in Alabama, it's not as common.

We very carefully ascend the steps. More homeless people are up here, but they keep mostly out of sight. At the head of the steps, I see a 2nd Floor Directory and, sure enough, there's ELP's main office to our right. The door's been kicked in and been re-attached very flimsily. I push with minimal effort and it swings in

To greet us are two naked women in a carnal embrace, their hands between each other's legs, and a much younger woman filming them. Both sapphoric performers shriek while the camerawoman grabs up a pistol and turns it on us. Mel freaks out and grabs for his shotgun way too slowly. I just hold out a calming hand at the camerawoman. "Chill, lady." I say it with just a touch of condescension, like it should be obvious we're not here for her or her starlets.

The two nude ladies scamper behind a tent and hide jiggly bits and scars. I can see hollow eyes and sunken cheeks as well as spindly fingers. One woman looks anorexic, and chemically so. The other has limbs just as skinny but a rubbery midsection that has tattoos that have been warped by age and wear. The camerawoman looks a bit healthier, though I suspect its only from shorter exposure to this lifestyle. Her jacket is more than a hand-me-down and her men's pants are a few sizes too big. As the performers hurriedly unstrip into sweatpants and multiple shirts, I address the camerawoman. "What are you doing?"

"Filming a porno," the woman/girl says with hatred. Fingers retighten on the handle of the pistol. "We got to do SOMETHING to eat." She speaks like she blames me for her plight. Not just me, anyone. Everyone. Her left eye is red and blood-shot, and patches of dull blonde hair are missing from her scalp. I can't tell if they fell out or were pulled out. Her skin along her hair is irritated and breaking out.

Poverty versus porno is an age-old debate and I'm not getting in the middle of it. "Look, we need some records from out of this place," I tell her with a look at the office. It's still full of filing cabinets and other storage bins. "You want to help us out?" She scoffs. "Make some money?"

Camerawoman looks uncertain. The thinner of her stars, however, shouts, "You got it!"

Mercenary work can be full of action. It can be glamorous and delightful, full of thrills and adventure. Or it can be stressful and terrifying. For every hot tub of grateful models, there's a shootout in some alley where you're sure you're going to be left for dead, alone and forgotten. For every rooftop chase, there's sewer diving. For every easy fight, there's a brutal brawl that leaves you shaken from your soul to your bicuspids. Those are the extremes though. Because a lot of the time, mercenary work is just tedious and boring.

People think street mercs know guns forwards and backwards. People think we're combat experts, trained in every form of martial arts and warfare. And, let's be honest, we are and that's true. But you want to know what serious mercs are also trained in: the Dewey Decimal System. The BISAC system. NLM Classification. The Library of Congress system. Hell, I even took a class with a rogue librarian (boy, there's a tragic line of work these days) on the Ranganathan's system.

You learn filing systems. Whether it's paper files or digital files, you learn how to navigate all the ways people organize their information. Why? Because we get hired a lot to deal with information. Always to find it, and then to conceal it, destroy it, ship it, send it, share it, something. Every job is different but I'm confident at least half of our jobs involve information. And information is always categorized. Always.

See, in the day of corporations, information and the ability to get it is tantamount to gold (definitely worth more these days, too). If you're smart, you learn every system of organization there is and you learn it fast. When you've snuck passed the cameras and you've got three minutes before security figures out you're in their system, you have GOT to find the targeted data. Every second you can shave off a search is that much better a chance you have to see tomorrow.

I say this because A) I once located a lost kid using just the spine of her favorite book and figuring out which library she frequented because of their filing system, so you best believe I work that into every conversation I can and B) because I probably clear 60% of the ELP office in the time it takes both performers, the camera girl, and Mel, to get through one shelf each. If you know what you're looking for, you can quickly discount whole racks of papers. If you don't know what you're looking for, you just flip through each sheet until you find something that looks promising. Still, even if they can clear one metal filing cabinet, that's a help.

"Hey, is this important?" asks one of the performers. Me and Mel turn as she holds up a manila folder with a hand that is solid black from so many tattoos. The pages inside the folder slip and they spill out onto the floor. She curses, but I start to pick up the sheets. "Sorry," she says.

"No, it's fine," I tell her as I look over the pages. "Actually, you may have found something."

"Do I get a bonus?" she asks. I can't fault someone trying to hustle me for every dime when she's resorted to doing porn for food.

"What is it?" asks Mel so I don't have to answer her.

"Terms of sale," I say as I begin scanning the page. Both visually and literally. My eyes make a line-by-line record of the document, just in case I need it later. "Looks like ELP was bought out, by Termagant Enterprises." I lower the page. I think this through for a moment. "Makes sense. Once Termagant became the cornerstone of all shopping on the internet, they started buying up the local retailers left and right. Usually after driving them out of business." Really, it's a standard practice these days. I check the net and confirm several wi-fi networks available. I start to hop online.

A quick search and I practically exclaim, "There's a Termagant warehouse outside of town?" I look at Mel. "Geez, no wonder your local economy sucks."

"Hey, them people gotta work," Mel argues.

"Exploiting temporary employment laws isn't work," I dismiss. I get some more files from the ground and read over them. "Termagant bought ELP's excess inventory, so if the CD's anywhere, it'll be at that warehouse." I look to the girl and women and sigh. "I don't have cash." The three look furious, but don't say anything. I think real quick and then suggest, "Do you like O'Tolley's?"

Under the bright lights of the garish fast food restraint, the three-woman porn team take their overloaded trays from the counter. "Can I get three fifty-dollar gift cards too?" I ask the woman behind the register. As she rings me up, I look to Mel who's sucking down a milkshake. "Do you know where the Termagant warehouse is?"

He shakes his head. "I can call Matt, though. He probably does. It's aways out of town, I can tell you that."

"What are your highways like?"

Mel scoffs. "I ain't gonna risk the highway patrol."

"Backroads?" I ask instead.

He gives it some thought. "Depending on where it is, we should be fine. Most of them are still paved, if cracked to hell. Definitely overgrown. 'Course, if it's it not in a civilized part of the state..." He cocks his head to the side, as if marveling at the danger. I've heard horror stores, but in my experience, they're usually watered down.

Cards bought and distributed, we leave for the darkness of rural Alabama. With a quick detour to the autoshop.

Pell City Alabama is a straight shot east from Birmingham. The Termagant warehouse opened up there in the first decade of the new millennium and promptly took over the local economy. It employed all the workers at stellar rates...until the local businesses started going out of business. Termagant offered great benefits, on-site resources, and early access to hot products. And like all corporations, once competition dwindled and regulation was loosened, those benefits began to fade. Quickly.

By the end of the second decade, the Pell City Distribution Center was little more than a slave farm. Everybody was making pennies on the dollar of minimum wage, without any benefits or job security. Exploiting temp-worker laws, Termagant would fire an employee just before 90 days, only to rehire them the next day, all to avoid hiring full-time workers. Underpaying the workforce allowed Termagant to create an entirely dependent community. They sold healthcare and food and housing, but at marked-up prices, requiring the workers to take out loans from the corporate bank. All at rates that seemed good unless they read the fine print, and even then, it's not like there was much choice. At the same time, Termagant kept up a vicious disinformation campaign to convince the workers that it was the union's fault, or migrant workers, or whoever the scapegoat du jour happened to be. Anybody but Termagant itself. And the corporation made money hand over fist all the while. I'd be more disgusted but, like I said, this is the go-to business model for most corporations these days.

The result is that the lands between Birmingham and Pell City are less country rural and more hellish landscape of redneck dystopia. Those who couldn't or wouldn't work for Termagant tried to live off the land, which turned them into little more than primitives. They took to feudalism and setting up stone-age forts with satellite TVs and trampolines in the backyards. So long as they didn't cause the corporations too much headache, the corps didn't hire mercs to deal with the problem or lobby the state government to do something about it. That means the locals prey on one another, or the rare traveler driving through their territory.

This is relevant the first time we come to a blockade.

A bridge crossing the Cahaba River is blocked with busted up, rusted vehicles. I'm pretty sure Mel's car-truck hybrid could either slam through them or just ride over them, but he slows, his great engine still growling under idle. "I don't think the bridge is going to hold the truck's weight," he tells me.

"Yeah, not with all those guys on it," I agree.

There's about ten deer hunters dressed up in militia costumes. They've got hunting rifles and revolvers, although one dude is sporting a machinegun that I'm pretty sure can't fire. "I'll handle this," I tell Mel before slipping out of his car. I glance behind us and confirm there are some more guys in the bushes a few paces behind the bridge. Pretty poor flanking, but it probably works most days.

I approach the main crowd ahead of us with my hands very casually up and away from my guns. "Sup," I call to the leader. He's a bearded older dude in a ducking-hunting jacket and camo pants. He looks like the type with more cars that don't run than do, and a penchant for girls younger than his daughters. "I need to get passed. How can we make that happen?" Just come right out and ask the toll.

"Depends on what you got," the guy tells me. "That car sure looks nice."

I feign considering it. "I dunno. Dude behind the wheel's pretty attached to it. And his guns." I give the leader a 'it ain't worth it' look. I look passed him at the blockade. "Those the best cars you got?"

Duck Dynasty looks back at the cars and laughs. "Not a chance."

"You know the roads out here are pretty rough," I tell him, just as an observation. "I bet their hell on your tires." The man looks at me with willingness. I look back at Mel and nod. The trunk pops and he gets out, his shotgun real obvious, as are his oh-so-impressive muscles. Sheesh, way to be subtle. Anyway, he goes around back and takes from the trunk a big truck tire. With some serious strength, he hoists it into the air and the tire slams onto the edge of the bridge, bouncing a few times before it comes to a stop a few feet from me and Phil Robertson. I look at the tire, at Redneck Prime, and back at the tire. "How about this and three more, for safe passage through your territory?" He gives the tire some serious consideration. "Common size, so they'll definitely fit one of your cars," I sweeten the pot. "100,000-mile warranty if you trust that sort of thing. I even kept the receipt."

The man nods slow. "You got a deal." I shake hands with a devil and count myself fortunate. I'll count myself legitimately lucky if he upholds his end of the bargain.

"That tire move was slick," Mel says as we rumble through backwoods Alabama. We've got no radio reception so the stereo's playing something from his phone. I can't tell what it is and I'm not paying close enough attention.

"Thanks," I accept, looking out the window. I see a cluster of trailers down a small ravine. One trailer's roof caved in. I'm not sure that's stopped anyone from living in it. I see kids playing in the dirt near the river.

"Those were nice tires, too," says Mel.

"It's not a bribe if it doesn't cost a lot," I observe. He's feeling me out. He's going to cross me. The only question is if he'll do it before, at, or after the warehouse.

I'm not sure monolith is the correct term for the Termagant Warehouse. I associate monolith with tall and while the warehouse is definitely that, it's bigger than that. In the neighborhood of four stories tall, it's probably two or three times as wide. Not sure how deep it is, but I'm guessing miles wouldn't be the worst measurement.

There's a cement wall with a metal gate that rolls into place. Not sure if they're trying to keep out cannibals or the state militia. Not sure which would surprise me more. There's a guard station but nobody there. My guess is the entire facility is automated at this point. I have Mel pull up to the gate and keep the motor primed.

I slip down out of Mel's car and approach the guard station. The (armored) glass of the door is cracked, a spindle web coursing through the material. I tap at it with my knuckle and pop out a few fragments. It takes some muscle but I'm able to knock in the glass enough to get at the door handle on the inside. The smell of refuse and death wafts through the hole.

Inside is a corpse. More skeleton than body, he's been dead a long time. There's food packaging around him, all of it junk food, the kind you'd get in the warehouse. He's bundled up tight. I'm guessing he didn't have anywhere else to live. I check the gate controls and try a few of them but get only declined responses. Easy enough to remedy.

I could hack the system. It wouldn't be that hard, but giant corporations pay a lot for top-of-the-line security systems. It would take a minute to be sure. Fortunately, corporations often can't allow for the human element, so it only takes a minute of digging through the corpse's pockets to find his phone. It's still got enough juice to turn on, so I check the signal settings and get the password. From there, it's a simple act of ordering the gate to open. It's rumbling back before I turn away. "Thanks, buddy," I tell the corpse, leaving him in his final resting place.

I climb back into Mel's car and he shifts it into gear. "You know this place has security systems, right?"

"I do," I tell him.

"What do we do when we have to deal with them?" he pushes.

I leave it at, "We deal with them." With a double-point of my finger, I urge him on. With only a bit of reticence, we start forward.

Greeting us through the gate is a massive parking lot full of abandoned cars. Some of them were clearly turned into homes at one point, too. Like with the security guard at the gate, I feel confident in assuming they're now caskets. There's a part of me that wants to go digging through the cars and see if there's anybody left, but another part of me – the part that's seen this sort of thing before – knows the ferality of any who might remain. Rather than look to help, I check all six of my guns to make sure they're loaded. Before today's done, there's going to be shooting.

The Termagant warehouse has a main gate at the front that looks big enough to house a space shuttle. The heavy metal doors part down the middle but forcing them open would be impossible. Next to the giant doors, however, are smaller human doors on either side. Both require keycard access, or wi-fi and a quick sixteen-digit hacking program. I run it as Mel and me walk to the door. As I reach for the handle, the door pops open in compliance.

Inside, we find signs of a riot. The initial room is cement with nothing but benches. No lockers or cabinets or anything. There's blood in a few corners, stains that have festered into mold. It's been a while but I'm guessing this was a serious brawl. You might think this was some inhuman horror from the eldritch depths, but it was probably just the last day workers were employed here. When even slave labor gets laid off, there are some sore feelings.

Through the foyer is another security lock (yay, hacking!) and we get a gauntlet of scanners. Metal detectors. X-ray devices (...aren't those illegal?). A bio-scanner (yep, those are WAY illegal). Even a cybernetic code sequencer (those are too esoteric to even have laws governing them). Geez, I've seen military facilities less secure. Black box military facilities at that.

There are cameras in every corner of the room, and a few in the middle. There are no blind spots, and no corner that doesn't have at least two vantages. Even more, some of the cameras move. I know because they move when we come in.

"Mel," I say and nod at the camera that looks at us. He cocks his shotgun. "Sup," I tell the camera before he can poke the bear with a stick. "We're here to get an item. We'll place an order and pay."

The camera just stares.

"Why are you talking to it?" Mel whispers.

"Because it pays to be nice to machines," I assure him.

"It's a camera," says Mel.

"It's not alone," I warn him. I lead Mel through the gauntlet of scanners, ignoring them when they make noises. Lots of bells and whistles and buzzers and alarms. I almost feel like a contestant on one of those kids' obstacle course shows. Only, like one of the kids that sucks and he does absolutely everything wrong.

We get to the next door: a metal door with security bolts, two of which have to be manually opened. The latches are loose. I'm guessing the result of fighting and damage. I'm just not sure on which side of the door the fights took place. I start to undo the locks but when I go to open the door, I discover its locked on the other side too. What the hell? Talk about fire hazard. Although, come on, this place has the best anti-fire system in existence. It's just not for the employees' benefit.

I juggle the handle for a second before Mel says, "Come on, man, pull."

"I am pulling," I insist.

"Let me," condescends captain muscle. He grabs the handle and yanks, then stops when he realizes just how sturdy this is. I see him check on me out of the corner of his eye and then he pulls again. He strains for a second, then he steps on the wall, trying to pull the door. Nada. "Damn," he curses, giving up without acknowledging his equal inability. "Well, want to find another entrance?"

"They'll all gonna be the same," I surmise.

"Can you hack it?" he asks.

I shake my head. "These are the manual locks."

"I don't see how we're going to get through," he says. "Shoot it?"

"That's 32-gauge steel, man." When he readies his shotgun, I go hide behind an X-ray scanner. Given there was a riot and these scanners are not just standing but in working order, I'm guessing they can take the ricochet of a shotgun blast. And they do! Click, bang, boom, ricochet. I peek out from behind the scanner and look at Mel. He glares at me like it's my fault, the door sporting nothing more than a scratch.

I check the roof. No tiles; just concrete. Concrete we might be able to shoot through since ceiling materials almost always need to be a bit porous, but I'd rather not waste the rounds or the time. We might be able to go back outside and climb the wall, but I doubt Mel's much of a climber. Whelp, only one thing to do. When hacking and brute force won't work, go to science.

"Come here," I tell Mel and we go to the X-ray scanner. I kick the machine and it doesn't budge. Oh, I'm going to enjoy this. "This is your fault," I yell to the camera that's been watching us this whole time. I punch the scanner's inner window, cracking the glass. "If you worked with us, we wouldn't be doing this." I reach inside and grab a whole bunch of wires.

"What are you doing?" asks Mel.

"We're going to polarize the door," I explain as I yank the wires towards the door. "If I'm right – and what are the chances of that happening? – we'll magnetize the door and it will repel the locks."

Mel stares with a dumb look. "We're going to what?"

I'm spending way too much effort tugging these wires. "Just...give me some muscle here."

It takes us almost ten minutes. The wires I'm pulling on eventually tear, so we have to start over. Once we've broken inside the X-ray machine, we basically have to dismantle it. That takes a hot minute, but it usually does when you're trying to take something apart rather than break it. The whole machine is eventually gutted and I'm able to plug the wires into the door like we're trying to jump a car battery.

"Here we go," I warn Mel before we touch the door with the wires. We heard a bang. "Cool," I say with pride. I try the handle and it doesn't open. "Crap, we just secured them further. And then I get to say the sentence hadn't realize I'd lived my whole life to say: "Let's reverse the polarity."

Mel stares blankly. "Let's what?"

"Reverse the...the polarity?" I repeat, less confident. "Go from positive to nega...nevermind." We switch out the wires and the flow of electrons. There's a slick unsheathing sound and the door half-pops inward. I grin like a fool. 3rd grade science and too many Star Trek reruns have finally paid off.

Of course, when we open the door I was so proud of unlocking, a team of security robots are waiting for us.

"Go left!" I yell immediately, strafing to the right. Reason and Respect, my two primary pistols, begin to unload on the primary two robots. They're big gray domes with red eye slits, looking like the portly cousins of Maximillian from the Black Hole. Mel goes left, pegging the two machines at the back that look like skeletons on treads. One of each turns to go after us.

Pre-weight-loss Max comes at me, shooting a current of electricity at where I was a second ago. I blast its projector with a shot from Respect, blowing the gun off and blowing a hole in its torso. I follow it with a shot from Reason, a precision weapon with more accuracy than a laser. The bullet goes right through the damage hole before Max can turn. I hear the ricochet inside and Max starts to fidget and spin before he falls over.

The Terminator Tank starts to rumble towards me, two giant hands reaching out. He may not have guns but he's all armor. I have to empty both clips into his torso before finally bringing him to a halt. People wonder why robots have heads and faces? It's so humans will shoot them there and not in their torsos where their actual processors are. Going for the head on a robot is dumb.

As I change out my magazines, I see a headless Max and a headless Terminator going after Mel as he retreats. I start to peg Terminator from behind. He's got thicker armor on the back (in case of a riot), so I don't score a full hit until I change out magazines again. He sputters and dies like his brother.

Rubenesque Max doesn't deviate from his target and chases after Mel as he retreats behind a shelf. I'm not getting through his armor unless he comes at me with a weapon out, and he's going to keep on his primary target, however arbitrarily selected he is.

It dawns on me to adjust his selection. I shout "Hey, robo...mall cop!" (look, they can't all be winners) and I start shooting at the shelves. Just firing indiscriminately at the merchandise. If I shoot up the box with the CDs, I'm going to be sooooo pissed.

It works because Maxi-weighs-a-million turns and comes right at me. Taser out, I rinse and repeat one shot from Respect and one shot from Reason. Down he goes, collapsing to the ground like a dropped brick. No shower of sparks or crash; just suddenly inert. "You okay?" I call to Mel as he comes out from hiding, sporting a few nasty electrical burns. He nods, out of breath and rolling his shoulder like he's trying to walk off the bad shock. "Okay, we got to move fast. More of them are on their way."

"How we going to find it in here?" he asks, looking at the warehouse.

This thing is all one BIG room. Giant. Colossal. Huge. Absolutely massive shelves are packed to the definition of dense, with almost no room between them. Little elevated retrieval bots zip on tracks connecting the shelves, removing objects at breakneck speeds and depositing them into waiting trucks that then take said products to be wrapped for shipment. Nothing has an interface. I could hack them but it would take time, and my attention, and the air is alight with the hum of robots approaching. The smooth cement floor is positively vibrating with the rolling treads.

I look behind us and see a few additional doors. "Come on," I say before dashing for the next door. I yank the handle and it's locked. It's also wood so screw that. I kick it twice and it breaks enough to force open. We slip inside before we see any other robots. We're in an office, so jackpot. "Secure the door," I tell Mel. I run to the nearest computer. I put my hand right on the computer terminal so I can expedite the connection.

I dive into the computer and find myself in a corporate office. That's just a visual representation, though. What's happening in reality is my brain is processing all the 0s and 1s and displaying it in a format my mind can process. I rush up to the main desk where a lovely woman with jerky, inhuman movements smiles with the uncanny-est valley smile ever. "How can I...you?" she asks.

"I'm looking for a discount CD sold at ELP music stores," I tell her. I quickly add, "I want all of them. All the CDs, all copies."

The woman smiles wider (which is so damn creepy) and starts to simulate typing. "We have no such CDs labeled like that. Can I interest you in—"

"Do you have a list of all unlisted acquisitions? Unlisted on the Termagant website?" I ask quickly. Having dived into a computer, I can't tell what's going on outside of me. The robots may have already overwhelmed Mel. This has got to happen quick.

"I do," says the woman with a smile that's fake even for a faux computer program. "I am afraid you don't have authorization to see that list."

I dive back out real quick to check on Mel. He's got the door blocked with a heavy desk and he's sitting on the desk, adding his weight to it. He seems fine otherwise. "Just a minute," I tell him and I dive back in. I'm back in front of the woman in the nice corporate foyer. I step back out of myself, like a ghost leaving a body. I see the world of code, halfway between the reality of computer hacking and the Hollywood version that makes it more dramatic, and thus more fun.

I review the drives and executable files in the code and look for opening keys. I change out some code using a fake diagnostic software, which is kind of like using modified RNA to change the DNA of a cell. I slip back into my simulated body and the woman smiles again. "Got that list of unlisted stuff?" I ask her.

"It's available right here," she says, handing me a tablet computer.

I take the tablet and see a list. Crap, it's long. Twenty-nine pages of just the products starting with the letter A, long. Okay, discard all the compilations. Discard the indie artists. Discard discounted versions of more popular collections. Slammin' Wrestling Hits? Who would buy this stuff?

I purge the list of like 90% of the titles. Anything that couldn't possibly be Eubanks' album, I purge. "Okay, pull all of this," I tell the woman and hand her back the tablet with the remaining titles. "I want every copy of every album on this list. Ready for shipment. Pickup on-site."

"Yes sir," she says with a voice that sounds way too enthusiastic. "How would you like to make your payment?" I suppose I could just hack this part too, but you think a corporation will kill you for breaking and entering? Imagine what they'll do to you for stiffing them on payment. I extend a credit card for Eubanks account (which is actually just auto-filling out the billing information in their system) "No problem, sir, this will take just a second," she assures me. The bill is a surprisingly small number. Given I'm buying a bunch of CDs, I'm worried the one I want isn't amongst them, but no time to worry about that now. Giant, armored, killer robots are on their way, if they're not here already.

"Order has been filled," she informs me. "The package is awaiting you at our facility. Go to the—" I dive out. We got killing to do.

I turn to Mel as he bangs in a bit from the robots on the other side of the door. "Ready?" I call.

"Whenever you are, boss," he says through the strain of holding the door.

I step back from the desk and hop once. "On three," I tell him.

"You mean," he asks suddenly, stopping my energy. "Like one, two, THREE, or one, two, three, then..."

"It's musical!" I yell at him. I count as I tap a pretend cymbal with one of my guns. "One, two, three, go!"

"Okay!" he yells back at me.

"One, two, three!" I yell and hop into a sprint. Mel rolls off the desk as I leap at the door and dropkick it. Sturdy wood goes spraying out as the door is knocked into Bloated Maximillian. There are six Tank Terminators this time and four Maximillians. We ain't winning this fight, and I bet there's still an order of magnitude more of them on the way. I backpedal out of the crowd, firing shots with Reason and Respect just to keep their attention. I manage to do that and ten robots turn to me like a crowd of hobos wanting your meatball sub.

Mel slips out and I keep backing up. The robots are quickly approaching, but I back into one of the order robots. I glance back and see a big-ish brown box with my name on it and Eubanks' mailing address. "Son of a bitch," I both say and think. I slip my guns into their thigh holsters, grab the box, and sprint for the door. "Cheese it!" I yell to Mel as we both start to run.

Tank Terminator gets in my way, so I hoist the box into the air. It sails in a tight arc (no spiral, though) and Mel catches it. He spins around another Tank Terminator and leaps ahead. He falls back as a Maximillian closes in, then goes for a lateral pass to me. I catch it and stiff-arm a Terminator before rushing around to the outside. We both run and make it to the door we came through, sliding inside as the robots rush to catch up. I'd be lying if I said there wasn't an urge to spike the box.

We don't stop in the security room, we run straight through. The far door is swinging closed but Mel grabs up a piece of the X-ray machine and throws it at the doors. It doesn't exactly block them from closing, but it slows them down enough for us to both dive through like we're trying to escape an explosion out of an action movie. The box gets caught though.

On the other side of the door, Mel and I blanch at the box caught between the closing doors. Thinking quickly, Captain Redneck grabs out a giant knife and slashes the cardboard shipping box. CDs spray out and I grab up all of them that I can. Mel does the same and we manage to get the majority of the discs. Our arms absolutely full of old-style jewel cases, we go racing out of the building.

Running like the most unambitious looters in the world, we make it to the car as we hear the whirr of drones from the rooftop of the facility. The drones are slim and sleek, but wide, like surfboards flying sideways. They're also armed with enough firepower to take out a municipal skyscraper. We don't have long before they start shooting, so we toss all the CDs into the floorboard of my side of the truck and Mel shifts into gear. I check the side mirror just before seeing the Vulcan cannon of a drone shoot off said mirror. Somebody screams "Holy hell!" and I'm pretty sure it was me.

Mel roars out from the space and races down the main thoroughfare of the parking lot. Two drones zip after us, raining down fire all around us, but fortunately scoring few hits. The roof has some tiny sunroofs in it now and we lose a couple of copies of 'Romantic Sea Ballads', but whatever. As Mel drives, swerving this way and that to avoid rapid gunfire like a water hose of death as well as plenty of grenade-quality missiles, I open the door and take out Victory. A small shotgun of a pistol, Victory's firepower isn't measured in kilotons but only because then it would be classified as a war crime to carry it. I pull the trigger and the drone explodes hard enough to ignite some of the nearby trees.

I think the other drone got scared, I really do, because when the smoking fire of its partner subsides, I don't see it anywhere. The corpse of Robbie the Robot crashes into the road behind us and Mel begins to slow down. I look at him, he looks at me, and we both laugh.

Few joys in this life can match surviving when it all goes to hell. As mercenaries – whether you're talking about street mercs, professional mercs, or just hired thugs – the thrill of making it out of a dead-end situation like that is simply indescribable. We all have our own way of celebrating but it's usually something along the lines of a cold beer and a warm body.

As we drive back through rural Alabama, I go sorting through the CDs on the floorboard. I discard quite a few that turn out not to be viable candidates (who names their punk album 'Sounds of Rain'?). I organize the rest into groups. There's not a single CD I don't have multiple redundant copies of, so assuming it was in the warehouse, we've got it here in my hands.

"You got it?" asks Mel as I sit back.

I just sigh. "I damn sure hope so."

As we drive, the afternoon settles into dusk. Fireflies begin to appear in the night, a multitude of them illuminating the dark patches of the trees. Leaves light up under their surprising numbers, making the night twinkle. Amidst gossamer draped from branches and the trees swaying in the cooling night breeze, the beauty of Alabama reveals itself. For a moment I forget about the poverty and harsh practices that have become so common, they're the culture. Instead, I see a natural beauty I'm not used to seeing in Sacramento. The sky is a rich color I don't know the name of and the air has a sweetness to it like a memory.

We return to urban life and civilization, such that it is. Mel takes me straight to the merc office, which is fine with me. I've packed some of the CDs into some of the pockets of my combat harness and I carry the rest. We go strolling inside to find Mat still behind the desk, filling out forms. He looks up and smiles. "How'd it go?"

"Well," I say, knowing full well how bad me and Mel look. "I'd like to settle up, please."

Mat looks more than a little delighted. I'm worried how many paying customers they get. He tallies things up quickly and hands over a legal pad with the numbers jotted all over. The final total is circled at the bottom. Of course, it's about fifteen percent more than I was quoted. I don't bother asking about the different charges. Whether they're made up or legit, I have to pay them or shoot both these guys. I don't want to do that. I pay. I even tip Mel 10%. Not quite fair but maybe it'll leave them with a good impression of out-of-town work.

"Thanks for your help, guys," I tell them both, shaking their hands and smiling. I collect my CDs and get on my way. I push through the glass door into the dilapidated parking lot of the shopping center forgotten by time, and definitely forgotten by customers.

There are six armed men waiting in the parking lot.

I sigh, still kind of smiling at the inevitability of it all. I notice the door doesn't shut behind me and I turn back to see Mel and Mat walking a few steps behind me. I just ask, "Really?"

Mat justifies his pending inaction with, "You're off the company's time now."

I've got my hands full of CDs (which, even seeing this coming, I should have known not to do) so I can't quick-draw on these guys. They've all got long guns (four shotguns and two rifles), so I bet I could drop four of them before they even started shooting. However, Mel is behind me. Even if I'm as good as I think I am and they're as bad as I think they are, this is a bad spot to be in.

"What do you want?" I ask, bored.

"The discs," says Mel. "And who you were selling them to."

Again, I sigh. "Okay," I surrender. I turn around to Mel and hold out the CDs. "His name is Adelphus Masters. He lives in Portland Oregon." I put the CDs in Mel's hands, switch on dark vision, and activate my virus sitting in the utility company's code.

Every light in the shopping center flashes bright and then goes dark. It's like a dozen lightning flashes all at once then total black. My dark vision buffers for the flash and then I'm the only one who can see. I whirl around with Reason and Respect, three shots with each and all of Mel's dudes are dead. After tipping this ass 10% on top of them already price gauging me? Yeah, I'm not shooting to wound.

Mel's dropped the CDs and is grabbing his shotgun when I shove him against the store front and put Respect to his chin. I slam his head hard into the glass hard enough for the chaotic pattern of cracks to reach the frame, then I get real close. I'm pissed. I saw this coming but it still pisses me off. "You're going to betray a fellow merc?" I accuse him. Actually, that's probably a poor stance to take. Mercs betray one another all the goddamn time. "You're going to betray a paying customer after the king's ransom I just paid you? What the hell's wrong with you, fool?"

Mat's fumbles out a pistol of his own and is putting it to my head. "Quit it," I just tell him, sparing him a glance and nothing more. When the pistol isn't removed, I slap it away and then punch Mel in the side of the neck when he tries to get his shotgun ready. I yank the gun out of Mel's hand and field strip it (not an easy thing to do when you've got a pistol in your hand). As I dismantle it, I toss parts and shells in all directions. I stand over him, Respect still in my hand. "The only reason I'm not shooting you – either of you," I make clear to Mat, "is because my bullets are worth more than your lives."

I collect as many of the CDs as I can in one scoop. I get at least three of each CD. "I'm putting a stop payment on that charge," I tell Mat. He drops his hands like that's just mean of me. I backpedal a good distance to make sure Mel isn't going to cobble together his shotgun or draw a backup weapon, but he looks like he's accepted defeat. Once I'm most of the way out of the parking lot, then I risk turning and walking (briskly) into the night.

Back in the hotel, I grab up my stuff and pack quickly. One set of CDs goes in my bags. One set stays in my harness. The remaining sets, I package for mail. One goes to Eubanks directly, overnighted. One goes to Macee's agency. Redundancy is your friend when it comes to transporting valuable goods.

Next, I call the airport and book the next flight to Sacramento. No, I don't care what airline. No, I don't care about layovers. No, I don't care about drink service. No, I don't care about anything except getting off the ground as fast as possible. I'm not even going to bother with trying to arrange an air marshal situation. I gots to go.

Lastly, I call a transport. They're like a taxi but where you don't run the risk of being dropped off at an alley to get jumped by a whole squad of junkies. Once that's confirmed, I grab my bags and make for the front desk. I check out (and buy some snack crackers because they've got nekot & peanutbutter). The transport is pulling up as I'm on cracker four of six.

Dude's car has flames on the side, which is kind of awesome. He pops the trunk and I throw my stuff in the back. When the door doesn't open though, I freeze. "No eating," he yells through the window. I scowl at him and shove the last of the crackers in my mouth. They're harder to savor but I manage. Off to the airport we go!

The door opens and the suspiciously young butler is there. "Mr. Rhest," he says with professional aloofness. He bows his head a bit and steps back to open the door wider for me. "Please, come in."

I'm straight from the airport. I got a bit of sleep on the flight, but not much because we had to fly over Texas. "Mission was a success...I think." I take out the CDs from my harness, having to dig through multiple different pockets. As I take them out, I push them into the butler's arm, quickly overwhelming him with the juggling act. "If any of them are scratched or won't play, I've got redundants that I mailed from the airport in Alabama. One grouping is coming straight here."

"Very good, sir," says the butler, still struggling to keep from dropping even a single CD. He manages with surprising grace. "Mr. Eubanks will be delighted, sir." His words are ecstatic but his tone is placid and even flat.

The blonde babyface butler leads me into a different room this time, a study. Giant walls of books head up to an abnormally tall ceiling painted to look like a cheerful blue sky. A giant window looks out over the side yard and Eubanks is staring into the distance. "Mr. Rhest, sir," says the butler as he enters the study. He walks with an awkward tilt to keep control of the CDs.

Eubanks wheels around in his manual wheelchair, the left wheel squeaking on the soft gray carpet. "Quick work, sir," says the old man, delighted. His voice is raspy. Next to him, he has two glasses. One's of orange juice, the other is of chlorophyll. Quite the odd combination of smells.

"It turned out to be relatively straightforward," I report to him. "I, uh, I hope I got it."

Eubanks develops a bit of a light in his expression as he wheels over towards the serving table. The butler is laying out the CDs for his consideration, setting out each jewel case like it's a priceless treasure. To Eubanks, one of them is. He only needs to glance at them before his eyes light up like a child on Christmas morning. His voice doesn't shake but his finger does. "That one," he says, pointing at one CD on the back row. The cover is a fairly affair with purple clouds of a thunderstorm and some generic font. Layout is like what a middle school student would throw together the day before a design assignment is due. "I remember it," he tells me with a smile. That time, his words tremble. He swallows tightly as his eyes tear up. "Won't you..." He gestures very generally at the butler.

"Of course, sir," says his man. The butler takes the CD with surprising care and, wearing white gloves as befitting his role, approaches a shelf of books. He lays down a very convincing masquerade to reveal a really nice sound system. When he turns it on, the room takes on a hum. Really, really nice sound system. Out slides a CD tray which I can't see but hear, the room is so quiet. I'm not sure Eubanks is breathing, he's so excited. The butler starts the CD with a beep.

"I hope this is it," says the old man, wringing his hands in his lap. He's quiet now. Humbled before the possibility he had thought impossible. I'm humbled by his eagerness.

In short order, rain begins to drift through the room. It's an elegant, delightful shower, like I can almost see the drops hitting forest leaves and dribbling onto the ground. It sounds like a soothing, gentle rain, dense and saturating. The kind of rain that makes you feel safe, not threatened. The kind of rain that all but requires inactivity and surcease. This is aural serenity.

Eubanks leans back in his wheelchair and smiles with a relief I don't think I'll ever know. Tears of quiet, gentle joy drip from the corners of his eyes. He's lost in happy thoughts, remembering every good thing that ever happened in his childhood. The CD takes him back to a time when the world made sense and he felt safe. I'm honestly envious.

Distant rumbles of harmless thunder echo in the rain while very subtle, minimalist tones of flue and violin play to accentuate the natural melody, to complement it. I look at the butler who has a pleased look on his face. He shifts towards the door. "Some water, sir?" he asks very quietly to me.

"That'd be great," I whisper back.

He departs and I share in the music with Eubanks. It's quite an experience to watch someone else reconnect with such a lost treasure. A flash of light gets my attention as a neighbor pulls in to their distant driveway. The sunlight contrasts with the music, so I silently cross the study and lower the blinds. I do it very slowly so as not to disturb the experience for Eubanks. The room is now in deep shade and thanks to the stellar sound system, it sounds like it could really be raining outside.

I walk back towards my place by the door, glancing at Eubanks again and that joyous, contented smile. It takes me a few seconds to realize that he's dead.

I approach him slowly and very gently touch his skin. With no response, I check his pulse, then feel for his breath. I'm feeling his heart when the butler returns, a frosty glass of water on a silver serving tray. He pauses at the door when he sees me over Eubanks.

"He's gone," I tell the butler, just over the sound of the rain. There's a very genuine sorrow in the young man's eyes as he places the tray to the side and joins me with Eubanks. With surprising medical skill, he confirms what I've said and seems resigned. "I'm sorry," I tell him.

He shakes his head. "It's fine." He doesn't speak like a butler, but a normal human. He cracks a smile, which is odd to see on a face I've only seen as professionally impassive. "This is, undoubtedly, the best way he could have gone." He sounds grateful as he looks down on Eubanks' smile. The old man is content in a way only sleeping children ever know.

Chip Masters, Ninja: part 4
A Crossworld Short Story

> *"Sword fighting is a little like making love. It's not always what you do, but what you say."*
>
> - Sword Teacher, The Secret of Monkey Island

Chip Masters leaned on his left hand, positioned to the side of the stadium seat. Looking down into the deep bowl of a stadium, he studied the runners as they lined up at the starting line. Around him, a vast host of people – most from Seir-reth but a few clearly from other city-states – were watching as well. There was a nervous murmur to the crowd, as well as plenty of anxious laughter.

Chip turned as Hatsumi sat down in the seat next to him, carrying two paper cones of popped corn. "I've got butter and caramel," he said, handing the butter over to Chip. Smooshed together in the narrow seats of the modest arena, they leaned forward over the railing separating them from the next row of seats two steps down.

"Did you place the bets?" Chip asked. He pointed at a plainswoman in the middle of the starting line. "I'm telling you, she can fly."

"If she does, she's disqualified," Hatsumi told Chip.

"I was speaking metaphorically," Chip said, covering his pale brow and sandy blonde hair from the sun as he checked the sky. "Who'd you bet on?"

Hatsumi scanned the runners for a second, his Asian-like features mixing as well as Chip's among the predominantly swarthy-skinned people of Seir-reth. "Uh...that guy."

Chip turned to his friend. "That guy? You don't even know his name?"

"It's not the person, it's the lane," Hatsumi said, sticking his tongue into the caramel corn and pulling out the popped kernels that stuck.

"That's gross," Chip complained, taking some of the treat off Hatsumi's cone. Hatsumi responded by taking some of the buttered corn from Chip's cone.

Over the middle of the field, a solitary ball of flame rose into the air. It began to spread, forming into thick bands in the air and shaped into numbers. Numbers that were systematically counting down. "Here we go," Chip said eagerly, bobbing up and down in his seat.

The instant the flaming numbers hit zero, a loud trumpet sounded. The racers broke from their starting positions, running down the track. Flawless form drove them as they grouped quickly. Chip and Hatsumi screamed in support, both of them soon jumping to their feet. The entire stadium rose and clapped and cheered, shouted and called. The racers arched around the first turn and the group shuffled. Leaders fell back and those behind began to move towards the front of the race.

"There he goes, there he goes!" Hatsumi told Chip, pointing. "I told you, it's the lane!"

Hatsumi's racer, with skin as dark as the twilight sky and speed like a tornado's wind, took to the lead along the second straightaway at the far end of the course. Hatsumi screamed, Chip unable to contain his own excitement. "Go, go, GO!" Hatsumi yelled.

The racer made it to the edge of the turn with almost two lengths between him and the 2nd place runner. He turned into the final turn and slowed down. Holding his arms up, he cheered to the crowd. "What are you doing?!" Hatsumi yelled. "Finish the race, you moron!" Chip's cheers had ended and he was laughing now, mostly at his friend.

As the racer turned to finish, he was passed at the last second by another racer. The pair raced neck-n-neck for the finish line but it was Hatsumi's racer who came in second. "WHAT THE HELL?!" Hatsumi screamed. He turned at Chip who had fallen back into his seat, laughing. Hatsumi scowled and threw his caramel popcorn at Chip. That only made Chip laugh harder. Hatsumi fell back into his seat and sulked. "What the hell?" he griped. Chip put his arm around Hatsumi and hugged him supportively, even as he chuckled.

Hatsumi sighed and ate some of the popcorn out of Chip's cone. "Geez, that sucks," Hatsumi griped.

"At least your guy placed," Chip consoled. "You can get half your money back."

"Yeah, I guess," Hatsumi complained. He picked some of the popcorn off Chip's desert clothes of layered breezy attire. He popped the kernels into his mouth. "So where's our contact?"

"Behind us," said Chip nonchalantly. "He's been back there for the last two races." Hatsumi turned and looked back and the tall man with dark skin smiled pleasantly and waved. "You've been a little preoccupied."

To the man, Hatsumi said, "Hey, what's up?"

Behind the railing for the next row of seats, a pleasant-looking man with deep tanned skin and black hair smiled back at him. He had an iced drink with him as well as a roasted vegetable on a stick. "I'm called Cadres," said the jovial man. He extended a hand to Hatsumi. "Like the shop." Hatsumi glanced at Chip who just shrugged, not knowing the name either. "I'm Kageryu's Chunin for Seir-reth, under Jorge."

Hatsumi took note of the thinning crowd around them, whole chunks of the stadium exiting between races to either place more bets, got refreshments, or simply satiated for the day. "So what's the deal? Our Chunin, Kagumi, said something about an extraction?"

Cadres nodded. He checked his own racing stubs, shuffling the tickets forwards and backwards. "It will be here, in Fades," Cadres told them as he arranged his bets as if that would change the outcome. "I'm making contact with him, get him through Seir-reth's territory, and we'll ultimately be smuggling him to Crossworld."

"You're making contact?" Chip asked, only half-turned to Cadres.

"What, you didn't think they were going to leave this to a pair of Genin did you?" Cadres laughed.

"A little bit, yeah," Chip said.

"That's why we're here, isn't it?" Hatsumi agreed.

"No," Cadres laughed harder. "You two are here to provide support to me and our defector if its needed."

"Why not use a local pair of Genin?" Hatsumi asked.

Cadres looked both amused and incredulous. "Training, obviously."

Chip and Hatsumi both glared at each other. "Of course," they said in unison.

Cadres leaned forward and patted them both on the shoulder. "Don't sweat it, boys. I still get this crap from Jorge. He still gets it from Kageryu."

On the field down below them, racers began to exit onto the track. Their names echoing through the air as they approached their starting points. Some waved to the people in the stands, others strutted with athletic focus. "This is a good time to go," the Chunin told them. "The crowds are coming back." He rose and began to slide through the seats, heading towards the stairs that divided the arena's sections.

Chip and Hatsumi looked to each other, less than enthused. Chip ate some of his popcorn by sticking his tongue into the kernels and eating whatever stuck. "That's gross," Hatsumi told him, getting up to go. Chip followed.

Outside, in the large town of Fades, Cadres walked with Chip and Hatsumi on either side. Through the market square, people walked in every direction at different speeds. Vendors were set up, selling products and services from across the spectrum of needs. Not only were the sales diverse, so were the people. Turban-clad desert dwellers of Seir-reth walked next to armored warriors from Crossworld and abnormal-looking figures from Tech-Noir, in outfits akin to the suits Chip knew from his home on Earth.

"His name is Alfin," Cadres shared with the pair as they walked, his knee-high boots kicking up only a bit of dust. "He's a low-ranking member in the Ember's League."

Chip slowed half-a-step. "Ember's League?"

"Local gang," Hatsumi told him.

"They aren't local; they're inter-city," Cadres told them. He turned around and, walking backwards, explained, "They've got agents in all five of the city-states and a lot of the smaller towns, like here in Fades. They're everywhere. Agent for agent, they may have more operatives than the Shinobi but that's just a guess. We honestly don't know."

Chip looked at Hatsumi and seemed impressed. "I didn't realize we had competition."

"Ooh, would we call the competition, though?" asked Cadres rhetorically before he turned back around. He bumped into a man who had been walking diagonally across their path. "Hey!" Cadres yelled in his face. "Watch where you're going!" He kept walking, the man he'd yelled at making a rude gesture as they departed. "Anyway," he continued, suddenly nonplussed by the encounter, "Ember's League is letting Alfin be extracted on the premise that he's going to be an informant for them. He'll report back to them periodically, but only to feed them information we provide him."

"This is crazy," Hatsumi told Chip. His blonde friend agreed with a nod.

"Spies versus crooks is always a bit of a head-spinner," Cadres agreed fraternally. "The point is, he's being extracted tonight. I'm making contact and staying with him; you two are to provide support."

"Is he trustworthy?" Hatsumi asked. "Are we letting a..." He did some math in his head. "...a triple agent into our midst, or a traitor?"

"I don't know, above my rank, and definitely above yours," Cadres told him. "Just focus on your mission."

"But why are we doing this?" asked Chip. "Why are we even involved? Does this guy have information that's critical to the Shinobi's safety?"

"No," Cadres told them. "We're not in danger. However, it is important to stay on the pulse of all information. Knowing information means helping information sources, sometimes even if their information is less-than-critical. It's to curry favor. Not just with a specific information source, but with future information sources." Chip and Hatsumi both tried to reason that out.

The three arrived before a stone building along an unremarkable street. Vendors lined the far side, while establishments continued passed the stone structure in both directions in a slight circle. "This is the Phosphooradin Tea House."

"Phosphooradin? What's that mean?" asked Chip.

"I don't know; it sounds made up," Cadres told him. "Point is, I will be bringing Alfin down that street..." He pointed down the street they had come, "to this tea house. We will be followed. I leave it to you two to obfuscate us, attack our followers, distract them, whatever you wish, so long as it does not draw attention to Alfin's departure and definitely does not reveal the Shinobi." He put his hands on each boy's shoulders. "You will be ranked on effectiveness, efficiency, and subtly. Probably in that order." He clapped both Chip and Hatsumi's shoulders. "Until then, the afternoon is yours. I strong recommend you scout your positions, set whatever traps you wish, place weapons, and generally prepare."

"We will," Hatsumi promised Cadres with the utmost earnestness.

The shop would have been a spacious eight-sided room were it not for the reams and reams of fabric that were draped all about. Folds of fabric spilled over one another, like the room was a giant collection of fountains, the flow of which was caught in time. The western-most wall was absent, replaced with two folding dividers for when the shop was closed. With the dividers open, the desert wind occasionally blew into the room but was absorbed magically by a trio of small blue stones that would glow whenever a gust kicked up.

Chip lounged on the sofa in the very center of the octagonal shop. A Gameboy Advance in his hands, he tapped the controls a bit with his thumbs, focused on the small screen. Behind him, the shopkeeper swept desert sand through the door and out into the daylight. The man paused and brushed his brow, then turned. In an aged and accented voice, he asked, "You are from Tech-Noir, yes?"

Chip glanced back at the man who had spoken to him. "Yeah," he lied, used to giving that as an explanation. "Not actually Tech-Noir, though. A little city outside called San Francisco."

"I don't know it," the man remarked offhandedly. He had deeply tanned skin and plentiful lines on his face. Scratchy white hairs stuck out from his chin and lip, like a poorly-shaved van dyke. He was about to say more when Hatsumi exited the dressing room.

Wearing a deep blue turban and a pale gray gown, Hatsumi nodded and grinned huge. "Huh? Huh?!" he asked with increasing eagerness. "What do you think?" He turned around, mostly showing off the belt that visually and functionally held the bland outfit together. "I think I look like a desert native, right?" Chip responded with a shrug. Hatsumi's arms fell. "You're no help."

Chip asked the shopkeeper. "What do you think?"

"Meh," said the old man. "It depends on if he is buying it. If yes, then of course, looks wonderful. You look like we look," he gushed. "If no, then no, you look like child playing costume-dress-up." He pointed at his own face. "It's the eyes."

"That's racist," Chip told the man.

"Is not," the old man said confidently back.

"I think I look good," Hatsumi decided. He went to a mirror and checked his reflection. He turned a bit, then gestured at the mirror. His reflection continued to turn, showing him off from every angle. "Yeah, this works. It totally works."

"Whatever you say," Chip agreed, focusing on his game.

"I think the dark brown belt and blue turban really hold the whole thing you really don't care, do you?" Hatsumi asked Chip. Chip just shook his head, lips pursed. "Are you playing with that thing again?" He started to come over. "What are you playing?"

"Final Fantasy 6," Chip said, showing him.

"What, again?" was all Hatsumi had to say to Chip. To the shopkeeper, he said, "I'll take it."

"Wonderful!" the older man suddenly gushed. "You look magnificent! You look like we look!"

"I heard you just a moment ago," Hatsumi told him. "I was right there."

"Yes, but that was then, this is now," the old man said as if it was praise. He headed to his sales ledger, Hatsumi following.

As dusk began to creep across the sky, Chip and Hatsumi stood at a vendor on the corner of the nearest cross street from the Phosphooradin Tea House. A purveyor of all varieties of dried fruit, the vendor was beginning to close for the night. Behind the counter, a dog with spikes extending from its shoulders laying defensively atop the man's sales chest.

Chip looked up, along the rooftops a street over. "If we've got fellow spies, rooftop seems the best route for them." He turned and looked down at the ground beneath their sandaled feet. "Does this place have a sewer?"

Hatsumi shook his head, crinkling his nose at the jelly-like fruit that was both spicy and sweet at the same time. He was sweating mildly from the spicy taste, the bottom of his turban a distinctive shade darker. "I think waste is removed magically? Or just transfigured? I don't know."

"So we've got the roads, or maybe the rooftops," Chip reasoned.

"Or the air," said Hatsumi, speaking dramatically to avoid having to keep his mouth closed. "They might fly."

"Not a chance," Chip asserted confidently. "The risk of being spotted is too great. And Seir-reth archers can take down anything they see." Hatsumi gave it a moment of thought and agreed with only a little hesitation. He resumed eating the fruit. Chip asked him, "You got any reanglers on you?"

"A few," Hatsumi said, sucking the juice out. He inhaled suddenly and winced tight. "Uh, wow, geez, that's intense." His toes curled up in his sandals and his eyebrows flared as his eyes clamped tighter. When the heat and pain subsided, he blanched with relief. "Whew." He handed the tough skin to Chip. "Want a bite?"

"Hell no," he scoffed at Hatsumi.

"Your loss," his friend coughed before popping the rind into his mouth and wincing all over again.

Nighttime.

Fades was a modest town, nestled between two roads that broke before it. One southern route headed into the endless sands and rocks of the southern deserts. The more-northern road headed straight east and to the very gates of Seir-reth. Whereas Fades was a modest village with roads and paths leading out in all directions, Seir-reth was a monument. Massive walls on the exterior of the city rode out of the desert like it was a mesa all its own. The city thrummed with life and even across the distance, its presence could be felt over Fades.

Fades itself was lively, although the evening was beginning to die down. As dinnertime passed into night and the evenings fires began to burn out, the city was beginning to calm. Tiny trails of smoke rose into the desert air, mixing into the soft breeze that carried the town's scent into the sky. Lights in windows and doorways burned bright while the long shadows of dusk had turned into the blanket of twilight. Stars overhead twinkled with not a cloud in the sky.

Alfin and Cadres walked down the street, the only two out. Cadres wore a Tech-Noir suit, carrying a black fabric satchel normally worn on the back. Gone was the visage of a harmless desert ne'er-do-well. Instead, the Shinobi Chunin looked every bit a responsible and upstanding businessman. He walked casually, while alert eyes very carefully searched his surroundings at all times. He looked unbothered by a single thing in the world while at the same time, he was aware of all.

On his right, Alfin clutched a large sack to his chest. In a red and white vertical striped desert dress, he turned frantically in every direction, panic clear on his sweat-soaked brow. He shuffled more than walked, as if too afraid to fully pick up his feet.

As they entered the intersection with the Phosphooradin Tea House in sight, Alfin slowed, paranoia getting the better of him. Cadres caught his arm, just above the elbow and pushed him into continuing to walk. The smaller man gave out a yelp of fearful protest but kept going. As they cleared the intersection, two figures rose from opposite rooftops. Dressed in a deep brown, like desert sand in shadow, the pair was almost invisible atop the earthen-tones of the rooftops. They carried deeply curved swords worn blade-out on their backs, the curve of the weapons cupping their torso.

With scarves across their faces, they watched Alfin exit the intersection. They reached into wide leather belts and drew out metal discs with subtle ridges on the exterior. The throwing weapons ready, they drew back their hands to attack, unaware of Hatsumi and Chip were right behind them.

Hatsumi kicked his target in the back of the knee, just as he was about to throw. The desert assassin dropped, too stunned to react. Hatsumi caught the throwing disc out of the air. Holding the weapon no bigger than a large coin, he yanked the assassin's mask over his eyes and slashed his throat. Had the blade not ended his life, the poison it had been soaked within would have.

On the other side of the street, Chip grabbed his enemy's hand and yanked it back. He pulled the man off his feet and slapped him onto the rooftop. Pinning him with a shoulder lock, Chip transitioned quickly into a chokehold and kept it locked well after the foe had ceased moving. Silently, he laid the man onto the surface of the roof and left him there. He looked across at Hatsumi. His Asian partner pointed at Chip, and then pointed to the tea house. He pointed at himself and swirled his finger. Chip nodded and leapt off the rooftop.

Landing a story below on the surface of the road, Chip rolled at the impact and came up in a brisk but casual-looking trot. He started into the intersection when a shadow moved against the still night. Chip turned to face down the road and snapped both his fingers. He pulled his hand down his face and in doing so, his vision shifted. Color drained from the world and he saw only endless dark tones. Purples and deep blues filled his world as near and far became cast against each other like a painting. All except for three figures in vibrant, unmissable green.

The shapes of the assailants were rounded and warped, like bubbles against the two-dimensional background of the rest of the world. Their movements were stilted but their attention was obvious. All three slowed when they realized Chip was looking right at them and their invisibility was gone. Chip dropped low and grabbed at his back, pulling from its sheath the straight-edged sword of the Shinobi. As the three dropped their façade, Chip's vision returned to normal and he rushed into the street at them.

A fight commenced in utter silence. The nighttime was not disturbed by the clashing of steel or the shrieks of effort and pain. All that was heard was the whipping of the wind as blades carved through the air, narrowly missing. Attacks were precise and calculated, as where the movements to avoid them. Less a berserk bombardment, more a furious dance with lethal consequences, the four fighters battled as quiet as a cloud.

Chip slashed at one man, missing by inches as the desert assassin leapt over the slice, landing in a roll that bought him space from Chip's blade. Another swung at Chip, who spun around the blade and slashed at the man's head. A quick duck and a retreat meant no hit was scored. Chip instinctively slipped suddenly to the side, avoiding being impaled from behind. He flipped backwards, landing a bicycle kick with his shin to the man's face.

Chip landed on his shoulders and flipped up to his feet. As he did, and his kicked opponent began to rise, Hatsumi dropped from above. Landing blade-first on

Chip's downed foe, Hatsumi's sword drove all the way to the hilt through the man's chest. The desert killer let out no scream or sound, only a whitening of his eyes as life left his body.

The two other assassins backed away from the two Shinobi, rethinking their strategy. Chip and Hatsumi rose and turned, squaring off with them. The only noise the droplets of blood from Hatsumi's edge dripping to the dusty road beneath their sandals. He and Chip backed slowly away, step by step. A wind brushed through the streets, noisier than them or their opponents.

As the desert assassins inched nearer, very subtly closing the distance, Chip released one hand from the handle of his ninjato. He slapped his thigh, the impact sounding like a shout in the quiet street. Immediately, Hatsumi disengaged. Lowering his sword, he turned his back to the pair of assassins and retreated, leaving Chip alone. The two desert killers weren't sure what to think and hesitated.

Hatsumi ran only a few dozen steps to the intersection and, once there, drew from a pouch on his side a single steel ball. He threw it down the street, then tossed a similar ball in the opposite direction. That accomplished, he turned back to the attackers and slapped his thigh just as Chip had done. Letting Hatsumi watch his retreat, Chip disengaged and broke into a run.

The two killers abandoned their third and gave chase. Chip sprinted ahead of them and leapt out of the intersection. Only steps into their pursuit and the pair of desert killers realized they were charging down the road they had just left. They stopped and turned and raced to return, only to realize they were facing the opposite direction yet again. They looked this way and that, angles changing on them and roads that should have been adjacent were paired opposite one another. No route led the way they expected and they found themselves bewildered and lost just standing still. Before they even grasped their own confusion, they also realized they'd lost all sign of the two Shinobi.

Through the swinging doors of the Phosphooradin Tea House, Chip and Hatsumi found bright candlelight and soft music. The crowd was tipsy with a pleasant evening, the crowd of businessmen discussing matters all their own. A single musician played strings in the corner as wait staff bustled about. In the corner opposite the musician, Cadres waved to the pair. He and Alfin were sitting with their backs to the establishment, a hookah and a large tea tray on the table. Chip and Hatsumi sat cross-legged on the cushions and reported, "All clear. Now."

"Good job," Cadres said, blowing smoke out through the corner of his mouth. "Why are two of them still alive?" he asked, as if a quiz.

"So they can tell of how badly they got beat by the Shinobi," said Chip, not unused to tests like that. "And maybe live in fear of facing us again."

Cadres nodded. "Not the answer I was looking for, but I like it. I was thinking 'because killing unnecessarily is a waste', but whatever."

The two younger Shinobi looked sidelong at one another. "Did Kageryu approve that?" asked Hatsumi.

"'Cause that doesn't sound like him," Chip agreed.

"And you've met the Shadow Dragon?" Cadres challenged in an irritated tone.

"Actually, he has," Hatsumi spoke for Chip. "They fought," he went on. "He survived." Chip smiled almost apologetically.

Cadres was genuinely stunned. "Huh," was all he could say. He looked at Alfin, who was totally lost by the whole exchange. "Well," Cadres started, trying to get back on track, and practically burst. "Really? You fought the leader of the Shinobi? Is he as tall as they say?"

"He's a good head taller than you, yeah," Chip agreed. "He's also kind of a dick."

"Well, yeah," Cadres agreed, as if it was obvious as the night is dark. He put all that aside. "Anyway, we've got more pressing matters." To Alfin, he said, "We've got to, uh, liberate his family's good luck charm."

"It is not a good luck charm," their contact insisted. The movement of his hand to emphatically express the urgency and importance was the first time his hands had left his satchel. "It is the Manasta Jewel."

Chip and Hatsumi looked at each other, neither sure if the name was supposed to mean anything to them. Their equally lost expressions were little reassurance. Hatsumi asked, "What's the Manasta Jewel?"

"The thing you two are going to go get," Cadres informed them both with a sarcastically contrite smile.

Chip rolled his eyes and facepalmed. "Christ, I could see that coming a mile away."

"The Manasta Jewel is a powerful artifact of the ancient world, and it is a family heirloom tracing my heritage back to the dawn of time," Alfin insisted.

"Yeah, we don't care," Chip told him.

"How big is it and where is it?" Hatsumi asked, on the same page as Chip and in just as much of a hurry.

Along a stone wall, a bird slowly walked on four spindly legs. The rear hips were small, but the chest and torso were much bigger, almost a giant plume of feathers and mass. Two tiny wings fluttered occasionally, while a long neck ended in a small head with a short, angled beak. The bird kept on its pace, eyes bigger than its mouth darting in every direction.

As it passed, a grappling hook landed behind its step. The bird turned and squawked quietly. It bent forward curiously and stared at the grappling hook, the rope trailing behind it. It squawked again and pecked at the metal hook. It snatched the rope in its beak and snapped it with ease. As the rope fell back to the ground far below, the bird pecked at the hook, loosening it and then throwing it over the side after the rope.

During the guard bird's distraction, another grappling hook swung behind it. Chip and Hatsumi climbed silently over the rope, disappearing over the other side of the wall.

The pair landed on the far side of the wall, amid some bushes and behind a tree. Hatsumi landed effortless, but Chip had to roll at the impact, causing leaves to rustle. Several of the guard birds along the perimeter wall of the wide compound turned and looked for the source of the disturbance. Hatsumi stayed close to the ground, the colors of his desert attire muting slowly. His ninja outfit - folds of cloth tied where beneficial and loose where useful - shifted from sand-colored to the color of shadowed soil like the ground he knelt upon. Chip, likewise stayed perfectly still, his breath barely disturbing a leaf. His own ninja attire darkened as well, matching the shadowed underbrush he lay amongst.

Almost one at a time, the guard birds lost interest. They systematically resumed their perimeter guarding, a network of sharp eyes pacing counterclockwise along the wall. The last of the birds was the one directly above the pair. It let out a squawk of disapproval, then resumed walking. Chip risked letting out a sigh and looked at Hatsumi. "They react to movement," Hatsumi whispered. "Be...patient."

They very slowly rolled onto their stomachs and at a hypnotic pace, they began to crawl out from the bushes. "Just...stay...calm," Hatsumi told Chip as they crossed the lush green field.

"Says...the...guy...who...just...HAD...to...use...his...grappling...hook..."

Hatsumi scowled. "I...brought...it...I'm...going...to...use...it..."

The pair kept shuffled on.

A narrow hall extended into darkness on either end. A solitary candle flickered in the breeze fed by distant exits. The fluctuations created a single orb of dancing light against constantly encroaching blackness. At the edge of the darkness, Hatsumi knelt and searched the shadows. Next to him and standing, Chip did the same. Hatsumi reached to Chip's leg and gave him a squeeze, then pointed.

Chip silently shifted his sword in front of him and, bracing himself, partially drew the blade. The newly-exposed steel caught the light of the candle and a bright spot reflected into the opposite darkness, falling right upon another desert assassin like those from the street. The man hiding in the shadows was taken by surprise and unprepared ready for action. Before he could draw his weapon,

Hatsumi had leapt by him, beheading him in a single movement. The ninja landed without a sound and turned, catching the falling head and then steadying the body as he led it gently to the ground.

Chip slipped passed Hatsumi and felt the wall. Finding the edge, he used a knife to carve into the soft stone just a bit, then he pushed against it hard. The door popped open, allowing Chip to get his fingers inside. He pulled open the door wide enough for the pair to see within.

Awaiting them was a room full of beauty. Jewels of all shapes, sizes, and colors were encrusted in the walls and ceiling. Golden foil covered the elaborate walls. Small piles of silver and gold were piled in aesthetically striking locations. Statues and works of art helped to separate the large room into corridors and aisles. Chip smiled at Hatsumi and they slipped inside.

Hatsumi pulling the door to, Chip took out a small gem from within his vest. He shook it a few times, then popped the top with the flat of his hand, causing the white gem to begin to glow from within. Its radiance began to build until it gave off more light than a torch. He held it up, giving them a better idea of the scale of the room. "Geez," Hatsumi breathed, taking in the opulence before them. "There might be more wealth in here than in the rest of Seir-reth."

Chip walked over to a life-sized statue of a woman, carved out of jade and encrusted in elaborate clothes made entirely out of jewels. The life-like statue had closed eyes and a down-cast expression. She had a third arm on her right side, holding a knife. Her other hands were held in a praying position. "I wonder who this is," Chip remarked.

"Don't worry about her; worry about the Manasta Jewel," Hatsumi said. He walked down the middle aisle, appraising the art of every variety. "I'm not sure how we're going to find it," he whispered.

"Alfin said it was big and purple, with silver flakes inside of it," Chip likewise whispered, beginning down the left side.

"There's an entire chest in here of just purple gems," Hatsumi said, gesturing at said chest as he passed it. "What's big? I mean, for a gem? The size of my fist? The size of my head?"

Chip gave up studying the gems and artwork. He began to turn around thoughtfully. "Where are..."

"Where's what?" Hatsumi asked as Chip robbed him of light as he rushed back to the entrance. "Where are you going?" Hatsumi asked in the dark.

Chip didn't answer for a moment, instead heading back around the far aisle of treasure. Hatsumi heard him shuffling with stuff for a moment, then a very quiet, "A-ha!" Chip stepped up on a chest, his face appearing between two statues dividing his aisle from Hatsumi's. "The Manasta Jewel is the size of a soccer ball and its diamond-shaped."

"Great," Hatsumi praised sarcastically. "What's a soccer ball?"

"It's the size of your head," Chip corrected. He hopped down off the chest and resumed looking. "That should narrow it down."

"How'd you figure that out?" asked his partner.

"This isn't about wealth; this is about collecting," Chip told him with a broad gesture at the extravagant room. "Anybody who collects this stuff is going to have reference material citing and describing how valuable it is."

"So you looked for a book that described the Manasta Jewel?" Hatsumi gawked.

"I checked the FAQ, yes," Chip responded.

Hatsumi sighed. "You are so weird."

The pair finished their respective aisles, coming to the far end of the room. There, situated in the corner between a giant one-edged sword the size of the guard birds outside and a mirror that showed no reflections, they spotted the Manasta Jewel. They paused before it and studied it for a second. Hatsumi cautioned, "It's trapped." Chip nodded. "I can do this," Hatsumi told himself and his partner.

He approached the jewel with his knife and knelt before it. The oblong purple gem sat atop a wooden pedestal equal in height to their knees. A single support leg rose into a circular cup that held the jewel from beneath, allowing one to casually look down into its largest facet. Hatsumi studied the leg for a moment, then knelt close and studied the cup through which he could see the smaller facets. He very gently touched the wooden leg with his knife and rocked back, uncertain. "I don't see any traps."

"Maybe it's not trapped," suggested Chip. "I mean..." He gestured at the rest of the room. "If somebody wanted this stuff, they'd have grabbed something else by now."

"I guess," Hatsumi said. He rose, put away his knife, and took the jewel from the pedestal. In doing so, the entire room erupted in a loud, grating alarm. "Or maybe I just suck at finding traps."

"No, you're fine at finding them," Chip argued as they both ran for the door. "You just suck at finding them before they go off."

They slid through the door and pushed it with their backs. The door was considerably harder to shut than to open, but with their combined might, they were able to shove it closed once again. They turned to run, Hatsumi tripping over the headless body of the guard. The Manasta Jewel went flying from his hands, its facets throwing fractal beams of reflected candle light onto the wall before it disappeared into the adjacent darkness. There was a loud clatter.

Chip and Hatsumi were panicked for a moment, terrified of the state of their quarry. Hatsumi quickly picked himself up and ran into the darkness, shouting, "Got it. It's fine." Chip slapped him on the shoulder as he ran by, the two charging through the shadows.

Around them, the alarm sounded. Like a screeching eagle, the sound emanated from the walls themselves, filling the compound with din. Along with the alarm's noise, though, soon came the stampede of feet as guards came pouring from the barracks. With swords and knives, axes and maces, hard men with scars of battle filled the exterior spaces, looking for intruders.

Chip and Hatsumi reached their chosen exit of the compound, only to see the men rushing into the garden through which they had entered. A dozen men of muscle and blades rushed not at the Shinobi however, but the desert assassins dressed like those from earlier in the night. Chip and Hatsumi froze, lingering with the safety of the shadows, as the compound guards fell upon the assassins.

"Huh," Chip remarked, mostly to himself. "I thought those guys were from here."

"Yeah, me too," Hatsumi agreed.

The two watched as four assassins fought the guards head-on. With the thick blades of curved scimitars, they parried sword and axe equally. They fought quietly, dodging multiple blows with acrobatic skill while chipping away at the greater numbers of guards.

"Amateurs," Chip decided, shaking his head, his arms crossed. "They're taking too long."

"Yeah, so are we," Hatsumi told him. With the Manasta Jewel in his arms, Hatsumi slunk back into the hallway and headed out the other direction. They passed the treasure room and headed on, arriving at an intersection of halls in the compound's inner keep. "Crap, which way to do we go?"

"Away from the noise," Chip said, regarding the stomping of feet. The pair looked quickly for cover, finding nothing reliably nearby. Instead, Chip leapt up onto the roof and slung his feet on some rafters. Hatsumi passed the jewel up to him, then as Chip rolled over onto the rafters, laying on his back so as to obscure the jewel with his body, Hatsumi leapt and pulled himself up as well.

The pair of Shinobi had barely disappeared when down the side hall came a dark-haired, swarthy-skinned man in a silk robe. Otherwise nude, he practically ran with a frantic look in his eyes. "They mustn't be gone," he was saying to himself.

A few steps behind, two of his wives went racing after him, both bundling up with more modesty than their husband. "What mustn't be?" yelled the brown-haired wife, the fairer of the two.

"The swords," he yelled after her, his voice disappearing down the hall towards the treasure room. Chip and Hatsumi both glanced at one another and decided to hear out the situation. They heard the heavy treasure room door open and then further exclaiming and the clatter of searching. "Thank Seyurn!" they heard the man breathe. "The swords aren't gone. My fortune, it exists on these blades."

"Bastard didn't even notice the gem is gone," Hatsumi whispered in disappointment.

"One man's treasure is another man's trash," was all Chip had to offer.

"Let's take out the trash," Hatsumi said, getting back to the matter at hand. He swung down on the rafter, dangling upside down as he looked back down the hall. It took a second for him to confirm the married group had yet to leave the treasure room. "We're clear," he whispered and he dropped to the floor. Chip rolled off his rafter and landed with all the noise of a feather.

Hatsumi checked in the four directions and decided on the opposite route from which the trio had come. Staying low and hugging to the heavy shadows, he led Chip down the path. But just as they began to make speed, the candles and torches on the wall all came alive as one. Flames burst into existence and the hallway lit to nearly daylight.

Up ahead, guards appeared, weapons already drawn. Chip and Hatsumi began to backpedal, only for more guards to appear behind them. Chip drew his sword from behind his back and said, "Move!" He burst ahead of Hatsumi and launched himself at the forward guards. He slashed high as he spun, then landed in a low crouch, still turning. The straight blade of his sword cut deep through the first two guards' unprotected thighs. Deep slashes through the thick of their muscle caused shouts of pain and then total collapse.

Chip came up with a sweep of his blade, slicing through another guard from gullet to nose, parting the man in half with the razor's edge of his sword. He turned his sword over in his hand as he swept it through the air and punctured through his most recent victim before the body could fall away, stabbing the final guard through the chest.

As Hatsumi ran passed, Chip grabbed Hatsumi's sword out from the scabbard across his back. Armed now with two straight blades of Shinobi make, he attacked the guards approaching from the rear. Holding both weapons in a reverse grip, the blades traveling down his forearms, Chip moved into the four's midst. He blocked strikes with the flat of his swords and then swept the twin blades in tandem, ending a life with every swing. He danced nimbly between the muscled men, negating their strength with leverage, surpassing their speed with timing. In only a few breaths and as many moves, left them deprived of their lives. "Let's go," he told Hatsumi who had ceased running and was staring, impressed.

The two rushed down the hall, mindful of the clatter of more footsteps. Unsure if they were being followed and running too quickly to worry about it, they spilled out into yet another courtyard. Waiting for them were not more house guards but more desert assassins. Just as surprised to see the Shinobi as Chip and Hatsumi were to see them, the four quickly tore free their scimitars and readied them for war.

"This is getting dull," Chip complained, tossing Hatsumi's sword into the air. Hatsumi dropped the Manasta jewel and, just as bored, snatched his sword out of the air. The two dropped defensively, ready to fight. Immediately, the four assassins began to back away, their masks hiding their expressions but not the budding fear in their eyes.

Hatsumi grinned, proud, and then his grinned darkened. "There are house guards behind us, aren't there?"

"Of course there are!" Chip chastised.

Both Shinobi turned, throwing handfuls of projectiles at the house guards. Hatsumi threw six-pointed throwing stars, Chip threw caltrops, and all failed to hit their targets. But the thrown weapons caused the eight guards to scatter, giving Chip and Hatsumi the chance to turn as the four assassins rushed them from behind. Hatsumi stepped back, blocking an overhead hack from a scimitar, only to skip back farther as a second blade slashed at his stomach.

Chip went straight at the nearest pair of assassins, feinting with a stab from his sword so that he could kick the leftmost of the pair in the face. He landed and rolled to keep from behind split in two by the still-standing assassin. He came up defensively but the assassin was impaled from behind by the house guards. They bypassed the other assassin, letting him join the other two facing Hatsumi. Chip had to backpedal to keep from being overwhelmed by the sheer number of the guards.

A guard with an axe chopped at Chip with a loud shout. He dove under the chop and rolled passed. Chip came to his feet, leapt up, and kicked straight back to hit the guard in the side as he turned. The big man stumbled into two others, the last guard coming at Chip with a sword.

Steel met steel for the first time as Chip blocked the strike. The force of the man shoved Chip back and the follow-up swing did the same. Chip slammed into the wall of the compound as the guards recovered and the rushing of footsteps signaled the impending arrival of still more armed men. "We got to get out of—" Chip was cut off by the guard slamming into him, trying to behead him. Chip blocked the strike and put muscle against muscle, a venture he was fast losing.

Hatsumi flashed by the guard, slicing out his hamstrings. The man yelled and collapsed. Chip grabbed up the Manasta Jewel, already a step into rushing after Hatsumi. Chased by both guards and assassins, Chip laterally passed the jewel as the two Shinobi ran straight for the wall. Hatsumi went bounding up onto the wide perimeter wall, the four-legged birds rushing along their patrol to intercept him. Hatsumi landed and stopped as if without the slightest momentum. Dropping the jewel, he spun around and dropped down onto his belly. Laying down, he held out his hand back down into the compound.

Half a step behind, Chip leapt up and kicked on the wall. He got as high as he could but wasn't even close to Hatsumi's hand. He landed and quickly tore free the scabbard of his sword, then stepped back and leapt again. Hatsumi caught the extended scabbard and pulled as Chip kicked up the wall, narrowly avoiding the blades of the assassins.

Hatsumi yanked Chip up as fast as he could. He barely got Chip within grasping distance of the wall when he let go of the scabbard abruptly and rolled to keep from being impaled by the beak of the first bird that arrived. Chip shouted and grabbed the edge of the wall with his fingertips. "Hatsumi!" he yelped, his grip giving.

Hatsumi spun on his shoulder, legs flared, to drive back the bird. He came up to his feet and leapt, kicking the bird in the head. It hissed and backed away as more birds rushed to its aid, squawking as they neared. Hatsumi grabbed Chip's hand to help him get a better grip, then slashed at the bird.

Chip pulled himself up onto the wall, just in time to slash defensively at the birds that arrived from the other direction. "What do we do?" Hatsumi asked, fencing with the sharp mouths of the birds. Chip looked over the wall at the rooftops of the buildings a street away from the compound. "No, Chip!" Hatsumi protested, right as Chip snatched up the jewel, grabbed Hatsumi by the shoulder, and leapt off into the city.

At the Phosphooradin Tea House, Chip rubbed a leaf against his scraped fingers, breathing sharply as the wound burned worse. The tea house was empty, devoid of even one other patron and only a single host who had fallen asleep in the pre-dawn hours. A solitary candle burned on the table Chip sat at as he scrubbed his wounds.

Opposite Chip, Hatsumi sat topless with a multitude of welts, cuts, and scrapes. He was using a larger leaf to scrub his own slashes on his forearms. He inhaled and stiffened, holding the leaf to the wound as long as he could before the pain grew to be too much. He yanked it away and let the clotting injury breathe for a moment. "Think Alfin will betray us?" he asked Chip.

"I doubt he'll ever know anything sensitive enough for it to matter," Chip said, still scrubbing his scrapes with the leaf. "This seemed more like a..." Chip's words stopped cold with sudden realization. "No," he whispered to himself.

"What is it?" Hatsumi asked, sitting up with paranoid concern.

"No, no, no," Chip repeated worriedly until he fished through all the pockets on his belt. He sighed with relief and took from his pocket his Gameboy Advance. He laid the portable game system on the table with some care, then reached over his shoulder to keep disinfecting the wounds on his back.

Hatsumi rolled his eyes and resumed tending to his own wounds. He groaned, then sighed with relief just after a loud joint pop. He feigned fainting with relief and slumped in his chair. Chip giggled, harder when Hatsumi had to sit up because he'd caught a cut on the backrest of the chair itself. "Don't laugh, ass." Hatsumi threw one of the leaves at Chip.

The leaf floated harmlessly in the air, then dwindled to the ground. "Hey!" protested Chip, catching the leaf before it touched down on the sandy carpets beneath their chairs. "These things are expensive."

Hatsumi looked astonished. "They're stolen."

"Right, so show some respect for how hard they were to get."

"I'm the one who stole them," Hatsumi further pushed.

"Exactly," Chip said emphatically. The confusion, combined with the late-night exhaustion, caused the pair to burst into giggles. They tried to get back to their wounds but couldn't stop the laughter.

When the curse of inanity finally did subside, Hatsumi confided to Chip, "I just...this whole thing...Cadress...it just seems like it was more an exercise than anything else."

"That is because it was an exercise," came a matriarchal voice. Chip and Hatsumi looked up as through the door of the tea house came Kagumi. The seasoned woman with indistinct Asian features walked past the host, making not a single sound as her bare feet padded along the wooden floor. Her normally silvering hair was a striking blue and she was dressed in desert attire befitting a widowed mother. She approached the table at which Chip and Hatsumi sat and helped herself to a seat. "You passed," she told the pair, adding, "Barely."

"Is there any other way to pass?" Chip asked, pushing a cup of tea from the silver tray to Kagumi.

Kagumi accepted the cup and took a sip, surprised by the strength. With a disapproving look at the two mid-teen boys, she informed them, "The fight in the Moogurush Compound was very poorly done. You barely escaped with your lives."

Hatsumi held up his right arm, showing the nasty cut along his side. "Yeah, we know." The slash matched others dotting his arms and legs.

"The grappling hook as a distraction was very well done," Kagumi nodded after another sip of the tea. She helped herself to a few of the shelled nuts complimentary with an order of tea. "As was the use of the re-anglers on the streets outside this establishment. Using them to avoid a continued fight against the rival spies was almost clever. Their involvement suggests possible movement by other forces beyond the Ember's League or the local criminal element. This is something we will have to investigate further."

Chip and Hatsumi looked at each other, a little confused but also hopeful. Chip tilted his head to Kagumi and asked "Will we be getting assigned here on a long-term ba—"

"Oh no," she almost laughed. Chip and Hatsumi were both let down. Hatsumi resumed scrubbing his injuries thoroughly but carefully. Chip collected his Gameboy and returned it to his pouch. "Your performance was adequate, until you reached the compound," their superior graded. "The first death of a desert assassin was where everything went awry." Kagumi told the two young ninja, "We don't leave behind bodies unless it is approved."

The elder ninja finished the tea in her cup and poured a bit more from the kettle. "Are you planning to ever sleep?" Chip mildly marveled.

She emptied the tea cup with a single shot and set it down, then informed the pair, "Cadres has extolled your virtues as operatives, limited though may be. You have done acceptably."

Hatsumi looked deadpan to Chip. "Such praise. I'm getting weepy."

Chip tapped his chest. "She really got me right here."

Kagumi rose from the seat and lastly informed them, "And the notion that the lane decides the victor of a race is positively foolish." She turned and began to depart, leaving Chip and Hatsumi to follow her back home.

Second-Hand Memories

Ayman Shedani dropped off the pull-up bar and ran to the barbell across the room. Sweat dripping from his dark skin, he grabbed the bar loaded with plates. Hands wide, he braced himself, focusing on locking his core and flexing his legs to maintain internal pressure. He recalled the expression 'like you're trying to make both kinds of calls of nature' and, with a smirk, hoisted the barbell over his head. His elbows shook and he wobbled a bit but he managed to lockout the barbell snatch. With overwhelming relief, he cleaned the barbell and dropped it onto the pads.

With a loud exhale, he collapsed onto the floor sarcastically. Laughing, he laid there in accomplishment. A few of the others in the hot gym joined him in laughing. His friend, Kevin Freeman, appeared over him. Offering a pale, freckled hand, Kevin pulled Ayman to his feet. "You alive?"

"No," Ayman snickered as the sweaty pair made their way to the side of the gym. The whole class was detangling from the workout of the day, sweat covering the floor where gymnastics, calisthenics, and Olympic lifting had been mixed in a furious, fast-paced workout.

Ayman got his and Kevin's water bottles out of the mini-fridge. Breathing hard but not quite panting, they moved away so others could their water. "What'd you pull?" Kevin asked, pacing to cool down. He didn't drink his water; he just squirted it into the back of his throat.

"Quarter bodyweight," Ayman waved off. "I'm not ready to start setting records."

"I hear ya," Kevin breathily said in the early morning. The pair paced over to the front of the gym, where garage doors were rolled open to let in the warm summer air. What had once been an auto-garage's parking lot now had cracked pavement dotted with grass. It also had a gorgeous view of an abandoned golf course across the street where nature had returned to reclaim its space. Crickets chirped under the final few stars in the bluing sky. A half-moon hung low, near the tops of the trees. "So how's work? Get the new chip reader fixed yet?"

Ayman sputtered his lips. "Are you kidding? No. It's the county, man, come on." He held his water bottle to his head, wiping his forehead with the condensation.

"Doesn't that mean cases are gonna back up?" Kevin asked. He leaned on the divider between two open rolling garage doors.

"I mean, the old machine still works, it just sucks," Ayman told him. "The interface is like a DOS program. The imaging is crap. But, again, it works. So long as I've got one machine to work, they don't make repairs a priority."

Kevin scoffed. "Remind me not to get arrested."

"You ain't got a priors' chip," Ayman told him. "Without a chip, it won't come across my desk."

"Yeah, but one arrest!" Kevin told him.

Ayman groaned. "You don't get a chip if you get arrested. You don't even automatically get a chip if you're convicted. The things are expensive. They're not gonna hand them out like candy." Ayman began to walk back into the gym. He passed under the boxy arrangement of pull-up bars. The dozen other workout aficionados were beginning to shower quickly in the half-stalls in the bathrooms.

"They're getting pretty generous with them, man," Kevin argued casually, following Ayman. "The other day, I saw one dude got one for unpaid speeding tickets."

Ayman nodded, irritated. "Yeah, I saw the same piece on The Daily Show. What they only mentioned once was that they guy had been doing over double. Like sixty-five miles an hour in a residential zone or something. And he had a bunch of prior arrests. Yes, for speeding," Ayman quickly defended before Kevin could argue, "but they were just as egregious and there was, like, twenty of them. AND," he further defended with a sarcastic finger to Kevin, "and it was part of a plea bargain the dude's lawyer negotiated."

Kevin looked unimpressed. "Dude, please don't ask me to defend this program," Ayman begged indifferently. "I didn't implement it. I got nothing to do with it except I read the chips. I make a report of it and submit it to the DA and the PD. That's it."

"So the police get confirmation, huh?" Kevin asked.

"Public Defender," Ayman corrected. Kevin shook his head, unconvinced. "Dude, I support the ACLU as much as anybody," Ayman promised, almost pled. "Even the ACLU signed off on this program. They said it was better than prison time, and it was better than ankle monitors and stuff."

"Yeah, I know," Kevin grumbled. "I just...Big Brother and all of that."

Ayman nodded, then giggled suddenly. "Dude, if you could see how my office works, you wouldn't be terrified; you'd laugh." He chugged some water. As one of the others came out of the bathroom, steam spilling out over the door, Ayman asked, "You want it?"

"Nah, I'm going to take the kids to the park when I get back," he told his friend.

"How the hell do you have the energy for that?!" Ayman marveled, collecting his bag from the corner of the gym.

"What, this?" Kevin laughed arrogantly as he swirled his finger at the gym. "This is warm-up."

"Screw you," Ayman laughed. "Later," he said, heading into the bathroom.

"Peace," Kevin said, getting his bag to head out.

Often one of the last to get his shower so that he could take his time, Ayman exited five minutes later in khakis and a light blue button-up. His bag slung under his arm, he passed through the gym, calling to the owner and trainer as he headed to his car. Outside, the morning was turning into true day. A bird flew overhead while traffic along the small road between the gym and the golf course was beginning to pick up.

Ayman clicked his door locks for his car as he neared, when behind him, a woman called, "Hey." Ayman turned as a lovely woman with red hair and dressed in workout clothes half-jogged towards Ayman. "Hey, sorry to stop you," she said.

"No, it's cool," Ayman assured her. "Uh...Kate?" he guessed.

"Karen," she smiled. "Kate's the Asian girl." Ayman snapped his fingers contritely. "So, I heard you and Kevin talking about the chip program." Ayman nodded. "You developed those?" she asked curious.

Ayman laughed a little. "Lord no. If I had that kind of money, you think I'd be driving this grocery-getter?" he asked her, gesturing melodramatically at his modest and dated car. "I'm a forensic data analyst for the county."

"Forensic analyst?" Karen repeated, confused.

"Yeah," said Ayman. "It's a five-dollar word that means I check computer data and body-cam videos."

Karen seemed disappointed. "Ah, okay." She smiled and said, "Cool."

"Why?" Ayman asked as she began to backpedal.

"I just...I just overheard you two and was curious," she said, already half-turned to head for her car.

Ayman nodded with pursed lips. "Cool. Cool." He threw his bag into the passenger seat and sat in the car. He pulled the door closed and sighed, irritated. "Man, I got no game." He cranked the car as he lamented the missed opportunity to make a connection. Pulling out, he headed towards downtown.

At Tropical Breeze, Ayman approached the dark wood-stained counter as three different blenders went full speed, mixing up high-content smoothies. "Can I get a Peanut Butter Tosser with extra protein?" he asked, putting a dollar in the tip jar. He handed over cash, got a receipt, and wondered over to the shelves against the far wall. Like the handful of others in the mostly empty smoothie joint, he milled about, waiting for his liquid meal. He spent that time eyeing the protein bars and jugs of powdered protein, trying to remember what BCAA stood for.

One by one, the symphony of blenders grew quieter, until it was just him and one other customer waiting on their mixes as the two girls behind the counter prepared them. Outside the big windows, cars went zooming by until one pulled up in front of the door. Stopping in the middle of the street, it got Ayman's attention. So did the man who got out and opened the door for another man. The car remained in the middle of the lane, next to two parked cars in the legal parking spaces. The driver stood by the car, not bothering to get back behind the wheel.

The man from the car came right inside the smoothie joint. A black turtle neck and a gray suit matched his gold rings, expensive watch and short white hair. He looked at the women behind the counter, as one brought the final two smoothies to the customers. He nodded to the pair of workers, towards the back. They immediately disappeared through the far door. The only other person in the smoothie joint took the hint and grabbed her frosty cup of fruity sludge and rushed out. Ayman looked to do the same, but the man stepped between him and the door. "Not you," said the older gentleman.

The suited man that looked equal parts distinguished and brutal pulled out one of the chairs nearest to the counter and sat at the small table. "Have a seat, Ayman." He gestured to the opposite chair. Ayman was too afraid to do anything but acquiesce. "You're a smart kid," said the man. He didn't actually make eye contact with Ayman, instead looking just off Ayman's shoulders or behind him. "Good worker."

"Th-thank you?" Ayman said. He was sweating now worse than he had been during his morning workout.

"Ayman, me and my boys, we got an issue," he conveyed. He spoke with his hands, leaning into his gestures. "One of my boys did something real stupid." He stressed 'real'. "Now, it has to be handled. But I feel like we, as his family, we should be the ones to handle it. You know? Keep it in the family. Keep it civil. Keep it quiet. You follow me?" That was the first time he looked at Ayman. Looked at him like he was imploring from one family man to another. "Your mom, your dad, your sister," he told Ayman very casually. "You want to take care of them, right? They do something out of line, you got to handle it but you want to be the one to handle it."

Ayman jumped when the man sat back suddenly. "It's like getting into a car accident, right? Little fender bender. Now the rules say, you got to call the insurance. But you don't want to call the insurance. Then your rates go up. Your fault or not, your rates go up. That's money. That's money you can be spending smoothies, so you can build up them muscles." The man reached over to Ayman with stunning smoothness and ease. He grabbed Ayman's forearm and squeezed him. "See that? That's hard work. And that's eating right. But you can't eat right if you don't got money because you're spending all of it on car insurance, just because some knucklehead rear-ended you." Ayman only nodded, terrified.

"Ayman, I want you to help me out," said the man magnanimously. Lines on his round face contrasted with bright eyes. "One of my boys, he did something dumb. He did something stupid. He did something he shouldn't have. He ain't getting off scot-free. I just need your help to make sure we – his family – we handle it."

Ayman stiffened again when the man reached with his right hand into his suit. From within, he produced a small white envelope. "This is an appetizer. Help me out, help us out, help my family out, and this is a tenth. A deposit. A down payment." He slid the envelope across the table towards Ayman.

The man waited a breath for Ayman to take the envelope. He glanced at it, at Ayman who remained motionless but with his eyes tied to the envelope. He took his hand back suddenly, again making Ayman jump. "I always like to pay when people do their job," he said. "Maybe overpay a little. I'm generous like that." His tone had changed ever so slightly. It was deeper. Fuller. Had an edge. "Do your job, I think you should get your fair share, am I right?" He didn't wait for a response of any variety. "But people who get paid and don't do their job…I got no time for them, you know what I mean?"

Whatever fear Ayman had felt before, it paled compared to now.

The well-dressed man stood, leaning towards Ayman and taking up some of his space as he did. He stood over the seated Ayman and buttoned the top two buttons of his gray suit. "I hope you're the top of man who does his job. I'd hate to have to find someone else to do it. But there's always options when people don't do their jobs." He patted the table like it was a pet. "See you."

The man turned and departed, getting into the car that was still blocking a lane of traffic. He didn't look back at Ayman or the establishment. He left like this was one of many errands he had that day, an errand he trusted he wouldn't have to think about again. It was that cold indifference that scared Ayman the most.

His eyes trickled down to the white envelope, sitting right next to his smoothie. It lingered on the table, white clashing with the deep stained wood, almost like a warning beacon.

Ayman parked his car in his space, not backing in like normal. He just pulled straight in, between a two-decade-old SUV missing a mirror and a little coup missing the runner along the door. His MP3 player plugged into a cassette converted for his stereo was still playing but the trumpet solo of the jazz was lost on him. He was staring at the negative space beyond his steering wheel but before the dashboard. His cognitive mind thought to brush off the dust from the steering column and the plastic screen protecting the speedometer and other dials. His animal brain was screaming in paranoia.

Ayman swallowed and turned off the car. The engine's silence was abrupt and scary. Ayman looked with jerks of the head in all directions, seeing absolutely nothing out of the ordinary and determined to see that as confirmation that something was amiss. He finally unlocked his door and began to get out, only to remember some movie he'd forgotten about, where a car exploded the instant the driver took their weight off the seat. Ayman was positively frozen for a good minute.

When he finally worked up the courage to get out of his car, he couldn't shake the fear of an explosion. He knelt on the asphalt and bent his head down into the floorboard. He looked under his seat and tried to see a bomb. Then he stayed kneeling, determined to memorize how the seat looked. He decided he would check again when he left work, and he'd know what looked out of place. He also dug out a soda can and a fast food wrapper that had been down there who knows how long.

Ayman crossed the four rows of parked cars towards the municipal building, a squat unassuming building with the proportions and color of the brick that it was made from. Three stories, not including the basement where Ayman worked, it was here that most non-detective policework was done. Forensic specialists and coroners were filing in for the day. They headed through the primary side entrance for employees, though only a few were around right now. Again, Ayman's mind invented a million explanations to justify his paranoia, but a glance at his watch told him he was simply a bit later than usual.

Through the white door full of windows, two uniformed police officers manned the metal detector. The seated one was on the computer, checking social media on one screen while waiting to man the scanner on the other. The standing guard was working a rubix cube that he'd been trying to solve for as long as Ayman could remember.

"Sup, Shedani," said the seated officer, scrolling along his feed. "How was the workout?"

Familiar faces and a friendly question helped dull the edge of Ayman's fear. "Fine," he said. He revised his statement. "Pretty good." He began to take off his shoes and his belt, placing them on the conveyor belt. He stepped onto the tube and let the scanners pass over him.

"You gonna compete in the games?" asked the officer with a snicker.

"Nah, man, I'm not that serious," Ayman chuckled. He began to redress himself under the following silence. He sat on the bench just passed the machines to tie his shoes. In the past, doing so had made him recall tying cleats on the soccer field in college but now, it felt different.

He looked up a little too quickly when the door opened and Dr Thomas shuffled in. The absent-minded medical doctor, he carried pressed to his chest a folder of papers that had clearly been blown half-open. He flopped them down on the scanner's conveyor belt, followed by his briefcase. Off came his jacket with elbow patches as if he was determined to look older. He stepped into the scanner and held out his hands a little melodramatically.

"Shoes, doc," said the standing officer. He'd put aside the rubix cube, preparing for the daily argument.

"Oh, forgive me, I'd forgotten," he said. He stepped out and hobbled on his bad hip to slip his shoes off. "Can't risk the chance I've got a bomb in my shoe," he told the two officers. He placed his shoes on the conveyor belt and returned to the scanner.

"Belt," said the officer as the scanner beeped.

"Should I drop my trousers too?" he asked.

"We go through this every day, doc," complained the seated officer.

"And every day, it's just as invasive," he argued.

Ayman left the senior official to pick his daily fight. He slipped the lanyard for his ID badge over his head and left for his office. He had to go down a half-flight of steps to the basement level, the temperature dropping a few degrees when he did. The hallway smelled of industrial cleaner more often than not and this morning was no exception.

The door to Ayman's office stuck, like usual, but with a kick to the base of the wooden door with the frosted window, Ayman was able to get into his office. He was supposed to lock it, but with everything already locked in cabinets and the door already so damn hard to open, he never bothered. His office was an ugly wood desk from a bygone era and a new-ish computer with a giant screen that hung on the wall. A half-submerged window that didn't open looked out on the southward-facing lawn at ankle level. The highlight of Ayman's day was when a squirrel or two would venture along his window.

His computer hibernating, Ayman swished the mouse and logged-in. He sat down in his office chair and looked at the near-solid wall of filing cabinets behind him. A mountain of documentation that needed to be kept for seven years after receipt. Each cabinet of blue metal was marked with dates when the contents could finally be destroyed, and the drawer repurposed for more recent work.

He turned back to the screen as his desktop appeared. "Okay," he said to himself, moving the mouse again to orientate himself. "What do we have today?" Just asking that question recalled the man in the coffee shop and it gave his hand pause. Ayman clicked on the office drive and summoned up a release program. Three files were pending review, the files' logo that of green circle with a white ball-and-tail, like some star in orbit around an alien world. Ayman downloaded the three files and selected 'Yes' when prompted to open the monitor system. The screen went black as if the system had crashed, and then an ugly, pale lime green cursor appeared. Ayman got up from his chair as a cascade of commands began to spiral rapidly down the screen.

He crossed the hall into the evidence locker. Sandra Moran was working the window, which gave Ayman a smile. The pin-up beautiful woman wore clothes designed to make jaws drop and had skills with makeup that would make movie stars envious. Today she was dolled up in a red suit with her black hair done up in a bun. Adding vibrant red lipstick and horn-rimmed glasses, she looked like sin.

"Ayman," she said in a sultry tone.

"Sup," he said, already taking the clipboard and signing in. "You got three for me."

"Yeah, I think so," said Sandra. She rose from her desk where she logged every last detail and went to a nearby rolling cart for the day's haul. She glanced for a moment, then grabbed a small plastic bag with three smaller evidence bags. "Here you go." She handed the bag through the armored window that divided her from the rest of the world.

Ayman accepted the bag, turned to leave, then came back. "Hey, look, I'm sorry to ask, and if this is too forward, I'm real sorry."

"I'm not going on a date with you," Sandra said with well-rehearsed precision and familiarity, not even batting an eye at the anticipated question.

"No, that's not it," he waved off. She seemed genuinely surprised. "What's with this?" Ayman gestured at her clothes. "You look good. I mean, good." There was real emphasis the second time around. "Better than usual. What's the deal?"

She just shrugged. "I felt good this morning. I like to look how I feel."

Ayman couldn't stop himself from looking down at her body and blushed. "You're gonna give somebody a heart attack."

"I look good," Sandra told him unapologetically. "I don't mind you looking. I get it. Just keep your hands and your comments to yourself."

"You think this is good work attire?" Ayman asked. He asked in a tone that was clearly conversational, even conspiratorial.

"Just because I'm good at my job doesn't mean I can't look good," she insisted, again unapologetically.

"No argument here," he insisted.

"Uh-huh," she nodded. "Want me to drop a pen and pick it up?" she teased.

"I'm not going to say no," he was quick to answer. She laughed and he told her, "I'll have these back by lunch." He knocked gently on the window as he departed, heading back across the hall to his office. With the evidence bag in his hands, now he shut the door and locked it behind him.

Ayman sat at his computer, thoughts of smoothies and Sandra drifting away as routine took over. He wrote his name and date on the evidence bag and tore it open, the surprisingly hearty plastic ripping unevenly. He jostled out the three bags within, writing his name and the date on each of them as well. He tore open the first bag and took from it a long, flat card about the length of a cell phone, but half the width or depth. At the far end was a small, circular disc with a mirrored finish roughly the size of a dime.

From next to his computer tower, Ayman pulled a small drive about the size of a paperback book. He slipped the card into the machine and two LEDs atop the reader lit up. On the black screen, more commands and prompts automatically ran. Ayman leaned back and watched the code work through itself, recognizing certain commands and prompts, and intuiting others.

Finally, the lines of commands cleared out and Ayman was left with a relatively clear screen with a few numerical options:

1 – Eject Card
2 – Documentation
3 – Video
4 – Other Recordings
5 – Observations
6 – Duplicate
7 – Erase
8 – Other
9 – Exit

Ayman clicked two on his keyboard and the screen shifted up slightly.

1 – Overview
2 – Full Documentation

This time, Ayman hit one. A cursor began to write out text like an old-world typewriter, letters appearing briskly but one at a time in sequence across the screen. As the cursor shot by, Ayman read quickly.

"Suspect arrested for speeding (68mph/30mph), most recent in a long history of vehicular offenses. Suspect challenged the arrest on the spot, and at arraignment."

Given the option to close the overview, Ayman did and opted for three. A small window within the black field opened. A pair of inverted video feeds showed someone at the wheel of a sports car, driving. Ayman entered a few unpresented commands and the pair of feeds inverted as flashing lights appeared in the rearview mirror along with a frantic search of the car. Ayman leaned close, crinkling his nose as he squinted. "Is that a joint?" he asked himself. "Dude," he groaned in disappointment.

He stopped the video as the car pulled over to the side of the road. He entered some additional controls and the video began to play back. The image was not crisp at all, but it gave a decent enough impression of color and movement. He played the video back to before the lights. A few more keystrokes and the video resumed. Ayman squinted again but couldn't see the dashboard of the car. He could see the double-digit digital display of the speedometer but he couldn't make out the numbers. He wound back the video farther and looked instead through the windshield.

He watched as street lights shot by, their glowing presence leaving streaking aftereffects. He chewed on his lip, still watching. Finally, he just sighed. He closed the video and hit five. A pre-derived form appeared on the black screen, the cursor quietly blinking at him. He began to fill out the form, most of the fields the usual questions: name, investigator ID, suspect ID, case ID, etc. Finally, at the bottom, was a larger field described as: Observation.

Here, Ayman spoke as he typed. "Feed from internal chip reviewed. Unable to ascertain specific speed of the suspect's vehicle prior to arrest. Likelihood of adherence to traffic laws unlikely based off attention to ambient information (specifically time between street lights as seen out the windows of the vehicle in the video feed). Guilt is not in question but severity cannot be confirmed. Recommend evaluation of the location where arrest was made, comparing distances between street lights for at least one mile prior to officer contact. If the distances are uniform, the speed of the suspect's vehicle can be ascertained and full charges can be app—"

The computer beeped at him. He groaned loudly and collapsed back against his chair. "Oh come on!" he exclaimed at the computer, not for the first time. "It's a damn official report. Why is there a character limit?!" He backspaced a few times and rewrote the final sentence. 'If distance is uniform, suspect vehicle's speed, and thus charges, can be confirmed'. Satisfied, he confirmed his entry and selected eight.

1 – Submit Record
2 – Command Panel
3 – Display Options

Clicking one, the black screen was once again filled with commands spiraling into action.

Thoughts of the smoothie joint came back to Ayman. He thought of the man's hands on the table, white skin with calloused fingers. Calloused knuckles. Old callouses. Callouses from decades ago. Ayman's eyes glazed over as he thought about what kind of man had to fight, but no longer needed to. Had he grown peaceful, or did he now have others who would fight for him?

In a moment, the thoughts faded and Ayman realized his computer was waiting, the blinking lime-green cursor waiting for him to pick one through nine. He hit one and the card ejected from the reader. Ayman took it, placed it in a new bag taken from a draw in his desk. He filled it out with all the pertinent data, then set it aside. He took out the next chip and slid it into the machine. Automatically, it began to read the data. It spun through the commands before it arrived at the nine options once again. Ayman hit two for documentation, and then one again for the overview.

"Suspect interviewed for leaving the county against orders of sex offender registry."

Ayman balked at the vagueness of the overview. Grumbling, he closed the overview, then opted again for documentation again, this time the full report.

"Suspect is a 73-year-old Asian male, widowed. Charged six years ago with possession of child pornography, allegedly obtained from a commercial site. Suspect maintained at the time of arrest that he was not aware of, and had no way of knowing, the site sold such images or that the pictures he purchased were underage. Pursuant to placement on the SOR (sex offender registry), the suspect is subject to periodic unannounced visits, which was the reason for this day's visit. Suspect was not home at the time of the visit. When contacted concerning the missed visit, he maintained he was at an early church service. Providing the name of the church, his attendance was confirmed but it was learned that the church in question was across county lines. Departure of the county for any reason is not allowed on SOR except with prior written approval from registry personal. In violation of SOR, suspect is to be re-processed for arrest and reincarceration."

Ayman's expression soured a bit. His hand on his lip, he rotated in his computer chair for a moment, staring. He checked the location of the arrest and minimized the window on the chip reader program. The switch from the primitive interface to the crystal clarity of the standard computer screen was always shocking. Ayman ran a few searches using commonly available web browsers. He located the suspect's home address where he had been living. Isolated and away from town, it was well outside any restrictions on the sex offender registry. A companion search found the church in question. It was across the county line. It was also the nearest church by over five miles.

He closed the browsers and went back to the chip reader. The blinking, green cursor was garish to look at once again. He exited to the primary interface and selected three for the video. He was immediately treated to the twin screens, this time orientated properly. The view was of the suspect in his car, driving along. String music was playing, so Ayman muted the video. He watched as the man arrived at his modest rural home, only to find three squad cars waiting.

The instant he exited his car, the uniformed officers came swarming around him. He held up his liver-spotted hands and followed their commands with total obedience. He was bent over his hood and handcuffed. What followed was a considerably montage of his possessions being searched with some callous disregard, all while he was interrogated in his driveway. Ayman's expression soured further until he was sneering at the officer doing the questioning.

Rather than keep watching, Ayman played back the footage. He guided it farther back from the automatic starting point, just one moment prior to police interaction which was the default setting. He kept going back, following the suspect all the way back to his church. Ayman smiled a bit as he undid the mute and listened to the old man singing a hymnal.

Satisfied, Ayman stopped the video and exited out before hitting five for observations. "Feed from internal chip reviewed. Suspect's guilt is confirmed," he said as he typed, "but well within reason. County line crossing is nominal and provides only access to reasonably nearby church for religious observance. Strongly recommend charges be dropped with no comment, or at the most, citation without penalty."

Ayman reviewed the details of the case for a moment, just to be certain, then returned to the main screen. Eight for other commands, he chose one to submit the record. Another cascade of rapid commands and quiet actions happening largely within the chip reader itself.

Ayman's eyes drifted down to the third and final chip. Unless something came in, which was unlikely as processing usually took some time, this was it. This chip contained what the man at the smoothie shop had been wanting addressed. Ayman's stomach wound tight as he waited for the computer commands to finish.

He prepared the second chip and placed it with the first, the bags on the edge of his desk. He sat back in his seat and stared at the screen for a moment, taking slow breaths. He didn't know what he was getting himself into. After a moment of readying himself, though, he stuck the third chip into the reader. Commands ran. Lime-green letters chased each other down his screen. And finally, nine commands. With an unsteady finger, Ayman selected two for documentation. He started with one for the overview.

"Suspect was arrested for violent assault of three persons at a gas station on East Riverton road. Pending charges include murder, battery, and sexual assault/rape."

Ayman died a little inside. This wasn't the first violent crime he'd reviewed but that never stopped them from being unsettling. Again, he flashed to the smoothie place. 'Did something real stupid'. 'We should be the ones to handle it'. 'Keep it in the family'. Ayman closed his eyes and regretted so many choices he had made to bring him to this moment. Even as he lamented his actions, he opted for the full documentation.

"Suspect arrived at the Gas 'n Gulp on East Riverton road, just past the metro stop. Suspect filled up with gas, paying outside with a credit card. He entered the convenience store and interacted with the attendant (DOA #1), possibly addressing him with racial slurs. While in the store, he also began to proposition a young woman (DOA #2), attracting the attention of the woman's boyfriend (victim #1). An altercation began and suspect bludgeoned the victim with wine bottle, before smashing two beer bottles against his head. He proceeded to bang the victim's head into the tile floor well after unconsciousness.

Suspect attacked the woman, tripping her to the floor and attempting to sexually assault her. When she resisted, he struck her repeatedly about the face and head. The store's worker attempted to intervene by shouting at the suspect, but he engaged the worker verbally and then chased him to the door. The worker tried to flee the store but the suspect pinned him to the door, removed the worker's belt and then choked him with it. The suspect forced the still-conscious worker halfway through the door and then slammed the door repeatedly on his chest and then head. Suspect returned to the semi-conscious woman and sexually assaulted her. Once completed, he ripped away her clothes and beat her with the worker's belt, then choked her from behind.

DOA #1, the worker, suffered multiple broken ribs and succumbed to intense cranial hemorrhaging caused by skull fracture and repeated trauma.

DOA #2, the woman, suffered severe damage due to physical and violent sexual abuse. She asphyxiated due to vomit and loss of consciousness.

Victim #1, the man, suffered severe cranial trauma and concussion. Currently in vegetative state with uncertain prognosis from medical professionals.

Surveillance video from the store shows agitated engagement by the suspect with the store worker, suggesting the use of racial slurs (audio is inconclusive and largely lacking). Suspect propositioned the woman with lewd and vulgar language, before striking her partner with only verbal provocation. Suspect refutes all charges and has been released on bail."

Ayman was sure he was going to be sick. Against his better judgment, he summoned the video. Despite it being his job, he regretted it. Twin video feeds played and Ayman was confronted with vulgar inhumanity. He watched first-hand as a man was degraded and a woman objectified.

And then the violence.

Clutching his fist, Ayman forced himself to watch what unfolded. His face shook as he tried to look away and he willed himself not to. His jaw shook and a tear ran down his cheek but he faced it all.

When the video mercifully ended, Ayman lowered his eyes and stared at nothing. He looked down rather than closing his eyes, for doing so brought a mental replay of the video. The video burned into his mind, a recap from the attacker's point of view, simply wasn't something Ayman ever wanted to relive. He couldn't recall ever having wanted to forget something so badly.

Exit.

Five.

But as the blinking green cursor hovered there, slowly flashing as it waited for input, Ayman's fingers didn't move over the keyboard. He remembered a smile and placed it back to the smoothie shop. He remembered the cold fear of facing the man who sat across from him. Without any thought, he turned in his chair and pulled from his coat's inner pocket the envelope. He opened it and saw the $100 bill and didn't need to flip through it to see the others behind it. He didn't know how many there were but he could tell just by touch it was more than a few.

Behind money were the images. The video. The violence captured and burned into Ayman's mind forever. Ugliness he would never be able to unsee. So he put away the envelope and took out his phone. Highlighting his mother's number, he sent her a text. 'Just wanted to say I love you'. He highlighted it, copy-and-pasted it, and sent it again to his father. Then his sister. Then he set the phone to the side and placed his fingers over the keyboard.

"Feed from internal chip reviewed. Suspect guilt is absolute. Evidence suggests all charges valid. Suspect appears to be a threat to anyone around him and is likely to repeat any or all crimes with little provocation. Recommend immediate apprehension with all caution. Sentencing is urged with all expediency."

He sent his report and ejected the chip. On simple, automatic motions, he sealed away the evidence, and then sealed it all together as per procedure. On the legs of the dispossessed, he rose and exited his office. Back across the hall he went, feeling the specter of terror but not terror itself. He went back into the evidence locker where Sandra was processing documents at the far end of her work space. "Done already?" she asked as she continued to write. She put the pages away and slid them across her desk. "That was quick."

"Yeah," Ayman said with an encumbered conscience. He slid the evidence bag through the window slit as Sandra approached.

She accepted the bag and saw the weight of the world on Ayman's shoulders. "What's up?" she asked, setting the bag aside and disregarding it for a moment. "Is everything okay?"

Ayman didn't respond for a moment. He stared for a breath, then told Sandra, "I'm going to take a half-day. I'm not...I don't feel...like..." He gave up and started to turn. "I'm going to go home." He was already to the door when he told her, "I'll see you tomorrow." It sounded like a hope, not a statement.

Ayman headed down the hall, his hands in his pockets. He didn't know if he was leaving for the day, or just for a while. He just knew he was leaving. He had a great sense of finality, like some page had turned. He exited through the scanner without a word or comment from the two officers. Everything was on autopilot.

He exited into the late morning with the sound of a single bird chirping loudly in the far-off distance. There was a rush of traffic to the air, but Ayman wasn't aware of any cars passing on the streets immediately nearby. He crossed the packed but motionless parking lot, chirping his car alive as he neared. He opened the door and sat down.

The instant his weight settled into the seat, before he'd even closed the door, the multitude of actions that could have been made lethal ran him over, bringing his every action. His body motionless, his mind went into overdrive as he reviewed his actions and realized where it all could have ended. Unlocking his car from afar could have triggered a bomb. Opening the door could have as well. Sitting down. Sliding the key into the ignition. The list went on like an emotionally abusive rollercoaster. Opening the door to his office. Just walking outside. His life was in a place new to him, a place of danger.

      Ayman looked out into the blue sky and took a deep breath. Resolved, he shut the car door, cranked the car, shifted gears, and backed out. There weren't many other options.

Trial By Numbers

"No real library has books in order," Carolyn grumbled to herself.

Dressed in blue jeans and a red Henley shirt, the city librarian pushed her braided hair back over her shoulders. Doing so caused a few beads in her hair to knock against each other as she glared at the lowest shelf of books. "Two masters degrees," she grumbled, beginning to pull books off the lowest of the metal shelves. "More years of college than I care to admit. All so I can play clean-up to a city library that's become the baby-sitting center of the city."

She glared up at the poster than hung from the white-tiled ceiling of the library, with the mayor proudly holding a book, his giant toothy smile hanging next to the simple word 'READ'. She went back to collecting the books.

With a stack almost as tall as her torso, she cupped her hands beneath the precarious group. With precision lacking from many professional dancers, she carefully rose, the tower of books in her hands teetering but not falling. She leaned back, the books settling against her body and she carried them across the stained carpeting of the library to the main circulation desk.

The big glass windows let in the last of the daylight, the city lights outside beginning to turn on. The office buildings that dominated the downtown area were beginning to dot with the offices of late-night workers while stars were appearing in the burnt umber heavens. Inside the library, the shelves were askew. Meant to create a dynamic and inviting layout, it instead provided a multitude of hiding places for young boys to giggle at nude illustrations and even the occasional drug user to engage in their preferred vice.

Carolyn dropped the chin-high load of books down onto the reference desk, having to step back from them as she flexed her back, trying to work the kink out. "Carolyn," came a grating, high-pitched voice. The librarian turned around, not wanting to see who she knew she was going to see.

It's not that Mary-Anne was a bad person. Not at all. She was very sweet. But she was also annoying. Very annoying. Obscenely annoying. If she wasn't so sweet, Carolyn would have wrung her neck many times for her incompetence or her inability to get to work on time or for her nasal voice or for any number of other transgressions that weren't enough to write her up for but more than warranted her immediate death.

"Yes," Carolyn said, rubbing her lower back. She heard boys snickering from the teens section which was never a good sound.

"There was a call from the district manager," Mary-Anne said, coming over to the books. "Oh, looks likes we've got more books to shelve," she said cheerfully. Carolyn considered strangling her then and there. Sadly, self-control won out.

As she turned to head off to her office, Dave strolled up. The high-school-minded college student looked at the books, then walked by. Carolyn watched him get almost past the desk, then tapped his shoulder. "Dave," she said, pointing at the books. "Books."

He turned to the books, then stepped back. "Oh, wow, man. More books?"

"Yeah," she said sarcastically. "This is a library. Books are what we do."

"Yeah, but I just put a bunch of books away yesterday, man."

"Dave, that's your job," Carolyn said. "You're the library page; you're supposed to put the books away."

"Yeah, man, but every day?" Dave asked. "That's like, I don't know man, a lot of work."

"That's why they call it a job," Carolyn said, her eyes closed. "Just put them away."

"Like in order, man?" he asked, looking back at the stack.

Carolyn's eyebrow began to twitch. She knew that a homicide wasn't far away, so she simply turned away and started walking. "What did the distract manager have to say?" she asked Mary-Anne.

The older woman paused, as if taken by surprise. "What?" she asked in a steep southern tone.

"The district manager," said Carolyn. "You said he called. What about?"

"He said he needed to talk to you about something," she said.

"What about?" Carolyn insisted.

"He didn't say," she said disinterestedly. "He asked if he could speak to you but I said you were busy."

"Mary-Anne, if the district manager wants to talk to me, come and get me," Carolyn exclaimed. "Did he say when he would call back?"

"No," she said, like she didn't process why this was a big deal.

"So he needed to talk to me, but didn't say when he would call back?" Carolyn summed up. "Am I supposed to call him or is he going to just drop by out of the blue?" As soon as she asked the question, she heard the sliding doors of the library swish open. "Of course," she told herself with a sigh.

Dillion Haufferman walked in stomach first. He wasn't an obese man. He was actually a bit on the skinny side, with simply a great bowl of a stomach that bulged out in front of him like some sort of bowling ball stuffed into his pants. He wore enigmatic octagonal glasses which clashed with his mundane light brown suit and unremarkable blue tie. Everything about him screamed man of intelligence but of far greater intellectual laziness. He was the living embodiment of wasted potential.

"Hey, Carol," he said.

She sighed, unwilling to correct him yet again. "Hey, Dillion. Sorry we didn't connect earlier. There was some confusion as to the schedule." She glowered at Mary-Anne but it was lost on the woman behind the circulation desk. "Do you want to go into my office?"

"No, I just..." He looked around the mostly empty library and stepped away from the desk. Carolyn followed. "The thing is," rambled the district manager. Carolyn looked at the clock on her desk as he spoke, rolling her eyes at the mere sound of his voice. "Parents have been complaining that their children are getting turned away from the library. Now, I know that's not possible."

"Well, sir," she said, as she rubbed her closed eyes. "If these are the parents I think they are, it's because their sons were looking at pornography. And not just the usual porno, but like the bad stuff. The kind of stuff that's illegal in most civilized countries."

"Did you get the addresses?" he joked. Carolyn didn't laugh. It wasn't funny the first time; it wasn't funny the fifth time; it wasn't funny this time.

"Dillion, we've got a real problem here," she said. "This library is becoming a day-care. I can't keep up with my responsibilities with all these--"

"Your responsibilities are to the patrons," said the distract manager.

"My responsibilities are to the library," she countered.

"The patrons are the library," he made clear with a patronizingly paternal tone. "You think it's the books?" he scoffed. "You have patrons and they need to be encouraged to come back, but they can't be encouraged to come back if they're getting ejected from the library."

"They're breaking library rules," Carolyn protested.

"Then stop them, but not so that they leave," he argued. "You have an obligation, under the new plan by the mayor, to make sure that you get as many kids in those library doors as you possibly can."

"They're not kids; they're monsters!" Carolyn shouted. Her voice carried and she did not care. "They tear up the books, kick the bookshelves, hack and abuse the computers, and start fights."

"And you need to make sure that they don't do any of that," said the district manager. "You are the manager. You can control it, can't you?" Carolyn was about to bite his head off, but stopped herself. Knowing it futile, she surrendered to the bureaucratic perspective. "Keep the kids in, keep the patrons in, and keep the trouble-makers out. It's not hard is it?" he summarized, checking his watch.

Carolyn just fumed.

With each click of the light switches, whole sections of the library fell dark. Like a cascading waterfall of shadow, the darkness fell over the library in systematic order. When the last of the lights went out, the whole place was cloaked in the deep purple of the urban nighttime. Without the electric buzz of the lights, without the wordless din of patrons, without the buzz of computers and elevators and all manner of other electric devices, the library was finally at peace.

Carolyn stepped out of the back room of the library and took a moment for herself. With a cup of peach-flavored fat-free yogurt, she walked to the desk to look out over the library. Her library. In the darkness at the end of the day, the space was finally as it should be. In order and at peace. Carolyn had to work to ignore the stacks of book that should have been reshelved and weren't. She had to work to ignore the stains in the roof and the patches of threadbare carpeting. She had to work to ignore the tattered spines and missing volumes from her shelves. Many flaws she couldn't see but knew were there. She refused to let them nag at her. For the brief surcease, in the dark and the quiet, the library was at peace.

Carolyn took a long breath and felt a certain sense of renewal, just being alone with the shelves of books. Ten million pages self rom the world and gathered close like chicks beneath a mother hen. She felt like the intruders had finally been cast out and her library was free from invasion. At least until they reopened again in the morning. Until then, the library was finally at peace.

With an angry grumble, Carolyn finished her yogurt, scraping the spoon along the edges of the plastic container to get every last bit of the peachy goodness. The thought of those doors opening and letting in more invaders caused her heart to skip a beat and her breath to catch in her lungs. She shuddered to think of one more day dealing with these people, as she did every night, and then again every morning.

The empty field of asphalt was Carolyn's only companion as she left the library. The parking field next to the library was full during the day, the spaces commanding a premium price. With dusk passed and the streetlamps and concrete all that remained of the vibrant city, the spaces were empty. Only a handful of cars sat alone in the field, the air still hot from the sun of the day. The nighttime breezes smelled of gasoline and fumes, like the energy Carolyn had left after her workday. Like the energy she had left after each work day.

There were three things Carolyn always left work with. Her keys in hands, a pile of books that she needed to repair, and a bad attitude usually tempered with a general hatred for humanity. She stumbled towards her car, today's pile of books reaching up to her chin. Carrying them with one hand, she jangled her keys to get access to the door key. She almost made it to the lock.

"Carolyn Chow?"

She stopped and glanced off to her left. In the Columbia nighttime, the world was only lit by the street lamps and the out-of-sync street lights that sat above the empty intersections.   Standing down the sidewalk from her was a man dressed in dark blue robes. With a long bushy white beard and a pointy hat, he smiled at her patiently.

Obviously the source of the question, she decided to proceed with her evening and unlocked her car door. She tossed her books into the passenger seat, then looked at him, a bad attitude brewing already. "What do you need?"

"So you are Carolyn Chow?" confirmed the man, approaching her harmlessly with a few casual, unobtrusive steps towards her. "The director of the main branch of the Columbia City Library?"

"Yeah," she said, pulling her leather jacket around her.

"Excellent," he smiled, holding his hands in front of him. "I would like to offer you a job."

Her eyebrow went up. "Do what now?"

"Working as a librarian, of course," he assured her, his scholarly tone reminding her of a bad professor she had back in college. "We are in need of a librarian of your magnificent qualifications."

"What makes you think I'm magnificently qualified?"

"Why your library of course," the man smiled. "It is positively infested with gremlins."

Carolyn stared for a second. "You say that like that's a normal thing normal people normally say." She looked him up and down and realized his robe was the most expensive costume she'd ever seen.

The elderly man didn't seem troubled by her disbelief. "Did you really think children and unconscionable patrons can make a library so disorderly? Oh dear me, no. You've gremlins everywhere. Agents of entropy, they are. If it's a system, a gremlin exists to muck it all up. And that you manage it so well..." He shook his head, in sympathetic awe.

"Explains a thing or two," Carolyn nodded. "So, are you crazy or just trying to take up more of my time than most people?"

"I am here to offer you a job to help us salvage our library," said the man with a pleasant enough smile.

"We? Who's we and who's you?" she pressed.

"We are the Institute of Higher Arcane and Occult Studies," he said. With a bow, he added, "And I am Merlin."

Carolyn nodded. "Riiiiight."

"Don't believe me?" he asked with a smile. "Then perhaps this will persuade you to consider my offer a bit more seriously."

And with a whisk of his hand, the world transformed.

The stars became reflections in a lake and the asphalt beneath her feet became clouds. The street lamps dripped away to become moss hanging loosely from ancient trees. The world swirled and twisted, not like a roller coaster but like a wrung-out sponge returning to its original shape. It wasn't so much disorienting as clarifying, like her ears had popped but for all her senses.

Carolyn spun around and looked out over the forest primeval. She saw a raven take off from a tree branch and go flying into the bright night sky. She heard twigs snap and things older than humanity move within the shadows of the forest. She gulped and turned back to the castle. It stood alone atop a great cliff, overlooking a huge, placid lake that reflected a silver moon far larger than any she could recall having seen. A winding stone path led up the hill, guiding the way towards the nighttime castle. Before it were rolling hills and perfect grounds while in the distance, ice-capped spires of far-off cliffs created the horizon. All of this against the velvety backdrop of the moon and the stars, while the light windows revealed the massive, incalculable size of the place.

Carolyn stared with wide eyes, unable to perceive what she saw. "This is the Central Office of the Institute of Higher Arcane and Occult Studies," said the wizard, turning to the librarian next to him. "And I'm but one of many faculty here who help oversee this fine institution."

"And you are?" Carolyn asked, staring at the wizard, struggling to break her gaze upon the castle. "Merlin. Right."

"My dear, you will come to learn many things," he said, putting his hand on her shoulder, leading her down the path towards the castle. "One key truth is that many of the great icons that you hold dear are in fact far more than singular fixtures of someone's imagination. We are in actuality manifested ambitions personified as individuals."

"Huh?" Carolyn bugged.

"To put it simply," the wizard smiled, a twinkle in his eye, "those who created us, were inspired to create us, by us."

"Huh? That doesn't make any sense."

Merlin glanced at her, puzzled. "It doesn't?" he said, somewhat startled. He thought about what he had said for a moment, then nodded. "Yes, quite right. It doesn't." He kept walking.

The castle they approached grew, broadening from a simple storybook construct to a sweeping marvel of engineering. It was a wide expanse, like an entire complex of buildings slapped together and surrounded by stone walls that appeared more decorative than tactical. Like some fairy tale construct brought to life, the castle was made of gray stone with red roofs. Towers and spires rose chaotically into the sky. Lights burned within arched windows and behind stained-glass panes.

Carolyn glanced back and saw the winding path of stone steps they were walking up. She expected to see only a short route but instead saw an entire road that headed to a staircase that descended a steep mountain. "Where did..." She looked again and realized she was looking out over a wild world far beneath her, along a path she hadn't walked. "What happened?"

Merlin stopped and looked back the way they'd come. "Oh, yes. I do so love mountains but they are a bit rough on the knees so I tend to skip them when I can." He resumed walking, the bewildered Carolyn unable to do anything but follow.

Merlin and Carolyn arrived at the castle, coming to stand before a giant pair of doors. The wizard reached into his pocket, pulling out jangling set of keys. He singled out what looked like a Hyundai door key and unlocked the castle doors with it.

Carolyn watched with an unimpressed look.

The old wizard pushed open the doors, revealing a large stone entranceway. Directly ahead of them, a flight of stone steps rose up. At the mouth of those steps were three gryphons who sat as ill-tempered guards at the entrance of the castle.

The gryphons eyeballed Carolyn, but to her surprise, they more vehemently scowled at Merlin. He smiled cheerfully back at them and began to ascend the stairs with the speed of a man defined by arthritis. "The Academy was established in..." He realized Carolyn wasn't following. He looked back at her, then followed her gaze to the gryphons. "Oh, think nothing of them. They are fine, charming beasts." He looked back at the trio of magical animals that scowled back at them.

"Are they the security?" Carolyn asked, staying close to the wizard.

"Oh no. Hat check," he said jovially. "But I'm afraid that beads in your hair are against their political affiliation so they don't really like you." As Carolyn touched the cheap beads in her hair, nervous they'd even been noticed, Merlin instead scowled at the beasts and kept walking.

"So this place is a magic academy?" Carolyn asked as they started up the story-tall flight of steps.

"Yes but think of it more as a magical laboratory for experiments than anything else," the wizard said. "Now, would you like the grand tour or to see the library?"

"Oh, I definitely want to see this place," she said. "The grand tour, please."

"Well, I'm afraid we're closed for the evening, I'm going to have to show you that tomorrow." He turned down to the right, heading off down a stone hallway. "Come along. To the library," he announced intrepidly.

Carolyn watched, feeling her blood pressure rising.

The doors parted ways, exposing a shadowy realm of chaos and disorder. Entropy was in full-effect in this singular space as cobwebs and dust floated across the lighted entranceway.

Merlin walked in first, his calm demeanor preceding him. Behind him, Carolyn walked in, her left eye twitching as she took in the sight of the utter devastation. They stepped into the circular landing from which the library spread out like sound waves from a speaker driven insane by mediocre cover bands. To either side of the doors were desks that sat unattended as they apparently had been for years.

A spacious landing was a step down from the doors. From there spread a positively massive library. Of a scale only approached in dreams, the library was several stories tall, with platforms and landings scattered among the towering stacks of endless books. Ladders of different heights dotted the space as did cobweb-encrusted candelabras, torch holders, and other hallmarks of a bygone era. Stone walls and slate floors were covered in a layer of dust. Huge bay windows dotted the far walls. The glass looked frosted, however and Carolyn realized it was from the dust that had accumulated across the panes.

To her right was a winding desk like an illustrator's French curve. The desk wound along the right side of the library and included several offices too dark to see into. Shelves and cabinets filled the underspace and Carolyn could see the layers of dust and cobwebs along the floor. " This is your library?" she whispered in horrified awe.

"Yes," Marlin nodded, looking around, his hands tucked in the sleeves of his robes. "I'm afraid no one comes in here anymore because of the disorder."

"This place doesn't look like it's been used in years," Carolyn said, looking over the side of the desk on the left.

"Well, we've just now freed up the funds to do something about that, ergo you're being here," he explained.

"Freed up funds?" asked Carolyn. "You just said I could name my salary." Merlin nodded, his bushy beard shaking a bit as he did. "What kind of funds got freed up?"

"My dear, you really must understand that our budget is not financial or monetary. It is far more...celestial." Merlin removed his pointed hat and brushed back a head mostly bereft of hair. "I'm afraid that if you are still accustomed to monetary compensation, then any explanation of the finances and budgetary systems of this establishment will take more than a mere conversation."

"So I'm too dumb to get what you use for money," Carolyn rephrased sharply as she neared a bookstack. She touched a heavy tome whose cover was heavy leather, bound tight with metal clasps. She pulled the book halfway off the shelf before the spine gave out in her hands. She stumbled back half-a-step, astonished to see the book's wooden spine still in her hand. She looked with horror at the shelf as the book slowly disintegrated before her eyes, pages falling out all over the slate floor.

Carolyn turned back to the wizard, mortified. "Yes, well, like I said: disuse and misuse. Once, long ago, this library was a place of some repute. It's knowledge and lore was unrivaled in all of known time and space."

"What happened?" asked Carolyn. Merlin didn't seem to follow. "To the library, what happened to it? You said at one time, it was known, it was unrivaled in all of known time and space."

"Nothing happened," he said with a bit of a scoff. "It's still well-known. Well-known, well-regarded, well-respected. Regrettably, well-known and well-respected is not the same as well-maintained. Well-regarded is not the same as well-traveled. A resource many rely on and trust in quickly becomes one that many take for granted. And a sterling reputation of excellence slowly becomes less a blanket authorization to continue to do good work and more a rational for a perfectly harmless budget cut." His sarcasm was obvious. "This library was the seat of learning. Now it is a repository of knowledge that is known, but the knowledge it holds is not." Merlin looked over the grand library like he was looking a lost love who had fallen on hard times. "This library has become as much a mystery as the mysteries this library knows the answers to."

"Yeah, well, this ain't the only place," Carolyn concurred. She began collecting the pages, but then just put an armful back on the shelf. She looked out at the great library, seeing still more beyond the door they had entered through.

She stepped down from the landing onto the floor of the library. She tried to take a second and grasp the sheer size. The smell of aged paper and dusty volumes was mixed with the acrid scent of candle smoke. The library was tall enough and wide enough to have its own circulation of air. "This place is huge," marveled Carolyn.

"Yes," Marlin nodded. He turned around. "Well, I leave you to it."

Carolyn's eye bugged out. She whirled around, staring up at the wizard. "Wait, now?!"

He stopped and turned back to her, brushing his bushy beard. "Well, I assumed you wanted to be left to work."

"It's like," she looked down at her watch. She stopped and held it up to hear ear. "Late!" she suddenly exploded. "Is there a place I can sleep and tackle this in the morning?"

"So you accept the position?" Marlin exclaimed. "Excellent. Wonderful. That's terrific news." He turned to leave.

"Merlin," she called after him. "Me. Bed. Sleep."

"Yes, what of it?" he asked.

"Where do I do that?" she pressed.

"Why in your room of course." he answered simply.

"And that's where?" she asked.

He blinked at her. "The same place it's always been," he responded absently.

"You didn't tell me where that same place is," she said with an accommodating smile.

He straightened up. "Oh. Dear me, I do believe you're probably right. Well then." He turned. "Follow me." She shook her head as she followed him out.

It was a small room, roughly the size of a dorm room, or a cell as she liked to think of it. Rectangular, the bed was against the fall wall, with a short table across from it. A set of dead flowers sat on the table. There was a bedside table next to the bed, one which was a good six inches taller than comfortable.

At the foot of the bed was a trundle case, while a chest of drawers sat right in front of the door, sticking out just enough for the door to not be able to open quite all the way. "I'm afraid most of your furniture was bought at a yard sale," Merlin explained politely. "Bit of a mish-mash of styles, really."

Carolyn stood in the door for a moment and just whimpered in surrender. She looked back at Merlin and asked, "How much do I get paid?" He blinked at her. "I do get paid, right?" she pressed.

"Of course, of course," he insisted with false-seeming confidence.

Carolyn looked wary of his assurances. "In money, right?"

"If you wish," he said, as though it was of no matter. "What would you care for your salary to be?"

Certain he was pulling her leg, she asked deadpan, "A million dollars a month."

He didn't bat an eye. "That seems rather unambitious, but I am certain we can make that happen. Though I think you will quickly find that monetary compensation to be of little interest." He smiled paternally, patting her on the shoulder.

"Then why would I want to do this?" she asked in astonishment.

"Why, the goodness of your heart." He smiled.

She stared at him for a moment. "I think I hate you," she finally decided out loud.

"Oh come now, there's no reason to hate me," he said, turning from her, closing the door behind him. "In time, you'll come to appreciate the charm of this place." He pulled the door closed. "Good night," he said as he pulled the door shut.

"Wait, wait!" she exclaimed. "Wh-what about my family? What about my stuff? My apartment! My car! I don't want to just leave it there. I'll have to pay for the overnight parking."

"You needn't worry about any of that," Merlin assured her, just barely leaning inside. "It is late and the dawn will be upon us. Trivial affairs like your belongings, your loved ones, and your personal life can all wait until you've had a nice rest." With that, he pulled the door shut, leaving her alone.

Carolyn looked back at her room, sighing. The stain-glass window across from her seemed to stare at her, while all the furniture seemed to not approve of her. Slowly, something registered with her. "How is this room being lit?" she asked, looking up at the ceiling. She saw no lights. In fact, she didn't see any lights anywhere. She held her hand against the wall, staring at it, not seeing a shadow.

One eyebrow went up as she pulled away from the wall. "Okay, dimmer," she said to the room.

The lights dimmed noticeably.

"Okay," she said. "Dark."

The lights went out.

"On."

The lights appeared.

Carolyn scratched her chin. "Off," she called, making the room dark. "On." The lights came on. "Off. On. Off. On," she said in rhythm. She smiled. "Off. On. Off. On," she said really fast as the lights rushed to catch up. "Off. On. Off. Off," she said rapidly again, grinning as the room got bright a second time. "Ah ha!" she exclaimed. "Got ya!"

The lights went out.

The chirp of songbirds awoke Carolyn, as did the gentle light of the dawn. She pulled herself off the pillow and looked into the window over her bed. Drool had laced the side of her mouth and her hair was a nest of tangles. She struggled to see, then reached around to the bedside table. She hit her hand and swore, remembering in her blindness how tall the table was. She fished around a moment more until she found her glasses.

With her vision restored, she sat up in her bed and looked out the window. The stained-glass window of abstract shapes was half-opened, letting in a sweet dawn. A gorgeous sunrise was on full display. The endless radiant beams of light were captured not only in the rich blue sky but also the silvery waves of the endless lake the castle overlooked. The far shores held trees that she could barely tell were swaying in the morning breeze.

For a long moment, Carolyn stared out the window at the beauty unmatched by anything she could recall having seen in her life. A strange melancholy came over her, like she had wasted so many days being anywhere else.

Realizing she didn't understand where 'here' was, she looked at her new bedroom. It looked no different from the night before, though perhaps a bit homier and inviting without the shadows of nighttime in its corners. She shuffled to the edge of the bed and hopped off, landing on the hard stone floor. She rubbed her heels and grimaced, then yawned as she looked around the room. She scratched her stomach as she looked at her surroundings, then shuffled to the door.

Still in her clothes from the night before, she shuffled out into the hallway. The castle corridor was warm, with candles and torches at regular intervals in both directions. Carolyn turned to pull her door shut, but found no indication of what room she was hers or how to differentiate it from any other room she might find. Two similar doors were within sight to the right, three more to the left.

She turned back to her door, only to find no manner of locking it or even securing it. She opened the door and looked back inside, and finally just sighed. Resolved there was nothing worth taking that she felt responsible for, she left the door ajar and headed down the hall. Trying to retrace her steps from the previous night, she backtracked along the way she recalled Merlin leading her.

As she reached an intersection that felt only halfway familiar, Carolyn yawned again. She smelled cinnamon and sugar, so she followed her nose. Down a different hall she went, padding along, wavering a bit as she walked. She yawned often, bumped the wall occasionally with her shoulder, barely processing anything except the growl of her own stomach.

Carolyn followed the scent of cinnamon and fresh-baked bread into a large cafeteria. Several wooden benches ran along the near wall while on the far side were wooden tables of a mismatched sort. Baskets of fruit and pastries were arranged in a haphazard pattern on the tables. Passed them were several carving boards covered in generous portions of bacon and sausage.

Between the entrance and the food were an array of seats around a variety of tables every bit as eclectic as the buffet. And just like the chairs and tables were a mishmash of every possible version of the word 'wizard'. Two older women in dark blue robes spoke over croissants and tea as they stroked the black cats in their laps. A young boy in a school uniform carried a wand and a bowl of cereal. A man in furs with a bone through his septum sat with a large full of sausages across from a man in vaguely oriental robes and a goatee that extended to his neck.

Carolyn spotted Merlin but made no acknowledgment of him. She instead crossed the dining hall for the serving tables.   Coming before the counter, she barely opened one eye enough to stare at the large frog-like creature with a hairnet that stared back at her. "Coffee," she groaned.

"Rippit," the thing croaked. "We don't have—"

Like lightning, her hand shot across the counter, grabbing the frog's collar. Her eyes flared open as she stared into the frog's giant bulbous eyes. "Coffee," she repeated clearly through clinched teeth.

"Just, just, just a minute. Ribbit," it squeaked.   She shoved it back, then stood still, fuming.

"I see you're getting used to the place," Merlin said, coming up next to Carolyn.

"Do you have coffee?" she asked without turning, her closed eyes locked forward.

"Well...no," he said slowly, considering the answer.

"Then don't talk to me for at least an hour after I get some," she said, her eyes flickering up just a bit.

Merlin considered her for a moment, then nodded acceptingly as he turned and walked away.

"That was...interesting," Carolyn said as she walked down the hall with several scrolls stuffed under her arm. Merlin walked with her, the tapping of his staff like a metronome. "I've never had an HR meeting quite like that."

"HR?" asked Merlin. "Ah." He put it together. "Human Resources. Yes, well, even for magical denizens of the realms beyond reality, we still must endeavor to optimize management."

"I guess," Carolyn agreed absently. "I find the lack of sick days troubling."

"You are not here to fill a position," Merlin told her. "You are here to perform a feat, and then to oversee the task of maintaining it. We don't care how your time is used to see the job done; simply that it is done. If you feel under the weather, well, rest until you feel right. A task is best confronted at your best, not when compromised from within. And if you are disinclined to work on a given day, it would be barbaric to ask you to do so."

She slowed to a stop. "So what if I just take every day off?" she asked of him.

He stopped as well, though seemed untroubled by the question. "Would you?"

"No, but..." She wasn't sure what point she was trying to make. She resumed walking.

"Vacation time, sick leave, all such are incentives and allowances for someone who would prefer to not perform a task but are required to do so," explained Merlin. "If yours is a task you would perform under your own delight without any insistence, then we can put our faith in you to do that."

"Huh," was all Carolyn could say.

"If your heart belongs to the library, we needn't ensure you return in a timely fashion," Merlin told her. "More likely, we will need to monitor you to take breaks and vacations when needed. With the right task, the right responsibilities, the right employment, one's work ethic will handle all the relevant matters. It is only with misplaced talents that one must be bribed and goaded."

Carolyn repeated herself. "Huh."

Merlin continued to guide her along, following down a winding path that passed through an enclosed breezeway. A gust of wind buffeted the trees in the small orchard within the castle walls but the breezeway itself felt scarcely a breeze. Carolyn was still focusing mostly on the scroll laying out her benefits. "What is this bit about funeral expenses?" Before she could get an answer, they arrived at the doors into the library. "This isn't the way we came yesterday—" She realized Merlin was gone and she was standing alone in the hallway before the library doors. She rolled up the scroll and stuck it under her arm with the others, then pushed through the doors.

Midday found Carolyn on the floor of the library, seated on a cushion she'd stolen from a chair behind the circulation desk. On the slate floor, she had a stack of books laid out around her as she tried to reason just what they were in order to construct an order to place them.

"How goes it?" Merlin asked from out of nowhere, startling Carolyn. The librarian jumped up and whirled around. When she saw it was Merlin, she just rolled her eyes and went back to her stack of books. "Finding everything in working order?"

"Not in the slightest," she grumbled, turning to glare at him. "And first up, I don't like wearing the same clothes two days in a row. I'm going to have to get some stuff from my house. And I need to let my parents know that I didn't get kidnapped. Well, that I did get kidnapped but it's cool. Apparently. Maybe."

"To be dealt with this evening, I assure you," the wizard pushed aside without worry. "How's the condition of the library? In times past, this library has been described alongside the word 'disaster'."

"Merlin, this isn't a disaster," Carolyn said, her eyes fuming alongside her breath. "This..." she said, her hands shaking as she held the pages of what had once been a book. She looked around at the shelves that spread out as far as the eye could see. "This isn't a library. This can't be your library. Libraries have some system of organization. They have structure and reason. They have books that hold together!"

"Well, yes," Merlin said, nodding his head. "You see, we've been having some trouble with book keeping since the academy opened."

"Trouble?" the librarian said. She snickered with a sick, almost maniacal tone. "Trouble is people not returning the occasional book on time. Trouble is a book shelf falling over. This isn't trouble." She pointed to the vast wasteland of magical texts. "This is a catastrophe. This is an insult to the very concept of organization."

"Well, there's no need to get snooty about it," said the elder wizard, a bit miffed.

"Haven't you ever heard of labeling?" Carolyn asked, getting red-faced in irritation. "Cataloging? Alphabetizing? The Dewey Decimal System?! I mean, come on. You're wizards. WI-ZA-RDS!" she yelled, slapping her palm with the back of her hand.

"Well," the wizard said, with a hint of embarrassment in his voice. "We did attempt an organization effort in the past." He looked away, his words coming with difficulty. "We tried to organize the library alphabetically. And as I'm sure you can appreciate, that becomes difficult when you have to work with multiple lettering and phonetic systems. And then there was the time we tried organizing it by author. I don't even want to talk about that."

"Look, Merlin," Carolyn offered up. "I don't even know most of these languages. Like, I can't even identify them. And I don't understand magic. And I can't organize anything if I don't have at least some idea as to how the subject matter works."

"My dear, magic is not science," Merlin returned. "It is, by nature, variable and argumentative against classification."

Carolyn sat back for a moment and thought. Then she looked up at Merlin, her eyebrow raising. "Is there a council of wizards here? Like the assorted heads of departments or something?"

"Of course," he nodded.

"What do you think they're up to right now?"

Like everything else in the castle, the group of magicians that stared back at Carolyn were strange and mismatched. On the far right of the semi-circular table was a middle-aged woman who was showing the wear of the years. Dressed in earthly green tones, she carried a tamed plant in a terra cotta pot along with a silver knife and a strand of golden rope. Next to the woman was a dangerous looking man dressed in black leather, a large and overly-wicked sword strapped to his back while a pair of futuristic guns sat on his hips. In the middle of the group was a wizardly-looking man not dissimilar from Merlin. Dressed in colorful rainbow robes, he stroked his bushy white beard occasionally.

Next to the wizard was a soothsayer if Carolyn had ever seen one. Dressed in a black cape with a red interior, the man had dark, striking hair with a few white stripes, while his captivating eyes seemed to blink just a bit too often. And lastly, at the far end was a polite-looking Korean woman sitting pleasantly with a bowl of cookies, her gray hair done up in a bun. Her cream-colored pantsuit had the broach of a kitty playing with yarn pinned to her lapel.

"Hi," Carolyn said to the group, glancing back at Merlin. "Um, so like how does magic work?"

The gathered figures of magical lore looked at one another with various glances. "I'm sorry," said the woman with the knife and rope. "Could you be a bit more specific, please?"

"I'm Carolyn Chow," she told them, stepping towards the panel of wizards. "Merlin here..." She looked back at the man who seemed to be beaming, as though it was a rare delight to be mentioned in conversation. "He, uh, contracted me to fix the library."

"We are aware," said the wizard in the center of the group, long fingers with knotty joints templed as he stared. His voice was deep, at the same time abrasive and strangely smooth like sweet-smelling cigar smoke.

Carolyn looked between the two wizards, certain there was a backstory here. "Yeah, okay," she dismissed it. "Well, in order to organize the library, I need to understand magic. I need to have some grasp of the subject matter that I am cataloging. I don't need to be a true expert but I need to have a basic grasp on what the library is meant to showcase."

"You ask after the very heart of all that is, was, was not, and ever shall be," said the central wizard in rainbowed robes.

Carolyn blinked and then gestured frantically right at the wizard. "Okay, see, right there. That's a categorization system: is, was, was not, ever will have not been or whatever you said." She looked to the council to get some notion that they followed. "You don't need to teach me magic, but I have to have some kind of an idea of how it works so that I can...I can...do my, my thing. Put the books in order make them available."

"Oh, she seems very lovely," deemed the Korean woman at the far end. She bit into an oatmeal-raisin cookie and smiled happily like a cat in a sunbeam.

"Child," said the lead wizard, "the magical arts are at best divided among the ten disciplines of the Ein Sof."

"Ten disciplines," Carolyn accepted without hesitation. "Okay, great. Cool. What are those?"

"The Ten Disciplines are an illusion," said the soothsayer with his black cape. "They are a diversion! From the true form of magic!" He seemed incapable of speaking without dramatically moving his hands.

"Childish boys," said the green-dressed woman. To Carolyn she began to speak when the central wizard snapped back at her. The pair began to argue with far more familiarity than seemed professional.

The din of conflicting voices washed over her like the surf. She chewed on their words for a moment, then put her fingers to her lips, whistling loudly and stopping all conversation. "Let's try this again," she demanded. She pointed at the Korean woman. "You. Fifty words or less. How does magic work?"

"Magic is a matter of inspiration," the woman said with a polite smile and a bow of the head, like she was proud to invoke her schoolgirl etiquette once again. "Magic is when the universe manifests it's will through the actions of those within the universe. It's--"

"And that's enough," Carolyn interrupted. She pointed at the man in black. "You. Magic. Go."

The man stood, his hand reaching back to his sword. "No one," he said with a harsh, raspy voice, "tells me what to do."

"Sit do-own, you fool!" called the soothsayer, his eyes wide as he pointed at the street samurai. "For lo, this woman is endeavoring to achieve, to excel, to accomplish the impossible!" He spoke in a pulsating tone, his volume and timbre fluctuating at every word and even syllable. "She seeks to complete the events which no act of magic could ever hope to achieve! She is trying to--"

"Thank you, thank you," Carolyn said, silencing the charlatan. She breathed out, then looked at the wizard. "In order for magic to be studied," she said almost rhetorically, "it must be broken down into simpler parts. What are those simpler parts?"

"They are broken down into five fundamentals," the man said with a grandfatherly smile. "And each of those five fundamentals are broken down into five elements."

Carolyn waited for them to expound. When they didn't she prompted with a slight roll of her hands, asking, "And they are...?"

"The core of magic," said the green woman at the far end, "is made up of the study of growth, decay, violence, static, and love."

"The elements that supersede all," explained the samurai in a crisp, clipped tone, "are the fundamentals which science claim to be motion and distance and time, as well as matter and balance."

"There are internal elements to be considered as we-ell!" dramatically exclaimed the charlatan. "For within, you have the mind and the body, along with the spirit and the soul, and one cannot forget that which defines the you that you are, what is known as..." He pulled his cape over his face, his eyes flashing with emotion. "The ego."

Carolyn looked over at Merlin. The wizard politely rolled his finger around his ear.

"Of course," came the kindly Korean woman, "the universe is made up of things far less tangible than that. The universe is governed by things like wisdom and courage and memory, as well as power and the ever-purveying sense of mystery."

"And then," said the wizard, "there are the elements that govern over all. Such forces as chaos and order. Truth as well, along with eternity and fate."

"Okay," Carolyn said, her mind reeling. "Um, what about neutrality?" she asked.

"There is no such thing," Merlin whispered. "Even if you do nothing, at some level, you are doing something. It is impossible to sit and not think. Even if you drive away all your thoughts, you are actively controlling them. Even if you do not move, you are existing. And no matter how much you may wish to remain neutral, if you are for something, you are against something else."

"So neutrality doesn't exist?" she asked with a deadpan expression.

"It's not a matter of neutrality not existing. It's a matter of neutrality being a misdirected perspective," Merlin offered. "Consider a three-dimensional object looking on at a two-dimensional object. The three-dimensional object may see the two-dimensional object as not being there, as being neutral to existence if you will, but that doesn't mean the two-dimensional object is not present. It's simply facing a different direction."

"So neutrality is just facing a different direction?" Carolyn asked.

"Yes. Whether morally or existentially, when you believe something to be neutral, you just don't understand what it's really in favor of."

"Okay," She said. She looked up at the council, then smiled. "Okay. I think I've got an idea." Carolyn turned and began to depart. She paused at the door and told Merlin, "Thanks," with a tight smile. Out she went.

Once the newest member of the staff had departed, the council turned and faced Merlin. He looked at them and gave them all a pleasant bow of his head. "If your pet project is attended to, we have more pressing matters at hand," said the central wizard. "The immediate future hangs in the balance."

Merlin straightened a bit. He brushed down his robes and made himself as presentable as he could for the task. The central wizard gave him a bit of a sneer of disapproval and then held up a cardboard menu. "We are under strife yet again over which lunch platter to order."

"I'll not have anything with meat," said the green-clad woman.

"Oh, I would so enjoy a salad," said the Korean woman with a smile. "And maybe a treat."

"Meat is the essence of life," said the samurai. "We cannot consider it a meal without sustenance for—" The arguing resumed.

Carolyn returned to her room late in the evening. With a plate of fruit and two cookies, she nudged open her door with her toe to find a laptop on the bed. She froze when she saw the computer, then looked back out the hall. She saw no one nor heard anything from the endless ring of stone passageways.

Carolyn approached the bed slowly, as if certain the slim computer was a trap of some kind. She said cautiously, "Lights up, please." The room gently illuminated.

She set the plate down on the bed-side table and turned the laptop towards her. The model and style was unfamiliar to her, but it seemed very new and very stylish. Curiosity got the better of her and she opened the top. A picturesque desktop awaited her but a program went immediately into action. Carolyn began to panic until a telecom program opened up and a simulated phone began to ring. "Uh...uh..." Carolyn stammered, looking for the cancel button.

The screen changed abruptly, showing a static image as an audio channel opened up. "Hello?" came a familiar voice over the laptop's rich speakers. It was the tough voice of an avid sports fan, a woman who owned more football jerseys than blouses.

Carolyn's jaw dropped open. "Mom?"

"Carol, honey, why are you calling right now? It's two minutes to half-time!" her mother exclaimed. "Is everything alright? The Panthers are 2nd and 8."

Carolyn's heart soared at the sound of her mother's voice. "Hey, mom, I just wanted to tell you I'm—"

"Hang on, hang on, they're going for it," she said. There was a pause and then Carolyn could hear the rush of cheers through the TV's speakers. "WHOO! Yes! Yes! YEEES!" She could practically feel her mom turn the other way. "Did you see that, Daryl?! Did! You! See! THAT!" Carolyn sighed and sat down on her bed. "I'm sorry, babe, what's that?" asked her mom, settling down.

Carolyn was equal parts mad, irritated, hurt, and delighted. "Nothing, mom. I'm just calling to check in."

"Well, aren't you watching the game?" she pestered out of the corner of a mouth that sounded full of chips. Her demeanor suddenly changed. "You aren't out on a date, are you babe?"

Even alone, Carolyn blushed. "No, mom." She kicked her shoes off and looked around her room. "I, uh, I actually got a new job. It's super, super-weird."

"Good for you, babe!" her mom cheered.

"Yeah, I think..." Carolyn shook her head and swished her feet in the air. "I think I like it? I'm not sure. It's weird."

"Where's it at?" asked her mom. "Is it another library in the system? Did you get that position at the university that you wanted?"

"No, not that one," Carolyn said. She wiggled back on her bed, her back to her wall. "I just...it just sort of fell into my lap, I guess. I didn't even know I was in the running for it and then it just...like..." She stared into the distance, gawking with incredulity at it all. "Just sort of happened."

The silence of the line was brief. "Well...if you like it. Do you have any coworkers you like?" asked her mother. "How's your boss?"

Carolyn scoffed abruptly. "My boss? My boss is an airhead." She reached over and grabbed the plate. "Oh my god, he's like the most scatter-brained guy ever..." The call went on for some time.

***

Unlike before, the library was lit and alive. Four people stood at the counter, waiting patiently. None of them seemed particularly engaged, only present and waiting. Carolyn ventured slowly into the library at first, still getting used to not only seeing other people in the castle academy but the types of people she would see. "Good morning," she told the four. She set down her plate of cookies from the breakfast cafeteria. "I'm guessing you guys are my staff," she said, getting their attention.

The crowd of four turned to her. Standing closest was fairly normal-looking woman with blonde hair that came down to her waist. Dressed in a long flowery skirt and a red leather vest, she smiled at the librarian. Behind her, at the circulation desk, a witch stood. Carolyn had to look twice to make sure she was seeing the stereotype correctly, but even the mole was present.

Standing next to the witch was a large, gray-skinned giant that had to be at least ten feet tall. With broad shoulders and thick, muscular limbs, he stared at Carolyn, making no sound. Lastly was a grinning fool dressed in a red bandana and tattoos. Nothing else.

Carolyn looked down below the grinning man's waist, then up at him. "Is there a religious reason for that?" she asked, with a demonstrative swirl of her finger at him.

"My magic flows from my body," the man said with a deep voice, his grin getting wider as he thrust his body forward a bit. The blonde woman and the witch both looked away, disgusted. "I'm not about to restrict my magic, now am I?"

"I wasn't referring to the lack of clothes," Carolyn said, one eyebrow going up. "I was referring to the pencil with the chewed-on eraser. It looks depressed." The grinning man looked down, his ego shrinking with company. "I'm Carolyn," the librarian announced. "I've been tasked by Merlin to get this place into order. Now, who amongst you has any library experience?"

All four raised their hands.

"How about in a library that made sense?" she asked.

All four hands dropped.

"How about in a library other than this one?" she asked.

All four hands stayed down.

"Oh boy," she sighed, rubbing her eyes. She took a cookie off the plate, broke it in half, and ate it quickly as she tried to get focused. "Okay." She rubbed her hands vigorously. With a clap, she smiled at the four. "I'm Carolyn Chow. I'm the..." She turned and looked at the door, more to process what she was about to say. The others looked over her shoulder, trying to figure out if she'd heard something. "I'm the, the head librarian of the academy." Having said that aloud, she smirked, then smiled. "Cool." With some renewed enthusiasm, she asked them, "And who are you?"

The fool spoke immediately. "I'm Rathbone. Mathematician and astrono-medium."

Carol nodded and shook his hand. "I'm going to assume that makes sense to you. Now, go put on some pants."

"But I—"

"Nope. No. Uh-uh." She didn't give him the chance. She pointed at the door and repeated, "Go." Like a sulking child angry his prank had failed, Rathbone went stomping up the stairs and through the door. "And come right back," Carolyn yelled after him before the door closed. "We've got lots to do." As the door shut, she turned to the remaining three. "Alright, who's next?'

"I'm Magpie Ravenwood," said the witch. Complete with green skin and a black dress made of discarded remains of many fabrics, the cackling old woman approached the table to Carolyn's complete apathy. She carried an ugly broom and an evil scowl in her eyes of unequal size. "Knowing and seer, am I."

"Terrific," Carolyn told her. "Blessed be. I'm going to call you Maggie. Is that okay?'

Magpie shrugged. "Suit yourself, lady."

The sharp contrasting tone jarred Carolyn and she turned to the other woman. "I'm Rael Knotting." The woman bowed her head a bit and smiled. "I'm a student of the organizational arts."

"Getting college credit then?" asked Carolyn.

Rael did a good job of hiding her panicked uncertainty. "I'm...not aware of any?" She seemed uncertain if that was the correct answer.

"Okay," Carolyn nodded. To the big, gray-skinned giant, she asked, "And you are?"

"Groth," sad the giant.

Carolyn nodded. "And you want to work in the library?"

"Groth like books," said the giant with a nod.

Carolyn nodded. "Okay," she said again. She rubbed her hands deliberately and exhaled. "So here's the plan," Carolyn started, looking at her small staff. "I want each of you to go into the library and get an armful of books." Carolyn looked at Groth for a second and said, "For you, maybe a third of an armful. Bring those books back—" She stopped when the library door opened and Rathbone returned, wearing his pants wrapped around his arm. "No. Put them on properly."

She didn't wait for him to get dressed. "Bring them back here," she told the others, "and we'll go from there. Got it?" Magpie's hand rose. "Yes?"

"Any topic?" asked the old crone with a cackle.

"Don't overthink this," Carolyn warned her. "We're working, not reading." She gestured to the library and let them break for the books. She turned back to Rathbone as he cinched up his pants. "Go grab some books and bring them back." He nodded obediently, almost exuberantly, and then went rushing down the long line of the library stacks.

Carolyn returned to her plate, had another cookie and some coffee, when Rael returned with some books. The others followed, with Groth the last to bring his collection of books to the circulation desk.

In Merlin's office, the great bushy-bearded wizard had a dozen wind-up toys set out upon his large wooden desk. Gnarled like it had been grown from a tree rather than carved, the desk had a smooth top with rings like the inside of a tree, but also living branches with leaves jutting off it from the sides. Upon this desk, several of the wind-up toys were bopping and sliding, kicking out and flipping forward. The wizard grabbed toy after toy, frantically turning the crank and setting the toy back down before moving on to the next.

The door to his office opened rather abruptly and Carolyn came in, pushing a metal cart whose wheels squeaked. The cart was stacked high with books as she rolled it right up to the wizard's workspace. "I need you to review these," she told Merlin. She took one look at his desk, then leveled a deadpan look of disappointment at him.

The wizard looked up at her and smiled sweetly. "It's magic."

Carolyn stared for a moment longer before allowing, "Sure." She laid down two large tomes. "My staff and I looked through these...all of these," she added, waving her hand at the whole tray, "and we couldn't figure out what school of magic they belonged to."

Merlin picked up one book and opened it towards the middle. He held the book away from him as eyes more ancient than mountains squinted. He turned the book a bit at angles and then set it down between the windup toys that had all fallen silent. He looked about his desk for a moment, then padded it with his hands. From above, a vine descended with a hand made of human bone. Pinched between the fingers were a pair of zany 60s-era reading glasses. "Ah, thank you," said the wizard, accepting the glasses.

Her hand on her hip that was cocked out to one side, Carolyn looked at the vine. She lamented how her life had come to be one where such a thing didn't just not phase her, it didn't even elicit any questions.

"Yes," Merlin said to the book as he turned a few more pages. "I can see the confusion." He turned the book around and faced the pages towards her. "In what form or format at your categorizing the library?"

"Five schools; Supra, Core, all of those," she told him. She swished her mouth to one side, ready for him to question her reasoning.

"Ah," he said, nodding, approving. She was a bit surprised. "This would likely be one of your Supra books. Time, I should suspect." He handed it over to her. He took the next book as she applied a sticky note to the front of the book older than any country Carolyn knew the name of. "And how many books have you identified needing categorization?" asked Merlin as he flipped the ancient pages.

"This is just from one shelf," Carolyn told him.

The wizard looked astonished. "One shelf?"

Carolyn faced him, ready to argue. "It's a big library."

"Yes," he agreed. "That you've made such progress is quite admirable." He opened the book and looked down his nose, through the glasses, at its pages. "I knew we were right to recruit you."

"Kidnapped is a bit more accurate," Carolyn charged unspitefully. Merlin smirked and nodded. She couldn't tell if he thought she was joking or that she was right. "I still want to talk about pay. And days off."

"Yes, of course," he said in the most dismissive tone she'd ever heard in her adult life. He closed the book. "Supra as well. Distance, I would think, although a case can certainly be made for Motion."

"We're getting a lot of that," Carolyn said, accepting the book and applying the sticky note.

"Distance books?" Merlin asked.

"No, books that 'could be this, but a case could be made for that'," she expounded. She looked at the wizard and he at her. She gestured with both hands at the cart, drawing attention to the dozens more books that waited.

"Oh," he said, rising, as if he had expected her to keep handing him one book at a time. He crossed the big desk, petting a leaf as he passed it. Doing so drew from the leaf a chime like a silver bell. "And how do you plan to remedy that?" he asked as he set about the task she'd assigned.

"I don't right now," she said, putting one hand on the desk and leaning on it. "We'll get the library in AN order, and then figure out afterwards if it is in the right order."

Merlin nodded. He smirked, turning the book to Carolyn. "Mencius' Treatise on Morality." The grand wizard tapped the bottom of the page. "He drew a comic. It is about hating the sun being in your eyes." He turned the book back to himself and re-read the comic. "I do so enjoy comic strips."

"You should have let me bring over some of the graphic novels from my old library," Carolyn lamented. The realization that she'd accepted her previous job as truly in her past gave her pause.

Merlin nodded and shut the book. He handed it towards Carolyn but just as she went to take it, he pulled it back. She thought it a joke but he had a very earnest look in his eyes. "Graphic...novels?" His left eyebrow went up.

Carolyn matched the expression sarcastically. "Yes," she nodded. She took the book from him. "Comic books?" she said, applying the sticky note and assigning the book a section. Merlin stood up, the idea seeming novel and increasingly revolutionary to him. Carolyn gave him a moment to figure things out, then soft-rebooted his mind by saying, "Just write the designation on each one and bring them to the library." She padded out with a million more things to do.

***

Under the soft glow of moonlight, Carolyn worked quietly.

A long piece of paper was laid out before her on the counter of her library desk. Carolyn had drawn a long line with the five major breaks of schools of magic. From there, she'd marked a series of three-digit numbers. To this, she'd added a host of other words, all scribbled through. An oil lamp burned next to her and on the counter by her side, nearest the door, Mesmaid snored. One paw in the air, it twitched occasionally as the cat dreamed.

The library doors opened and in strode Merlin. He had a happy smile on his face and carried a brown paper bag that smelled of apple cinnamon. Spotting Carolyn, he asked, "How are you finding matters, my dear?"

"Chaotic," she said, disappointed. She pointed at a stack of books that lay obviously yet to be addressed. "Two of your wizards came in here and made quite the ruckus."

"The twins, I presume," Merlin said, looking at the books. He picked one up and nodded. "Yes, I should imagine so." He set it back down and then appraised the great silent and dark space with approval. "The library appears to be slowly gaining the shape you envision."

Carolyn looked up from her page and considered the library. The scent of musty air remained, as did the slight air of antiquity. Given its dark shadows and aged features, she was confident it would never lose that appeal. The thought of that made her smile. "I hope so," she decided.

Merlin tilted his head, coming around the counter, the floorboards or his knees creaking as he did. "And what is this that you toil at?" He craned his head further to see. "What are these numbers?"

"Divisions in subject matter," said Carolyn. "I'm trying for something similar to the Dewey Decimal System, but since this is all totally new and bizarre to me, I'm having to make it up as I go."

"The best kind of magic," Merlin grinned paternally.

"What?" asked Carolyn, not sure she'd heard him.

He waved it off. "Nothing but trivial mutterings of an old man," he assured her. With a sweet smile, he told her, "I am delighted that the task is yours, and that you are in command of the task."

She wasn't sure how to take that. She waggled her pen at the shelves. "My staff and me will keep at it, but I think we're mostly going to be categorizing the books as they're checked out." Merlin just nodded confidently. Turning back to him, Carolyn asked, "Sound good?"

His smile slowly widened with great approval. "Sounds excellent." With an affectionate scratch to Mesmaid's big belly, the wizard saw himself out, leaving the librarian to work her magic.

Block-Rockin' Beats

The violin didn't produce music; it produced emotions.

Eli Demarcus leaned back in an expensive desk chair, bulky headphones cupping his afro. His eyes closed, he listened to sounds that transcended music and were the aural recreation of dreams. Each masterful stroke of the bow created music unimagined by any human mind. The melodies and rhythms transcended notes and time signatures, becoming instead swirls of thoughts. They left the mind blissfully numb before the beauty.

Eli opened his eyes to water-stained roof of his apartment. The ugly beige stain, edged with brown, always looked different each time he stared at it. Now, driven by the music that played through his headphones – music that was transforming his world and his very existence – the stain came alive. Forming into a rabbit, he watched it hop about like a playful dream. Bounding around the white featureless landscape of his ceiling, it played joyfully in a manner only animals know.

Eli closed his eyes again and drank in the music, absorbing it rather than listening to it. The violin slowed, the piece coming to a close. When the final stroke of the bow concluded, silence and emptiness followed. The world felt hollow, like an echo with no noise.

Strangely morose after the music had concluded, he turned in his chair to his desk. The record player's arm was lifting automatically, shifting over to the resting bench. Eli tracked the cords to his computer, the screen dark. He sat up and moved the mouse, causing the display to show the digitization program compiling, finishing the transfer of violin notes into computer code. Here, Eli smiled, a curl to his lips on one side of his face. "Here we go," he said with a grin.

Sitting up in his cushy desk chair and enthused, he activated a mixing program. Importing the music file of the aged record, he began to splice it out without even needing to hear the music. The display of the solitary violin performance was sufficient. He laid down a simple beat and added a reverb for effect, making the violin sound like it was playing in a spacious hall. Reverb gave the intimate music a sense of majesty. With just a moment, Eli played a trial snippet to see what he had created. His smile only grew as the fruits of his labor began to present.

***

The crowd went nuts for the new hotness.

Eli bounced to the rhythm, not of the music but of the crowd itself. A sea of people stretched out before Eli as he manned the DJ booth, turning controls and adjusting the feed, reacting to the energy of the crowd and amplifying the effects in real time. He bopped along, one ear covered by his headphones. Eyes watched as much as ears listened; not sampling; merely observing.

Strobe lights flashed over the sea of people. Lasers descended and moved and patterned lights spun. The crowd twisted and writhed in the musical cloud. And Eli's smile of pride was real.

With a rattle, the whole refrigerator shook when Eli opened the hard metal door. A pronounced lack of cold came from the fridge and the shelves were mostly empty except for some half-finished takeout and a few cans of cheap beer. Eli scoffed as he pushed the door shut. "This party's lame, man."

"What do you expect?" asked Dierdre as he checked the cabinets over the fridge. Straight out of some 1950s sitcom, the fridge kept rattling back and forth, especially when the 6'4" cross-dressing Dierdre stepped on his thick-soled platforms. Long nails trailed along the cabinets that held surprisingly little crockery and even less food. "William doesn't entertain much. He barely even lives here. He practically lives at the club." Dierdre barely pronounced consonants, making his speech a swirling vortex of soft syllables. The broad shoulders of a weight lifter didn't match the speech pattern, just as they didn't match the neon-green backless dress, but Eli assumed he wasn't the target audience for Dierdre's attire.

"The club's a migrant art instillation," said Eli, pushing the fridge a bit, curious why it was rattling. "He just makes parties happen whenever he can find the spot."

"More to it than making parties happen, brah," said William as he muscled by. With a build similar to Dierdre's but lacking the height, William showed the signs of recent stress with a subtle gut that proceeded him. "What's you guys looking for?" As he asked, he pulled open the cutlery cabinet to reveal a tray of cookies.

"Let me guess: there're gonna be peanuts in the lint trap," Eli teased.

"Ice sluice from the freezer," William corrected. He chewed with his mouth open but smiled with child-like friendliness. He readied to toss a cookie at Eli, aiming for his mouth. Eli was legitimately curious if they could manage the feat but caught the cookie with his hand instead.

"You got one for me, baby?" Dierdre asked William.

"One what, honey?" he asked back with a flash of his eyes and more laughing.

"Ooh," Dierdre delighted. "Maybe in a moment we'll find out, but baby, I have GOT to eat something."

"I got some pizzas coming; threw in some chicken wings too and one of them cookie-pizzas," William told them both. He sniffed a nose used to but not quite addicted to cocaine and said, "Sorry about the refreshments. I haven't been home all week." To Eli, he said, "Good thing I didn't get that dog like I wanted. Glad she went to a real home, huh?" Eli agreed with a nod as he checked the time. The after-party was always a unique experience. No two were ever the same. Without segue, William asked, "Say, man, what was that Mozart thing you played tonight?"

"What Mozart piece?" asked Eli as he followed William. Plastic tray of store-brand cookies in hand, William lead two of his DJs into the parking lot of his townhouse. A circle of cars had been parked together in the nearest spaces and his sofa had been brought out from the otherwise empty living room for some comfortable seating.

"He means that violin piece," Dierdre explained, eating a cookie from the tray, nibbling on the ends in a counterclockwise fashion. "It sounded like Stephane Grappelli on methadone."

"Yeah, what was that?" William asked walking backwards to the rear of his couch. He had another cookie that he ate with his mouth open, holding the tray to make the option available to anyone. The cluster of two dozen DJs, club-goers, and ravers responded lethargically.

"I don't know," Eli said, slender hands in the tight pockets of his jeans.

"What do you mean you don't know, baby?" asked Deirdre, like he was worried Eli was having a depressive episode.

"I mean I found this record. Old record. Got no label. It's got 'Brod' written on one side. B-R-O-D. That's it." Eli shrugged youthful shoulders.

"Brod?" William said with a bit of a sneer, not liking mysteries. To Deirdre, he asked, "Honey, you're my walking encyclopedia."

"Yeah, but I don't know," he said. He asked Eli, "Is that the artist or the producer?"

"No, not a label," Eli further explained. "The thing's, like, scratched on the side. Like somebody took a key to the side of a car. That kind of a deal. B-R-O-D."

William's round face hung forward, genuinely unsure what to do with this information. "Weird." Deirdre nodded, with a similar expression.

"Yeah," Eli agreed. "But shoot, this Brod person sure knew his stuff because...yeah." He gestured at the music from tonight. "I'm gonna find some more. This is good stuff."

"Yeah, you do that," William told Eli in a strangely ominous tone and a coy smile.

Eli's gaze grew cautious, suspicious, and hopeful. "Why?" William averted his eyes and avoided the question. "Why?" Eli pressed. William looked around at the others in the cluster of cars. A few had pilfered from his tray of cookies but most had barely noticed.

"Deirdre, honey, would you handle these?" William told the big man in the little dress.

"Sure, baby," he said, taking the tray. He gave Eli a hopeful look and walked around the couch, finally getting the attention of the others.

As the rest of the party descended on the cookies, William walked a few steps back towards his house and towards Eli. "This little migrant thing," he told the slender DJ. "It's about to go seriously migrant."

Eli tried not to get his hopes up. "What? You're going to throw another party in NYC?" His heart skipped a beat at the lucrative possibility.

William shook his head. "No, brah, so much bigger." Eli laughed, unsure what else to do. "I partnered with this company in Asia. They make soda and stuff. They got me going out to a nine-city, four-nation tour. Thailand, Cambodia. That kind of stuff."

Eli did a doubletake. "Holy crap."

"Yeah, brah," William whispered. "I got to supply the talent; they're supplying the party. I got to supply the talent," he repeated. "I got to supply...the talent," he emphasized again at Eli. "Get me some more of that violin stuff, man. Get some more and we're going to frickin' Thailand."

The deal was sealed with a handclap.

***

Eli scrutinized the record very carefully.

There were no designations on it, no marks or serial numbers inscribed anywhere. Aside from a few blemishes left by long-lost adhesives, there was no label or decoration of any kind. The disc was just slightly oblong, only noticeable when held out to be inspected. The ridges were very pronounced and rough, rawer than any commercial record Eli owned. The comparison alone prompted him to look at the mountains and mountains of such records which filled his tiny apartment.

In the warm light of the day that filtered through faded curtains, Eli considered the records like they were silent experts. He decided he needed a consult.

With a jangle, Eli stepped into the cigar shop. A wood-paneled establishment on the back of a nowhere street, it smelled of aged tobacco and clean steel. There was a whiff of brandy and other comfort liquors in the air while several clocks ticked in perfect unison.

The grandfather clock, to the right of the sunny door, was open. An old man with well-groomed white hair turned the key to wind the clock. He noted Eli enter and sniffed. "Mr. Demarcus." He pulled the chain of the clock with a satisfying clack of each length and shut the door. "What brings you here?" He locked the door with a ring of keys, all locking antiquated things.

"I got a record for you to hear, Mr. Ales," said the college-aged man.

"A record?" responded Ales, with skin the color of bleached parchment. He walked back behind the counter and removed two glasses. "Did you drive?" Eli shook his head. The man old enough to be Eli's great-grandfather poured two very short glasses of brandy. He pushed one vaguely towards Eli and let the other be. He began to head to the back of the store. "What's this you have? I'm not much of a man for modern music." He shouted to be heard as he disappeared into the back.

"Yeah, but this is obscure. This is weird," said Eli. He took the glass and sniffed it. The scent burned his nose and he hesitated.

"Obscure? Weird?" said Mr. Ales as he came back around, a laptop under his arm. He set it on the counter next to the small brandy glasses. "Hardly a thing a man like me might know a thing about, but I'm flattered you thought of me." He laid out the laptop and opened it, a lovely pastoral desktop appearing. He plugged a turntable on the counter into the laptop and speakers in the cigar shop came to life. "Regale me, Mr. Demarcus, regale me."

As Ales had a sip of his brandy, Eli set the record on the player and let it begin to turn. The needle arm moved on its own, sensing the weight of the disc. It placed itself with robotic precision and the speakers crackled as the audio began.

With the first notes, Eli could see Ales felt the same thing. Those first long strokes of the piece were like being grabbed by the soul and pulled aloft. Memories of things forgotten were laid before them both as the music that came through those speakers reached right inside of them.

Ales forgot about his brandy and was lost in the haunting mystery that was the violin. Amid the imperfections of the recording, cutting strokes of the bow slid through the air. Melodies were piled atop one another, cascading quickly into a torrent of experiences far beyond sound. Music and memory fused and transposed, until both men at the counter were feeling life rather than hearing music.

For Eli, his eyes drifted to a case where cigars were stacked in a humidifier. Inside the glass case, Eli saw the cigars begin to twist and roll. What had been a box of indulgences rose into a snake. A hooded beast like nothing on this earth turned from its coiled position. A pair of dangerous eyes twisted and focused on Eli, not quite threatening him but aware of him and mindful of his distance. The snake slithered its tongue once and its hood began to grow, expanding wide.

A distant horn awoke both men.

A near-collision outside the shop shocked them both. They realized they were panting. Mr. Ales' hand was shaking when he pulled the needle arm off the record. The music stopped with a hint of a scratch and the shop was empty and lifeless. Air made hot by glass cases and stocked shelves, felt like it was settling ash after an eruption. The world was flat and unimpressive without the bittersweet sorrow of that violin.

"Wow," whispered Eli.

"Wow, Mr. Demarcus?" Ales said, his face flushed. "You act like you've not heard it."

"Sure sounded different last time," said Eli. He wiped his brow, surprised he wasn't sweating. "Sounds different each time."

"It is amazing how important the context of art," said Mr. Ales. He removed the record with great care, with reverence. "A book read at night instead of the morning. A movie seen on vacation as opposed to a work night. A painting seen as a poster in a dorm room instead of in a gallery showing." He slipped the record back into the generic case Eli had bought. "Context is almost as important as the art itself."

"Too true," Eli said, agreeing more and more with each passing second. He accepted the record and asked, "You know who it is?"

"Oh no," Ales said gravely, shaking his head and his puffy white hair at the same time. "I've heard..." He could only shake his head.

Eli smiled in disbelief. "Come on, man. You've heard recordings of James Hetfield playing chopsticks when he was, like, fifteen. You've got Michael Bublé's school plays. You've got Mozart pieces nobody knows exists. Come on, man. You've got Victor Borge's audition tapes. You don't know this? Mussorgsky's work before he was famous and Vivaldi's Arias after the death of Charles the 6th. This? You don't know THIS?!"

Mr. Ales nodded, almost proud. "I don't know this." He gestured to the record precisely the same way Eli did. "Mr. Demarcus, you've got something quite unique here." His eyes shone when he told Eli, "I'm not sure I even know what this is." He took the glass of brandy and accepted a sip. As he sipped, he stepped back from Eli and his record. "Is that jazz, or is that baroque? Is this a solo performer or a group?"

"Well, it's definitely a solo," Eli said, one of the few things of which he was certain.

Ales was not so confident. "Is it? What I heard included note schemes that no one person could perform."

"Ever heard of John Stump?" Eli asked rhetorically.

Ales snickered. "John Stump? You're referring to the Tribute to Zdenko Fibich, I assume."

Eli nodded. "The Death March, the part that's supposedly impossible to play." He took out his phone. "I can find, like, five videos of people playing it right now on YouTube."

"Tribute was written as a parody," Ales insisted quickly, stopping Eli from his digital search. "The notations include jokes like calling for a duet of gongs."

"Which would be kinda sick," Eli nodded.

"But no, this is different," Ales insisted, putting his hand on the record. "This performance...what I heard...it included melodies that a single violin cannot produce." He spoke slowly and emphatically as he looked Eli most earnestly in the eye. "This is either a joke," he told Eli, "or something truly phenomenal." Ales took Eli's brandy glass, was about to sip, then paused. Eli gestured quite happily for his host to partake, so he did. "I trust," said Ales tightly after emptying the glass, "you have worked your digital magic and examined it?"

"It's legit," Eli assured him. "This isn't a...this was recorded from a live performance. None of the usual little tells of a recording or a digital work are there. I mean, it COULD be..." He just shook his head. "But nah, man. This is a guy. One guy."

Ales backed away from the counter again, arms crossed over his suit vest. He thought as outside, the city street was mostly quiet. "You might speak to some of the old listeners over on Heide Street."

Eli couldn't place it. "Heide Street?"

"You might be forgiven for thinking it Little Germany," Ales nodded. "It is a neighborhood formed by immigrants of rim nations during World War II."

"Rim nations?" asked Eli, half-sneering at the bizarre term.

"Nations on the outskirts of larger, more famous, more powerful countries," Ales explained, his arms still crossed. "Every child knows Germany, but Luxembourg is a bit more esoteric. Slovenia, Moldova, Estonia. These were just as ravaged by the war but they had not the political power and influence as, say, France or Finland."

"Yikes," said Eli. "So it's just a community of immigrants?"

"Not is. Was," Ales told him. "The horrors seen by many are, understandably, guarded from grandchildren. Now there are only a handful of shops that would carry the hallmarks of the old community, of the old world. Still..." Ales smiled. "The old endure and what they've heard is unlike what we of the modern world might know."

Eli was a little amused by Ales referring to himself as being of the modern world, but he gave no hint of it except to smile. "You recommend anybody in particular?"

"I'm afraid not," said Ales. He collected the two brandy glasses and said, "Good luck in your search."

"Yeah, thanks," said Eli. He collected his record and began to head out. "I'll let you know what I find."

Only as the door was shutting did Ales' smile fade and he answered, "That's quite alright."

The smell of onions and pepper assaulted Eli as he stepped into the deli. A few eyes drifted to the skinny young black man who hedged at the door to look around, seeing old eyes and leathery faces with deep lines. Nothing was said, though, and the patrons returned to their conversations and their meals. "Can I help you?" called a much older man behind the counter. He had a gruff face, like he had been bored since dawn of last week.

"Yeah, hey," Eli said as he headed to the counter. "You know Ales? Mr. Ales? Runs the cigar shop on—"

"Yeah, I know him," said the man. His heavy accent had a husky tone, an abrasive element born of regular but light smoking. "He send you here?"

Eli nodded. "Yeah, I'm trying to find something."

The deli proprietor gestured to the shop. "I got sandwiches."

"This is about music," Eli told him. He slung his backpack off his shoulder and unzipped it. "I got a record with no label. I'm trying to find out who did it."

The proprietor was clearly intrigued. "What kind of music? I don't do any of the new stuff."

"It's old," Eli told him. He glanced when the door opened, the bell over it jingling as a couple came inside. "Just a bunch of tracks of violin pieces. I know classical but I don't know any of these. They're original. All of them."

The proprietor looked very intrigued. "Ales sent you to me?" He laughed, a strange expression for such a naturally dour face. He pulled off his plastic gloves and yelled something in a language Eli wasn't sure he'd ever heard. Another man about the same age appeared from the back. The proprietor kept speaking in a European language, the two clearly arguing, as he untied his apron. A vertical striped shirt and brown pants out of style by multiple decades led Eli into the backroom.

The back room was full of cardboard boxes of produce and meat ready to be sliced. A cooler and a fridge stood next to each other. Opposite them was a small cot with two heavy blankets. Next to it, a set of bedroom shelves which included a record player. "My brother, he gets headaches. Migraines they call them." Nothing else was said as the owner turned on the record player. He stepped back and gestured for Eli to take over.

Eli slipped the record from its protective sleeve and set it on the turntable. He manually set the needle and stepped back. From an embedded speaker of the ancient player, the strokes of the violin began. Whatever the deli owner heard, however, it was not entirely unfamiliar. The man's face contorted with strained recognition, like he was trying to recall where this music had last entered his life. "You know it?" Eli asked, considering the question rhetorical.

The deli owner's head nodded up and down while his mind was a thousand miles away. Wherever it was, it wasn't good. He removed the needle abruptly and took the record from the turntable. "I'm not helping you." He pushed the record into Eli's hands and pointed. "Get out."

"Whoa, wait, what is it?" Eli asked, not sure if he was certain this was a joke or just hoping.

"No," was all the old man would say.

"Dude, just give me a name or something," Eli begged.

With a finger held forward, the old man stared earnestly to Eli. "No." He pointed over Eli's shoulder. "Get out." Eli couldn't bring himself to argue. He exited onto the street, backing out from the deli. He looked at the unremarkable front, not sure what he'd just experienced. The record under his arm, he began to walk down the sun-bleached street in the afternoon.

Eli made it only a block until he spotted a pair of older gentlemen playing chess in front of a bar. The 'open' sign was unlit but the front door was open. He approached the pair and asked, "Hey, can I trouble you guys for a minute?"

"Bar opens later," said the man facing away from him. He was an ancient man, like a great action hero candle that had melted. A flat cap sat atop a head with less hair than came out of his ears. His words were almost unintelligible, the accent was so thick.

"I'm looking for somebody that knows music," Eli asked.

"Music?" laughed the other old man, with a mustache like a parody and a plaid corduroy jacket. "We don't listen to hip hop much." He was a little more intelligible but the accent was still an obstacle.

"Nah, it's a violin solo," Eli told them. "Dude at the deli got spooked listening to it. We didn't even make it a minute." He looked down at the two men as both of them turned and faced him. "Y'all wouldn't know anybody interested, would ya?"

Three minutes later, in the empty bar lit only by the sun coming in through the windows, the mustached old man set a dusty record player on the bar top. "My granddaughter, she got me an iPod. Little white thing." He spoke as he set-up the record player. "I have music on there. So much music. Music I didn't think anybody knew anymore."

"Rawhide," said the other old man, still wearing his cap atop a head covered in old age spots. He mimicked riding a horse and the rhythm of the old song. "Rolling, rolling, rolling," he sang, then laughed, then coughed.

"Yes, but not," said the mustached old man, finally plugging in the record player. "I've got music on there. So much music. I can play anything. All the music. If I can find it. The screen, it's so tiny. And the controls, they don't make sense. That wheel. Such a mess."

When he clicked on the record player, speakers throughout the bar crackled and a subtle hum overtook the air. "Let me see," said the old man. Eli handed the record over to him. He took it with knobby fingers, joints that had been broken decades ago. He accepted it happily but when his eyes fell to the center, he saw BROD carved in the center. "Where's the label?"

"No label," Eli told him as he waited.

Eyes dulled by age but not devoid of awareness looked at Eli. Across the rims of heavy glasses, those eyes were guarded and cautious. Hands that shook from age now shook from something else. "You know what Brod means?" asked Eli.

The old man didn't speak, he only set the record on the turntable. His watch jangled as he set the needle on the bleed. The speakers crackled loudly, the echo passing back and forth through the bar. Wood paneling and mismatched tables and chairs are created a décor that could only be called eclectic.

The violin began. Long strokes with a bow like a straight razor across the wrist. Heavy notes punched inside of Eli's chest and grabbed his heart. The music was different in the bar. Same notes, same rhythm, same melodies, different impact. Long shadows deepened. Reflections moved in a still world. Eli saw his own eyes staring back at him in every surface.

The man in the hat, with a burst of speed that would have impressed a college athlete, pulled the needle off the record player. The mustached man was panting, sweat on his brow. He had been too catatonic to do the same. To Eli, he said, "That's cursed music."

"Cursed music?" Eli asked, not entirely in disbelief.

The mustached old man grabbed the record with effort, a pained look on his face. "Go somewhere else." He handed the record gruffly across the bar to Eli and the smaller of the ancient men grabbed Eli by the elbow. With strength more appropriate for a lion than an octogenarian, he pushed Eli through the door.

"Guys!" Eli yelled. "I just want to know who—" The door was slammed shut in his face.

The smell of dusty paper didn't inspire confidence as Eli walked into the used bookstore. Another half-forgotten store that catered to the mostly ancient community, it was helmed by an old man in a dark brown jacket with patches on the elbows. He noticed Eli enter and seemed intrigued. "Yes, young man?" He looked ready to give directions to somewhere more prescient to the life of the young.

"Hey, sorry to bother," Eli told him, his thumbs in his backpack shoulder straps. "I've been all through this neighborhood trying to get some info and nobody wants to help me out."

"I'm terribly sorry to hear that," said the old man with a hoarse voice. "And surprised. We're normally a very friendly community. Welcoming, we are."

"Everyone's been real friendly," Eli was quick to acknowledge, "until they hear my music."

The old man smiled kindly. "We're not much for dance music here, I am afraid. Except for maybe something from our youth." He gestured at the store. "I'm not sure I have a volume here for this millennium."

Forgetting his quest for a moment, Eli looked at the store, seeing the crooked spines, warped jackets, and torn binding. He could smell the entropy. "How do you do it?" he asked. "How do you..." The words didn't exist for him.

The old man understood the question even without words. He smiled bittersweetly. "We're from out of time," he told Eli poetically. "We were moving forward, but tragedy tore us from our world." He spoke better than the others, but he shared their accent. "Ripped from all we knew; our lives have become – for many of us – all about finding some shred of what we knew. If we can find it, no matter how small, we cling to it. We guard it jealously, for fear of knowing what it's like to again lose it."

"When you're young, you seek to run," explained the old man with words worn deep by his own mind thinking them but never saying them. "You wish to gain momentum. Trip and fall, proverbially of course." He laughed gently, as did Eli. "Trip and fall and you often need your parents and your family and your community. They help pick you up and you work to regain that momentum. You pursue change. But fall without family. Or fall together with your family. Fall with your community and momentum stops being a thing that propels you forward. It becomes something that takes you away from what you needed. What you need."

Words heavy with need told Eli, "This isn't a store. It's a museum. It's a museum to the memories of the people who need a place to hang their recollections. They have to have something to hold onto. A book from home. A scent. A smell. Maybe just even an arrangement." He looked at the store, to the store. "My shelves haven't moved since I opened half a century ago. And they'll stay precisely where they are until I am gone. Not for business, not for me, but for the people."

Eli was awe. "How do you stay open?"

The old man smiled kindly, and sadly. "I find a way. I help, I get help." He smirked. "I don't expect a man of the millennium to understand it, but businesses don't have to be about money. Money is nice, but businesses can be about services. And sometimes the service that is provided isn't the service advertised."

Eli felt strangely humbled and he wasn't entirely sure why. The weight of the statements hanging over them like a cloud, Eli took off his backpack. "I have a record. It's got no label; just the letters B-R-O-D etched into one side. It's just violin music, nothing else. It's old. I played it for a bunch of people here, in this community. The only answer I've gotten is that it's cursed music."

"Cursed music?" repeated the owner of the book shop. Eli set the record before him. The old man took the disc from the sleeve and ran fingers over the four letters. "Hand-carved, I would guess," he described them. "I don't have a record player, I'm afraid."

"That ain't a problem," Eli smiled. He took his phone and cued up an audio player. "I copied the music. I been using it for some dance music." He smiled at the old man, but while he got a smile in return, it was more polite than genuine. "People my age got a place for your world in our lives." The book owner was touched. Eli pressed play and began the melody.

Even a digital copy of the haunting notes carried much of the same might. The violin pushed out all other sounds, and then all other thoughts. It swelled like a cancer, taking over all emotion until those notes were the focus of Eli's mind and heart. As he stood at the counter of the ancient bookstore, he felt books begin to sing, like the dead calling to their kin.

"That's enough."

Eli was awoken from the musical fixation. His thumb silenced the music. He could see the distress in the old bookseller. Eyes that had seen nightmares had heard one now. But it wasn't just the music that had unsettled him. "You know this stuff," said Eli. It wasn't a question or an accusation, but a realization. A confirmation.

The old man took a long, slow breath. "I do." There was a tear in his words. "Ezekiel Brod."

"Brod?" Eli perked up.

"You see it now spelled with an E or an AU or..." The storeowner didn't bother expounding. "You see Smith with a Y." He shrugged heavy, burdened shoulders.

"Who was he?" Eli asked. "Who was Ezekiel Brod?"

There was a tightness in his throat as he tried to speak. His eyes darted about as he searched for where to begin. "Many of them...they didn't know where their neighbors had come from," said the bookseller. "They knew only that they found themselves in cattle cars, riding towards the camps."

The bottom fell out of Eli's soul.

"I know of Ezekiel Brod because of my father, because of my uncles." The bookseller took from old pants that ceased to fit properly a wallet aged with use. From the wallet, he took a piece of fabric pressed between laminate to preserve it indefinitely, permanently, for eternity. He handed over a small pink triangle. "My father wore one of these. Ezekiel Brod did as well."

Eli was hesitant to even breathe, the magnitude of what he'd discovered on that record so much greater than he had been prepared for. The bookseller accepted back the pink triangle, returning it to his wallet. "My father works, as do my uncles." His words shifted, as did his tone. He wasn't recalling but reliving. "Brod, he works, but he also is made to play the violin. An officer in Hitler's forces has Brod play. Play for the workers, play for him, play night and day."

Well worn, hungry lines on the bookseller's face grew more tired as he remembered a story burned into his mind. His memory recalled it like the needle recalled cursed music off the record. "When the Allies came, the Jews were freed and given aid," explained the bookseller with a broad smile. "The Romani, the resistance fighters, all freed." The smile darkened. "The others...not so much. Many were moved from the concentration camps to the brigs of military bases. Not an improvement one would hope for. Less freedom than merely slightly less inhumane. Brod was one of them. Brod was brought to the United States but was denied access."

"Why was he brought here?" asked Eli.

"To be tried for sodomy," said the bookseller with clinical detachment. "He was a criminal. Gays received no sweeping pardons like so many Nazi soldiers. So they were tried – sometimes in Europe, sometimes in America – but they were tried. My father, he was what they now call bisexual. Before his trial, he managed to meet a woman. The details are..." The bookseller smiled and said with old-world dignity, "They are for another time." Again, his smile darkened. "Brod was not so lucky. I don't know if he was admitted to the United States or not. He wasn't then; he was to be returned to Europe."

Eli swallowed, worried. "Maybe he's still over there." The bookseller only smiled tightly, enjoying the optimistic impossibility.

The smile faded like the sun disappearing behind a twilight cloud. "Memories are long," he said with a whisper in shadow. "Many who hate then hate now, but their hate is for themselves. They hear this music and they hear not the beauty of it, not the incredible skill of it. They hear their own inhumanity. They hear their abandonment of their own. They hear their own backs turning on one in need."

"So that's why they call it cursed?" Eli tried to reason, whispering. "Because they feel bad for leaving Brod without help?"

"Men of our caliber can scarcely imagine what it was like in those camps," the bookseller warned Eli. "Most would give anything to never think of those moments. Most, when death took them, were grateful to be free of the turmoil and torment. To survive took something powerful. Love of family, love of home."

"So what did Ezekiel Brod love?"

"I don't know. I never met him," the bookseller admitted with equal parts lament and gratitude. "I would hope a kindred spirit, a person of tremendous beauty that could inspire a love that would endure. But a gay man in Europe in the 1930s? His was a hidden life." The bookseller tapped the countertop and turned away. "No, there are suspicions of something more desperate that saw him through the camps."

An ominous fear overtook Eli. "What do you mean?"

"A Jewish slave was working twenty hours a day, only to be plucked from torment so that he may engage in a beloved pastime? Playing for a Nazi officer perhaps, but it was a luxury to say the least." The bookseller shook his head. The shadows of aged lines darkened, as did his tone. "No, if you find anyone who even knows the name Ezekiel Brod, you'll likely hear whispers of a deal he made."

Eli felt a chill in his soul. "A deal?"

The bookseller smiled at his cluelessness. "You know music, sir. What does the name Robert Johnson mean to you?"

"Blues player," Eli answered without effort, without thought. "Allegedly sold his soul to the devil." His words tumbled more slowly out of his mouth. "They think Ezekiel Brod sold his soul?"

The bookseller only shook his head, uncertain of the truth. "Would it be so hard to believe? That a community racked with guilt for their dereliction of responsibility to one of their own would concoct some myth to justify their behavior? Or perhaps," he added cautiously, "would it be so hard to believe that a man devoid of all hope would look to his music and offer anything so that it might save him? Could you blame him?"

"The Devil isn't real," Eli stated, insisted, needed.

The bookseller didn't argue, only said, "Theology isn't my area of interest. Nor is demonology." He gestured to his bookstore and offered, "But I can point you towards some books if you would like." He cracked a smile as forced as it was brief. "You've heard the music," he told Eli, his shopkeeper façade falling again. "Can you tell me you are one hundred percent certain there is nothing unnatural at play?"

"Absolutely," Eli insisted as firmly as he could force himself to seem.

The bookseller only nodded. "You are a man of confidence. More confidence than I have."

Eli found himself second-guessing, thoughts of the impossible notations he'd seen on his computer. He looked down at the record disc and stared at the grooves of the music. "If it is cursed, should I destroy it?" he asked, the words drifting from him like a ghost rising from another's grave. The bookseller grew wary of that question. "Destroy maybe the man's only remaining legacy?"

The bookseller was quiet for a long, long time. He approached the disc like he might approach a viper. "Demonology as I said is not an area of interest for me.

However, I know enough of the world to believe it ill luck to destroy a cursed object. Curses tend not to be destroyed, merely passed on."

"I don't want some demon in my house," Eli said quickly.

The bookseller nodded. "I would find a safe place, and leave it there. Never to be seen or heard again."

"And the music?" Eli asked. "Is that safe to play? Like, if I got it off the record?"

The bookseller surrendered a sad, sympathetic smile. "You are looking for absolutes when there may be none. You seek rules to protect you when there may be none, where there may never have been any." The bookseller stepped back from the counter, from the record, from Eli. "The decision is yours. I am not you, but I would not play that music. But I am not you. The decision is yours."

TEACH THE SKY 2018 SHORT STORY ANTHOLOGY

Robots: Zeta Danger, part 4

Stormdive's eye twitched as he read the report. A transparent data screen extending up from his left forearm, it read short, clipped text of only the most basic information of the day's headlines. No pictures, no exaggeration, no explanation. Just facts. Cold, unfeeling facts.

Stormdive dropped his robotic hand, letting the feed deactivate automatically. His body was made of hard edges on the inside and curved edges along the sides. A pair of wings extended behind his shoulders almost like a cape, in line with a pair of pauldrons for shoulders. The nosecone of his vehicle mode stuck out from his chest, the stubby nose of an aircraft seeming to point his way.

With a scowl, he sat back against the boulder and stared at the sky. Endless blue above called to him, a freedom in the sky unlike anything found on the ground. Near him, two other robots looked at the Rebel. "What is it?" asked a thick, blocky robot with a desert camo color scheme.

"Deadon was just captured," Stormdive lamented, staring into the endless blue sky overhead. His accent stood out, with a flowing tone that contrasted the hard and clipped words of the desert dwellers. His thoughts soared above his terrestrial body as he added, "Eastbound and Parker were captured before him."

"Deadon?" asked the blocky robot in a Westrion accent. "Isn't that one of the Warbots?"

"I am one of the Warbots, you imbecile," Stormdive snapped. "How'd you miss that?" The thick bot didn't respond. As if what little sympathy he had spent, Stormdive turned and faced over the rocky embankment. The deep gulf between long mesas in the rocky Westrion expanse whistled with the late morning wind. A burst of dust went skating against the three bots, tiny grains of sand pelting their metal chassis.

"Is the Central Authority trying to round y'all up?" asked a younger bot, a flier like Stormdive. Rotors stuck out from his back, keeping him from sitting on any of the rocks and small boulders that dotted the top of the canyon mesa.

"Apparently, Twister," Stormdive said with too much sarcasm. He looked up at the sky again, like it was home. "I mean, I guess it makes sense. We're..." He scoffed and shook his head angrily. "The Rebels depend on us, to say the least." He looked out across the canyon, into the endless desert of stalwart mesas and hidden canyons. He looked at the desert not unlike he looked at the sky.

"If that were true, why're you here with us, robbing an energy shipment?" asked the blocky bot.

"Staying under the radar, Rockyroad," Stormdive practically sang. He stood and looked over the rocks. Passed them was a deep ravine, at the base of which were long-rusted tracks for a transport. "Now what are we doing again?"

Rockyroad glared at Stormdive. "Do you pay attention to anything?"

"Only the important stuff," he remarked.

"We've got three teams," Rockyroad repeated for the umpteenth time, pointing around the deep ravine with the barrel of his blaster. "When that transport comes down, we jump on it and bring it to a halt. You fliers are to engage any defensive drones it lets out."

Stormdive nodded. "And what if the transport isn't a vehicle but a robot? What if it's Iron Horse?" He looked right to Rockyroad. "You think all nine of us can take Iron Horse?"

"You think they're going to send Iron Horse along this backroad just to deliver an energy shipment?" the leader of the assault asked condescendingly.

Stormdive smiled to one side. "I think you underestimate the Central Authority."

"I think you need to know your place," Rockyroad snapped. "You're hired help here."

Stormdive smiled with a cruel edge. He looked to Twister and urged the young boy, "If that train reconfigures, you run."

"I ain't no c-coward," Twister said defiantly but nowhere near confidently. Stormdive chuckled at the crowd he'd found himself among. "You think the CenA is going to come for you?"

"Eventually," he said with absolute certainty. "Me and Systema. Her, then me, or me and then her. Or maybe they got whole teams going after all of us." He scoffed nihilistically. "I mean, it makes sense. We ARE the Warbots. And we're not together right now. Divide and conquer and that stuff."

"Transport's coming," Rockyroad warned the crew with a steely growl. He stared across the ravine, seeing a flashing light. He suddenly jerked his head back to Stormdive. "Why you got to say that its Iron Horse?"

"I don't know that its Iron Horse, fool," Stormdive exclaimed back at him. "I'm just saying there's a chance."

"They wouldn't send Iron Horse," Rockyroad argued. "He's one of the Centurians."

"He's part Centurian, but yeah." Stormdive's mocking tone only irritated Rockyroad more. "That's what I mean. If they're sending a transport this far out of the way, by this antiquated of a path, they're trying to make sure nothing gets this energy. The CenA, the Central Authority, absolutely would double-down and make sure they sent a bot capable of handling whatever got thrown at it. That means somebody like Iron Horse."

"It's not Iron Horse," Rockyroad argued.

"How do you know?" Stormdive asked, enjoying the uncertainty and anguish his questions were causing Rockyroad. He chuckled. "That's what I thought."

The air took on a roar of pressure and the throb of supersonic vibrations. "Here it comes," said Rockyroad. "Get ready." Stormdive slapped Twister on the shoulder as he looked down into the ravine, practically salivating at the coming action. "Here...it...comes..." said the gang's leader. The instant the train appeared, he yelled, "Go!"

Rockyroad leapt over the rock and reconfigured at the same time. The robot's chest came forward as his legs kicked back. His arms came under his body and by the time he slammed into the wall of the steep ravine, the four wheels of a rugged, all-terrain jeep made contact. The squeal of rubber was echoed by similar vehicles all descending in unison, tracks of smoke and dust flying down in their wake.

"Here we go, kid," Stormdive yelled. He leapt into the air, doing a flamboyant backflip as he went. Stormdive's arms and legs folded in and down as his snub-nosed cone extended above his head. His body became one long, slender cone, ending in an aerodynamic tip. Two wings were all that differentiated the jet from a missile. Once in jet mode, Stormdive cracked the sky with a burst of force and flew over the ravine. Cackling madly, he strafed the rocky edges with blaster fire, doing little more than knocking loose pebbles and filling the ravine with din.

Emboldened by his fellow flier, Twister stepped up onto the rocks and reconfigured as well. His arms went over his shoulders and head, while his legs twisted up under his hips. Tiny wings sprouted from his sides as the rotors on his back extended to more than twice their resting length. Spinning rapidly, Twister's rotors took him into the air and he laughed, firing wildly as well.

At the base of the ravine, beneath the cacophony of blaster fire, Rockyroad and the others reached the bottom. A pair of desert vehicles with gun-placements on their backs stayed ready while the others reconfigured into their robot modes. Weapons bristling, they ran to the cargo cars and blasted open the doors. Within were rows of insulated batteries, cooled to near-absolute zero. Rockyroad began to hyperventilate at the sight. "Alright," he called to the others. "Let's get these—"

He was cut off by three attack drones launching out of the train's engine. Tiny eagle-like interceptors, they swung tightly around as small but deadly Vulcan cannons extended from beneath their bodies. Eight spinning barrels began to whirr just as they started to pepper the air with blaster fire.

The lead drone only got off a few shots, however, before Stormdive came spiraling down out of the sky and eviscerated the drone with his own blaster fire. The tiny flier erupted in a massive explosion from unspent charges and the other two drones peeled off. They rocketed up into the air, heading for their new target. Stormdive laughed as he flew straight up, heading high into the sky.

Once he reached purely vertical, he shifted form and came to his robot body. His upward propulsion gone, he instantly began to drop. He glanced over his shoulder as wind whipped and slammed his arms down on both sides. His fists took out both drones with a gravity-powered clothesline. They exploded but he dropped faster than the force of their deaths. With a quick shift, he reconfigured again and was flying casually by the time he returned to the ravine.

The bandits were unloading batteries by the armful and throwing them into one another's storage placements. Stormdive dropped onto the roof the train and walked down the hub. He giggled and fired into the train. Rockyroad jerked his head up at the blaster fire. "What are you doing?!" he yelled, his arm full of batteries. "That's not a security station. Them's medical transport."

"You don't know that they don't have CenA guards in there," Stormdive laughed. He fired again. "Besides, this will make sure nobody comes out." He kicked the roof. "Huh!" he challenged. "Come out, CenA!" He kicked the roof again and laughed. He fired behind him as he walked off the car, blasting for the sake of blasting. He dropped down off the storage car's roof and stepped inside. He grabbed a couple of the remaining batteries and laughed. He tossed one into the air, spinning it before catching. He opened a port in his chest, putting he batteries away for later.

When he hopped out, he saw Rockyroad and the others still loading up the last pieces of their treasure. He yelled, "We good?"

"Yeah, we're good," Rockyroad said, stuffing himself to the gills with batteries. "You and the boy, take the route back to the hideout."

"Will do," Stormdive said. He reconfigured on the ground this time and burst into the sky like a space rocket. He reached the blue heavens above and spun as he ascended. "I love easy jobs," he broadcasted to Twister as the helicopter started to follow him.

"Me too," came a female voice from the far distance.

Stormdive barely had the chance to shift his attention before two blaster bolts tore through the air just behind him. Flying out of the west was a blue and silver flier. Embedded rotors in wings on each side of its chassis spun almost silently as the flier closed on them. Stormdive had no mouth to smile but his laughter conveyed his delight. "Let me guess: the CenA stooge that got Deadon."

"You got one right," said Setter as she fired again. "I'm not Central Authority and I'm no stooge. I got Deadon, though. As well as two other Warbots."

Stormdive flew in a wide, vertical circle to try and come behind Setter but she strafed to avoid being caught from behind. "You a bounty hunter?" he laughed. "CenA can't even send their own people after little ole Rebels?"

"Why risk losing a jack when an ace will always get the job done?" Setter asked, firing two missiles. They immediately arced back and went screaming at Stormdive. The narrow jet jerked his wings vertical at the last second so the two missiles skated within inches of his body without making contact. "Nice move,

Rebel," Setter praised caustically, turning and firing blasters. Stormdive avoided them with ease.

"Stormdive!" yelled Twister, just barely catching up with the pair.

"Stay out of this kid," the Warbot called. "I need to stretch my wings and this loser will do nicely."

"Underestimate me at your own peril, Warbot," Setter told her prey. Maneuvering above him, she reconfigured. Her rear tail opened and out extended a pair of legs. The rotored wings shifted back behind her shoulders as arms extended out, one hand holding the humming blade of an energy sword. Setter dropped straight out of the sky, slicing through the air with the powerful sword. She nicked Stormdive right on the rear wing, along the tail of his circular body.

"Yeow!" he yelled, diving at bank to keep from getting further slashes. Setter reconfigured and fired futile blasts after him. "Holy crap!" he called, dodging and weaving. "Kid, give me some cover!"

Twister blasted at Setter with his forward gun batteries but she slipped between the twin shots with little concern. "Stay out of my business, son," Setter yelled back at Twister as Stormdive disappeared into the horizon.

"Stormdive's my crew!" Twister yelled.

Setter banked suddenly, inverting herself to come at Twister from straight above. "That just makes you collateral," she told him before blowing off his rotor. Twister screamed in pain and dropped out of the sky. Trailing black smoke of serious injury behind him, the young brigand fell to the ground. He reconfigured at the last second and managed to touchdown on his feet, then rolled to lessen the abrupt impact.

Twister came to a screeching halt far from the point of impact, his rotors completely blown off. His chassis scratched and banged up badly, he groaned, unable to move for a moment. Just rolling over was an effort. When he finally caught his breath, he looked up to see Setter walking towards him.

The female robot had her sword in her right hand, her blaster in her left. An all-business scowl crossed her face as she aimed the blaster at Twister. The boy's eyes shone and he held his hands open in surrender. "Let me make this perfectly clear, son," Setter told him. "Stormdive is my prey. You get between me and him again and I will end you." She lowered the blaster. "He isn't worth your loyalty," she promised him earnestly.

"H-he's part of my team," Twister stammered defiantly, his hands still held up.

"Then where is he?" asked Setter. "Why isn't he here to help you?"

She left the youthful robot to ponder that question. She reconfigured into flier mode and rose up into the sky, heading in the direction Stormdive had disappeared.

Night.

Twister arrived at the ancient hotel in the middle of the dead town. Forgotten by the ages after a nearby mine of tin had gone dry, the town was little more than a husk of forgotten memories. It was as dead as the dreams of those whom had once lived there. No lights were on and no movement was to be had. Once-sturdy structures of modern design had fallen into disrepair through the years. The once-fashionable décor becoming ugly with time and wear.

Twister pushed open the door of the hotel's entrance to find light inside. A single lantern burned brightly off one of the new batteries. The windows were blacked out and sleeping pads were laid in the corners of the room. Rockyroad sat under the light, carefully arranging the batteries in neat, even piles. At a nearby table ruined by erosion, four of the crew were already gambling with cards, passing off charges to be owed once their share was paid out. In the corner, crackling light from a welding torch sparked and sizzled as the final bots did repair work.

"Where's Stormdive?" Twister asked, looking exhausted. He approached Rockyroad and flopped down behind him.

"No one knows," Rockyroad said, still counting. He pointed to a far stack. "That's your pile if you need to charge."

"Yeah," Twister said eagerly, grabbing a black brick from the pile. He opened the rubber top and uncoiled the wire beneath. He plugged the battery into his system and exhaled slowly as light returned to his body. Dormant systems went active, one by one as he felt renewed. "An Authority bounty hunter jumped us."

The card game stopped. Even Rockyroad turned to Twister. "She just wanted Stormdive, though. If she cared about our heist, she didn't say anything."

Rockyroad went back to distributing batteries. "She can have that lout. He's more trouble than he's worth."

"What a rude thing to say," said Stormdive. Again, all eyes turned to the entrance as the Warbot entered with a flair for the dramatic. With the doors thrown open behind him, the flier strode into the hotel lobby with weaponizable overconfidence. "And after all the good luck I've brought this team." He went right to the batteries and yanked one up. He tore off the entire rubber top and plugged it directly into the port on his side.

"That weren't your pile," Rockyroad told him.

"Who cares?" the Warbot scoffed, laughing. "Make it my pile. Or take one out of my pile. They're the same thing." He turned and paced in the shadowy lobby. "Hey ya, kid." He thumped Twister in the chest. "Thanks for the help with that CenA bounty hunter."

"You ran," Twister accused.

"Of course I ran," he confirmed with an incredulous laugh. "I was injured, badly. Her lucky shot damn-near split my fuselage. And I knew you could handle that twit." He popped Twister again in the chest. "I believed in you." His confidence and good mood soured a bit. "Was I wrong to?"

Twister balked. "N-no. I could...I just felt—"

"Who cares?" Stormdive laughed. He turned and faced them all, pacing back up to the rear of the lobby. "We did it! We got the energy! We've got enough charges to last until this time next cycle. Longer. And with plenty to spare!" He jammed his hand at the massive pile that Rockyroad was divvying up. "Look at that haul!" he cackled. "I don't know what you bots are so glum about, I really don't."

"We're glum because some Central Authority bounty hunter is on our tail," yelled Rockyroad. Getting up, he abandoned his loot division in favor of the more pressing matter. "Now we got to splinter to avoid her tracking us."

"She ain't tracking you," Stormdive derided. "She don't care about you small fries. She's after the main course." He thumbed at his own chest. "So you leave her to me and you just..." He flittered his fingers at them. "You go on about your business and I'll take care of our little latcher-on." He looked at and spoke condescendingly to Rockyroad. "Don't you worry that pretty little face of yours." He grinned and reached up to gently paddle Rockyroad's cheek. The bandit leader had enough.

Surging forward, he grabbed Stormdive around the throat and drove him into the wall. Blaster to the Warbots' face, Rockyroad growled. "I'm getting real tired of your attitude," he seethed.

Stormdive giggled. "Aww, is that so?" His amusement seemed to know no end. He leaned close to Rockyroad's face as well as the barrel of the blaster. "Shoot," he challenged slowly and with great mirth. "Buuuut...look down first." Hesitant though he was, Rockyroad glanced down and saw on his chassis a small metal ball. With smooth edges that contoured right into the sides, the icosahedron was a deep brown, like wet mud in deep shade. The outermost side of the fist-sized ball was blinking very subtly. "That, right there, is a cerebral bomb," Stormdive explained. "And in case the role of 'cerebral' is lost on you desert-sucking losers, you should be able to figure out the bomb part."

Stormdive shoved Rockyroad back and he went stumbling back a few steps. At the table, the others had risen, more in fear than defiance. "That, right there, is connected to my noggin'. Oh, oh!" Stormdive giggled when Rockyroad went to yank the ball away. "Don't do that!" he challenged gleefully. "Pull it off and it will blow. Your feet might be left. Head may land somewhere still inside city limits."

The table was overturned as the card players all leapt up in terror. The sound of welding came to an abrupt stop as the pair turned, too scared to even get to their feet. Twister felt his fluids freeze, his whole body going numb. His eyes, like those of the others, were locked on that explosive latched to Rockyroad's chest. Their leader froze too. He swallowed, stunned by Stormdive's insane audacity.

"Anyway, as I was saying," Stormdive paced away, no longer feigning fear of Rockyroad. "That little doohickey there is connected to my brain. My brainwaves keep it from blowing up." He grinned and laid clear, "You have a very, very vested interest in my continued survival." Stormdive walked right up to the stack of batteries and plucked up another one. He sniffed it, as if checking the vintage, and then tossed it callously back onto the pile. He looked at Rockyroad as if he'd forgotten the bandit existed. He waggled his fingers at the pile and encouraged, "Finish up. Then I'll be out of your hair."

"And this thing?" said the leader.

"Falls off in a day or two, once I'm out of range," Stormdive said glibly. He headed for the corner.

"And what's to keep us from incapacitating you and driving off, leaving you?" asked Rockyroad. Stormdive didn't answer. He smiled wide and laid down in the corner, as if he was incapable of being happier. At a loss, the bandit looked down at the tiny blinking metal ball. He turned back to the pile of batteries and resumed working.

Twister watched the whole exchange from near the door. He finally settled into the floor and leaned back into the adjacent corner. He could only watch the Warbot, trying to understand him.

***

Not long after dawn, Stormdive landed on a rocky outcropping. At the foot of a massive, spanning canyon that wound through the Westrion expanse, the outcropping showed a wide view of anything and everything for kilometers. The jet reconfigured. As it did so, blocks and blocks of batteries came tumbling out of storage.

Landing on his feet, Stormdive began to toss the batteries into a small cave. Once they were all inside, he bent down and looked into the cave, seeing ten times as many batteries of all shapes and sizes. The cave was half-full of nothing but batteries, their hum of energy almost imperceptible. Stormdive chuckled, but then his chin shook. Laughter turned to paranoia and he brushed the batteries. "Don't go nowhere," he told the energy store.

The Warbot slid out of the cave just as he heard rotors. He whipped his hands down, causing two blasters to extend from his forearms. While he expected the bounty hunter, instead Twister revealed himself. Flying up to the outcropping atop a mesa towering over the canyon, the young bandit reconfigured and became a robot right before Stormdive and his twin blasters. The Rebel dropped his weapons and let them recede into his armored forearms. "What do you want, kid?"

"You left as soon as Rockyroad finished distributing the batteries," Twister said. "I wanted to..." He looked down nervously. "I wanted to...to learn from you. I want you to teach me."

Stormdive laughed. "Teach you what?"

"How to...how to be smart," the boy said. "You put that explosive on Rockyroad. I never seen anybody do something like that. I never ever would have thought of that."

"Kid, when you're one of the Rebels, you pick up all sorts of tricks," Stormdive bragged.

"Then teach me to be a Rebel," Twister asked.

Stormdive grinned. "Sure, kid. But to be a Rebel, you better know what you're getting into."

"I-I do," Twister insisted. "The Rebels, they're fighting the Central Authority. Because the Central Authority wants to control everyone."

"Close enough," Stormdive told him condescendingly. He turned and looked out into the desert and inhaled deeply. "I think maybe what you need is to meet some other Rebels."

Twister's eyes lit up. "Yeah, okay," he nodded eagerly.

Stormdive paced on the outcropping. "I got to think here for a second." He faced up, his arms crossing over the jet's nose sticking forward from his chest. "Where are some of the teams?"

"Teams?" asked Twister.

"Most of the Rebels operate in teams, like I'm part of the Warbots," Stormdive explained. "Different teams have different specialties." He mentioned that as an afterthought. He paced for a moment more. "Nightmares should be north right about now. Fly north, and I mean due north, until you get to the snows."

"You can't take me?" Twister asked, a little scared.

Stormdive was barely able to contain himself. He glanced back at the cave to his back and panic filled him. "I-I got things to do. I got other places to...to check on."

The glance wasn't lost on Twister. "What's in the cave?" he asked, making the mistake of stepping towards it.

In a flash, Stormdive had Twister's throat in his hand, the barrel of a blaster in the boy's face. "DON'T YOU DARE TOUCH THEM!" he screamed. His eyes were wide with madness, his hands shaking with fury. "They're mine, you understand! Mine! Don't you dare! Don't you DARE!"

"O-okay," Twister stammered, absolutely terrified. He dropped to his knees, too afraid to even stand. "Okay, o-okay, I'm sorry."

"They're all mine," Stormdive burned into the boy's mind. "Every last cave! Every last battery! Every last charge! They're all mine! They are ALL mine! Don't you understand me?" The blaster's hum began to grow. It was a hair's breadth from firing.

"I won't," Twister almost begged.

"I will kill you," the Warbot made perfectly clear. Twister only nodded.

Stormdive shoved Twister to the ground and backed away. He whipped his other hand forward, the second blaster revealing itself. "Go," he told the boy. "You go and you fly and so help me, you forget you ever saw me or mine. You ever see me again, you pretend you don't know me. You ever breathe about me or mine, I will carve you up." Both blasters were set on the boy. "Go. GO!"

Twister scrambled to his feet and leapt off the outcropping. Reconfiguring into helicopter mode, he soared into the air, heading south as quickly as he could. Stormdive let him get out of sight, then finally dropped his arms. The blasters receded and he turned to the cave.

Turning, he dove inside. He began to pull all the batteries from the cave, filling the outcropping with the cave's contents. His hands shaking, terror on his face, he looked around the foot of the canyon. "Nobody's going to take you," he told the batteries like they were children. He shook, clutching an armful of batteries. "I'm not going to run out," he stammered hysterically. "I'm not going to run out." He leapt into the air, reconfiguring with his batteries stored away. He shot into the distance, heading west.

The cave in the wall of the ravine was hard to see. Hidden behind the natural folds of the rock and dust, it wasn't until it was seen from beneath that it could be spotted. From it crawled Stormdive. His body covered in dust, he shoved the last of the batteries into the cave and backed away. He looked fearfully in all directions. Once he was certain absolutely no bot had seen the new location of his most recent stash, he pulled a rock halfway over the cave, obfuscating it further.

The ravine was a narrow canyon, little more than an eroded crack in the ground. The stony walls of the canyon rose up dozens of meters, smooth and flush with a clean break in the world, followed by the erosion of centuries since. The boulder-strewn valley floor was awash with small basins were water would collect. Pocket-marked holes dotted what was little more than a desolate, unremarkable corner of nowhere.

Not satisfied with the look but content to leave it be, Stormdive reconfigured and took off into the sky. A thin streak of a vapor trailing behind him, he coursed through the endless cloudy sky, heading towards the west. Once he evened out to a comfortable cruising speed, he began to hum to himself. He triangulated his location using the various peaks and mesas of the Westrion Expanse. He was then promptly shot down.

The blaster bolt struck Stormdive in the right wing, blowing a hole out through the very center. "What the hey!" yelled the Rebel as he dropped to his right, plummeting for the ground. Air zipping past him, he reconfigured into robot mode. The port that had been his primary thruster in flier mode became his feet and they fired twin mini-jets. They didn't cease his descent but slowed it to a manageable speed until he dropped hard onto the desert floor.

The Warbot coughed as the dust from the impact abated and then he laughed. "Well, that's a fine how-do-you-do." He picked himself up and winced. He touched his wing and inhaled sharply when doing so caused intense pain. "Damn," he observed at the damage. A hole the size of his fist had been blown through his wing. Fragments of metal were gone, making an on-site repair out of the question. He transitioned his attention to his surroundings, looking for some sight of his opponent. He saw nothing in any direction, but with the canyons winding through the expanse, that meant little.

Stormdive whipped his hands forward, the blasters coming out. "Come out, come out, wherever you are!" he yelled to the endless open expanse. "I know you're out here!" he screamed with sudden hysterical bloodlust. "Does the little CenA bounty hunter want to come out and pla-ay?"

"I don't play," said Setter, rising up in flier mode from behind the nearby canyon. So small, barely a vein running through the land, it was almost invisible, only meters behind Stormdive. He whirled around but Setter didn't shoot at him but the ground he stood atop. Her blasters took out huge chunks of the rock and metal that made up the planet. Breaking along fracture lines, the ground gave out beneath him.

Stormdive fell into the canyon in a call of surprise. He fired his rockets but did little against the falling debris about him. In addition to slowing his descent, he began firing straight up into the veritable avalanche that was cascading down atop him.

Falling more than a hundred meters down the deep, narrow canyon, Stormdive fired upwards the whole way. Boulders burst like bubbles all around him. When he finally slammed into the ground, his left foot thruster bent in sharply. Stormdive screamed in agony and grabbed his leg. The rocks and ground, little more than dust and pebbles at that point, fell about him but he was oblivious to all but the pain.

Rocking back and forth, the Rebel flier clutched his leg, delirious in his agony. As he grew used to the pain and the sting of its newness wore off, he snarled furiously. "I'm going to rip your circuits out one by one, bounty hunter!" he screamed above.

"I'd like to see you try," called Setter, her voice ricocheting off the canyon walls. There was no sight of her however.

Stormdive stood and tried to fire the rocket of his left foot. A blast of flame came out but the pain intensified. He yelped and grabbed his foot again. "Is this how the CenA conducts its business?" he yelled to the sky. "You wound, then hunt down like a scavenger?"

He turned to head down the canyon, away from the crash site, only to have Setter put her sword blade to his neck. "I'm not Central Authority," she told him coldly. "I merely took a contract."

Stormdive smiled cruelly. "Hunt the Warbots down."

"Hunt you down," she told him simply, indifferently. The blue and silver robot pushed him against the wall of the canyon, the sword blade still against his neck, ready to slice through critical wires and tubes that would end him. "Hands out," she told him. Stormdive slowly smiled, recognizing the routine. He extended his hands wide, his grin equally extending.

Setter never took her eyes off Stormdive as she reached to her side. From a compartment built into her waist, she took a glowing fragment, a purple incandescent square. "Don't move," she warned, the blade still at his neck. She placed the purple square on his hand and Stormdive flinched at the electrical sting. She removed another fragment, keeping the blade at his neck. She shifted towards the other blaster and Stormdive's smile moved to one side.

The blast of missiles from his chest blew Setter off her feet and slammed her into the far side of the canyon. Stormdive was likewise blown off his feet, the backlash of the missiles and the force of the explosion doing almost as much damage to him as Setter. He crawled on the rocky base of the canyon and tried to get moving. He hobbled quickly and tried to reconfigure, but fell flat when his feet wouldn't align.

Setter was on him in a flash, her weight on his back and her hand on his head. Her blaster was buried deep against his neck, ready to blow his head from his torso. "That. Hurt," she growled, smoke rising from her chassis.

"That was the point," he seethed, his face buried in the ground. "You aren't taking me anywhere, CenA."

"I'm taking you or I'm taking your lifeless husk," Setter told him fiercely. She got up off of him and yanked him up by the nap of his neck. "Your choice which."

His arms bound behind his back, Stormdive lay face-down on the surface of the world. Dust blew into his face as a southerly desert wind picked up. He spat out the dust and strained against the electric cuffs on his hands. He looked behind to his hands bound at his waist. The cuffs were half-loops of metal with burning electric arcs completing the circle. The irritation became pain if he even twitched against the restraints and their magnetic hold was far beyond anything he could hope to force.

He looked beyond the cuffs, staring hatefully back at Setter. A small blow torch extending from where her hand should have been, she worked meticulously on his foot. "That's it," he snickered with pleasure. "Just a little to the left, please."

"Shut up," Setter cast at him, her entire front marred with damage from the missiles. "I'm only fixing you up so I can march your worthless carcass to the pickup."

Stormdive laughed. "What? These mesas too hard for your buddies to navigate?"

"No, they just aren't going to go that far out of their way to pick up trash like you," Setter said. "Now shut up before I rupture your Achilles actuator."

"Oh, you'd be carrying me for sure," said the Rebel. He looked into the sky and saw a tiny dot overhead. A grin crossed his face and he said, "Course, that's assuming you can keep a hold of me."

Setter knew a threat when she heard one. She turned from her repair job to see Twister descending rapidly. She stood and drew her blaster but not before the young bandit began to pepper her with shots. She called out in pain, barely able to return fire.

One shot from Setter's blaster caught Twister in the rotor, forcing him to reconfigure and land in robot mode. With Setter distracted, Stormdive rolled onto his back, using the rocky ground to tear the purple incandescent square from his left hand. Pain like he'd never fathomed ripped through his body and for a second, he considered shooting off his own hand. But even through the pain, he managed to taking aim over his own shoulder. The blast suppressor gone, he shot Setter. Together with Twister, the two fired on her repeatedly, driving her to the edge of the canyon. The ground gave out beneath her from his blast and she fell with a shout. There was a long delay between the collapse and the sound of the rocky collision below.

Stormdive chuckled with delight, then rolled onto his face and screamed. "Get these things off of me!" he yelled into the ground. Twister ran over and figured out the restraints with only a glance. The instant they were off, Stormdive rolled onto his back and screamed again, this time grabbing the hand he'd used to fire on Setter. A residual glow was left by the blast suppressor and he rocked in pain. His eyes opened frantically, as did a module on his forearm compartment. He reached into his arm and grabbed wires. Tearing them free, he howled again, then fell silent.

Twister watched Stormdive sit for a moment, then cringed when he heard a sickly laugh rise from beneath him. "Eastbound better be able to fix this." He rose awkwardly, his hand now limp were wires dangled loosely. He tested the stability of his left foot, deciding it was adequate. He took a step and winced but determined the pain was tolerable. "Thanks for coming back for me, kid," he told Twister, patting the boy on the shoulder. In a chatty tone, he asked, "There a town I don't know about nearby?"

Twister stared at the edge of the canyon, the gaping hole in what had been a flat edge. "N-no," he stammered. Remembering himself, he swung back around to Stormdive. "I didn't come back to save you."

"I don't care why you came back," Stormdive laughed. "You did. That's what matters. That's all that matters." His gaze grew a touch distant. "Nobody cares about motivations, just actions."

"You nearly killed me," Twister said at Stormdive's back.

"No, I threatened to kill you," Stormdive clarified like he was correcting a spelling mistake. "I don't 'nearly kill'."

"I wanted your help!" Twister yelled.

"Wanted, or want?" Stormdive screamed suddenly, whirling around. "You still want to meet some damn Rebels, then you check that tone, you ungrateful little brat, and you start walking!" Stormdive turned and his tone was completely conversational yet again. "You ain't flying with that busted rotor and I got a bum wing." He kicked his heel against the ground, almost enjoying the pain. "I can't even reconfigure on this thing." He turned suddenly to Twister. "You don't have a third form, do you?"

"No," said Twister, his face twisting in revulsion at the mere suggestion.

"No," Stormdive repeated, understanding. "Yeah, I figured not. Just checking." He began to walk, still heading west. "We have a hike ahead of us. Best get walking."

"The nearest town is rotations away," Twister called.

"I repeat: best get walking," Stormdive repeated.

"Except you're going in the wrong direction," said Setter.

Stormdive and Twister both turned as Setter's flier form came raising up from the canyon. Rotors sparking as metal ground against metal, her wings shifting as she wobbled in the sky. She none the less managed to ascend over the edge and reconfigure. She didn't turn into robot, however, but shifted down onto four wheels. Squealing at impact, she shot forward in vehicle mode and slammed into Twister. Rolling over him as he shouted in pain, she raced over him and went right for Stormdive. He turned to fire but his blasters were too late.

Rather than run over Stormdive as she had done Twister, Setter leapt at him. Fire bursting from beneath her chassis, she reconfigured as her forward momentum carried her right at her prey. Slamming both feet into Stormdive's chest, she knocked him hard onto the ground and he went skidding across the desert floor.

Landing unsteadily, Setter turned and fired her blaster back at Twister, startling him as he tried to get up. She turned back at Stormdive and shot him as he was in mid-rise as well. The two thieves stunned momentarily, Setter ran at Stormdive. Just as he got to his knees, she leapt at him, entangling his neck with her arm and swinging around him. She landed in a crouch, partially hiding behind him and her blaster to the back of his head.

Twister finally got to his feet, a chunk of his chest plating missing. Circuits inside sizzled, electricity subtly arcing out from time to time when he moved. He saw Stormdive with a blaster to Stormdive's head and froze. Setter held the position as long as she could before her leg gave out and she dropped to a knee. Damage taking its toll, her ravaged body was starting to give out. "What's your play now, CenA?" Stormdive asked cynically.

"Trying to talk myself into bringing you back alive," she warned him.

The grin of Stormdive was never more evil. "What a wicked thing you must think yourself. But you're nothing but a hypocrite and a fool." To Twister, he yelled casually, "Shoot this pile of rust." Twister could only swallow, terrified. "Shoot her!" Stormdive yelled at him. "You wanted to be a Rebel. Be a Rebel. Kill the Central Authority stooge."

"You pull a weapon and I will end him," Setter told Twister over Stormdive's shouts. "Him or you. Or both of you."

"She isn't a killer, boy," Stormdive laughed. Setter elbowed him in the back of the head. It only made him laugh harder. "Oh, brutal you might be, but a killer? Please. If you were a real killer, you'd have killed me by now. Or the boy. Or, like you said, both of us." He turned to Setter and laughed in her face. "You're not a killer. You're pathetic!" Setter gently settled eyes of pure loathing on Stormdive. His grin returned with condescending intensity. "Prove. Me. Wrong."

In the momentary distraction, Twister took his chance. He held up a blaster and curled his finger around the trigger. Instead of getting off his shot, though, Setter beat him to it. Whipping her hand out, a single blast tore through the air and Twister's head equally. A sizzling hole was all that remained where an eye had once been. Through the chasm in his head, the far end of the desert could be seen, until he teetered and fell summarily.

Stormdive's smile wasn't abated. If anything, he looked elated. "You murdered a child. In cold blood." He looked like he couldn't have been more delighted.

"He raised a blaster," Setter told him. "He was armed. He had a weapon."

"A weapon of irritation, to a grizzled CenA bounty hunter like you," he responded. She stood and put her weapon back at his head. The presence of the blaster, the proximity of the death is threatened, had no effect on him. "And you telling me you couldn't have adjusted the intensity? You couldn't have...shot to wound?" he asked with a curl to his words. He giggled. "Oh, you are every bit as pathetic as I first thought. Better to be a weak coward with some consistency than a blubbering fool who does whatever she's told."

"You would do wise to keep your own advice," Setter warned him. She pulled him to his feet. "Now march."

"Sure thing, killer," he told her conversationally, like the accusation was a pet name. He began to walk, heading still towards the west. Setter walked behind him, sparring a subtle glance at the body of Twister, still face-down in the dust.

Through the wide desert, the pair walked slowly. Stormdive made no effort to outrun or fight Setter. He kept strolling easily along, smiling into the bright sunny sky, letting the heat rain down on him in unyielding pain. The dust and sand they kicked up as they walked for stretches over soil, then metal, then stone, then back. The harsh, open sky was aloof to the pair of robots as they walked. Heat vapors turned the horizon and the distance into shimmering, twisting illusions. The blue sky was washed out by the heat. Even the mesas of stone that towered over the canyons and fields of nothing seemed to be melting.

"See this is part of why I hate the Central Authority," Stormdive told Setter as he walked ahead of her. "Why capture us alive?" he asked her, laughing cynically, nihilistically. "It makes no sense. What are you going to do? Throw us in prison?"

"I don't know and I don't care," she told him, deadpan. Her body was sizzling from the heat. Her joints groaned painfully from heat expansion.

"If you're going to throw us in prison, we're just going to live at the expense of society," he told her like his questions weren't rhetorical. "And we both know the CenA values individualism and personal identity and sovereignty of the mind!" he mocked with an increasingly high-brow accent. "They ain't gonna reprogram us against our will." He said that with the opposite accent. Now he scowled, honest derision making him sneer. "So why not just kill us?"

Setter didn't engage him.

"That's what the Rebels would do," he told her, his smile gone. "They're honest like that."

"They, not you?" Setter asked him.

"I'm a Warbot," he told her, glaring at her over his shoulder.

"You say that like it makes a difference."

To that, Stormdive's gaze glassed over. "At one time it did," he admitted. Still walking, he expounded. "We're not mercenaries, but we're not regulars either." His walking slowed to a shuffling. "We're somewhere between loyal and aligned."

He stopped entirely. He turned to Setter and looked earnestly at her. "I guess maybe the Warbots are like you." Where Setter might have said something pithy, she only stayed silent. "How far differently must things have gone for us to end up on the opposite sides we're on now?"

"You really think the Warbots could work for the Central Authority?" she asked him. "You really think YOU could work for the Central Authority?" she specified.

Stormdive faced away. "No," he whispered. Some of his nihilistic bravado returned. "No, I guess not." He resumed walking. "I guess the Rebels were the only option for us Warbots. We're too powerful to be CenA and we're too opinionated to be unaligned." He scoffed and admitted, mostly to himself, "I guess we didn't have a choice."

He stopped again and faced back the way they'd come. "If we didn't though, I wonder if we would have picked the same." He stared. "That boy...he picked."

"You think he picked right?" Setter asked him.

Stormdive turned and walked again. His steps were far more hateful. "Whether he did or not, it doesn't matter now."

"These things itch," Stormdive complained, scratching with his bound hands at the blaster suppressors on his wrists.

"I don't care," said Setter. She paced behind Stormdive, her blaster drawn but not readied.

"I'm just saying," the flier griped. "They itch. It's like rust or something." He scratched. "Can't you take them off? I've been pretty compliant." He didn't get a response. "Come on, they itch."

"I don't care," she repeated, staring into the east.

Stormdive pouted angrily. "Can't you get me some water? I'm going to overheat."

"I don't care."

"Well, what about some—"

Without turning her head to him, Setter shot the ground right in front of his foot. Stormdive shrieked and leapt off the rock he'd been sitting upon. "What the hell?!" he yelped. Her point made, she grabbed his shoulder and shoved him back down onto the rock.

The ensuing silence didn't last long. On the horizon, a spot of silver appeared against the intense heat vapors. Stormdive noticed it and asked, "What's that?"

"Your ticket back east," Setter told him with relief.

Rumbling out of the east came a giant silver train. Rolling along the ground as if on a set of tracks, the smooth and polished train arrived right before the pair of robots. "Hey, is that Iron Horse?" Stormdive asked. he laughed and said, "Hey, we was talking about you just yesterday."

He didn't get a response. Instead, a door opened on the side of the second train car and from it appeared tendrils. "Hey, what the!!" yelled Stormdive as the clasps of the tendrils grabbed him. "Hey, this is cruel and unusual!" He continued to protest as he was pulled into the train, his voice disappearing as soon as the doors shut.

Setter strolled coolly towards the train. She gently tapped its silver frame, leaning on it emotionally and physically. "You okay there, Sunsetter?"

The use of her full name, and the anger she attached to it, made her smile. "Shut up, Iron Horse," she told the train. Her smile faded. "Just a bad day."

"Bad how?" asked the big bot, its voice echoing as if it emanated from the entire surface of the train.

"I'm just not quite as sure I'm on the right side," she said. She practically shoved off of him and started to walk west. "It's not about right, though. It's just about the job."

"Say it all you want, Setter," Iron Horse told her. "You'll never believe that." The great engine within the train started powering up. The mammoth machine began to course slowly back around, beginning its wide turn to head back into the east. Setter kept walking west until the sound of Iron Horse began to fade. Still walking, she glanced over her shoulder in his direction. He disappeared into the horizon and she was alone in the endless desert expanse.

Robert V Aldrich

Carved
(inspired by Pygmalion and Galatea by Jean-Leon Gerome)

Rock doesn't bleed.

I step back from the stone form, barely aware of my feet stepping on the scattered chisels and pebbles. I stumble, but I don't really notice. I just stare at the rock, stare at the chip made in its form, stare at the cut I inflicted.

Blood.

Red blood.

Red blood, dripping out of the rock.

I reach out, touching the stone, touching the blood. I touch it, as if that's the only way I can be sure. But I'm sure now. It's blood, on my fingers, coming from the rock. It's just a bit, barely more than a few drops, but it's coming from the rock.

I step back again, looking at the half-completed sculpture in my workshop. The hot air off the parking lot wafts in through the wall of open windows of the warehouse that's both my workshop and my home. But none of that registers in the moment. There's blood coming from the rock. City sounds of twilight, horns and traffic, foot traffic, flitter in through the dusty light. But none of that registers in the moment. There's blood coming from the rock.

I reached behind me, scraping my fingers over my desk to find my cell phone. When I don't find it, I turn around to look at the cluttered collection of art books and photos, dog-eared corners and scribbled notes, a menagerie in its own right. I don't see my phone. I turn back to the rock, to my sculpture, to see the blood drying.

I look up at the powerful lights that are casting down onto me and the rock. I don't see anyone. I look around, nearly falling I spin so fast. But there's no one. In the vacant warehouse, full of my paintings and previous sculptures and judgmental empty space, I am alone. Just me. And the rock. The rock that's bleeding.

I turn back to the bleeding rock, taking a deep breath. I rub my chin, then take a few steps towards it. My tray of tools is still there, next to the mammoth stone. The floor is littered with dropped and discarded utensils of my art. I stop just a few meters from the giant rock, considering it.

The human-shaped form is already well established. It looks strangely androgynous, with the right arm held up, like an old-time crossing guard. A faceless head is aimed forward while the left arm is lowered, almost deformed. My hopes of abnormally shortening the left arm are halted by the blood.

I reach down to the floor and, by instinct alone, I collect a hammer and chisel. I look at the stone and I put the chisel's blade to the stone. I look at the blood stains, then at the rock, my heavy breath sending the dust scattering off the stone arm.

I put my hammer to the chisel's base and I close my eyes. Carefully, I chip the rock. I find myself holding my breath. I have to will myself to exhale. I look down at the stone and I see the stained blood, but no new blood. I take another breath, holding in my chest. I wipe the sweat from my forehead with the back of left hand, then I chip again. The stones chip and a piece of the rock falls down.

Rock Rock Rock Rock Rock Rock Rock Rock Rock Rock Rock Rock Rock Rock Rock Rock Rock Rock Rock Rock **Skin Skin** Rock Rock Rock Rock Rock Rock Rock Rock Rock Rock Rock Rock Rock Rock Rock **Skin Skin** Rock Rock Rock Rock Rock Rock Rock Rock Rock Rock Rock Rock Rock Rock Rock Rock Rock Rock Rock Rock Rock Rock Rock

I stumble back.

The breath in my chest turns as hot as the wind from the empty summer parking lot.

When I finally release the air in my chest, I nearly collapse. My knees are shaking. I don't even notice that I drop my chisel and hammer.

I stare.

I just stare.

I can only stare.

At the rock.

At the skin.

At the skin, encased inside the rock.

I have to take my glasses off, wipe them off on my shirt the color of errant paint strokes, then put them back on to make sure I'm seeing what I'm believing. I wipe my face, feeling the grime on my cheeks. But the feeling's lost on me. All I can do is stare.

It's either a few seconds or a few hours after I finally get the strength to approach the rock again. The sculpture is so close to being done, but the fracture in the stone has ruined it. But I can't care. I just stare at the skin. Soft and vibrant, it looks natural. But the rock is pressed up against it.

I swallow hard then look down at the ground for my chisel and hammer. Gathering them up with shaking hands, I reach back up to the arm. I follow the fracture up to the shoulder joint and I choose the one juncture. I hit. Careful. Precise. Where the control comes from, I don't know. My movements are accurate but I feel anything but. The chisel slices the rock like the biting cold on a spring morning. The stone cracks like the dawn.

The rock breaks.

The stone falls, making me jump back.

The rock falls to the ground with a loud crash. The tray is pushed back, but doesn't fall. I do. I collapse to the reinforced industrial floor, closing my eyes to the sound. I'm forced to listen to the resounding echo of the crash as it circles my warehouse. Pebbles and shards of rock go scattering, as do chisels, hammers, picks, brushes, and all manner of my tools.

In a matter of moments, there are only two sounds left: My heavy fearful panting.

And the arm moving.

It takes me a moment to realize that my eyes are open and I'm not imagining things. I look and I see an arm moving. Sticking out of the rock, where the left arm had been, is a feminine arm. I take a deep breath, staring at the arm. It's moving around, not wildly, not desperately, just...curiously. It touches the rock, as if not understanding what it is. Fingers unfamiliar struggle to grasp the world they feel solely by touch.

And then, the wind.

I can see the goose bumps on the arm as it stops, staying perfectly still. I hold still too, guarding my breath as the hot wind flows like a brushfire into my warehouse. It rushing up against the rock, my sculpture, the arm. The arm freezes, then reaches out towards the wind, holding its fingers desperately wide. It waves its slender arm in the wind, as if trying to touch every inch of the vibrant, hot wind.

I stand. I worry that the arm will know it, but the arm doesn't stop moving in the enduring wind. I take a breath with each step towards the arm. A few steps and I have to move over the crumbled remains of the stone arm that fell. When I get within a breath of the arm, it stops moving.

I don't know how, but I know it is aware of me. I hold my breath until it burns in my chest once again. My knees shake and I'm afraid that the wind will knock me over. But the arm stays still.

It's afraid.

I release my captive breath and I see the goose bumps again. The arm suddenly flares out towards me. Without any thought, I step back, falling over the stone husk. On the floor, I watch the hand continue its search for the source of that brief breath from me.

It takes me another few moments to stand. I start on this side of the stone, but I step around it, putting myself just outside the arm's reach. I take another deep breath and let it out at the arm. Again, the arm reaches out towards me, across the bulk of the stone's vaguely female form. Its fingers flare out, coming within a few inches of my chest. I can feel the air it displaces as it reaches unsuccessfully for me.

I reach passed the hand searching for me and I brush the arm itself.

The arm flails suddenly, blindly, fearfully, desperately, trying to find the touch. I stumble back, but I find the courage to keep standing. The arm keeps reaching out, grabbing at air and nothing else. I take another breath, then with an explosion of will, I grab the arm. The hand freezes as fearful as my heart, but I hold the arm. I touch the forearm, gently running my hand over the smooth, unblemished skin. The hand stays as still as the stone from which it appeared as I touch it, running my fingers over its smooth skin.

Slowly, my pulse slows below a heart attack's rate. I take control of the hand. I step forward. I put the hand to my chest, letting it feel my shirt. Fingers unused to sensation twist and turn the fabric, delighting in every sensation as it touches my t-shirt, my collar, my skin.

As it searches my chest, I look at its inner arm. I see the cut where my chisel struck too deep. I look over my shoulder at my chisel on the floor. Guilt runs through me. When I turn back to the arm, it reaches up. It touches my chin, then my lips. I hold my breath as it searches, straining to reach. Against my own mind, I step forward, letting the hand search.

It has to know what it's touching. It has to. It moves too gently, too carefully, as it searches every inch of my face. It delights in every motion as I let it feel me. I turn my head, looking at the chisel again. I look at the rock and I make my decision. I decide. For both of us.

I step away from the arm, trying hard to ignore its sorrowful search for my lost presence, pained in the sensationless absence. I gather up my chisel and hammer and turn back to the stone. I go against everything I ever learned, everything I ever taught myself. I look for the weakness in the rock. I look for where it will fall apart. I look for the tiny points that will bring it all crashing down.

I step forward, touching the hand. I let it touch my face again. I let it find some sense of familiarity in my presence. Then, I step closer still. I come next to the stone. The hand wraps around and underneath my arm, feeling my back. I try to ignore it as I put the chisel to the stone, my mind set on finding weaknesses in the sculpture.

With a single hammer strike to the blunted butt of the chisel, the neck cracks. The hand freezes in fear. It remembers the strike that cut the skin. But I take the hand in mine. Rough, dirt-covered skin mixes, intertwines with soft skin as flawless as a newborn's. I touch the fingers to my face. I hope it understands. I hope she understands.

I put the chisel up farther on the shapeless, amorphous, androgynous head. I strike. Pieces of the rock chip off and fall away. I hear the crack. I drop the chisel and the hammer and grab the cracked rock. I try to pull it, feeling the stone give way. I take a deep breath.

The rock falls. The front of the faceless head collapsing to the ground, while the back tumbles opposite it. There are loud crashes in my workshop, crashes lost to me.

Blue

Her eyes are blue. They stare up at me, filled with so many emotions. So confused. So joyful. So frightened. I reach down and take hold of her hand. Even with her face half-covered by the remains of the rock, even with her dark hair still tucked deep down inside the soft stone, I lift her hand to my face, letting her touch me. She feels my lips, finally able to see me. Her lips curve up in a joyous smile and I smile back.

I lower down, even with her hand still on my face, to I regain my chisel and hammer. I stand up before her again and hold the chisel before her, so she can see it. She's confused, but when I place it to the stone that still covers her face, she closes her eyes, bracing herself for pain. I hold my breath as well, carefully striking hammer to chisel to stone. It takes me several very gentle strikes, little more than taps, to finally chip away enough rock for the rest of the head to fall. When it does, it takes part of the chest with it.

I jump back as stone falls where my feet had just stood. The pieces of rock rattle and shake across the floor. When I look up, I see her take a deep breath, her bare breasts heaving with the effort. She writhes in orgasmic pain as her chest moves again and again, tasting the free air and knowing liberated breath.

Now her left hand is fully free and she moves it, drinking in its movements like they are miraculous. She reaches up to her own face, feeling her lips and eyes. She looks at me, right at me, and tries to convey what she feels. More than anything else, I see her smile.

I move back towards her, coming right in front of the statue. A statue that was rock and is woman. Her right arm still captured within the stone, along with her abdomen and beneath, she looks at me, her face filled with emotions. I smile at her, laughing in joy. She mimics me, smiling as well.

I step closer to her, letting her left hand touch me. She touches my lips, with her fingers, her eyes closed as she's over taken with emotions.

"Th..."

My eyes go wide, appalled. I try to say something. I try to breathe but nothing takes. I can't do anything as she holds my face, her eyes holding my soul in their gaze.

"Thank..." she manages out. "Thank you."

Without even noticing it, she pulls me down. Before I know it, our lips meet.

Robert V Aldrich

Rhest and the Long Walk

Being a street merc isn't all gunfights and cyberwarfare. Sure, the movies make it look like being a street merc is some kind of action-packed job with non-stop thrills and adventure. And sometimes life can move at a breakneck pace. But most jobs are far more mundane. For every corporate espionage job – where you have to scale a bio-dome and get through eleventy-gazillion layers of security - there are more personal jobs. Jobs where you have to shake down some stalker, stand guard while an abused spouse makes a run for it, or just walk kids to and from school. Some jobs get even more personal than that. Trust me, I know. My name's Rhest. I'm a mercenary.

Tuesday mornings at the agency are always slow. I don't know why Tuesday of all days, and why just the morning. Some days, the place is absolutely empty because everybody's got gigs and we've got a wait list for the next batch. Other days, we've got a good cycle of people coming and going. But man, it seems like every week, come Tuesday morning, more of the regulars are here than not.

See, while the life of a street merc can entail tremendous action, there are also periods of unending downtime. It's during those times that most street mercs meet their end. Not immediately, not directly, but what gets you killed starts when you're bored.

I've known a lot of mercs that could handle a gunfight no problem. Fistfight? They could beat the most badass hand-to-hand fighter you can name. Breaking-and-entering? Identity simulation? Whatever you want them to do, they could do it so easily, you'd swear it was magic. Anything at all...except wait for the next job. It's amazing how an hour of waiting at the staffing agency can turn into 'hey, let's run down to the bodega and get some beers'. That turns into doing an easy job buzzed. That turns into doing a not-so-easy job buzzed. That turns into doing an easy job drunk. That turns into dying on a not-so-easy job because you were drunk. Sure, the gunshot killed you but you wouldn't have been in the situation to get shot if you hadn't been three sheets to the wind.

Thus, most mercs who are around for more than a year have some structured way to spend the time. Some are classy and play chess or read, but that's a bit too passive for me. Plus, there are a couple of psychics who work at the agency. Playing chess against a psychic is about as much fun as playing basketball against a giant in a wind storm. Others mercs do crafts. No, I'm not kidding. Jacob Hart might rock a pair of mini-guns on his power armor but the dude knits like you wouldn't believe. He knitted me a pair of socks for Secret Santa last year that if they hadn't been set on fire, I'd wear every damn day. You ever wear socks made out of super-special Irish Alpaca yarn? It'll change your religion.

Don Mathis likes to practice card tricks. John Keller is working on a comic book (and has been for nine years and we've yet to see one completed page, but that's neither here nor there). Sandra and Xi run a wholesale auto-parts website. Frank works for a Q-and-A company that does nothing but the answer to the most random questions you can imagine. Ralph is painting water colors. At least three guys are trying to get some broken appliances to work. I say this because some days and especially Tuesday mornings, the staffing agency – this den of combat masters, street thugs, and deadly assassins – looks more like a daycare center.

Me, I like to spend my time coding. Despite carrying six pistols, I'm really a hacker by trade. I like code and programming. If I didn't hate wearing a tie, I could probably get a halfway decent job as a corporate coder. I do some contract work for a few corporations, or rather for friends who work for some corporations. When it's slow, I'll set up with my laptop in the corner of the agency – which is just a repurposed store front in the forgettable corner of a forgettable shopping center – and I start gluing together 1s and 0s.

As I'm trying to decide if I want my program to have a neural interface or if a keyboard GUI will be adequate, Macee's phone rings. She's an older woman, but still with plenty of vitality.   She puts down the romance novel she was reading behind the counter and picks up the phone. The phone's so old, it has a cord. Where did she even find that thing?

"Macee's Staffing Agency," she says, her voice as aged and leathery as her face. It's only a second before she grabs a chewed-up pencil she uses mostly to fill out crossword puzzles. She begins to scribble, which is not something she does often. She's got one of the best memories I've ever seen, and she doesn't have any cybernetics at all. Me and a bunch of the others all perk up when we notice the scribbling. "Okay, honey. And what's the pay?" She only nods. "No, I understand. Which hospital?" Medical transport. Interesting. "It's okay, I can take care of that. Just tell me, what's your absolute ceiling?"

Some mercs lose interest. Anytime Macee has to ask what's the absolute most a person can afford, that means we'll be working for peanuts. Heck, I'd be lying if I said it didn't deflate my interest a bit. "Don't worry, honey, I'll see what I can do. Call you back." The instant she hangs up, Macee bellows with lunch-lady volume to the rest of the agency, "We got a Long Walk."

'Long Walk' is a term mercenaries use for one of two types of operations. The less common operation is where we will be escorting a criminal to the local police to turn themselves in. Usually, this is face to an erroneous charge or something similarly contentious. The catch is that, for whatever reason, they fear they'll be killed before they can arrive into the protective (snicker) arms of the law. Strangely, when they arrive at the Law, the crime they are turning themselves in for is often so serious, it will likely end up in a death sentence. But that type of Long

Walk happens a whole lot less. It's pretty rare. What's the one that happens more often?

We need to escort a woman to an abortion clinic.

Despite being a perfectly sound and sometimes medically necessary procedure, abortions remain a contentious issue. Protestors still line up outside of clinics, denouncing the women who make the walk. The fact that there technically isn't an 'abortion clinic' and they are protesting outside of medical offices that provide a wide variety of services, and thus the women walking in can be there for any number of non-pregnancy related reasons makes no-nevermind. The walk can be dangerous and thus, street mercs get hired.

Macee calls again. "Long Walk."

It's an unspoken rule that male street mercs take a step back from these jobs. We let the women and non-men have first crack, but the agency is almost entirely men currently. When I glance around, I see only two women here and neither of them seem interested or inclined. So I join a small cadre of hands that go up.

"It's a morning job, nothing fancy," Macee tells us like a substitute teacher telling the kids today's a reading day. "Who'll do it for base pay?" Hands drop, but not all of them. "How about a flat rate?" Macee asks aloud. A few more drop. Macee holds up her fingers, indicating the flat-rate in question. Me and like three other guys are left with our hands up. The three of us look at one another and more or less finish the negotiations with some glances, gauging our respective interest. The way their hands drop essentially announce to everyone else that I won the bidding.

I save my coding progress, close out my programs, and bring my laptop over to Macee's counter. My laptop's got an armored frame over a burnt umber chassis with a metallic finish. It's Nightmare Custom Rig, which means it's the size of a Gutenberg Bible and holds two times as much data as the combined knowledge of all humanity. Plus, it's got a full-sized keyboard and anybody who says they can code on a mini-keyboard is a liar. Macee writes on her pad as I approach, teasing me, "Tuesday doldrums making you desperate?"

"Easy jobs make for a higher success ratio," I tell her as she hands over the number. I take out my cell phone and start dialing.

"You still got a hand unit, Rhest?!" teases Jacobi. Jerkass. Despite having more cyberware in my brain than most server farms, I still use a hand-held cell phone. I don't want my dreams trademarked. I walk around Macee's counter so I've got a modicum of privacy. The phone rings twice and a young woman picks up. "Hello? My name's Rhest. I work for Macee's Staffing Agency."

"Hello, thank you for calling back so quickly," she says. Her voice isn't shaking, but I can hear the fear in her words. She's quiet, not quite whispering but close. I can tell it's a volume she's practiced at using.

"No problem," I tell her with a smile. "Macee didn't give me much details on the timeline of the job. When were you hoping to get moving?"

"I can do it anytime this week," says the woman on the other end of the line, just a little quickly. "The earlier, the better. It just has to be during the day."

I quickly call up my Heads-Up Display, a whole host of readouts appearing as transparent characters superimposed over my vision. I check the time and ask, "Is now early enough?"

I'm outside the Regency Skyline Community. It's a gigantic bio-dome about the size of six city blocks and stands somewhere in the neighborhood of ninety stories. Not the biggest bio-dome in Sacramento but it's one of the nicer ones. You know, of the public bio-domes. It's a pretty simple block of a building, with smooth edges and a flat top. Solar panels dot the spaces between floors to maximize energy reception. Every ten or so floors, the building ducks in a few dozen feet, with an exterior area (they're usually used for either landing pads or communal gardens). The lower levels are noticeably clear of most of the usual graffiti you find in this part of the city. There's only the newest spraypaint and tags. That means the industrial concrete walls get cleaned often. That's a sign of some respectable money.

I'm outside, watching the entrances and exits. Some bio-domes have dedicated metro stops, where part of the stop is open to the public but part of it is dedicated access only. The rest have nearby stops, which includes the RSC. That means the giant bio-dome has manual entrances: sliding doors that open with a keycard, keycode, or you speak to security.

There are security guards posted periodically, roughly one every city block. The guards inside don't look like elite special forces, but they do look like the kind of people paid enough to actually be good at their jobs. Light gray shirts with dark gray pants and hats for uniforms are a good indicator that these guards are serious, but so are the fitness standards. Requiring people to maintain a certain bodyfat ratio seems Draconian, but it also entails that you pay them enough to put up with that kind of thing.

The security stations likewise aren't a joke. Placed periodically around the exterior of the bio-dome, they've got the hidden lenses of security cameras with few blindspots. Good designs. Their aesthetics are more like information terminals at metro depots than mini-jails. They're also clearly armored with cement up to waist-height. All of this suggests money spent where it makes a difference. That kind of judicious expenditure also goes hand-in-hand with judicious hiring.

Now, it's bad mojo to just walk right up and be all 'I'm a merc and I was hired by a resident'. That causes problems on a lot of levels, not the least of which that mercenary work is technically illegal (hence why I work for Macee's Staffing Agency, not Macee's Mercenary and Assassination Emporium). Even if the guards are cool (and they don't look it), odds are I'm being hired because something about this woman's situation is sketchy. Overbearing husband, kids she doesn't want to share the cookies with, something. So I got to be low-key.

'Now Rhest', I hear you ask, 'aren't you wearing a combat harness, low-level body armor, and sporting six pistols?' Yes. Yes I am. But the trick to entering without an invitation isn't to look a certain way; merely to go unnoticed. So I just have to go unnoticed.

I see Little Johnny step out from behind a pillar. Red baseball cap, hoodie that's at least one size too large, sneakers held together with tape, the half-dead expression of the over-educated youth as they confront a lifetime of social immobility in the face of staggering corporate greed, really expensive cell phone. Johnny shakes his spray paint can and pushes a stencil to the pillar. I don't actually know the kid's name is; I just know I paid him some serious cash to tag the pillar. He'll barely get started before security springs into action, in which case he'll run (I told him if they do chase him, he can keep the cash). The important thing is that several security guys will be off-position for a moment.

As soon as paint hits the wall, there's a pulse in the local network. I'm not connected to the wi-fi or anything (connecting to public wi-fi is like having unprotected sex with the entire internet) but I still monitor the data exchange. It's one of the ways you know a cyberattack is coming. Well, there's a sudden addition to the local data traffic. That means a sensor was just tripped and an alarm somewhere is going off. I turn and check. Sure enough, the guards at the booths on either side of Little Johnny's chosen pillar turn. From each booth come darting two uniformed guards. They run at Johnny, shouting, "Hey!" Why do they do that? Anyway, I've now got two sliding doors to choose from. I pick the farther of the two because inside the bio-dome is a security checkpoint and the farther door has a pillar I can step behind.

As I near, I activate my cybernetics and reach out to the local wi-fi. I send out a pulse signal that hits all the nearby video-collecting devices. They all do a soft reboot. Takes less than a minute. It's not even static; the screens just go flat for a second and boom, they're right back to it. Now, if somebody really ambitious wants to inspect the code to see what caused the soft reboot, they won't find anything because part of the virus I just sent out includes a self-cleaning, self-terminating protocol. Granted, if they REALLY dig, they'll find evidence of the virus but I'll be hella gone by then.

Into the bio-dome I sneak and I slip right by the security guards on the interior. Through the doors is a spacious promenade of shops, escalators, and corporate art. Ads buzz in the air on screens set to just about every surface. Some are static images; others are videos that play on a loop. There's a brisk traffic as lower middle-class people come and go, although since it's late-morning, I can't imagine where this many people have to be going right now. Amid all the foot traffic and people coming and going, no one notices me going for a security access door. Another virus pulse and the door pops open for me. The sturdiest door in the world won't do all that much if you're dealing with somebody who can basically make keys out of thin air.

Through the door is a security deployment hallway, probably meant for when there's a riot. It's a long tunnel with narrow walls, a low ceiling, and no decorations. There are reinforced pipes running along the ceiling and single bulbs of bright light spaced regularly. The air hums with the movement of water, electricity, and everything else that passes through those pipes overhead. I hear footsteps but don't break stride. I spot somebody's lunch in a legit metal lunch pail. There's a jacket and a cap with the RSC logo, so I grab up the sandwich and slip on the hat. I take half a step, then backpedal and leave a ten-dollar coin. I'm stealing somebody's lunch. That's just mean. Least I can do is buy them a replacement.

I resume down the hall, opening the sandwich to see what's in it. As I do, two security guards come down the hallway at a brisk pace. I just look angry that somebody in this world eats a bologna sandwich without cheese. What kind of godless heathen is this? My casual stride, distracted affectation, and clever costume of a uniform ballcap means the two dudes just run right by me. They definitely saw me because they lean to get by in the narrow hallway, but they barely even slowed as they passed me. Unnoticed, remember?

Floor 49.
Seven times seven.
It's a floor of religious significance to those in the Christian Faith because...reasons. I don't know. I get that definite vibe when the elevator doors part and, lo and behold, there's a religious mural right in front of me. It depicts a bearded white guy with blue eyes and a dove on his shoulder. There's a golden halo encompassing his head. Around him green meadows full of animals and what I'm guessing are clouds of golden light? I can't really tell. Those big doe eyes are staring right at me, watching me no matter which way I move. It's really creepy.

The mural is painted on the simulated stone wall and in front of it is an incense shrine that looks suspiciously Buddhist but I doubt I could tell the difference. The ceiling is painted to look like a blue sky with little angels and cherubs flying about. It's really good work, too. Not Michelangelo, but more than an art school dropout.

The doors on either side of the hall have all sorts of cutesy little signs and decorations. Wreaths and chalkboards with bible quotes written on them. Little woodland signs that tell me 'Mr and Mrs So-and-so live here'. It's all quite quaint, if a little suburban for my tastes.

Bio-domes are like apartment buildings for people rich enough to be able to afford all their monthly bills. The floors in the hallway are carpeted and it looks like they get cleaned at least once a year. The walls are painted with care, with the lips of fixtures like lights not marked. The lights don't buzz and only one or two flicker. I get the impression those will be fixed soon. The people who live here probably don't have gold-plated toothbrushes or personal shoe buffers. They probably have to work for a living. But their workspaces are probably air-conditioned and they can probably go out to eat without checking their bank account and deciding what bill to delay paying.

I go down the hall to the first intersection and take a right. Down that a little ways until I get to apartment 103-F. The door is light green. A little stencil family of six. Lot of kids for an apartment. I can't recall the last time I saw a bio-dome with units larger than three bedrooms. At least, not until you got to the top-most layers.

I knock quietly, then remember I'm still wearing an RSC hat. I take it off and look around, then settle the hat on a statue of a turtle crossing guard with a sign reminding me to be considerate of my noise. I'm not sure if he's there because of the bio-dome or whatever bunch of religious zealots live on this floor. Not sure which would surprise me more.

Through the door, a young woman calls, "Who is it?"

"My name's Rhest," I tell her through the door. "You called about a pick-up?"

I hear more than one lock undone and the door opens. A young woman with frizzy hair in an ankle-length denim dress steps out. She practically slides out the door and pulls her purse through with her. "Hey," she says nervously as she slings her purse. She locks the door back. She looks down the hall in all directions, more than once. She whispers when she says, "Let's go." Trusting, lady. I guess we're doing this.

I gesture for her to lead the way. We start back the very way I came but when we reach the intersection, we're met by an older woman. She's wearing a jogging suit and has a sweatband on her head. Two-pound dumbbells are in her hands as she speedwalks around the corner. When she sees us - who am I kidding - when she sees me, she slows. "Katie..."

"Hey, Mrs. Tenet," Katie says nervously. "This is..." She turns to me, gesturing like she's introducing a boyfriend she's embarrassed of. I can see the panic and shock in her eyes as she realizes she has no excuse or lie planned.

"I'm Rhest," I tell the woman, extending a hand and giving her a big smile. "I'm Katie's escort." Katie's face goes pale in horror, like I just outed her. But I keep on, saying, "She's taking a shift at the Oak Park Community Center. It's a sketchy neighborhood; Oak Park asked me to provide her an escort."

Mrs. Tenet beams. "Well, how sweet of you." Katie plays along as best she can manage and smiles modestly. The older woman steps around Katie and squeezes my hand. "Good to know there are still a few gentlemen in this world." I smile back and nod appreciatively, then Katie and me start passed.

Mrs. Tenet begins to get back into the stride when she calls back, "Will Katie be back in time for service tonight?"

I turn back even as I keep walking forward, calling, "She should be." We turn the corner and our smiles fade. "She seems nice," I tell Katie a little sarcastically.

"She is," Katie whispers, withdrawn. She looks nervously about, constantly checking ahead of us and behind us, glancing down long and lonesome hallways as we go. We arrive at the elevator foyer and wait in silence for our car. Katie keeps an unsubtle vigil. Every sound draws her attention. Every hint that someone might be moving in any direction causes her to look cautiously. It sends her long brown hair flapping about her shoulders as she looks through her bangs. The whole time, I stand still and wait, watching the elevator. It takes a long time. We are almost fifty stories up.

The elevator finally chimes and the doors part. Thankfully, there's no one inside. "Thank god," Katie whispers and slips inside. I step in and Katie flashes a keycard before she presses for the parking deck.

"I didn't drive," I tell her.

"Yeah, but there'll be fewer people," she says, glowering at her reflection in the elevator panel. She's quiet and all we have is the sound of the elevator quickly swishing through the floors in a vacuum. In time, somewhere around a floor in the mid-thirties, she volunteers, "The church owns the whole floor." I just nod. It's not unheard of for a tight-knit social group of one variety or another to all move into the same community or bio-dome. And if they can arrange to get a floor to themselves, so much the better. Hands in front of me, I rock on my feet as I think my way through the next few steps. She asks, "Do you know the Wilson Women's Clinic?"

It takes me a second. "Uh...I'm sure I do." I bring up a search engine in my Heads-Up Display and run a fast internet search. "Found it," I tell her. "That's kind of far. There are three clinics that are closer. And they all do...they all offer full-range service."

She nods, doing so causing her hair to shimmer. I bet her locks have never been colored once. "I know," she says. "But my family's at one of those closer ones. I don't know which one. Most of the church is." Through her bangs, she clarifies to me, "They're protesting."

The job is making more sense by the minute.

The elevator stops and the air hisses. With a fifty-story altitude change, the elevator pressurizes before opening the doors. When they do part, we're both hit with the smell of exhaust, erosion, rust, and all the scents of modern deregulated vehicle standards.

The RSC's parking level is in a thin layer of smog. The air looks like somebody's left their car running in a garage as they wait to asphyxiate. My lungs kick their filters into gear, but Katie begins to cough slightly. I undo one of the pockets on my combat harness and produce a paper breathing mask. It won't help a lot but it'll do something. She straps it around her head and follows me into the smog.

We're walking a good distance when we hear an engine roar. I spin around and see headlights. I jump back as Katie turns to see a car shooting straight at us. I grab Katie and pull her in between two nearby parked cars and the commuter shoots by, flashing us the bird. If my bullets didn't cost more than some cab rides, I might take a shot.

I start to resume but Katie's visibly unnerved. I turn back to her and she stands up slowly, her hands literally shaking. "Drivers have a hate-hate relationship with pedestrians in this city," I tell her. She only nods sheepishly, brushing her hair back from her face.

We resume walking, heading towards the north-facing exit. "At least we're not on bicycles," I joke as we walk, trying to calm her down. "The only thing drivers hate more than pedestrians are bicyclists." She doesn't laugh or even seem to smile. I give up and we keep walking in silence. As we do, she walks closer and takes my hand. Her eyes cast down, she stays half-a-step behind me, as if by instinct. Or conditioning.

The metro ride is quiet. In spring, the metro cars are rarely comfortable. Either the heat is still on and it's too hot, or the AC is on and the seats feel like ice. Katie doesn't seem to mind, though. She sits next to me, hugging her elbows in thought. She stares into space.

I've done Long Walks before and each one is different. I don't really have any idea what she's going through or what she's thinking about. Sometimes it's the husband or boyfriend that she's going to upset. Sometimes, it's thoughts of the child inside her. In Katie's case, I'm inclined to think she's reflecting on how her family will react. I don't know if they know she's pregnant. She doesn't look it. Given how freely available contraceptives for both men and women are these days, her family must keep pretty tight reigns on her. Or maybe this is one of those statistical anomalies. Who knows. All I know is my client is worried and we've got a long ways left to go.

The metro car doors slide open and I rush to take the lead. I can tell Katie's surprised when I step ahead of her, but when she steps out, she sees why: a small squad of people are standing at the landing of the opposing escalators out of the station. They're holding signs announcing that the medical professionals working at the Wilson Clinic are murderers. Katie freezes in shock, but I take her shoulder and guide her into motion. We start for the up-escalator.

The metro-station is a giant domed space, not unlike some sort of negative space rotunda you might see in a state capital building. The walls are a dark concrete or cement, I don't know which, with little ridges built into just about every surface to buffer and void the sound caused by the trains. There are two different metro lines that cross at this stop, meaning there are two levels but we're on the top-most level. The escalators out onto street level are immediately within sight, to our immediate north-west. It's pretty much a straight shot, which would be nice except there's no meaningful way to get there without walking right passed the protesters.

It's a cadre of middle-aged types in conservative attire, holding hand-made signs. One of them has a wi-fi scrambler, which is irritating. It's a device protestors use to block wi-fi signals. They do this so you either have to pay attention to them and can't get distracted by checking the net, or so you can't look up the very things they are claiming. To me, a cybered-up street merc who can see wi-fi signals like most people can see fog, it's like somebody walking around with a strobe light.

Somebody in the protest group is paying attention because she moves towards Katie and me. She practically smacks Katie in the face with a pamphlet, saying, "The Wilson Clinic murders babies!" Katie accepts the pamphlet, keeping her eyes averted. She just nods and tries to keep walking. No such luck.

Another protester steps in front of her, this time a man and this time not so friendly. "You're not going there, are you?" he asks, like he knows the answer.

When you deal with a direct confrontation, there are three ways to handle the situation. The first, and easiest, is just to ignore it and walk around. You don't give any kind of response, you don't argue, you don't refute, you detour and go. It's surprisingly effective.

The second response is to acquiesce and engage with the person. You can either agree and do whatever it takes to get them to shut up, or you can argue and make your counterpoint. It's up to you. This is problematic but if you're feeling froggy, why not jump?

The third response is to up the ante and go on the offensive. If they come at you with a Six, come back at them with a Nine. You escalate things above and beyond whatever they bring and you find out how badly they want to be an ass. It's dangerous and its tricky but it also tends to have some permanent effects. Permanent effects are the prep school word for consequences.

Katie goes for option number one, which is to step around the guy and keep walking. Katie is smart. I follow Katie, mostly because she's my employer at the moment, and also because this is the job. I'm here to get her to the clinic safely, not argue points with religious kooks. But then the man steps back in front of Katie again and yells, "You are, aren't you?!" Then he goes for the age-old line all idiots use on women. "SLUT!"

Respect is in his face.

I carry six pistols on my person at all times. My two primary pistols – Reason and Respect – are paired weapons that ride on my upper thighs for easy access. They look very similar but they aren't identical, especially in function. Reason is a tactical pistol with plenty of rounds, precision to spare, and has enough power to shoot through a car. Respect kills cars. You know, in movies, when that loose cannon cop takes out the big-ass gun that's supposed to be so powerful, it's immoral? Yeah, that gun wishes it was Respect. That gun wants to be Respect when it grows up.

See, the thing is, I don't do subtle. I'm a street merc and subtle is for people who actually spell out the whole word 'mercenary'. Street mercs are a lot of things and today, I'm hired muscle. I wear a combat harness in my day-to-day life. I walk around the streets of Sacramento with six pistols. I don't do subtle. So when I am tasked with protecting somebody, I'm not going to go the executive protection route and be all 'sir, please step aside'. No, I'm going to show this loser exactly who and what he is dealing with because sometimes shock & awe is my job and – just so we're all crystal clear – I don't do subtle.

Brother Love here practically jumps back. A well-reasoned argument might make converts from non-believers but a gun to the face says 'shut up' like nothing else. I walk forward passed Katie and threaten the dude away from her. The half-dozen other protestors have all fallen silent as we stand in a little circle of tense fear while around us, the brisk urban air is flying. People in the metro station are all slowing, lingering in morbid curiosity to see what's about to happen. Few things draw a crowd like impending violence.

Of course, nothing is going to happen. Respect might be the thunder after the lightning but them bullets are expensive. And it's one thing to draw a gun, it's a whole other thing to actually fire it. The worst I might do is pistol-whip this jerk. No, I just want to get things off on the right foot and that foot is the one I'll put up his ass or anyone else's that tries to give us flack.

I have to wiggle the barrel a bit before they get the picture and make a path. Once Katie's route is clear, I lower Respect and eyeball the protester. Once I hear her get onto the escalator, I give him the ultimate disrespect and turn my back to him. I make a show of very casually reholstering Respect as I get on next, a few steps behind Katie. As I ascend, I turn and look back at him and make very clear when we come back, I either won't see him or I just might be the last thing he sees.

The escalator is long. The sloped tunnel is almost like a leaning building. We lose sight of the bottom before we see the top. The slanted walls are covered in ads, some of the video screens plastered with flyers for bands that have long since come, gone, and broken up. Most announce those moments in musical history will be playing at clubs that have since closed. The air smells of stale pastries and fresh motor oil. Lights flicker and buzz.

"Why did you draw your gun?" Katie asks me. She can't look me in the eyes and speak at the same time.

"To make my point," I let her know as I keep an eye out ahead of us and behind us. "I don't want to talk to these people. They've got nothing I want to hear."

"Is your mind so made up?" she asks me. I'm surprised. But then, maybe I shouldn't be. She's been steeped in this culture for her whole life. Somebody like me, somebody pretty much counter to her believes in every way, is probably very confusing.

"I never seen or heard of anyone change their views because they were shouted at," I tell her. "I've never seen anyone believe something different due to shame, either being shamed or seeing someone else be shamed. All it does is reinforce the beliefs of those who already believe like you." I look down the tunnel as the bottom level finally disappears. "These people, their protesting, it isn't social commentary or ethical protectionism: it's puritanical masturbation. They're not changing minds. They're bullying and they've convinced themselves the power trip they feel is a religious high and not the rush of cruelty."

Sadly, things take a turn for the worse. As we ascend the escalator, we heard a dull roar, like the rumble of traffic or a Black Friday Stampede. It's only as we crest to the top that we see a few hundred people just off from the landing. They're all carrying anti-clinic signs, all chanting loudly anti-medicine slogans. We've just walked into the middle of a rally.

We reach the top of the escalators and I stumble, not stepping off the platform fast enough. Katie is unsettled too, but I grab her and guide her over to a corner. We hide in a cubby that's got vending machines for everything from sodas to snacks to metro tickets to small pistols. The protestors can see us, but between the dribble of traffic coming out the metro with us and being sequestered to the side, we've got a second.

I spot the clinic on the far side of the square. We could circumnavigate the square which would spare us a bit, but we'd still have to walk through part of the crowd, just to reach the front doors. I don't know if they specifically design women's clinics this way, or what, but there never seems a convenient, subtle entrance. There's no good way to do this. I don't explain that to her, but summarize my assessment by telling her, "We need to do this tomorrow."

"I'm not sure I'll have the nerve," Katie says. Her voice is shaking already. She's terrified.

"Let's go to another clinic," I suggest, I urge, I insist.

"I-I can't," she says. "I don't know which one my parents are at. If they...if they see me..." She lets out this light shriek, like a pre-scream and grabs me. For a tiny girl, her grip is like iron. It hurts to have her hold me, practically shaking in terror. "I can't," she says to herself. She tries to take a step but her feet won't move. Jaw quakes and her face warps as she tries to keep her terror in check. Every battle I've ever been in probably paled to the one she's fighting with herself right now.

Somehow, someway, she digs deep and pushes forward. She starts through the metro landing, keeping her hands close to herself. I want to grab her and take her to a different clinic or take another route but at this point, doing so will get us noticed. The last thing this woman needs is more negative attention and she's insisting on leading the way right into the thick of it.

Coming out of the metro stop is a city park about half-a-block in size. It's shaped like a trapezoid, extending forward and widening until it abuts an office building. Several stories tall, it runs into the distance, becoming a part of a multi-corporate structure. Similar small buildings, most less than a dozen stories tall, surround us as traffic flows along the two legs of the park.

The park itself is a staggered set of levels, each with grassy plots, benches, and quite a few tiny-ass trees that really just need to accept that their bushes and be done with it. Big trees don't grow in Sacramento. Or maybe it's just the litter and pollution caused by all the noise and shouting.

Some of the chanting is turning towards Katie. Eyes are casting towards her, seeing the young woman approaching a medical clinic. They also see the dude behind her sporting combat armor and guns. There's a fifty-fifty chance they'll focus on me, which is what I'm hoping for. If I engage some of the protestors, I might draw their ire and, more importantly, their attention.

I get pre-empted by a middle-aged woman with gradient-tinted sunglasses. She gets right in Katie's face and yells "Baby killer!" Katie pauses and clutches her purse straps. I move between them, sliding an arm between Katie and the woman. She screams "Baby killer!" again and several of the other protestors get involved. "It's got a soul!" I put my hand on Katie's back and push her gently forward, trying to urge her on. We're more than halfway through the park now.

A problem with protesters of all stripes is that they tend to get so wrapped up in their protesting that they see anybody not directly part of their protest as complicit in what they're protesting. Worse than 'if you aren't with us, you're against us', it's more like 'if you aren't with us right at this moment, you are and have always been against us'. No activist that I've seen has any monopoly on binary thinking like that, so I'm expecting it as we wade into the crowd.

The crowd of protesters are closing in around Katie and me and I'm starting to think about drawing a pistol. It's poor form to draw a pistol and shoot it in the air but it's amazing what a high-caliber gunshot will do to give you some breathing room. Drawing a gun against a person can be an effective (and rewarding) tactic but drawing a gun on a crowd never ends well. Plus, in situations like this, you got to keep your hands free. Free for what?

Stopping bricks.

As Katie is wading through protesters who are absolutely certain she's guilty of a gazillion sins already and that the best way to change her course of action is with shame and threats, I'm right beside her. My left hand is having to practically hover ahead of her, to part the sea of protesters shouting threats and even obscenities at her. Man, they're amazingly certain she's here for an abortion and not, I don't know, a pap smear or a mammogram or something.

I spot the brick right as it sails over somebody's head to my right side. It's a good throw. I'm guessing whoever tossed it played high school football. My right left hand raises and the brick hits my bracer. The brick cracks against the composite, high-impact plastic armor over my forearm. I sweep my hand around and catch the brick that's falling. If I knew for absolute certain who had thrown it, I might throw it back. Doing so would be dumb, but it would guarantee all the ire goes to me and comes off Katie. But since I don't know who threw it, I just keep the brick with me.

Everybody reacts when a brick is thrown. For a few people, it's a moment of crystallization. They realize they just went from protest to the cusp of a riot. For some people, that's a step too far. For others, it's a step not far enough. Some people shout cheers of support. At least one person yells, "You missed!" like it's a joke. People are all looking around. The unified chants turn into a cacophony of confusion. Everybody's turning, everybody's moving, and it becomes a swirling vortex of sensory overload. Katie gets swept up in it all and I don't blame her. It's a lot. Still, we're committed and we've come farther than we still have to go. I put my hand on her back and push her forward. I can't say I guide her because I'd never guide a person into this pit. I'm just urging her to the fastest route out, which is sadly straight ahead.

We get still more static once we reach the steps. It's just three steps up to the clinic entrance but it's amazing how hard it is to make that ascent with people yelling at you, who refuse to budge. Still, I manage to wedge my arm forward and guide Katie into the space it helps create. We make it to the door and I pull it open. I don't hit anybody with the door but I'd be lying if I said there wasn't some temptation.

The instant the door shuts and we get that medical disinfectant smell, the crowd outside doing their rhyming chants becomes a dull, constant drone. Katie's in shock. Her hands are shaking. "It's okay," I tell her, dropping the brick in the corner and opening the door out of the vestibule and into the office proper.

The office is made up of light gray walls and a sandy-colored carpet. There's a flat-screen on the wall playing some cooking show. Cheap wooden tables have ancient magazines and a few coloring books: kids and adults. There's a receptionist behind an armored window. Nobody else is in the clinic waiting room, so when Katie approaches, the receptionist slides open part of the window and smiles, "Good morning."

"H-hi," Katie stammers. "I..." Her jaw shakes. She's still in shock from the walk. "I'd like to see a doctor."

The pair begin to exchange information, with Katie being handed a data pad to fill out. The receptionist has to speak up a few times to be heard over the chanting from outside. I leave Katie to handle the Ts to be crossed when it comes to insurance and all of that. I don't know what patients are required to have at this point. This is an unaffiliated clinic, which is one reason why there's no hospital security. These people are one step up from a free clinic (or a pre-funeral home as they're more commonly known). They help a lot of women who are uninsured, homeless, or otherwise lacking in resources (IE 97% of the female population). Still, they have to ask.

I keep an eye on the crowd as Katie fills out the data pad. I start to lean an elbow on the lip of the medical window but it groans immediately. Guess it's not rated for cyborgs. With all my cybernetics, I weigh more than some motorcycles. I watch the people, their chanting, their signs, their angry scowls. As Katie continues to handle the bewildering forms on the data pad, I half-turn to the receptionist. "I thought protesters had to stay back at least five meters."

The receptionist sighs as she fills out data on her computer. "Not if they're protesting based off their religious views. Like, two-thirds of the social activism laws don't apply under those circumstances." I nod and go back to watching them. I doubt anybody in the crowd can see me through the windows, but I can see them. They're a rowdy bunch for being so religious.

"What agency are you with?" the receptionist asks me. She's got artificial eyes, but they're pretty high-end. The whites are actually a steely off-white. I see that with some club-goers these days. I guess she's a party girl when she's not on the clock.

"Macee's Staffing Agency." She nods, still inputting data using two different keyboards, her attention jumping from screen to screen. I ask, "Do you guys contract security?"

"No, but we get some mercenaries who volunteer time for tax benefits," she tells me. "They mostly volunteer on the weekend. That used to be when the protests were the most intense, but now it's kind of random."

"Yeah," I acknowledge, looking at the crowd again. Their chanting continues. "I was not expecting this."

"I come to work every day expecting this," she says, just as Katie returns with the data pad.

Because there's nobody in the clinic, Katie gets taken into the back almost immediately. For a moment, it's just me and the noise of the crowd. I see people looking through the windows but with the glare from the daylight outside, I don't think they can really see inside. They think they do. The crowd is yelling at the facility and chanting. I thought they prayed at the facility, but I guess that depends on the church. This vitriol is pretty acerbic. It's also pretty active. You'd think they'd calm down after a few minutes or get tired, but no, they keep going.

The door opens and another woman enters. She's wearing a heavy coat and has tired eyes with heavy wrinkles on her face. She sees me and glares, but doesn't stop walking straight to the counter. I move to give her plenty of room and privacy once the receptionist comes back. I'm curious how she got through the crowd unhindered. She's alone and a bit on the older side, so why didn't they give her any brouhaha? Maybe they think she's too old? But then they'd have to ask why she's coming here, since they refuse to acknowledge other medical procedures happen in this place.

She talks to the woman in a terse tone, her voice as scraggly as her hair. She uses vulgar terms to describe a labial lesion. I feel a little bad for eavesdropping, but only a little. She looks at me, abruptly and angrily. I return the glance with my own of defiant indifference. The receptionist finishes doing whatever it is receptionists do and takes the data pad back from the woman. They keep talking and I decide to step away. She might be meaner than rusted barbed wire but she still deserves some privacy.

I never really got people who worried about their medical privacy. I mean, I get that you have to worry about insurance and medical scammers and stuff, but that seems a forgone conclusion anyway. And it's not like it's hard to get somebody's medical information and medical history. And the attempts to make it private just seem to be a problem for those who would already respect it, you know?

And it's not like corporations have much respect for the law, the letter or the spirit of it. I know anarchist hackers with more morals than even your shining star of a corporation. Plus, it's not like medical care is scarce. In Sacramento, cyber-docs are on every corner. You can buy inoculations and VR drugs in most gas stations and neurotropic chemicals are available for drone-delivery 24 hours a day. Most cancers are handled with out-patient treatment. Amputations are considered a mild inconvenience in an age of cybernetic limbs.

But all of that's structural injury, and universal body parts. Everybody's got an arm. Internal matters specific to the female population, majority though it be, are still something that is grossly unrepresented. If you want a better-looking vagina, that can be handled in an afternoon with maybe a day or two of bedrest afterwards. But if you're a woman and you want to get something south of the bellybutton fixed by someone who actually works on humans and not horses or carburetors? That's surprisingly scarce. And a crowd of angry judgmental asses trying to make you feel guilty for looking after yourself, trying to shame you for treating your body as anything other than a disposable baby oven, is far from the only problem.

As I consider the mathematical quandary of my meat-to-metal ratio, I go over to one of the tables and select a coloring book. They've got some generic pattern books, with fractals and mandalas, but I never liked those. I like the color to have context. I select a coloring book of Heian-era Japan. That's pre-samurai which is cool. After looking around for a second, I'm disappointed to find they only have crayons, not colored pencils. That stinks. I flip through a few pages to find one that hasn't been drawn in yet. I take out a switchblade and whittle the end of the red crayon to a sharper point, then lean over to start drawing.

As I put wax to paper, I glance up again. The woman who came in is sitting with her back to the far wall. She's reading in a data pad. I check the receptionist and she's typing still, doing the work of three people at once. I glance back over my shoulder and check on the crowd. Still ornery and irritating. I take a second to relax and color.

The explosion isn't powerful but it does cause a push to the air. I'd guess a grenade. I drop the crayon and stand up, Reason and Respect coming out immediately. A lot of people complain that using two guns at once is a bad idea, but those people aren't here and I am, so two guns it is. Besides, shooting in two directions at once is of surprising benefit when you're dealing with a crowd.

I check outside and the crowd of religious protesters is scattering. They're running in half-panic, bent over and retreating away from the sound and force of the explosion. The square is emptying of people who are retreating in a surprisingly organized manner. No stampeding that I can see. What I can see is fire from somewhere by the metro stop but I can't tell what's on fire or really even how big a fire it is. I see thick black smoke rising over the rain guard of the stop itself. I rush into the vestibule and check outside. The crowd has left behind a bunch of their protest signs and there's trash and litter everywhere. The sidewalks of the adjacent streets are likewise emptying. Gunshots are commonplace enough in Sacramento but explosions still get a crowd to move.

The fire is by the metro station. The wall that partitions it off from the rest of the street is on fire, which is cement. Maybe it wasn't a grenade but a cocktail or something else improvised? Or maybe it's a chemical grenade. I activate my visual spectrum, a transparent menu appearing inside of my vision. My eyes start to shift through the filters as I highlight different viewing types. Normally this takes longer but I wrote a program a few Tuesday mornings ago that lets me get a quick preview of what I'd see if I did fully activate these filters.

The first one I go to is thermograph. The world flashes faster than an eyeblink and suddenly I see a vast array of heat signatures. I see body temperature, ambient temperature, exhaust trails, etc. I see the flames too. Nothing unexpected there. I switch to gas sensors. The glass of the vestibule makes this tricky, but my eyes look for unexpected changes in air density. It's not real accurate and again, looking through the glass wall of the clinic front further complicates things, but if there's a sudden push of, I don't know, argon or xenon, that might give me an idea about the explosive or at least the accelerant. I don't see anything unusual, so it's a moot point. I cycle through half a dozen visual spectrums and decide to go back to standard visuals. The high-def vision of my standard visual settings is shocking compared to the previous, low-res spectrums.

I back out of the vestibule, both guns still ready. I only glance to the wary receptionist as I rush to the western-most side of the medical office so I can see out the windows. From this vantage, I can just barely see around the side of the partition that separates the metro stairs from the road that runs along the park and the offices. The cement is coated in something that's burning hot and fast. It's giving off a lot of smoke but there's nothing nearby to really catch. Some old posters and fliers, maybe? The explosion didn't do any real damage except scraped up some pavement and caused an awful din. Maybe a few windows are cracked? The fire's going to do more damage to the finish of the metro station and, having been on the metro station in this town, that's not exactly going to stand out among the graffiti and vulgarity. Was the grenade meant for a person? Who would try and kill a person with a grenade? Grenades are area-effect weapons. They take out groups. They aren't precise or subtle. They're loud and they—

They're loud.

This was a distraction.

I turn and look at the old woman in the coat against the far wall. She looks right at me, crosses herself, and explodes.

The impact of the blast shocks my system. I don't lose consciousness exactly. I just sort of blink and I'm outside. I'm in the road and my left side is badly scraped up. There's pavement in my skin. My pants are on fire and I'm disoriented enough that I don't really seem to mind at the moment. I just kind of pat them down to kill the flames like I'm bored.

My vision is shaking as my digital systems begin to reboot and relaunch. My vision clears up and crystalizes and I see the gaping chasm of death where the Wilson Women's Clinic once belonged. I was blown clear of the clinic when the suicide bomber detonated. I don't know if it was a cyber-bomb or something somebody had put in her surgically. I just know there's only black rubble and flames where a place of medicine once existed.

I pull myself off the pavement and stumble back for the clinic. Protesters are appearing from around the block and from down the street. Reason's holster was blown clean off my combat harness, but I can at least put away Respect. My right foot is strangely numb and I feel blood. My systems are taking stock of my damage and it's not trivial. I'm in trouble.

I climb up the steps in total silence. My hearing was turned off either from the explosion or due to the explosion. Or maybe my ears are ruined. Wouldn't be the first time. And it's not like cochlea surgery is a big deal. But that's for another moment. Right now, I'm more focused on the waiting room of the clinic. The books are all gone, blown away or perhaps just evaporated by the force and heat of the explosion. Some chairs burn, others just combusted on the spot.

The receptionist's office wall was blown in. The receptionist is right behind it, or the charred remains of what's left of the receptionist. The left side of her face is completely burned away. Her eyes look fine but her skull is charred. Her brain is on fire. Her expression is placid though. I'm hoping she didn't even notice when it happened. Those multi-chrome eyes spark, though. The left iris cycles through settings, opening and closing again and again. It's caught in some kind of diagnostic loop before it finally dies like the woman. The finality of those eyes going motionless is more chilling then the scent of burned flesh.

The cheap walls are burning and the smoke hugs the ceiling. I hold my breath, which I can do for up to six minutes thanks to a reserve oxygen tank in my lungs. I step over brick and cinderblocks that fell from above. There's furniture strewn everywhere, some of which is from the offices above. Wires hang from the roof like entrails from a disemboweled victim.

I slip into the back of the office, behind the receptionist's armored space, to where the treatment rooms are waiting. Or were waiting. They're small and there's only a few and they're all on fire. Medical chemicals burn the heated air. Multi-colored smoke surrounds me. Medical gauze and disposable gowns are already dying out, they burn so easily.

It only takes me a moment to find Katie. She was blown into the far wall. There isn't very much of her left. Both her legs were broken by the impact. Her head's turned unnaturally on her shoulders. The side of her head is subtly but firmly flattened. Her eyes are open but both eyeballs have been burned out of her head. The doctor is dead as well. She was standing when the explosion hit and she was thrown not into the wall but into the doorframe. Her back is broken, warped around the frame almost like something out of a cartoon. If I saw something like this in a movie, I'd laugh at the comical special effects, too exaggerated to be real. But they are real. They're both dead.

I can't hear the people outside, but my system is still picking up their noise. Sound vibrations and non-auditory sensors and other highly technical things. Emergency systems that make sure that in this moment of quiet horror, I'm not spared the awareness of the chanting.

It's the crowd from outside. They're the ones chanting. What they're chanting, I don't know. I can't immediately tell. My system isn't being that specific; it's just identifying the semi-harmonized noise. The crowd has returned in the wake of the bombing. They're outside, just beyond the reach of these medical flames, burning up this house of healing. They're outside, in the remains of the public park, chanting. Praying. Praising.

They're cheering.

The voices outside are cheering.

They're proud. They're proud that Katie was killed. They're proud that Katie was murdered. They're proud that they murdered someone in order to show how wrong murder is.

Rise of Team Demon

"I don't know where Alec Walters is," said Ramona Blacken.

Seated at attention in the very middle of the room, floor-to-ceiling windows circling her vision, Ramona worked to focus on the men and women at the semicircle table between her and the windows. "I don't know why he broke into Neo-Bio," Ramona went on. "I don't know why he accessed those machines, I don't know why he...he used them in that way."

"In that way," spoke up the man directly across from her. Thom Duvall, the leader of NIST. A clipped tone to his words underscored his anger. In a pressed suit every bit as crisp as his attitude, he set interlaced fingers forward on the white table. "You understand that he connected a cloning unit with the spectral cartographer. Their software is incompatible. Completely," Thom emphasized, his face resting against his hand. He sat like a hawk, poised and patient. He was picking spots in Ramona's answers, sizing her up like a mugger would size up a victim.

His look wasn't unlike those of the people around the table. Eleven men and women sat in the semi-circular table in the sterile white room. The window behind Thom, like all the windows in the room, showed the hard radiation from the artificial sun. Through the haze, the far side of Duralee was lost to distance and smog. It became nothing more but the indistinct distance, a vague openness that Ramona's eye could mistake for a sky.

Those around the table were predatory like Thom. Their eyes were sharp and keen minds, trained to sniff out weakness and exploit it, and their gaze was united on her. Expensive haircuts and semi-useful jewelry, top-end cybernetics and cutting-edge fashion, but none of it hid their bloodthirsty demeanors. Data tablets covered the table that Ramona sat before but not at. She had no access to such reminders or resources. She faced the combined might of the entire Neo-Bio Corporation determined to fix all their blame upon her.

Ramona's expression softened, not in sympathy but in disinterest. "Thom, what do you want?"

The man stiffened. "For the purposes of this review, it is inappropriate for you to refer to me by my first—"

"Alec is smart," Ramona assured him. Her confidence wavered. "Was smart," she corrected half-heartedly. Her eyes fell to her hands, her skin darker than those across the table from her. She was born a few shades darker than all of them, but a childhood spent in the toxic light of the artificial sun had intensified the difference. It contrasted with the light brown security uniform she wore now. It wasn't a uniform befitting her rank in NIST, the Neo-Bio Internal Security Team. It was the uniform given to the rankless, those who would be disposed of shortly.

One of the women to Ramona's right sat forward. "You say that like he is gone."

Ramona chortled. "He's not in the city. We'd have found him." She glared at Thom and corrected, "Excuse me. YOU would have found him."

"Is that a declaration of your termination of your position here at Neo-Bio?" asked a man to her left. "Your role as assistant to NIST leadership is not lightly thrown away."

"The Neo-Bio Internal Security Team is our most important security assist," said the woman who had spoken just a moment ago. "They are the bedrock of this corporation. Without NIST, our absolute confidence in our security would be called into question, would be compromised."

"Can't have that, now can we?" Ramona whispered to herself, fighting not to give in to bitterness and street acumen.

"What was that?" asked Thom, picking up on her mumble only from his fixation.

Ramona looked up from her thoughts and stared right back at Thom. "You're enjoying this, aren't you?" she asked him specifically. She smiled sardonically. "It's nice to have the importance of NIST - it's oh-so-crucial nature – spelled out over and over and over again." She turned her eyes on the corporate suits in the room and barely contained her sneer.

"So you recognize the importance of NIST's work," the woman pushed. Ramona nodded, more of an acceptance than a confirmation. "Then you can appreciate why these steps must be taken." The woman smiled the most inauthentic smile Ramona had ever seen. "We aren't singling you out."

Ramona's eyes glazed over and she shook her head. She looked out passed Thom's head, through the windows. Outside was the spanning city that was her home: Duralee. The wretched city was a garish, filthy brown, the color of yellowed materials and rust. At this height, inside the Neo-Bio main offices, Ramona could make out the curvature of the city. The endless urban expanse gently sloped upwards until it completed a sphere, with the city surface following the interior.

"I've been around enough," Ramona said quietly, her eyes dropped off the city. "I know how this is going to go down." She looked at Thom, looked right into his eyes, looked right through him. "I've been on that side of the table more than once." She shook her head at the inevitability of it all. "I don't want to quit. I don't want to be fired. But I know I don't really have a say in it, do I?"

Before any of the other experts could recite prepared lines for just such an assertion, Thom spoke ahead of them. "You aided a thief," he told Ramona personally. She said nothing. "You helped distract our security forces, on the night when they were already stretched thin thanks to the racing championship that you two organized. All of this so that he could violate the sanctity of the Neo-Bio

Corporate Complex." Ramona snickered at the word 'sanctity'. "This further allowed him access to top-secret technolo—"

"Alec Walters, a respected leader in the community and the owner and captain of the most decorated racing team at the Duralee Track, came to me with a business opportunity that Neo-Bio could NOT ignore," Ramona snapped. Her glare was so intense that raising her head caused her short-clipped hair at her chin to shake, the shimmer from the lights on her dark locks doing nothing to mute the burning anger in her eyes. "He had arranged an unheard-of business opportunity: to bring a Gold Sovereign Cup team to the local track and compete against a local team. To have our name attached to a Gold Sovereign Cup race, win or lose, is beyond invaluable." She laughed. "We made more per minute off that race – a race Alec Walters arranged – than we lost in the entire evening trying to apprehend Alec. As for helping obscure him, I'm the one who ascertained the compromised sensors that helped him gain access to the complex. I'm the one who risked exposure to pursue him. I'm the one who – in my own, personal vehicle – tried to run him off the road as he made his escape." She sat back, leaning against the chair and crossing her legs. "If you were to ask me – and I note, after two weeks of hearings, you still have not – I would say everything connected to this inquiry has been a huge waste of resources."

"That's enough, Ramona," Thom ordered.

"Alec Walters did no harm to this company," she told the collected board of well-to-do corporate types. "He broke in so he could use a machine we had mothballed. He broke in after multiple attempts to pay to use these machines which we had mothballed."

"Ramona," Thom barked, louder.

"We could have just charged him and he'd have paid it," she kept on, indifferent to Thom's protests. "He made us a fortune and then did little more than ignore the 'do not walk on the grass' sign. Shame. On. Him."

"RAMONA!" screamed Thom, leaping up abruptly, on the verge of losing the last vestiges of control. "I won't be ignored or dismissed, you arrogant little bitch!" Ramona very deliberately took her time rolling her head towards Thom, making him wait before she confirmed that he had her attention.

Thom's eyes twitched, a vein throbbing in his forehead. His face flushed with rage, he stated for all the world to know, "Alec Walters broke our law. There is no breaking our law." Ramona sighed slowly, disinterested. Around the table, the others watched the nonverbal exchange between the two, afraid a murder was about to be witnessed. "That thief violated our company, sullied our resources, and undermined our authority as the future of this city!" He seethed, panting hatefully. Around the table, others were looking at the corporate leader who had broken with decorum.

Ramona was unperturbed. Eyes locked on Thom, she smirked with disdain. Her gaze rolled slowly off him and she looked at the others around the table. All well-dressed, all well-maintained, all corporate. "If you're going to fire me, fire me," she told them. "If you're going to demote me, demote me. Just get it over with." She looked right at Thom. "I'm simply sick and tired of hearing you talk."

Ramona walked passed the empty assistant's desk outside her office, noting the sterile work space that had been vacant for half a month. She slowed only for a moment as she hoped for the best for her assistant, then headed passed.

With a large, empty box in her arms, Ramona pulled open the manual door to her office with no trouble. Inside was a spacious office, much taller than it was wide. The pristine space looked out over a sweeping vista of the gorgeous and cultivated Neo-Bio campus. The healthy and green corporate space clashed with the ugly brown and rusted husk of a city beyond. The red tint to the windows made the artifice of the city of Duralee seem even more unnatural. A few plumes of smoke from the factors between her building and the edge of Neo-Bio's corporate perimeter disrupted the view.

Despite its size, Ramona's office lacked most hallmarks of a personal space. A framed poster to her left, showing the wear of age, proclaimed Team Demon the Duralee Track's Bronze Sovereign Cup Champions. A handful of framed photos dotted the mostly-empty shelves by her desk. All the photos were of Ramona and her friends and family.

One photo caught her eye. On top of a filing cabinet, the steel frame matched the sleek form of the furniture in her office. In the photo, Ramona was dressed in the Neo-Bio cap and gown, showing that she had completed their rigorous initiation and education program. She was arm-in-arm with Alec Walters, both of them smiling. Taller than Ramona by half a head, Alec had lost a bit of his urban tan but still had the permanently-squinted eyes of city life. The data ports need for racing were visible between the muscles of his neck. Most of all, however, she fixated on the smile of her friend.

Ramona slapped the picture face-down, angry. The office door opened behind her. Ramona barely had to glance back before she clamped her eyes shut and worked to summon the strength not to start throwing hands.

"We're going to find Walters," Thom told her as he let himself into her office. His suit jacket was unbuttoned, his hands in his pants pockets. Creases of fabric were about as casual as he got. "It won't make the public news when we do."

Ramona just nodded. She choked up as she began to collect her photos, placing them carefully but quickly in the box she'd carried in. Once the shelf was emptied, she set about removing her few personal belongings from her desk, a task that took only minutes. "All my passwords have been changed, so my replacement shouldn't have any problems getting into my files."

"We'll have to go through them," said Thom. "Make sure you and Alec didn't—"

"Oh my god, what is wrong with you?!" Ramona yelled, whirling around at Thom. "For the last time, just like the first, just like the hundredth, I did not help Alec. I did not aid Alec. I did not..." She gave up. She turned and resumed clearing out her office. "I tried to capture him. When that didn't work, I tried to stop him. When that didn't work, I—" She choked up. "I tried to kill him." She stopped and spun around to Thom. "I tried to run him over in my own Specter. My. Own. Specter. A car that was completely totaled, I might add, and for which I have not received one ounce of compensation." She continued packing up her things. "Asking me the same question, again and again, is not going to change the answer. It's not going to change the fact that I did not – DID NOT – help Alec."

Thom only allowed, "We'll see what he says." Ramona scoffed quietly, by which Thom was equally amused and insulted. "You doubt we'll find him."

"Neo-Bio has a lot of resources," Ramona allowed. To Thom, she said, "But Alec has intelligence."

A shimmering sign of humanity appeared in Thom's eyes as he stared at Ramona. "You betrayed us," he leveled at her.

"I did everything I could," she countered, returning his glare. "Neo-Bio is betraying me." She turned and walked across her large office, the light of the day coming in through the windows separating her and Thom. "Just like Alec." She took down her framed poster but paused. "At least he had a good reason."

As she returned to the desk and her box of belongings, Thom asked her, "Why did Walters betray you?"

Ramona turned to her former boss, surprised by his tone. Only a hint softer, it was a question, not an interrogation. Without thinking, the name almost escaped Ramona's lips. "Sam--" She caught herself, swallowed, and answered instead, "Same thing anyone betrays their city for."

"And that is?" pushed Thom, his hard tone returned

"If you knew, I wouldn't need to say it," she said. She stood up straight, her box in her arms. "And if you don't know what it is, saying it wouldn't make any sense to you." She walked around Thom, leaving her office for the last time. "Get the light, would you?" she asked as she left him behind.

Ramona's pictures rattled in the plastic bin labeled 'Neo-Bio Resident Removal'. The letters were bright and vivid, so much so they shone back at Ramona in the reflection of the metro window. The rusted train car vibrated painfully, kicking up and down as it rumbled ungracefully along the tracks. A gap in the door opposite Ramona let in the caustic daytime heat. Several bags from fast food stalls were crumbled and ruined by residue, collected in the corners. The metro smelled of spray paint fumes and baked mold.

As the train rounded a turned towards the next station, a divider wall flashed by. A solid block of posters advertising the match between Team Demon and Team Devastator were still vibrant. More than two weeks removed from the titanic match, the posters were still all over the metro stop. The doors opened with gasps of pressure and the squeal of rusted metal. Exhausted people came and went. Meanwhile, Ramona looked at the metro stop like it was an art gallery. Posters of the epic race dotted walls and pillars, covered some windows and even a few of the screens that played advertisements nonstop.

As the metro car kicked into motion again, the doors sliding closed and a mechanical voice coming unintelligibly over the speakers, Ramona realized she hadn't noticed which station they were leaving. She looked up at the digital map, part of which had been magnetized into uselessness. She saw the complicated network of stops and courses and tracks and routes and all the multitude of places there were for her to go.

And she had no place to go.

Ramona looked down at the hard box in her lap, slowly realizing she carried everything to her name. A panic hit her. She instinctively clutched the box closer to her as she looked around the metro car with a totally different gaze. Survival instincts buried deep thanks to a civilized, corporate life, returned to her. Paranoia and territorialism struck her.

"No, let go!" yelled a girl's voice.

Ramona turned sharply and saw a young girl fighting with an older boy. The pair were tugging on a stuffed animal, an old and raggedy thing. The boy's artificial leg hissed as actuators dug his metal foot into the ground. His height as well as his cybernetics gave him better leverage. He pulled and the girl yelled before she smacked him with a hand missing a finger. Their mother, whom Ramona hadn't noticed because her complexion matched the graffiti and trash of the metro car, sat forward and hit them both. She chastised them and then sat back, allowing them to renew their fight, albeit more quietly.

Desperate, Ramona got off at the next stop. She didn't care what it was, just to get away from the rush of urban sensations she had forgotten. Before the metro car had even come to a complete stop, she rose and carried the box to the door.

As the doors slid apart, Ramona was struck with a sobering realization. On the sign directly before the doors, a blue arrow – faded and covered in graffiti – announced the direction out and towards the Duralee Track.

As the double doors of the metro closed behind her, Ramona turned around in the cavernous metro stop. One of the hubs of public transportation in the city, it was situated a block away from the track. A dozen small business stalls dotted the metro stop, none of which were operating. Trash had collected in the corners of the cement stop, as had a few of the city's homeless population.

Ramona's footsteps proceeded her as she headed up the steps to street level. She exited out into the harsh daylight but didn't need to look around. She followed the specter of her own thoughts towards the Duralee Track.

A massive cement structure, huge pillars held up the center stands high above. Wide, open halls would lead crowds through the ticketing booths, through the security checkpoints, through the vendors and concessions, into the tens of thousands of seats beyond. Only now, they were empty. The great, towering spaces were still. Grand entrances, big enough for the hopes and dreams of the depressed, were vacuous. Long halls divided by massive pillars that would hold up the sky, empty save for echoes. Advertisements rolled on screens with cracked and fritzing monitors. Speakers buzzed, the roll of automatic advertisements lost to the dusty air. Silent but not noiseless, lit and yet filled with shadows, time had done nothing to Ramona's memory of the enduring monolith of the track.

Ramona breathed the air, taking in the scent of crowds and dust, people and the city, oil and machinery. The scents of home. The clack of shoes weighed down by her possessions echoing ahead of her, Ramona walked paths that her feet remembered but her mind did not.

She arrived at a ticket desk, but found the terminal empty. She stood on her toes and looked through transparent window. Someone was asleep in the stall, a jacket pulled over them. Concluding it was a worker, Ramona slipped passed. She glanced up at a harmless security camera as she did, but then kept on. She wound through stone steps, the metal railing rattling as she passed. She spotted security in the distance, large men with obvious cybernetics. She heard one say, "She's fine", recognizing Ramona from ages passed. It only added to a growing sense of isolation from the present. She turned up a familiar stairwell and into the stadium she ascended, only to find her way into the bright daylight that looked out over the track.

A seven-mile circuit, the Duralee Track was made up of multiple obstacle courses that would test the teams of drivers as they fought for position. A large gap existed at the northern end of the track where a pair of loops over ten stories tall were being moved off the track, to be replaced with another obstacle for the new season. Nearer obstacles were familiar, not just to Ramona's eyes but also her reflexes.

Hot wind blew off the track, winding along the steps. The chain link fencing rattled at the base of the lonely seats. Across from her, inside the center of the track, a high-rise sat silent and dark. Behind the glass windows, the well-stocked and well-maintained box seats for the corporate account holders and other wealthy looked out from a better vantage than the city dwellers could ever hope to glimpse. A strange bitterness set into Ramona as she looked at the windows, trying to find the Neo-Bio box. All she could see was the painful orange reflection of the artificial sun at the very center of the city.

Ramona's head led her in turning and she looked up to the height of the seats, to where the track offices waited, quiet and dark.

Ramona walked slowly up the stairs into the meeting room. In the kitchenette opposite her, John paced. The track owner had an external phone in his hand, and he was turned away from the stairs. In ugly brown pants and a striped blue-and-white shirt, suspenders and an unkempt mustache completed the look of a short-statured scam artist. The hiss of hydraulics and the brass-plated hand did nothing to dissuade that impression.

The track owner glanced at Ramona, ready to yell at whoever was disturbing him. Instead, anger melted away when he finally recognized her. "'Mona," he said. Into the phone, he said, "I'll call you back." Whoever he was talking to say something snide, because he followed it with, "Yes, I will, I swear!" Another comment, less snide and more vulgar. "Yes, this time I mean it." He clicked the phone off and looked at Ramona as she set her box on the dinette table. Wobbly legs struggled with the trivial weight. "Fancy meeting you here," he said in a city accent. He glanced at the box and read off of it, "Resident Removal. That mean Neo-Bio gave you the pink slip?"

"Something like that," Ramona said as she paced in the office she had once known like a second home. Her mind drew incomplete memories off every detail.

"I thought corporations didn't fire; you just...disappeared," said John. He turned back to the kitchenette and continued brewing coffee.

"There are different protocols," was all Ramona would say. She came to the edge of the kitchenette, where the ancient carpeting was stapled into the warping tiles. "Besides, some corporate types think exile is worse than death." John only chortled. "Who was that?"

"On the phone?" asked John. "Oh, that was Hazel. He's interested in booking Team Demon to do an appearance at his track in Pozal."

"Another city. That's...exciting," Ramona said. John shrugged indifferently. "Well, I mean, the Duralee Track's got the hot commodity right now. Team Demon just beat Team Devastator, the Gold Sovereign Champs."

"Yeah, which debatably makes Team Demon a Gold Sovereign team, but maybe not," John told her. "The League is still reviewing the rules. And in the meantime, everybody and everything is in disarray. We got Bronze teams challenging Copper teams, Iron teams saying they can beat the Steel teams. It's chaos." He tried the coffee and approved of its minimal awfulness. He applied a liberal amount of seasoning from a hip flask he made no effort to hide. "Great time to be a fan. Oh, it's so exciting!" He was sarcastic. "Lousy time to have to actually run things." He had some coffee and remarked, "And run them, I do."

He began to shuffle towards the windows that looked out at the track. Grime had collected in the corners but the daily radiation had burned the center of the windows rather clear. "Now that Alec just up and disappeared, we're not even sure Team Demon's going to race again." He faced through the window at the track. "The furlough that they're recovering isn't going to hold much longer." He turned back around to Ramona. He glanced at her box of belongings, then at her. "Neo-Bio kicked you out." It wasn't a question, but a precursor. A prompt. "You know what they did with Alec?" Ramona was confused. "Rumor has it that Neo-Bio grabbed him for some reason."

"Neo-Bio's looking for him too," she told John. "If they find him, I'll be the last to know about it. I doubt anybody will know about it."

"Where'd he go?" John asked.

Ramona shook her head. "I have no idea."

John took his time staring at and through Ramona. He had another sip of coffee. "I'm not sure I believe you." His bluntness took Ramona by surprise. She readied to defend herself but John continued. "Neo-Bio might hang on to Alec and use him somehow. Team Demon's valuable. You said yourself: they're the hot commodity. Nothing corporations like more than a hot commodity."

Ramona stood still as John began to approach her from the window. "Right now," he told her with words loaded like a gun with no safety, "things are hanging on by momentum and inertia."

"Those are the same..." Ramona just kept quiet.

"Everybody's waiting for something to happen," John practically accused Ramona. "Everybody's waiting for Alec's next miracle and when it gets out that he's gone, there's gonna be hell to pay."

"The track has other teams, John," Ramona reminded him.

"I'm not talking about the track!" he yelled suddenly, startling her. His face flushed, his eyes shook with more fear than anger. "I'm talking about Duralee. I'm talking about the city. I'm talking about this stinky, rotten, ugly city. This city's more than this track but this track is its heart and if this heart quits a-beating..." He paced backwards from Ramona. "You think people are gonna be okay when they learn that Team Demon disbanded right after winning the biggest race in history?" He smiled a grin of crooked teeth as yellowed as the sky. "You look out that window and tell me these people can handle a letdown like that."

Ramona couldn't stop herself from looking out and seeing far beyond the track. The city extended into the haze, as if the endless slums and corporate retreats melded into the haze and pollution. "The team disbanded?" she asked, her voice a ghost.

John nodded. Callously, he added, "Now imagine how them out there are gonna feel." He nodded to the stadium when he said that. He turned and began to depart. "Maybe they'll riot. Or maybe they'll all just sit down and finally not get up again." He sniffed back some congestion as he descended the stairs. "Personally, I give the city a month. Maybe less."

Ramona was left staring through her own reflection.

In the garage doorway, Ramona teared up nostalgically at the smell of engine grease and motor oil.

The familiar scents were coupled with those of rust, metal, rubber tires, and hard-working but inefficient cooling jets from the wall vents. The air hummed with electricity and the whirl of cooling fans on computers that dotted the garage.

Four vehicles slumbered in the nearest of five bays, each divided by a thick, solid pillar. The floor was a textured mix of metal plating and cement. Chemical stains dotted the ground, especially under the vehicles. Towered tool cabinets on rollers were all locked and pushed to the walls. Their metal paint was chipped from age but mostly use. The diagnostic computers were in sleep mode. The garage was stagnant.

Nearest was the large, boxy tank of a racer. Six wheels, with four in the back, it was the heaviest and largest but not lacking for speed. In the middle were the two standard racers. Four wheels, low to the ground, and everything one could want in a vehicle. Lastly, at the next-to-last space, a three-wheeled racer. What very little it lacked in stability and power, it made up for with maneuverability to spare. All four racers were black with red highlights, the colors of Team Demon.

Ramona was hesitant to break the seal on the memories but willed herself to step into the garage. She looked around at the oil-stained floor, dust and debris blown in and clumped among the clutter here and there. She set her box of belongings onto a rolling seat used to work on engines. Making sure the balance would keep her things from falling, Ramona left the box and stepped further into her own past. Instinctively, she reached to wind up her black hair, only to remember it was no longer passed her shoulders but cut short. She touched the back of her neck as if to remind her of the time that had passed since she'd last been down here. Her fingers rubbed against the cyberjack at the base of her neck and she lingered there, fingers brushing the edge of cool metal.

"We missed you."

Dotson stood in the doorway, an arm leaning on each side. With the light from the stairwell outside, he was rendered a partial silhouette. Ramona smiled at her friend and approached. "It's good to see you." They embraced and hugged just a second longer than customary. Rather than greet each other, for a second, they leaned on one another, supported one another. Grieved together.

When he finally drew back, Dotson looked over Ramona and smiled, overjoyed and bittersweet at the same time. "I've got to be honest, I've never been so glad to see you. Like, ever."

Her own plight forgotten for a moment, Ramona grew worried. "Why, what's going on?"

"Well, you're Neo-Bio security. You know Alec's disappeared," Dotson told her.

"Yeah, but I'm not Neo-Bio security. Or, not anymore." She glanced at her box.

Dotson followed her glance and then reeled. "Holy crap." He wrestled with that for a moment. He turned to Ramona, about to bombard her with platitudes and offers for help but she stopped him.

"I'm...I'll be...let's, one emergency at a time," she said. "You go first. You said...what's going on? Beyond Alec...leaving." She choked up just a bit to say it aloud.

Dotson backed up from her, his hands in his pockets. At a loss for what else to say, he summarized it for her. "He left me everything."

Ramona's eyes opened wide, then her jaw dropped. "He WHAT?"

Dotson nodded. "Yeah. Everything, and I mean everything." He sat back on the hood of the first vehicle. "The racers, the team, the garage." He laughed. "He even left me his apartment." He laughed again, almost delirious at the implications.

For a moment, the fortune at play was forgotten and Ramona felt her heart break yet again. "I guess he really isn't coming back." Rage entered Ramona's mind. Her jaw clinched tight enough that her teeth began to grind. "I hope she's worth it, Alec," she whispered spitefully.

Dotson looked up, not sure if she'd spoken. Ramona hedged off him asking by saying, "Hell of a fortune, Dotson," she said.

"Yeah," he confirmed at the understatement. "I don't know what to do with it. I don't even...I don't even know where to start." Ramona turned away. She hugged her elbows to her side. She tried to speak but it was unsettling to her to see Dotson's handsome, chiseled face so morose. "Lancer thinks we should call it," he told Ramona. "He thinks we should sell the vehicles, sell the team, and just..." He shook his head, staring off.

"And Berri?" asked Ramona.

"The opposite." Dotson chuckled. "I guess Berri's always been the anti-Lancer. He thinks we should stick it out. Recruit two or three new members for Team Demon and try to soldier on." Dotson laughed again, an edge of paranoia and fear in his laugh. "I mean, we did just beat the Gold Sovereign Cup Champions. The track manager is already fielding requests to book us at other venues." Dotson admitted to her, "I don't know what to do, Ramona."

Ramona's instincts kicked in warily. "Well," she said, partitioning off her emotions, "it sounds like you've got a fortune handed to you. You can hire somebody to advise you. I'd recommend Decker. He's got the corporate contacts. He's always been a good guy and he's about the only person I'd trust to not take the money and run."

Dotson looked up at Ramona and admitted, confessed, "Ramona, I need help." She readied to chastise him for putting her in such a spot. "I need YOUR help," he stated absolutely.

The honesty was too much for her. Ramona punched him in the arm, nearly knocking him off the racer's hood. The strike made Dotson wince and inhale sharply but he didn't otherwise respond. "Dammit, you come at me like this?!" Ramona yelled, her professional, corporate demeanor gone. "You come at me, like this, after he left?! After he abandoned us?!"

Dotson chewed on lashing out. His square jaw clinched and he struggled to keep from exploding at her. "The same might be said for you," he told her as patiently as he could.

That stung and Ramona backed up from him. "When I left Team Demon, I pursued a different career." Dotson's placid face told her the difference was immaterial to him. "I gave notice. I let you know in advance. And I was still in Duralee."

Dotson told her, "You were part of our team, you were part of our family." He tossed his hand up, vaguely at the door. "And then you weren't."

"So I was just the trendsetter," Ramona said unfairly. Dotson didn't respond to the barbed comment. She regretted it immediately and had to look away from Dotson, to avoid his hurt expression. "I'm sorry, Dotson. I really am. I'm sorry he left. I'm sorry you got saddled with this. But this isn't my world anymore." She started to leave, but hedged at the door. "I'm...I'm not a racer anymore."

"Yeah," he acknowledged. But then he nodded towards her box of things. "But you're not Neo-Bio Security either." She looked over her shoulder at him and he pled. "I need help."

"Dotson," she lamented warily, looking away from him. "Don't do this. Don't try to pin your hopes of..." She paced from her, the clack of her steps on the garage floor echoing off every metal surface. "I don't know what I'm doing. I don't know...anything." She laughed her own sick, heartbroken chuckle.

"I do," he told her. Their eyes met. "I know this team matters. I know it's important. It's not just...it's more than just a sports team to this city, to these people. I can't let it just fall apart. I won't."

"Alec left," Ramona said, not even a whisper.

"Alec wasn't the team," Dotson insisted, more determined than certain. "He owned it, he was the captain, but...but he wasn't the team. He wasn't Team Demon."

Ramona snickered, disgusted in the presence of optimism. "Sounds like you've made up your mind." Dotson gave her observation a thought and realized she was right. Ramona faced the stairwell out, the metal grated steps that wound up and down the long vertical shaft. She took another deep breath and backpedaled into the garage. "What do you want?" she asked. "Not 'help'. Don't say 'help'. Specifically. What do you want?"

Focusing, Dotson considered the task at hand. "Help me convince Lancer to stay on. He was Team Demon's playmaker. We can't replace him. After that, help me audition new drivers. The team operator, Basin, he knows his stuff and he's good at taking command of a situation on the track, but he doesn't have the instincts for the team dynamic."

"Do you plan to recruit from other Steel Teams?" Ramona asked.

He shook his head. "No, I don't think so. The Steel Sovereign Cup League is the first pro rank. By the time you're there, you've been racing for a while and you're probably with a team that's got corporate sponsorship which might transfer with a contract. Too much trouble, especially for a racer who probably already is used to working a certain way. No, I think we go to the amateurs."

"The Iron League?" asked Ramona.

Dotson nodded. "We recruit from the Iron League," he told her, knowing her willingness had a time limit. "Anybody from Steel or higher will be set in their ways. We need somebody who has some skill but whom can adjust and join the team. We can't start from scratch, so that means the person has to learn to work with us, less the other way around."

Ramona thought about it and nodded. She took off her Neo-Bio security jacket and pulled over a rolling stool for engine work. She sat in front of Dotson who returned to the hood of his own vehicle. "We'll need a manager."

"We will?" Dotson asked, then grinned. Ramona seemed confused. "I wasn't sure there was a 'we'. And I wasn't sure you would be part of the team."

Ramona hedged and could feel her face go flush with embarrassment. She looked at the tri-cycle in the docking bay and finally let out a laugh. "Well, I mean...it was originally MY racer."

The way she swallowed as she stared at the racer scared Dotson, and he wasn't sure why. Rather than push the sensitive issue, he returned to the task at hand. "For manager, I think that role pretty much has to go to Decker. I can reach out to him," Dotson said as his only viable option. "And as for the team, I was thinking we hold an open audition. Let some kids run the course and see what they do." He expected Ramona to counter but she nodded, agreeing with the decision. "Those that look promising, we invite back and have them run the course with the team. Whittle the list, rinse and repeat, until we've got something that cooks."

Ramona continued to nod. She shrugged and told Dotson, "Sounds like you know what you're doing."

"I need you to watch the races," he told her, refuting her confident assessment of his skills. "I need you to see what I can't that he...that he could." She looked away again. Rushing to stay focused, Dotson laughed as he said, "But it all starts with convincing Lancer not to quit."

Ramona stood up and said, "Let's go see him."

Dotson panicked a little. "What, now?"

Ramona started for the door, picking up her jacket as she walked. "No time like the present, Dotson." He glanced at her box still on the rolling seat and couldn't help but smirk. Unaccustomed to optimism in recent days, he embraced it as he rushed after her.

Dotson's rapping went unanswered. He waited for a moment on the front step of the suburban house, then knocked again. "I'm sure he was home," he said, bending to the side to peek in through the adjacent window. Ramona watched him fret, then sighed when he knocked again. "I'm not sure where he could—"

Ramona banged on the door with an open hand and yelled powerfully, "Open up, Lancer! We know you're in there!"

Dotson winced at the volume. "Do they teach you that in security school?"

"No, that's natural talent," she assured him without hesitation. She smacked the door again, loud enough for the impact to echo across the neighborhood. A pleasant road in the middle of a cultivated neighborhood, the house looked like it should belong to a middle-class family instead of a racer.

The door parted a crack and a thin but muscled man was behind it. A beautiful face perfectly between masculine and androgynous was framed by shoulder-length blonde hair. His eyes were wide and his mouth hung open as he said in surprise, "Ramona?"

"In the flesh," she told him with a smile.

Lancer seemed hesitant to believe her, but he stepped forward and gave her a hug. He looked to Dotson and his expression warped in stunned shock. Dotson only nodded, agreeing. "C-come inside," Lancer told them both, gesturing for them to follow him.

Through the door was a suburban home meant for a small family. A sunroof let in filtered sunlight, cleaning the radiation so the glow felt pristine and clear. The solid beam fell on an old woman who sat in a lotus position on a small rock garden in what had been the living room. "Oh!" Ramona exclaimed. "We didn't disturb your mom, did we?"

"No, she's been taking meditation very seriously," Lancer told them. "She's oblivious to the world while she's meditating." He guided the two of them down the hall to the back of the house where a spotless kitchen looked out over a patch of land with actual soil. A few fragments of dried, dead grass remained but otherwise, the yard was a dustbowl.

"What happened?" asked Dotson as he approached the window.

"The storm killed the grass," Lancer reported. "The night after the race, it rained so heavily, most of the grass drowned. We're not used to getting rain like that." He shrugged narrow shoulders. "I bought the wrong kind."

Ramona saw her chance. "Well, we've got an opportunity to help you pay for reseeding it."

"Yeah, it'll be easy to pay for it once I sell my racer," Lancer told her, knowing where this was going already. To Dotson, he said, "Come on, man. We've been over this. I'm done." He clapped his hands together. "I'm out."

"We need you," Dotson pressed.

"Castor's living his brother," Lancer began to rattle off.

"Castor's what?!" Ramona balked. She swung around on Dotson. "You're letting him move back in with Dylan and the rest of those losers from Team Synthesis?!"

"We'll deal with Castor," Dotson said, as much to Ramona as Lancer. "Basin too, assuming he hasn't drunk himself into a stupor." Ramona scowled at Dotson, just barely keeping from throwing a punch. "Berri's still in," Dotson told Lancer. "I am too. Decker's going to manage."

"Did he say he would?" Lancer demanded, insistent on clarity. "Did he actually say those words, to you. 'Dotson, I am going to manage Team Demon'?"

Ramona checked with Dotson and saw him hedge. Angry in her own right but desperate not to lose the momentum, she said, "Yes." Lancer was as surprised as Dotson. "Decker's going to manage. He's on-board. There's some stuff he's got to clear up with Ars Technologica; declare secondary employment, list possible conflicts, stuff like that. But Decker's in." The momentum took her. "I am too," she announced.

Lancer's face went so wide in surprise, he did a double-take. "Wait, what?!" He looked at Dotson who was trying to seem pleased and not overly delighted. "I-I thought you just brought her to persuade me."

Ramona nodded to both her old friends. "I'm...I'm going to leave Neo-Bio," she half-lied to Lancer. "I'm going to come back as the team captain." She smirked and gave an uncertain look. "I mean, that is, if you guys will let me."

"Holy crap," Lancer whispered. He looked to Dotson. He hid his surprise and looked expectantly at his friend. Lancer grew tense, then looked towards the front of his house. He finally sighed and closed his eyes. "Alright," he acquiesced.

"Yeah!" Dotson shouted, startling Ramona. He grabbed Lancer around the shoulders, hugging him tightly. "Oh thank you, man!"

"Yeah, but you've got to deal with Berri," Lancer told Dotson as he wedged himself free of the hug. To Ramona, he told her, "He's not going to be thrilled that you're re-joining."

Ramona only shrugged. "Yeah, well. He doesn't have to be thrilled; he just has to stay on the track." Three friends shared a moment of hope.

The afternoon was alight with fires coming from a towering building. Once the site of a mid-level corporation, the multi-story structure of cement and metal was now a shanty town. Tattered blankets and cheap materials made up the homes that were now on fire. The poisonous glow was visible across the entire city, the black smoke rising up towards the bright light of the artificial sun.

Ramona and Dotson both looked to their left, watching the flames burn as they walked. The air was buffeted by the heat and the shouting as survivors tried to escape with what few valuables they had to their name. Nearby shantytowns watched in horror, knowing stray embers could mean their communities were next. The corpses of previous dried-out husks that had once meant jobs and livelihoods were a promise of how the tower would soon look.

Dotson coughed as some of the smoke billowed in their direction. He faced away until the urban winds carried the black smoke in a new direction. Reprieved, he found himself looking at Ramona. She noticed and smiled on the left side. He averted his gaze and looked upwards, the sky above them almost obfuscating the city that rose up in the distance. Dotson asked, "How much of that did you make up on the spot?"

"Huh?" asked Ramona.

"You haven't talked to Decker," he explained. "And are you really in? Are you really back on the team?"

"Decker'll come around," Ramona assured him and she kept walking. Dotson did as well, but he looked back at the flaming structure they were passing. Worry filled him as guilt spread about just walking by. He turned and caught up with Ramona, leaving the fire to burn itself out.

The wall next to Berri's door was molded with tiny black speckles, like a poor paintjob that had been forgotten halfway through repair. The sound of data streams was coming through the thin walls and the floor felt unsteady at more points than not. Dotson knocked again, rapping a few times on the door, the frame itself rattling. "Berri, it's Dotson. Open up, man."

"Did you call him?" Ramona asked.

"His phone charges by the minute, him and the caller," Dotson said. "He keeps it off most of the time anyway." Ramona nodded.

The door opened and Berri halfway stepped out. He fixed entirely on Ramona, his expression that of angered shock. "What's she doing here?"

"We need to talk," Dotson told Berri.

"Not with her we don't," Berri insisted.

Ramona tried. "Berri, I want to—"

"You left!" he yelled at her.

Berri opened the door completely and stepped out, fixating on Ramona. He asked in disgust, "What's she doing here?!" The question was for Dotson alone.

Rather than let herself be muscled out of the discussion, Ramona addressed Berri and his issues straight on. "I had a chance!" she stated emphatically and loudly. "I had the chance to go work for a corporation. I had the chance to make real money and make lasting change."

"Change for yourself," Berri accused. "We were a team! And he le—you left us!"

"He left me too, Berri!" Ramona yelled back. Her eyes watered up as she looked him up and down like she was reconnecting with a long-lost sibling. "Look, I'm sorry that I went to work for Neo-Bio. I thought it was the chance of a lifetime. I really did. And I didn't know how bad it felt to you. But I know now. Oh god, I know now." She wiped her tears away with her palm. "I don't think you're ever going to get Alec back. But you got me back. And if you don't trust me, fine. That's fine. But give me the chance to get that trust back."

"You don't deserve that chance," Berri said, stepping right in Ramona's face.

"None of us like being abandoned, Berri," Dotson said, a little too loudly so as to get his attention. "I was there when Ramona left the first time. I was here with you when we realized Alec left us. How do you think the fans are going to feel when Team Demon leaves them?"

"We can still save the team," Berri told Dotson, looking from Ramona for the first time. "You own it. It's all in your name. We just got to get Lancer, and some new guys. We can survive losing a member." He turned and buried his glare right into Ramona. "We've done it before."

"Berri," Ramona told him, her tone hardening. "I'm back on the team now. You need to just accept it." Dotson was about to question Ramona's tone when Berri punched her. The blow knocked Berri's red dreadlocks around his neck and into his face as Ramona slammed back into the opposite wall.

Dotson exclaimed in surprise. He was about to move when Ramona kicked off the hallway wall and tackled Berri at the waist, knocking him into his apartment. Dotson sighed as a neighbor's door opened. A young girl peeked out to find out what the noise was. She looked at Dotson. He waved and said, "Domestic dispute." She only went back inside. Dotson sighed as, through the door, Berri yelped, "Quit it, quit it!"

Dotson slipped into the messy apartment as Berri and Ramona wrestled for position. He stepped over the pair as Berri tried a submission hold he'd seen once long ago, while Ramona had already countered it. They both shouted and exclaimed in pain, hitting for pain more than damage. Dotson crossed the apartment into the kitchen and opened the fridge. Seeing few edible options, he called, "Do you have any fruit?"

"Ow!" Berri yelped. "Top shelf! Ow! That's my nipple!"

Dotson opened the shelf next to the fridge and discovered a half-full bag of dried apple chips. He took it down and had a bite. Deeming them acceptable, he returned to the living room where the match was still underway. He unbuttoned his suit jacket and sat down on an ottoman that clashed with the chair before it. He had a few more chips and waited things out.

It took Berri and Ramona a few minutes before they were both panting and out of breath. Ramona had an ugly black eye beginning to form and Berri's nose was bleeding, red blood dribbling into his red dreadlocks. Both were bruised all over and their clothes sported a few rips. They were scowling and glaring, hatred seething between them. "We done?" asked Dotson.

"You left!" Berri yelled up at Ramona.

"No, guess not," Dotson accepted with an eyeroll.

"I had to leave!" Ramona yelled as she got on top of Berri. A split lip was resurrecting a childhood lisp. "I couldn't let the chance slip by."

"We needed you!" Berri yelled, punching Ramona again, hurting her but not doing any damage.

"And that's part of why I'm back!" she yelled. She pulled off of him, huffing and glaring, just like he did at her. She checked her nose and confirmed it was bloodied but not actively bleeding. She wiped her blood on his sleeveless shirt.

"Just like that?" Berri asked, laughing incredulously. He slapped her hand away. "You expect us to welcome you back, just like that?"

Dotson was about to speak, but Ramona simply smiled and asked, "Would you want it any other way?"

The answer was Berri's slow, resisted, unwitting smile.

The door opened, letting in a line of light that widened. The noise from the hallway ads echoed into the small space. The ceiling sloped dramatically due to the surface of the roof, it hid the condo's deceptive size. A couch sat underneath the UV-tinted windows, a rug laid out over the floor. There were no ads in the private space, no video players or news feeds. Only a stark silence that was rare in city life.

Ramona stepped inside, her Neo-Bio box in her hands. She set it down and clicked the light switch, but no illumination came. "When I got the notice of ownership, I suspended the utilities," Dotson told Ramona as he shut the door behind her. The dusk light was burning down on the city, the radiation from the artificial sun slowly dwindling. "I messaged the companies. They all get turned on at midnight."

Ramona approached the windows and looked out on the city. She could see the curve of the city from that elevated vantage. With the daylight dwindling, it was easier to see into the far distance. The buildings and streets, the manufacturing centers and trash dumps, all rising with the curve of the city. She smiled as she enjoyed minor vertigo until she reached the edge of the windows and looked at the distant side of the spherical city like it was a real sky. "I kind of like it like this." She exhaled deeply. "A fresh start."

Looking around the living space, she was amazed at the furniture and electronics still in place. It was clear the home hadn't been lived in for several weeks but it felt far from abandoned. "It's weird, to be in Alec's...to be here, knowing he isn't." She turned around to Dotson and asked, "Are you really okay with letting me stay here like this?"

He gestured noncommittally. "I mean..." He looked around at the three-room home. "I only learned this place was mine last week. I didn't even have the...strength, I guess, to..." He looked at the place like it was the corpse of a friend. He admitted, "I certainly don't have any plans for it."

"Well...thank you seems inadequate but thank you," said Ramona. "I don't think I even have enough money to rent a room for the night, much less until I can find a job." Her eyes trialed out to the city beyond the windows and she felt a pang of terror at the prospect of even finding a job to pursue.

"Let me guess: unpaid leave ate all your savings?" Dotson asked. Ramona neither confirmed nor denied it. "Aren't you going to get severance pay or something?" he asked. "I mean, you were at Neo-Bio for years."

"Corporations run by different rules," she told him, like she was admitting a truth she'd turned a blind eye to. "They're garnishing my wages and savings to pay for the investigation into my termination. When it's all said and done, they'll send me a bill for the remainder."

Dotson just scoffed. "Geez."

"Yeah," she nodded. "And there's going to be hoops to jump through to get the bills formally observed. Because if I don't, once I pay them off, Neo-Bio can be like 'oh, we forgot the other half of the charges'." Ramona turned back to him and smiled sardonically. "The fun is just beginning."

"Joy," he said with a deadpan. He extended a key. "Well, you can..." Ramona took the key from him, curious about his averted eyes. "I mean, the place is paid for. And so's my place, so..." Dotson stepped back awkwardly.

Ramona's eyes narrowed, her smile curling. "Errol, what is it?" The use of his first name threw him and he stammered. "Come on. Out with it."

"I'm glad you're back," he admitted with a whisper. "I-I missed you." Once he'd finally said it aloud, he glanced at her, checking her reaction.

Now it was Ramona who stiffened. She swallowed hard and wanted to speak but had no idea what to say. "I..." was all she managed.

Dotson, his eyes averted like a nervous school boy, turned away. "It's a nice place," he told her, leaving her behind to wrestle with the realization. "I, uh, I was always curious why Alec kept it after his parents died but, I mean, I have to admit that it's really nice. Owning – actually owning – property in Duralee's not a small thing either."

He went into the next of the three rooms in sequence. "He owns several of the garage spaces, too. There are two commuters – an Aja two-door and a BTX 300. I don't know what happened to his Specter." In the front room, Ramona was still trying to unwrap the emotions Dotson had revealed.

Back in the final room, where the small single bed sat, Dotson found the wooden desk where Alec wrote in a paper notepad. Bereft of all other fixtures, the desk seemed to exist solely for the notepad. Curious, Dotson opened the pages to find pages of hand-written notes. Cursive and print lettering paired off, almost like it had come from two different people.

Unable to stop himself, Dotson read through page after page, discovering whole conversations carried out in the notebook. He then flipped to the front of the journal. "Hey, Ramona?" he called. She appeared in the doorway and, as he turned to her, she saw the notepad. Her hands dropped, as did her jaw. Dotson asked her, "Who's Samifel?"

Robert V Aldrich

Chip Masters, Ninja: part 5
A Crossworld Short Story

"A Black wind howls...one among you will shortly perish."
- Janus, Chrono Trigger

"What the hell is that thing?" asked Chip Masters.

At the tall wooden fence, a moose-like animal was consorting with cattle. The animal was as tall at the shoulder as any person Chip could recall having met. It was a stocky beast with thick shoulders and knobby knees. Its skin was spotted with rough patches of leather-like armor, between which grew tufts of matted brown hair. Atop its head was a rack of bony spikes that looked less like a moose's antlers and more like the gnarled branches of a haunted tree.

Separating the wild animal from the domesticated cattle was a fence made of whole tree trunks. Five trunks high, it was a daunting fence meant for animals and capable of keeping out many vehicles. Behind the fence's lengths, a few cows mooed at the moose. They were cows like the animal was a moose, with stockier bodies, noticeably broader hooves, and their own stubby horns like those of a miniature triceratops.

Hatsumi was walking with Chip, the pair leading a pack horse loaded with boxes. They were both dressed in denim pants with goat-skin vests beneath heavy leather jackets. Befitting the western-most expanses of the territory, the pair of teen boys looked the part of locals. Just as Hatsumi began to answer his friend, though, a great bellow came from the field. Both boys came to a stop, the horse with them, as a massive bull came over the hill in the field.

The bull was the size of a small tank and of a similar build and disposition. Impossibly wide and made of imposing muscle, the multi-ton animal came galloping towards the moose, bellowing again like it was charging into war. "Aww, damn man, this is about to be good," said Chip with the grin of a delighted troublemaker.

The bull came tromping at the moose, approaching the fence with decreasing speed but greater presence. The moose swung its head left and right and paced laterally but didn't yield. It approached the fence as well and rose up onto its rear hooves. Tall enough to practically step over the fence, it slapped its front hooves together and slammed them down onto the ground with enough force for Chip and Hatsumi to both feel it. The two boys laughed in awe.

The bull was not impressed. It came charging right up to the fence and stopped just short of tearing through it. It bellowed again, causing the very air to throb and pulse with its might. Not as tall as the moose but much thicker, it clamped its feet up and down, stomping the fertile soil of the field. It snorted fiercely at the moose and smacked the vertical posts of the fence.

"Think they'll fight?" Hatsumi asked, eyes huge at the sight of the two behemoths about to throw down, only a few posts of wood separating them.

The pair of heavyweights snorted and called at each other, pacing up and down the fence, threatening one another. Moments ticked by and an increasingly bored Chip noticed their pack horse had wondered to the opposite of the hard-packed dirt road to graze on some wild flowers. Chip confirmed she was okay, then checked on the moose and bull. They were still going back and forth. Disappointed now, Chip clapped Hatsumi's arm and said, "Come on."

"Man," griped Hatsumi. The pair retrieved their horse and resumed walking down the path. It wound between two fields, one fenced and one not. Dense forests were paired with rolling hills of crops in the early seasons. A few workers could be spotted in the far distance here and there but the air was devoid of the sounds of human life. Insects chirped and under the blue sky as endless as the day, the warmth of spring caused flowers to open and gentle breezes to turn the tall wild grass.

"I think this is the farthest I've been away from home," Hatsumi shared as they walked on.

"We're on the western edge," Chip remarked, recalling the map of the territory. "We're as far away from home as anybody can get." The walked with the wind towards the west, leaving the fenced fight to resolve itself.

Hatsumi opened the chest and slid it across the wooden table to the farmer. A tall man of sinewy strength, he wore similar denim pants and goat-skinned vest as the two travelers. He opened the case and took out a pair of orb-shaped vials full of transparent liquids. He popped the cork on the bottle in his right hand a took a sniff, then jerked back and gave a cough. As the man checked the contents, Chip remarked, "Ariesta leaves, cold formula, sundown potions, drying nuts. Enough medicine for a small hospital." Chip took out a vial of clear liquid with a slight green tint. "Mostly, though, it's a whole lot of...whatever this is." Hatsumi took it out Chip's hand and returned the vial to the chest along with all the others.

"Yep, looks good," said the man. He gave the boys a weak salute. "Tell Kagumi she has my thanks."

"Our Chunin didn't exactly fill us in on this," Hatsumi said, glancing at Chip as if for his agreement. "She said you are part of the Shinobi, but...not?"

The man closed the small chest and turned from the boys. He set the chest on a wooden shelf made from local timber, by local hands. "You don't know about Acan Samul and his defection?" Hatsumi and Chip looked clueless. The man didn't work hard to hide his disappointment. "Well, I'm Acan."

"Yeah, we kind of deduced that," Hatsumi said.

"Context clues," Chip added, tight-lipped.

"I betrayed the orders of the Shadow Dragon, Kageryu himself," explained Acan with lament. "Leader of the Shinobi," he clarified with some gravity.

"Dude, we're ninjas," said Hatsumi, gesturing to himself and Chip. "We know who Kageryu is."

"And I don't think he actually leads the Shinobi," Chip remarked. "He's like a silent partner who just shows up occasionally and tells people what to do."

"Like a step-parent," Hatsumi suggested.

"Or the Pope," Chip countered.

"I'm going to guess that's a funny reference where you're from," Hatsumi teased, deadpan. The pair turned back to Acan. "So you disobeyed orders. What over?"

Acan's smile told volumes, of a convoluted scenario involving way too many factors. "Nothing important," said the farmer with a dry throat and eyes that, for only a moment, glanced into the past. "Not now anyway." He rearranged the shelf's books and crockery to not hide the chest, but merely make it appear as if it had always been there. "Sure seemed important in the moment though." His words had a shadow of remorse but not regret.

"So you got kicked out," Chip said. He thought about it for a moment. "I suppose there are worse results. I kind of figured we killed anybody who tried to leave."

"We usually do," Hatsumi told Chip.

"It's true," said Acan. He brushed back stringy brown hair in an act of exhaustion. Midway between Hatsumi's Asian features and Chip's fairer European complexion, Acan looked more like a transplanted desert dweller than a native to the cooler climate. "I was part of a group that carried out removals."

"You were an assassin?" Chip half-marveled.

"You're all technically assassins, just like you're all technically spies," said Acan. He walked around the dinner table in his two-story cabin. The small windows were open, the shutters propped open with latches. "Regardless, after I disobeyed, I found myself without a place to call my own." He looked at the house. "I felt compelled to get as far away from home as possible and, well..." He gestured to the cabin. "I was halfway through building this place when the others arrived. They got mad at me for getting here first and I got mad at them for getting here at all. If Matilda hadn't been among them..."

Chip whispered loudly and sarcastically to Hatsumi, "I think that's his wife."

Hatsumi comparably whispered, "I think you're a moron."

"You're both right," Acan told them in matching tone. Chip grinned, thought about it for a second, then scowled. "She and I got paired. Had some daughters. Had some fights," he said, mostly to himself as he glanced at a basin full of used plates. "It's hard out here on the western edge," he told the two shinobi. "My time among the shinobi gave me skills that were needed, and the know-how to hide those skills so nobody asked too many questions." He looked at the chest on the shelf that now looked like little more than merely more decoration. "Still, medicine-brewing was never my strong suit."

Acan laughed, self-conscious and self-aware. "Sorry. I'm not usually this chatty. It's just been a while since I've been around any shinobi." He fell quiet as he thought over the recent past.

"Well what is this stuff?" Hatsumi asked. "I mean, neither Chip or me are healers, in any sense."

"We've got a fever that's starting to go around," Acan told them. "Nobody here understands epidemiology, herd immunity, stuff like that. They don't understand that they can have no symptoms and still carry the disease. We're about to be the start of a major epidemic for the western edge if it isn't stopped." He looked again at the chest. "Fortunately, it turns out I was still in good standing with a lot of the Genin I'd trained with. Some of the second-rank ninjas, the Chunin, like me too. The Jonin don't like me."

"That's okay; nobody likes the Jonin," Chip told him. Hatsumi nodded, like that was an understatement.

"The strains of command, I imagine," said Acan. He rose, about to say something more, when the front door of the cabin opened.

In came a buxom woman with a hat adorned with local wild flowers. Rosy cheeks and shining eyes, she saw the two young men and beamed. "Acan! We have company?!" She squealed and ran right up to the two boys.

"Matilda, this is Chip, this is Hatsumi, and those are still dirty." The last remark was aimed at the dish basin.

"Not now, honey," Matilda dismissed easily and out of habit. She shook the hands of both ninja, grinning hugely and infectiously. Her hand-shake was of farmer's stock and practically rattled both boys out of their boots. "Girls!" she called back at the door. She told Chip and Hatsumi, "These are our daughters: Heva, January, and Cadria."

Heva and January were closer to adulthood than childhood but they still wore freckles behind their long hair. January wore a long skirt over denim pants, while Heva wore slacks similar to her father's. Cadria, the youngest of the trio, wore a green dress against which her blonde hair looked golden. She was missing a tooth from her smile as big and bold as her mother's.

Chip paused for a moment at the girls. "January, like the month?" he asked, pointing at the middle girl.

Matilda and Acan were both puzzled for a second. "No," said the woman. "Like the queen of Crossworld." She gestured at herself. "That's where I'm from."

"So are we!" Hatsumi grinned. He shook Matilda's hand again. "Not Crossworld exactly, but from around there. Just north."

"Oh," Matilda beamed. "You HAVE come a long way. Are you from one of the eastern villages?"

"No, more towards Tech-Noir," said Chip. He checked subtly with Acan to see if he was worrying about being outed as a former Shinobi. Rather than worried, he had a curious look as well and it was fixed on Chip.

"They're from one of the smaller villages between the two city-states," Acan said toyingly. "It's called Earth." Chip did a double-take. Hatsumi wasn't as shocked but stumbled in playing it off.

Matilda only kept smiling. "I don't know it, I'm afraid." She patted both boys on the shoulders and said, "Well, they should most definitely stay tonight. Tonight at the very least."

Now it was Acan's turn to do a double-take. "Say what?"

Heva, the oldest of the three daughters matched her father in word, expression, and shock. "Say what?"

"That's right!" squealed Cadria. "They have to come to the dance."

"They're still going through with it?" Acan exclaimed. "I told the elders...th-the fever!"

"Nobody that's sick will be coming," Matilda waved off. Acan went ahead and surrendered, incredulous. "You two should both stay for the dance tonight!" she told Chip and Hatsumi. January and Cadria both brightened at the prospect. When neither ninja spoke up in direct protest, Matilda clapped her hands together excitedly and beamed. "It's decided!"

"What, no!" Acan protested. "What's decided? Nothing's decided!"

"Yeah, nothing's decided," Heva agreed, following her mother up the stairs to the second floor. Acan ran up right behind her.

Chip and Hatsumi were left with January and Cadria in the spacious single room that was the entire bottom floor of the cabin. Awkwardly, they shifted on their feet for a moment before Hatsumi waved at the two smiling girls. "Hey," he said.

"Hey," said January, turning her red hair between her fingers.

"Hi," said Cadria, with a similar look at Chip. Given her age, she looked less seductive than her elder sister and more like a child playing pretend. The two ninjas looked at one another and swallowed nervously.

"This is a bad idea," said Chip as he tied the heavy hiking boots that completed the frontiersman look. He rose and studied the way they felt. He crossed his feet as he lifted his hands, then began to shift his way to his right, going through the careful movements of a karate form.

Behind him, Hatsumi came up the ladder to the barn loft and saw Chip. "What are you doing?"

"Tekki Nidan," said Chip.

"I love how you say that like I know what that is," Hatsumi said, giving Chip the space to do the form. He had taken off his vest and jacket, and let his undershirt breeze open. He crossed around Chip and went to a small water basin they'd set up in the corner of the farm attic. "I'm not thrilled about staying for some farm festival-thing with a bunch of sick-os, but I'd rather sleep in a bed than on the forest floor." He looked at the two pallets of straw with multiple blankets thrown over them. "Or, not beds but whatever these are."

"Matilda's trying to pimp us out to her daughters," said Chip as he brought the form to an end, his feet shoulder-width apart and his hands crisp before him. He wiggled his right foot suddenly. "I swear, something's in these." He began to untie the boot again.

"Well, between the two of us, we're one-and-a-half good-looking guys," Hatsumi joked. He waited for a reaction but got none. "Really? No comeback?"

"What? I was complimented," said Chip. "You're a stone-zero, so I figured you thought I counted as more than one good-looking guy." He feigned being touched. He put his hand to his heart and whispered, choked up, "Means a lot, buddy."

Hatsumi accepted the insult reversal and sat on the lip of the straw pallet. He winced and realized he'd sat on his straight-bladed sword, thankfully still in its sheath. "Still, we've got plenty of time before we have to be back home. It's not impossible Kagumi tailed us, but I seriously doubt it."

"It's more likely she got one of the regional Chunin to monitor us," suggested Chip. He was sitting on the floor, his hand stuck inside the boot as he felt around the sole.

"If she checked up on us at all. She hasn't been riding us all that much of late," Hatsumi speculated, checking out the window at the afternoon beginning to skirt towards dusk.

"Maybe she respects our skills," suggested Chip. "We've been delivering consistently."

"Yeah, maybe," said Hatsumi, drifting slowly away in thought.

Chip gave up and stood, slipping the boot back onto his foot. He took a few test steps, felt nothing, and was even more confused by the disappearing irritation. "Besides, it's not like spending tonight in the village would be a waste. We could spin it as working on our ability to blend in." He walked over to the solitary window that looked out over Acan's home. The ninja-turned-farmer was calling in some fowl to their shed. "Like you said earlier, this is about as far from home as you can get."

A thought hit Chip and he turned over to Hatsumi. "How'd he know about Earth?"

"I don't know," said Hatsumi. He stood up and twisted and bent until he popped his back. "He may have been stationed there or something. Or recruited. Astrokel isn't the only recruit Kageryu uses. And if he was a Shinobi assassin, he's more than competent."

"Still..." Chip pondered. "How often do people get stationed on other worlds?"

"I don't know," Hatsumi half-exclaimed. "I don't even know how many other worlds there are. A dozen? A million?" He just shrugged, then stood. "Come on, man. We've got a dance to get to."

"Yay," Chip said unenthusiastically, following Hatsumi to the ladder.

A platform had been built at the valley between four hills. The sloping land gradually dropped to a flat space that emptied out through a ravine that headed into the woods beyond. At that platform, four posts had recently been raised, the fresh and untreated wood starkly lighter in color to the aged and stained wood of the lasting platform. From the posts were strung lines of lanterns, where candles burned behind paper shades. The shades were multi-colored, throwing a festive glow over the small valley.

Next to the platform were several long tables where food was laid out. Families were bringing a handful of dishes each, setting them out in a communal meal. Couples and families set up blankets around the platform and a dozen or so of the locals were setting up on the edge of the platform itself, preparing instruments for music.

Chip and Hatsumi set down the large chest, both nearly collapsing with the effort. They stood up, panting, as Acan and his family walked passed. "Don't you have pack animals that could have done that?" asked Chip.

"Yes," Acan confirmed happily. He set down a small platter of candied eggs and turned to the two disguised Shinobi. "Just put that right over there," he said to them, directing them to place the chest at the far end of the tables.

Hatsumi and Chip looked at each other glumly and contemplated murder. They decided instead to do as instructed and picked up the chest with a three-count and carried it awkwardly to the edge of the platform. The red chest with golden highlights groaned under the considerable weight the whole way until they set it down in the soft grass.

As soon as it was set down, Acan came over and unlocked the chest with a key. He opened it and confirmed the tiny chunks of ice were still okay. "We carried an ice chest over a mile?" Chip remarked.

"What's a mile?" Hatsumi asked.

"Two and a quarter kilometers," Acan answered as he shut the lid. He turned the key back the other way and the key gave off a chime like a silver bell had been struck. He pulled the key out and opened the chest to reveal the ice was now full of glass bottles of various liquids. Acan picked up one of the bottles and smacked the top with his palm. The rounded top of the bottle revealed to be a lodged sphere that dropped down into the bottle proper. He took a sip of the liquid and nodded. "Good job, boys."

Chip took one of the bottles and studied it. "You guys have soda?"

"They're not carbonated, but yes," Acan said, opening the bottle for Chip.

As Chip took a sip, surprised at the vague sarsaparilla flavor, Cadria came by the boys. "Thank you, father," she told Acan as she shut the chest and then reopened it. A different variety of bottles were available and she selected something with a shock red color to it. As Acan headed over to join Matilda on their blanket, Cadria tried twice to pop the top, then handed it to Hatsumi and looked expectantly. He accepted the bottle and opened it for her, handing it back. "Thank you," she said far too sweetly, and she walked off.

"What the hell have we gotten ourselves into?" Hatsumi asked Chip.

Before Chip could answer, Matilda came over to the boys and looped their arms in her own. "Now I want you two to have some fun," she gushed at them as she led them around to the front of the platform as the band began to tune up. A few of the young people were gathering onto the platform under the lights. A few started to dance while the sky overhead continued to darken. "Our village is a happy place and you two look like you could use some merriment."

"Merriment?" Chip repeated, checking with Hatsumi. With surprising strength, Matilda pushed them both up the stairs towards the platform. They went with her physical insistence and joined the other young and single types. The platform had a large red circle painted in the center, a band of checkered blue and gold around it.

January came to Hatsumi and took his hand. "May I have this dance?" she asked.

"Th-there's no mu—" The farmer's daughter didn't take no for an answer. She yanked Hatsumi into the red circle, slapped his hand on her hip, and began to saunter about with a lively step. Chip snickered, almost laughing, until he spotted Cadria coming for him. He quickly spun around and looked for anything to warrant taking him off the dance platform. He grabbed for the utility belt hidden under his vest and the smoke bombs beneath but he wasn't fast enough and Cadria caught his hand.

"Let's dance!" she squealed with uncomfortable, childish delight. With a strength that belied her youth and size, she tugged Chip out into the dancing.

As the evening wore on, Chip found himself at the food tables, looking up at the clouds. One of the musicians sat apart from the others, an older woman with deep lines and only a few lingering locks of faded brown among her otherwise silver hair. With an unremarkable woodwind, she played quietly on the far side of the dance platform. Her notes lost to the band, the effects were not.

Above her, the cloud that hung above the valley was shifting colors. Like a watercolor come to life, the cloud hung lower than a fluffy tuft of vapor should and didn't move with the refreshing evening breeze. It shifted with pastel highlights, as though lit from some distant sunset. All the while, the woman swayed with her own music, creating a swirl of colors unlike any Chip had seen.

As he watched the performance, a young child came over to the woman. She smiled and ceased playing, the two talking. She beamed as the child spoke and then nodded enthusiastically. As the child ran back to his parents, the musician resumed playing and the cloud began to take on green hues. The favorite color came to prominence as the woman catered to the request.

Heva came up beside Chip, filling a small wooden bowl with another round of crispy leaves from a native tree. Chip noted her and moved to give her better access to the bowl. "Thanks," she said cooly.

"You're not much of a dancer," remarked Chip. Heva only shrugged, black curly hair clashing with her blue dress. "You also don't seem thrilled to be married off by your mom."

Heva checked back at Matilda as she and Acan danced together on the grass by their blanket. Fireflies flashed in the interim space between the devoted couple and their watching daughter. "Mother loves being married," she said before biting a crisp. "She loves..." Uncertain of the best word, Heva took a leaf straight from the plate and crunched it. "She wants us to be happy."

"Nothing wrong with that," Chip said.

Heva didn't argue. She only said, "I'm just not really the marrying type."

Chip only nodded and agreed. "Nothing wrong with that either."

Heva ate another crisp, then turned to Chip abruptly. About to speak some critical truth, the noise Chip heard was instead a gong. His confusion was shared by Heva, though, because she turned to the far edge of the valley. A man in a sharp suit with a red vest came briskly towards the platform. The music stopped, as did the dancing. Chip looked to the platform where Hatsumi was caught with Cadria. The young girl's playful and incompetently-flirty demeanor was replaced with real worry.

"Sorry, folks," said the man who had rushed to the platform. He dashed up the steps and removed a short stovetop hat. "We've got to end the party early."

"What's going on?" asked one of the older boys near Hatsumi. His question was echoed by many others in the crowd.

The man said, "The Nightstorm's heading back."

The title, enigmatic to Chip and Hatsumi, was clearly known to the others. After only a moment of shock, they quickly began to collect their belongings. Hatsumi checked with Chip and ran to join him, letting questions come later. He leapt down off the platform, him and Chip going for the chest, but Acan called to them. "Leave it."

Hatsumi and Chip both let it drop. "No problem!" Hatsumi declared. He and Chip ran to help the family grab the rest of their belongings and rush out of the valley.

With a flip of his wrists, Chip sent the blanket fluttering over the bed of blankets set atop the straw. In the next stall to him, Hatsumi was sitting on the edge, untying his shoelaces. They both heard the barn door open and several of the farm animals react favorably to an arrival. "Hatsumi? Chip?" It was Acan calling.

The pair went to the rickety ladder as Acan began to ascend. With a candle in-hand, he rose up onto the loft level and asked, "Are you two comfortable?"

"Yeah," said Chip.

"It smells like methane, but yeah," Hatsumi said with a crinkle to his nose.

"I didn't get the chance to say it before but I wanted to thank you both for your discretion," Acan said as he set the candle aside. "I don't hide much from my wife but I've never felt it beneficial to explain my background to her."

"No man, we're not going to snitch," said Chip. In the ensuing silence, he realized the colloquialism didn't translate for his partner or their host. "I, uh, I did want to ask you about this whole Nightstorm-thing. What is it?"

"It's just a storm," Acan told them. "It comes down off the mountains with these really intense gusts of wind but..." Now he shrugged. "It's not a big deal. It picks up around midnight and it happens for a few nights in a row periodically but that's it. The people of the village just personify it as some figure. It's a common thing," he said predominantly to Chip.

"Are you sure?" Hatsumi pressed. "I mean, I know not everything in the world links back to magic but an entity that travels with the wind isn't exactly unheard of." Chip's head slowly turned on a swivel, leveling a terrified look at Hatsumi.

Acan only shook his head. "I've seen it all but I haven't seen any evidence there's anything to this. It's just a bad storm."

Chip took the opportunity to ask, "What about Earth?" The segue confused Acan. "Were you stationed there? How do you know about it?"

"Yeah, Kageryu placed me there," Acan told him. "I stayed in a city called Kabul." The name didn't mean much to Chip. "Actually it wasn't Kageryu, it was one of the other dragons. One of the twins, Bahamut or Tiamat. They requested it. Something about how the line of ninja on Earth was deteriorating or something."

"The line of ninja?" Chip asked. "Are the ninja a lineage, or an ethnic group?"

Acan's absence of an answer was obvious. "I don't know," he told Chip. "But on Earth, I was an assassin and an investigator. A spy. I wasn't a researcher or historian. Your Chunin, Kagumi would likely know more."

"Yeah, if she'd answer a question," Hatsumi remarked.

The comment made Acan chuckle. "Yeah. Forest spirits are a quiet bunch."

"Forest spirits?" asked Chip, as much to Hatsumi as Acan.

"It's what my wife calls the ninjas," Acan told Chip. He rose from where he'd been leaning and told the two boys, "Get some sleep. Rest well."

"You too," Hatsumi told him.

"Yeah, good night," Chip told Acan. The pair stayed still until they heard him depart, then looked at each other. "Let's go find the Nightstorm," said Chip.

"Uh, yeah," Hatsumi agreed, already grabbing his boots.

The blustering wind that blew under the night sky was intense and intermittent. Strong, fierce pulses of wind were punctuated with moments devoid of any movement at all to the air. With the town's windows shuttered and all the residents hidden away, the trail was dark. No stars in the sky to provide light, there was no shadow or contrast.

Chip slipped around the edge of a building at the town's center. The heart of the village was made up of a scattering of buildings, different from the homesteads only due to their commercial purpose. Chip checked down the street in both directions, then drew back to the wall. "I can't see a damn thing," he whispered.

"Here, let me," said Hatsumi. He slid around Chip to the edge of the building. He leaned out and, eyes longer trained by the Shinobi, checked the dark world of the windy night. While he looked, though, Chip listened. As another gust of wind buffeted around them, the air moving in a new direction, Chip caught a sound. He turned into the wind and held up his hand, protecting his eyes from the coursing air.

Noticing Chip's displaced attention, Hatsumi asked just loudly enough to be heard over the wind, "What is it?"

"I hear something," said Chip. He pushed away from the wall, leaning into the wind. He discarded safety and secrecy and walked into the very center of the town. As if at the wind's most intense, Chip was forced to a knee in the gale force Hatsumi followed him, squinting and protecting his eyes. The darkness shifted and pulsed with the wind, as if the torrential air currents displaced light and darkness along with the air. His hand went for his sword which he wore on his back, the handle over his right shoulder.

Through the air, Chip could hear a hum. It was almost impossible to identify against the rushing in his ears but the more he focused, the more he worked to block out the ambient noise, the more he could discern. Like some celestial choir warming up their voices, he could almost make out ten thousand voices quietly readying themselves for their first note.

Chip closed his eyes and listened to the hum. He began to hum as well, trying to find the pitch. He danced musically around it for a moment, then raised his own voice. Just as he heard Hatsumi shout, "Chip!", the wind evaporated.

In eerie stillness, Chip opened his eyes. The world was alight, as if filled with the dusky light beneath a full eclipse. The air was absolutely still and scalding hot. Between his feet, the surface of the world had been broken. A fissure wormed through the ground, centimeters narrow and impossibly deep. Within the fissure was not darkness or even magma, but pure light. A radiant prism that cascaded noisily out into one pure burst, shooting into the sky like limitless energy rising into the starry heavens.

Chip followed the crack in the ground, tracking it up through the village center. The burning light made no sound yet it drowned out all other noises. It cast now shadow but it drove out all light. It had no sensation and yet it burned just to be in its presence. The break in the world extended almost out of sight, into the forest beyond the town. Yet through the silhouettes of the trees, Chip could see movement born not of the shimmering light but from life.

"Hey!" Chip yelled, running for the forest. The light beneath him began to flicker and fade, strikes of wind hitting him as the world shifted between two planes. The tangible world he knew and the darker world of harder hues and unforgiving absolutes. "Hey!" Chip yelled again, racing with full speed of Shinobi running.

He ran to the edge of the forest and leapt through the first line of trees. The split in the ground was greater here, a deepening chasm that let out light brighter than a sun. It was an act of harmful strength for Chip to look even towards the light. Hand up and eyes squinted, he danced his gaze around the light, trying to make his way.

At the cusp of the chasm, he saw a figure. Taller than him, and exceptionally thick, the masculine form was made of might. Brawny shoulders and thick joints stood motionlessly at the edge of the broken world, staring down into the light. A tunic fluttered at his thighs and a pair of short swords hung from a thick belt. Recognition but not placement flashed in Chip's mind and he ran for the man. "Hey!" he yelled. His hand went for his own straight-bladed ninja sword, worn at his side.

The figure turned and a pair of glowing red eyes set beneath short black hair turned back to Chip. He saw the steely gaze and powerful jaw of a forgotten enemy. Chip exclaimed, "Octavius!"

One brilliant flash and Chip fell to his hands and knees. Rain pounded on him like a mob, icy chilling water battering him abruptly. He screamed in shock and pain and fell to his hands and knees as the intense wind blew through the forest trees. There was no sign of the break in the world, no evidence of the light or of Octavius. Only the bone-chilling cold of the storm and the intense, unforgiving night.

"Octavius," repeated Hatsumi with equal parts trepidation and panic-stoked awe. "Xelex's agent." He placed the bowl of hot water in Chip's hands and held them against it, letting the warm water give him some feeling back. Beneath a heavy woolen blanket, Chip shivered. Out of his rain-soaked clothes, droplets of rain still dribbling out of his darkened hair, the paler of the pair shivered. "You're sure?"

"Dude tried to kill me the first time I came to this world," Chip repeated, his teeth chattering. "I know who Octavius is." He opened his eyes and looked across the farm loft at Acan who moved little and said even less. "Your Nightstorm is a demon's right-hand man."

Acan exhaled slowly. He checked the window out from the loft which overlooked his home. The shutters closed, he could hear the rain battering against it. A few droplets made it in through the barrier's edges. "We've had storms, but never a storm like this." To Chip he asked, "You said he had...there was light coming out of the ground?"

"It was like a crack in a cartoon, like an earthquake," Chip explained, gesturing with fingers still red from frostbite. "Only instead of fire and stuff, it was light."

Almost desperate, Acan asked, "And you're sure it was Octavius."

"Kageryu's big-breasted bimbo, Astrokel, brought me to this world on accident," Chip yelled at Acan. "I ended up in the middle of a goddamn war between Xelex and the Shinobi. I practically fell right on top of Octavius and the dude tried to murder me. Trust me, I know who he is."

"Acan, we have to report this," Hatsumi apologized.

Acan countered defiantly, "What do you think Kagumi will do?"

Before he could continue with his rhetorical question, Hatsumi corrected him. "We aren't going to report this to Kagumi; we're going to report this to Kageryu."

That stifled Acan's attitude, but only for a moment. "And how do you plan to do that?" he asked. "The Shadow Dragon is an inconsistent thing. The Shinobi will go a hundred years and never see or hear from him. He sleeps for eons at a time, and comes and goes with whims more unpredictable than the breeze."

"Oh yeah, he's a flighty dick, but still," Chip argued.

"He's in charge, and he's the only one with the might to stand against Octavius," Hatsumi said. Chip opened his mouth to correct him but decided now wasn't the time.

Beside himself with hesitation, Acan ventured, "The storms are rarely single-night affairs. If Octavius is the cause, then..."

"Dude, what is your problem?" Chip asked defiantly and at an end of his patience. "Why are you so afraid of us reporting this?"

"Because I don't want the Shinobi here," Acan called back, his voice raising. He glanced instinctively at the window and towards his house on the other side of the night. "I don't know what Matilda would think of me. A-and I'm exiled, remember? I don't know how they'll respond to a former member."

"You sure didn't seem so hesitant to ask for medicine from Kagumi for what looks like a couple of dozen people with the sniffles," Hatsumi said. He stood and moved protectively between Acan and the chattering Chip.

"Asking for some medicinal trinkets from a friend is a far cry from reporting the agent of an interdimensional demon," Acan said. He paced back, trying to envelope the whole of the issue. "If the Shinobi come here, I will be outed. If the Shinobi come here, the village will be exposed and, and in danger and..."

"The village is already in danger," Hatsumi told the older man. "I mean, I'll concede we don't know what Octavius is up to but can you think of ANY time that Xelex or his agents have been seen that sorrow and misery didn't soon follow?"

"These storms have been happening for a long time," Acan dismissed. "We've never suffered any ill effects in the long term."

"Yeah, and you can Russian Roulette more than once before you lose," said Chip.

Acan looked at him, confused, then at Hatsumi. He only shook his head, used to such obtuse colloquialisms from Chip. "The threat may not be to you," Hatsumi implored to Acan. "Or it may be so gently levied against the village that you haven't noticed the toll it takes. Xelex's machinations can be remarkably subtle. And if there is anything Octavius is known for, it is patience and unyielding determination."

Acan wiped his brow and sighed. "Just...just give me a night," he asked of them. Practically pleading, he explained, "Give me a night to confirm what you, Chip, have seen. The three of us, we can lay our eyes upon Octavius. If we...if it is..." He relented. "Then report it you must." It almost pained him to say that. "But indulge me. Let us, let me, be sure."

Hatsumi looked back at Chip. The blonde boy shook his head and looked away. Hatsumi turned back to Acan and nodded. "Okay. We'll give you tomorrow night."

Hatsumi surfaced from the hot water with a gasp, nearly shooting out of the pool. He laughed as he exited the water, then flopped back with a great splash. A wave of the steaming water went spilling out over the rocks and sprinkling on the grass beyond.

"I love hot springs," Hatsumi said, backstroking to the edge of the crystal-clear water. The small stone outcropping in the middle of the dense forest was surrounded by trees. In this sylvan privacy, Hatsumi and Chip unwound. At the edge of the water, Hatsumi looked across the modest pool and asked, "How are you doing?"

"I still can't get this chill out of me," Chip said. He was pulled in on himself, as if he were still in the blistering rain. Even as the water steamed around him, he gave off the tiniest shiver. He opened his eyes and looked down. Through the clear water, he could see the rocky ground going through to the base of the pool and the cracks from which came the water. "We've got pools like this on Earth, in Yellowstone," Chip remarked in thought. "They freaked me out. I had no idea how deep they went."

Hatsumi looked down at the craggily break in the stone floor, darkness just beyond the edges smoothed by watery erosion. "Afraid something would swim up and grab you?" he teased.

Chip smirked. "I used to think that was a silly idea. Then I came here." He laughed, as did Hatsumi. Their laughter was spiced with a few giggles from beyond the edges of the hot spring. Both of them rose a bit and surveyed the area. It was only when they saw their pants yanked off the bush that they spotted their stalker.

Out from behind the bush appeared Cadria. The young girl had some of their clothes bundled up in her arms. With a mischievous grin, she giggled at them and then turned to run. With surprising speed for a girl so young, she dashed into the woods, disappearing into the dense forest.

"What the holy hell?" Chip asked as he stared into the forest. He looked back at Hatsumi who was just as astonished.

"I guess this is her idea of flirting?" ventured Hatsumi.

"Who gets a husband by stealing his belongings?" Chip asked, getting out of the water. He went over to the bush and checked around it. "Oh good, she left us our shirts and our shoes." He started to roughly brush himself down with the flat of his hand, trying to wring off any excess water. Hatsumi made a series of gestures with his hand and then winced as his body went flush. His normally pale skin flared

red for a moment as if he had a body-wide infection. The water on his skin evaporated. His skin returned to normal and he dropped forward, light-headed and in pain.

"Yeah, you need to stop doing that," Chip told him, draping Hatsumi's shirt over his face. He began to pull on his own shirt. "That ninja hand magic doesn't seem worth it."

"Samijitsu is a hallmark of our Shinobi training, oh god why does it hurt so much?" he groaned, holding his head.

"Maybe because you had a body temperature of a hundred and seventy damn degrees for ten seconds?" suggested Chip as he tied his shoes. He looked down at his bare thighs. "I guess this prank was predicated on us having no shame."

"I'll concede you're shameless," Hatsumi grumbled as he pushed up from the bush. He returned to the hot spring to rinse his face.

"Hey, I have some shame; I'm ashamed of you," Chip teased. He looked around the area, remarking, "Thank goodness we didn't bring any of our gear." He was about to say more when singing rang through the woods. Chip gave a tiny shriek and covered up, blushing from head to toe. Hatsumi saw and snorted, trying to keep from laughing out loud. "What is that?" Chip asked.

"If it's another wood nymph, I'm leaving right now, Octavius or no," Hatsumi told Chip as he walked passed him. Hatsumi led the way through the woods, pantless thighs making them cautious about passing through the underbrush. They carefully followed the singing that echoed off the trees, only to discover another hot spring. There, at the edge of the pool, January lay stretched out.

Singing just a bit too loudly to be solely for herself, she was bent over as she unlaced her boots. The effort to be sultry and attractive was more gawkish and off-putting. As she hummed and sang wordlessly, her long hair fell down into the hot water. She cursed to herself and stood, getting a face full of water-logged hair. The heavy locks smacked her hard enough to make her stumble and she fell over her own basket of bathing materials.

Hatsumi stared, utterly dumbfounded, as Chip facepalmed.

January recovered herself and resumed singing. She was almost on-tune. She kicked off her boot, a feat that required several flicks of her foot. When it finally went flinging across the grass, she bent over again to untie the other boot. The difference in height between her feet caused her to stumble and she nearly fell over with a shout.

Chip whispered, "Oh my god, I've had enough of this crap."

"It's kind of flattering?" Hatsumi half-suggested with a disgusted expression.

"Yeah, to have prostitot steal our clothes and this middle school strip show?" Chip asked. "I feel gross just knowing this is happening." He turned and snuck off from the tree they had hid behind. Hatsumi agreed and followed.

At the edge of the forest, the spacious daylight just a few more steps beyond, Hatsumi and Chip found Heva waiting. The long-haired eldest daughter of Acan and Matilda had blankets wrapped over her arm. As she saw the two approach, some distance still between her and them, she rose from the tree she had leaned against. Making eye-contact with the pair, she let the blankets drop from her arms, then departed the forest.

The two Shinobi gathered the blankets and wrapped them around their waists. Heavy fabric that could easily double as storm curtains, the two wore the blankets like armored kilts.

"She's the only one really marrying age and she's not interested," Hatsumi asked to Chip.

"I think there are three options," Chip posed to his friend. "She's a mature person who is in no rush to jump into arbitrary milestones of adulthood. Or she has taste and thus doesn't find us attractive."

"Very likely," Hatsumi agreed.

"Or she's a lesbian," Chip finished.

Hatsumi looked confused. "She hasn't shown much artistic skill."

"That's thespian, moron."

Hatsumi looked after Heva for a moment, then back to Chip. "What's lesbian mean again?"

"A woman who likes women," said Chip.

"Oh," Hatsumi nodded. He thought for a moment, then looked even more confused. "How would that even work?"

"It's a good thing you're cute," Chip teased with a disappointed shake of his head. They started out of the forest.

Matilda opened the cooking closet to reveal a large cast-iron bowl. She took it from the middle rack at waist height above the embers burning in the metal tray at the base of the closet. She used magnetic stones to lift the metal bowl off the rack and set down in a waiting mold at the edge of the table. It fit perfectly and the table began to groan with comfortable heat expansion.

Acan removed the metal lid off the bowl, the smell of rich vegetable stew filling the house. Hatsumi and Chip both instantly found their mouths watering. Sitting opposite the three daughters, their eyes were locked on the meal. "Honey, you have outdone yourself." Acan scooped up a plate and served it to Cadria first.

"I'm glad you boys decided to stay for a few days," Matilda told Chip and Hatsumi. "It will give us the chance to have some more company." She smiled at Acan civilly, then at her daughters, almost like daring them. Chip and Hatusmi noticed the look and both swallowed tightly.

"It is nice to have some help with the chores," Acan acknowledged. "Maybe we should consider hiring some workers," he proposed. "We've got the space, and we definitely could benefit from the additional hands."

"I was just thinking how nice it is to hear the pitter-patter of friendly feet," Matilda told her husband.

As the two talked, Chip felt a foot toe against his own. He glanced at Hatsumi who was stirring his stew. Chip tried to pick up on some subtle clue he should take notice of but didn't see anything. He felt the nudge against his foot again. He checked Hatsumi again, studied the way he stirred his stew, the way he was breathing. He watched for some indication of what his partner was trying to get him to pay attention to.

The next contact with his foot wasn't a gentle stroke of a toe but a kick to his shin. Chip barely kept from calling out in surprise, only to realize it wasn't Hatsumi. He looked across the table at Cadria. She batted her lashes at him, an act which looked less enticing and more like she had something in her eye. A sense of panic and mild revulsion stuck in Chip's mind and he forgot about eating.

"I'm just glad the barn is comfortable," Matilda was saying as the dinner carried on around Chip's awkwardness. "Of course, I think we might want to consider some expansions to the house." Matilda looked at Heva and nodding goadingly. The eldest daughter looked around, certain there was no way her mother was talking to her. "Don't you have something to say?"

"...no?" said the otherwise reserved young woman.

"About you and this one," Matilda lead on with a nod towards Hatsumi.

"What about this one?" Chip asked with a rush as he yanked his foot under his chair.

"I've seen the chemistry between you two," Matilda told her daughter and Hatsumi.

"What chemistry?" Heva, Hatsumi, and Chip all asked in unison.

"Honey," Acan spoke up. He made a calming gesture.

Matilda turned her head with a huff. "Well." She seemed genuinely upset. "I suppose the barn is adequate after all." Chip looked at Acan, demanding an explanation, but the former ninja didn't have the reserves to make eye-contact. "Still," said Matilda, her tone softening, "with the storms, I'd hate to think of you out there in the wilds, going back to Seir-reth, when the rain started."

"I don't know about the rain, but coming here was a pretty smooth trip," Hatusmi told her as he batted his lips with a napkin. "We're mostly glad that you—"

He was interrupted by a distant gong striking. The air throbbed with the far-off note, the silence that followed each strike growing more intense and ominous. Chip and Hatsumi both looked across the table at Acan. The head of the household buried his fear and averted his eyes.

Little more was said at dinner.

A torrent of rain pounded against the shutters of the barn. Dressed in the dark blue of his Shinobi attire, Chip paced. A straight-bladed ninjato worn at his side, he walked back and forth across the loft on split-toe tabi sandals. His steps caused the wood to creak a tiny bit, the chill of the rain making the world seem small. The lantern over the straw pallets swung gently. Shadows were tossed about the room. The stuffy air wasn't entirely devoid of occasionally chilling tufts that blew through cracks and slits.

Chip spun abruptly as Hatsumi ascended the steps. He wore a dark green outfit similar to Chip's, only with more armor. The loose clothes meant for action were tied at the joints, ensuring movement was never impinged. Hatsumi wore hard ceramic greaves and bracers as well as spaulders and chest plates sewn into his deep green ninja outfit. He pulled down his rain-strewn cowl and removed the ceramic half-mask over his mouth. "It's seriously coming down."

"I thought this was just supposed to be winds and stuff," said Chip, returning to his pacing. He looked at the window shuddered tight against the storm. "And where's Acan?"

"Checking on his family," Hatsumi told Chip in a hard tone. "Come on, man."

"Yeah, well, we're waiting on him solely because he wanted to investigate," Chip grumbled, recognizing his own impatience. "If it is Octavius, what do we do?"

"Run," Hatsumi laughed, assuming stating the course of action was rhetorical. "I've known people who have fought Xelex's harbinger. Most of them aren't around anymore."

Chip checked the window again and sighed. "I've beaten him."

"Yeah," Hatsumi acknowledged. "And you can play Russian Roulette more than once before you lose too." Chip didn't look back at him but Hatsumi could tell he was smiling in spite of himself.

They heard the barn doors open and the animals below called out gratefully They both went to the edge of the loft and looked down. Acan turned from shutting the doors, wearing the clothes of a Shinobi Chunin. All black, his outfit mirrored Hatsumi's with hard plastic armor, more befitting a SWAT officer from Earth. He pulled his cowl down from his face and looked up at the two boys. They looked at him and needed to say nothing.

The rain didn't fall so much as pound against the three ninja as they clung to the building's wall. Near the village center, they knelt by the rocky base of the building and let the lee side of the structure give them some shelter. Hatsumi pulled down his ceramic half-mask and yelled over the gale force winds, "How long are we going to search?"

"Last time I heard something," Chip yelled back, at the front of the trio. "Something in the wind. I don't..." He didn't know what else to offer.

"Like Xelex laughing at us?" Hatsumi scolded.

"What did you do after you heard it?" asked Acan, behind Hatsumi. "You hummed, right? You tried to—" He covered up as a gust of wind brought more rain against them. The lip of the building broke and water began to pour relentlessly on them as if they were beneath a waterfall.

Chip grabbed Hatsumi and pulled out from the running water and they ran to the very heart of the village. Acan ran to the rear of the building but found himself bombarded with rain. He growled in irritation and covered his face. Realizing the boys hadn't followed him, Acan checked back to the front of the building. He saw them in the village center, in the middle of the intersecting roads.

About to race to them, Acan heard a window opening. He glanced to one of the neighboring businesses and the residence above. He spotted shutters being pulled open, to check on the world outside. He quickly dashed across the rear of the building, around to the far end. Once he was hidden from prying eyes, he ran with preternatural speed. Feet remembering long-ingrained skills, Acan was at the front of the building in a flash. He turned to look down the road where Hatsumi and Chip had been, only to find them gone.

The crossroads at the very heart of the village was empty.

In absolute stillness and throbbing heat, Hatsumi and Chip saw the dark silhouette of a figure at the very edge of the chasm of light. The ground broken right before them, warping and winding through the center of town, the light from deep within was blinding and painful. Where the light shone, the buildings eroded. Aging years in a matter of seconds, Chip and Hatsumi could see the whole village beginning to waste away.

The world beyond the blinding and scalding light was drab and flat, even as it wasted away beneath accelerated entropy. The sky was eroding, clouds and stars replaced with existential apathy. The air choked in their mouths, acrid and hostile. Their very breath felt pained while movements felt stiff and disjointed, like they were passing through waters of different densities and different temperatures.

"What's causing that?" Chip asked of Hatsumi. Even as a whisper, his voice carried like a shout. Not only did Hatsumi hear, so too did Octavius.

Ahead of them, half-hidden by the chaotic intensity of the light coming from the broken chasm of the ground, was a figure turned away. His head was down, staring into the endless intensity of the light. When Chip spoke, the stoic figure's head rose and he turned from the chasm. Shoulders like boulders and arms like granite, he faced the two Shinobi. Gray skin and short, curly black hair paired off with dark eyes with the subtlest glow of red. He wore a white tunic befitting the two Gladius swords that hung from a dark leather belt on his waist.

"Why do you interrupt me?" asked Octavius. His voice was like cast iron and resonated with other-worldly might.

"What are you doing?" Chip yelled as if the wind was still howling.

"We need to go," Hatsumi said, grabbing Chip's arm and unsuccessfully trying to pull him away.

"Listen to your friend," Octavius warned Chip. His glance towards Hatsumi chilled him to the core.

"What are you doing?" Chip yelled again, wrenching his arm free of Hatsumi's grip. He drew his sword and, with a glance at the village decaying around him, called, "Why are you doing this?!"

"I'll suffer no further delays," said the gray man. He turned and faced back into the light.

Chip ran for Octavius, holding his sword ready. He swung with the force to slice apart wood but connected with nothing. Octavius was suddenly beside Chip. He caught both his hands with his left and punched Chip in the face with his right. He grabbed Chip behind the head and yanked his head down into his knee, ending the fight immediately. Chip's dazed body was tossed to the ground, blood draining from a broken nose.

Hatsumi looked at the downed Chip, discarded like a bad thought, then at Octavius. The figure was only a black outline to Hatsumi, save for the pair of red eyes that were now fixed firmly and completely upon him. "And what will you do, child? Help your friend? Or join him in his suicidal foolishness?"

Terror filling his eyes and stealing smoothness of action, Hatsumi nonetheless reached for his own sword, beginning to draw it. The ring of the blade leaving his scabbard was drowned out by a new, deeper voice. "There's a third course of action," it said. "The one he should have taken to begin with." Octavius turned when through the soul-shattering light stepped Kageryu. "He should have called me."

With speed beyond human potential, Kageryu grabbed Octavius' collar and yanked him forward. At the same time bending his own arm, the towering man pulled Kageryu right into his elbow. The blow struck Octavius in the face and sent him stumbling.

More than a head taller than Octavius, Kageryu wore a sleeveless variant of Chip and Hatsumi's ninja uniform. Powerful arms with deep tanned skin twisted with sinewy muscle as Kageryu flexed his shoulders, as if warming himself up for a fight. An indistinct complexion and a casual intensity, the ninja stepped to keep himself between Octavius and his subordinate. Kageryu's eyes flashed with their own might as he fixed the full force of his intentions on his foe.

"What calls the attention of the Shadow Dragon?" asked Octavius. He drew the gladius from his right side. "I thought I was beneath you." He drew the gladius from his left side. "Have you really nothing more befitting your celestial mind than to meddle in my mundane affairs?"

"I don't keep the counsel of Xelex's stooges," Kageryu snarled.

"No," Octavius told him a cold, indifferent tone. "You merely lie to children and send them to do your work for you."

In the instant Kageryu glanced back to Hatsumi, Octavius attacked. He slashed with the gladius in his right hand, then thrust across his own arm with the gladius in his left. Kageryu dodged the first, then parried the second and responded with a punch. It was a quick jab with no commitment but it still knocked Octavius off his feet. He landed roughly but kept rolling over his shoulder and came to his feet. When he rose, he showed no signs of damage or injury.

Kageryu approached slowly, steps of tabi sandals like gunshots in the absolute silence of the bright world. Hatsumi ran in a wide arc around the fight and to get to Chip. He grabbed him up and shook him lightly, waking Chip with a start. "We've got to get out of here," said Hatsumi. He pulled Chip to his feet and slung an arm across his shoulders.

The sound of steel striking steel was like a gunfight in high speed. Kageryu faced Octavius with an absolutely massive katana, a weapon of such length and heft, it was more a polearm than a two-handed weapon. Even for his great size and muscle, the weapon looked a hair too big on him. He wielded it with skill and ease, however. Yet against Octavius, he struggled.

Octavius' paired short swords moved like a dervish. He fought with no flair or style, only function. He kept pressure against Kageryu, slicing constantly, the backswing of a strike only a wind-up for the following blow. Each step a kick, trip, sweep. Every shift in balance, no matter how subtle, an offensive measure. His relentless attack had Kageryu on the retreat for a moment, but only a moment.

With a burst of force, Kageryu blocked a strike and the connection of the blades flashed with light and sound. The world transposed for a second, light becoming dark and dark becoming light. Octavius was thrown back and it gave

Kageryu ample opportunity to turn his blade on him. Before Octavius could react, Kageryu ran Octavius through, driving his massive katana all the way to the hilt.

No blade pierced Octavius' back. For a weapon nearly as long as Octavius was tall, there was no exit wound. The agent of Xelex looked up at Kageryu's haughty eyes and glowered. He spoke something to the Shadow Dragon but even in the silent world, the words were lost to Chip and Hatsumi.

Like a wisp of nighttime cloud blown away by the dawn breeze, Octavius faded from sight. Disappearing off of Kageryu's sword, he was gone in the span of a breath, leaving the towering ninja holding his complete blade once again. Chip and Hatsumi both suddenly realized they were alone in the silent world with Kageryu. Chip looked back but saw the crack in the world gone. "Wh-what happened?" he asked.

Chip's voice carried like a gunshot in the flat world. A seamless, featureless world of shadow and mixed hues of nothing was all around them. The sky above looked indistinct and the ground beneath their feet was featureless and void. They were in an endless vacuum of color, devoid of even meaningful darkness.

"You got your ass kicked," Kageryu told Chip, approaching. He put a finger to Chip's forehead and agony struck. Chip screamed in pain for only a second, then dropped to his knees. With the pain came sensations. Rain was pouring down on him, washing blood from his face. Wild winds were a cacophony of natural sounds. Chip could breathe through his nose again and with a simple touch, he could tell it had been reset. He faced into the rain at Kageryu who stared down at him in displeasure.

The great Shinobi barely even glanced up at the sky and the rain lightened almost immediately. Dwindling to a drizzle, the ceasing storm revealed the state of the village. The buildings were broken and eroded. Rotted wood had crumbled under its own weight. Walls were taken over by vines. Cobblestone paths were destroyed by weeds pushing up between the stones. Trees ruptured through buildings that were little more than crumbling corpses of rotted materials. As if forgotten by the ages, the entire village was wasting away. Chip and Hatsumi stood with Kageryu in the heart of not even a ghost town.

Hatsumi turned in disorientation, not grasping what he was seeing. The forest had encroached into the town. The farmland overtaken by nature. Fences had fallen from disrepair and the buildings were full of mold. "What happened?" To Kageryu, he asked, "What was that, my lord?"

"Oh, you do remember your manners," quipped Kageryu. With eyes suddenly wide with realization, Hatsumi bowed his head and backed away from Kageryu. "I don't mean...I don't need that!" he chastised. "I just...come on, I'm me." He gestured at himself like he was a big deal.

"What was Octavius doing?" asked Chip, the pain of instant healing subsiding. He pulled himself up onto unsteady legs, his joints stiff like he'd been asleep for a full day.

Kageryu paced away from the pair for a moment. When he finally looked back at Chip, he said, "You're an idiot." He looked at Hatsumi. "But you should know better. You don't engage the agents of Xelex." Hatsumi averted his eyes in shame. "You should have contacted your Chunin as soon as you even suspected involvement. Katie would have told you—"

"Kagumi," Chip corrected.

"Kagumi would have told you to leave immediately," Kageryu amended without hesitation.

"Yes, my lord," Hatsumi accepted. Chip did not.

"What was Octavius doing?" he repeated. Chip gestured at the decayed and destroyed village. "Was this his doing? Or yours?"

"Careful," Kageryu warned lightly.

"You knew Octavius was up to something," Chip all but accused Kageryu. "You wouldn't have shown up so abruptly if you didn't already know and were watching. And if Octavius was up to something by extension, that means Xelex was or is up to something. What was he doing here?"

Kageryu's admiration for Chip's bravery was almost equal with his irritation with his irreverence. "Gathering." He looked at Hatsumi, as if to see if he had any additional questions. Hatsumi's eyes were still cast down, as was his head in obedient deferment. Back to Chip, Kageryu expounded. "He was scraping lichen off the cave walls. Gathering mushrooms in the forest. Checking for loose change in the gutter."

Chip couldn't follow. "He was farming?"

"As accurate a description as a million others," Kageryu told him. "You're a square attempting to comprehend a cube."

"Sir." It was Hatsumi. His voice was timid but he still willed himself to speak. "What of Acan?"

For the briefest moment, Kageryu's expression softened. For the briefest moment, there was genuine remorse in his eyes. "Acan never existed."

"So he was a plant?" Chip asked, not following. "He was some actor you planted, or somebody else planted to—"

"Acan existed," Kageryu corrected harshly. "Acan existed, until that fight, and then Acan never existed."

Hatsumi understood and stiffened in abject horror. "He was erased from existence."

"Every person in that village was transformed," Kageryu said. He spoke down, specifically to Chip. "Every life was altered. Most didn't escape with existence. Even their memory is gone from those who might have known them." He backed away from Chip with disdain. "You're fortunate." He didn't expound on the multitude of ways that was. When he looked up, Chip and Hatsumi did the same. The wild forest that had overtaken the forgotten village was gone. Instead, they looked up into the three towering trees of home, the Shinobi stronghold. Bridges were strung between the three mighty trunks, great structures built of living wood between the branches.

"Return to your team," Kageryu told them curtly, with a nod towards the arboreal metropolis above their heads. "Kagumi will likely not remember your assignment. You may be punished for going off-site without permission. I'll make sure it's not too harsh." He faded from sight, not unlike how Octavius had disappeared. The last to depart was his tone of condemnation.

Hatsumi covered his face and dropped into a squat. "I can't believe it." He let out a long and deep sigh of relief. "We were this close to being dead. Deader than dead." He dropped his hands from his head and looked expectantly and accusatorily up at Chip.

Chip remained standing. He looked at the bridges that crossed between the skyscraper-sized trees that were the heart of home. Ninjas crossed, a few glancing down at the pair. None addressed them or even made any appreciable note of them. Content they were somewhat safe, Chip indulged in a sigh as well. "Every time I've had any dealing with Octavius, it's gone very badly."

"It's worse with Xelex," Hatsumi warned him. He rose and shook his head, in awe at their good fortune and bad luck. He was quick to add, "There's a reason we have a standing policy not to engage the demon, or his agents." Needing to let it drop, Hatsumi clapped Chip on the shoulder and said, "Come on. We've got to go check in." He started for the nearest of the three trees.

Chip lingered. He stared into the middle distance, towards this most recent run-in with Octavius and the specter of Xelex operating in the shadows behind him. Something ate at Chip but unable to identify it, he turned and followed Hatsumi into home.

Robert V Aldrich

Healing Prowess

Evein's palm was glowing slightly as he stopped the blood flowing from the cow's hind leg. Evein sucked out of the corner of his mouth as he worked, the light flickering a bit from his palm. "Come on, not too much," he said to himself as he circled his hand a bit over the cut.

The slash in the cow's hind quarters began to bleed again, but only a bit. Barely even a drop issued forth from the wound longer than Evein's forearm. "There we go," said the young man. The glowing from his palm ceased and he sighed with contented pride. He patted the cow on the back, causing it to moo loudly in protest. The sudden noise startled Evein and he recoiled.

The two farm boys sitting on the fence laughed at him. Like most of the country boys, they were shirtless and wearing denim pants. The boy in overalls sitting on the top of the fence nearly fell off, while his partner lodged between the second and top rung laughed from a more secure position. "Not one for cows, are you, healer?" teased the middle boy.

"I'm not used to big animals," Evein tried to defend, smiling self-consciously. The farmer boys hopped down off the fence and began to round up the cow. Evein collected a small bag of glass bottles holding an array of ointments. "Give her half of..." Evein leaned awkwardly to see beneath the cow. "Give him half of this tomorrow morning and the rest tomorrow evening." He handed over a vial of green liquid. "It will release the magic binding the wound and redirecting the blood."

Overalls accepted the vial and nodded, giggling noticeably less. "Thank you, healer," he told Evein. He mimed tipping a hat and then turned with his kin to lead the cow across the pasture. Evein snapped closed the brass clasp of his bag and slung it over his shoulder. He turned and looked around the field for a moment, disoriented by the sweeping green grass and tall trees that bowed in the late spring wind. The scent of ripening fruit and wild flowers filled the bright day.

Evein finally spotted the others dressed in white cloaks like his own. Trimmed in various colors, the class of a dozen were gathered around a great sow in an adjacent field. Kneeling over the sow was Def Alis. The instructor held his hands apart, his index fingers and thumbs extended to form a rectangle over the sow. Within his hands was a watery image of the pig's inner body.

As Evein neared, Def Alis was saying, "Do you all see it?" He asked not as a question but to make certain. He saw Evein joining the group and asked, "What do they see?"

Evein balked at being put on the spot like that. He looked at the internal image created by Def Alis' hands. He saw the sow's ribs, her lungs, and her assorted organs. The arteries and veins appeared to be in the right places and in working order. The pig's heart was pumping normally, if a bit slow since she was asleep. Her breath was— "A malignancy," Evein half-exclaimed, startled by the sight.

"Very good," Def Alis nodded, his approving smile crinkling his graying temples. "She has an abnormal growth in her lung. Cancer." The one word spoke volumes to the students. "Do you see it?" he asked again to the other students. Now a few students ventured the bravery to admit they did not. "Kalic, where is it?" The student, a year younger than Evein and two years behind him in studies, pointed at the image.

"What lobe?" asked Def Alis. When Kalic hedged, as did the others, their instructor released his hands. The image faded like a drawing in sand eroded by the surf. "This is why we come out here to study," he told them all. His was a patient tone, illustrating not that they had failed but they were in fact learning a truer lesson than porcine anatomy. "When you must label pages in a book, you think only about those pages. Seeing the animal in action, learning the intricacy and brilliance of its construction in person is—"

He was interrupted by the pig passing gas in her sleep.

The students all giggled and laughed, even Evein. Def Alis couldn't keep a straight face either. He succumbed to a chuckle. "I think we're good for today," he decided. He looked at the clear blue sky as the wind brushed back black hair with just a few strands of dignified silver. "Take this to heart," he told his students. He pulled back his white robes, the hem of his sleeves dotted with red triangles. "Books and practice and reading will take you a long, long ways. But the instant you are in the field – literally – your knowledge will be for naught. Your skills, your understanding, your magic, they won't be able to help others. Or worse, you'll know a healer's truest nightmare: to do harm." He let that statement hang over them like a curse, ever-ready to descend upon the inattentive. "What heals can hurt. Unless! Unless you learn to apply it. You need to be out here, in the world, helping people, helping animals, helping plants, helping life. Only then will you understand just what the books seek to teach you." He brushed down his robes and added, "Or you might even teach the books a thing or two." Some more giggles from the students. "Dismissed."

The students all let out a chorus to "Thank you!" and turned to head south out of the field.

"Where are you going?!" Def Alis exclaimed incredulously. The students froze and turned back to him. "The school day isn't done! Just because I brought you out into the field doesn't mean you don't have to get to your next class." He teased them in a sarcastically mocking tone, "Y'all don't get to go into town just because you're in the field." He pointed towards the campus. "Get."

With decidedly less enthusiasm, the students – all a spectrum of ages and ethnicities – turned and began to head back the dusty road towards the stone castle in the distance.

As the first orange light of dusk slipped through the windows, Def Abersoth came around to the table and lit a lantern. He let the wick catch to a healthy flame, then returned the glass enclosure. Evein was sitting at the table in the library, one of the few students who came up to the third-floor medical library. He had two large tomes laid out before him as well as a drawing pad stretched across his legs.

"What's this then?" asked Def Abersoth, coming around the table. He had to hold back a waist-length beard to see the drawing paper. A mountain of a man, the library's curator was also the coach for several of the school's sporting groups. A fan of heavy things and moving them, he could be mistaken for a two-legged oxen or a small hill if he sat motionless for long enough.

"It's an anatomical drawing," Evein said. He held the paper to the curator.

The big man took the drawing and squinted. "I don't have my glasses," he griped to himself, holding it so he could see in the daylight and not have to rely on the candles. The drawing was anatomically correct down to the placement of lymph nodes. "This is how you study?"

"More like meditate, really," Evein said as he accepted the paper back. "I started drawing when I was a first-year and it helped me keep all the parts straight."

"Very nice," Def Abersoth nodded. "You should consider a past time as an illustrator. We've dozens of manuscripts that could benefit from some illumination. Really helps make the—" The library curator was shhhed by a student.

"I'm not an artist; merely a hobbyist," Evein admitted sheepishly.

"What exactly do you think the difference is between the two, then?" Def Abersoth asked. "We've books in this library that would want for illustrations that good." He tapped Evein's page before seeing himself off. Evein looked down at the page. The figure was a simple construct, drawn with different colors to signify different structures: red for arteries, green for organs, so on. It was hardly a masterpiece.

"May I join you?" came a woman's voice.

"Yes, of co—" Evein said absently before he realized who had spoken.

Before he could react beyond dropping his mouth open, Maestro Sara sat down across from him. An older woman of exquisite beauty, she was without her customary headdress. Blonde hair, silvering with life, was tied in a pair of pigtails that brushed at her shoulders. She was without makeup and her flushed cheeks were all the more obvious. "Are you alright, ma'am?" Evein asked.

The leader of the school laughed. "Yes, I am fine. I went to play a round of racquetball with Def Almo." She rubbed her eyes which stung from sweat. "I told him not to let me win for once. He very generously illustrated my arrogance in my skills." She was shhhed by a student. "They're strict around here," she remarked with an amused glance. "I happened to notice you as I passed and I wanted to speak with you. Specifically about Premier."

In a flash, Evein rolled up the drawing paper and set it aside. Likewise with such speed did he close the books and place them on the corner of the table. He sat forward, hands dutifully together, as he gave Maestro Sara his undivided attention. The woman looked amused at the scene and remarked, "Oh but could more efficiency be applied to chores." To Evein she levied a more serious look and she breathed out. "I have...reservations."

"I'm the best choice, by far," Evein insisted to her. "I'm two years out from my apprenticeship. I've already logged over a hundred spell casts beyond my assignments and I've also logged over a dozen extra surgery hours. I help in the kitchen, I maintain some of the herbs, I've even helped Def Sampson and Nnamdi teach their classes."

The Maestro only nodded sagely. She sat back in the chair and set her hands on her stomach. "I understand. There's no doubt that you are a strong candidate. Perhaps, academically, the strongest candidate we've ever had. Academically." The stipulation made Evein nervous. "Yet there is a difference between knowledge and knowing."

"And the Premier student must know," Evein asked.

"The Premier student must possess both," the Maestro told him.

Evein tried not to become agitated. "Then who is the stronger contender?"

The sound of distant commotion caught Maestro Sara's attention. "There isn't a Premier every year," she said off-handedly as she got up. The remark struck Evein hard, but the growing din subsumed his attention. Outside the chamber, the clamber of rushing feet up the stone steps grew louder.

The Maestro led Evein to the door of the library chambers just as Def Alis rushed up. "Hunters. Looks bad."

Maestro Sara turned into the library and called, "Absersoth, your robe if you please." The big man took of his white robe with golden highlights and handed it to her. The Maestro held up the massive blanket of a coat and handed it back. She looked at Evein, judging his size. He looked down at his simple tunic and denim pants beneath. He gave the Maestro a nervous smile.

Moments later, Maestro Sara descended the stairs into the main keep of the school. She wore Evein's white robe, trimmed with light blue triangles along the cuffs and hem. Evein followed, looking decidedly out of place without a robe like all the other staff and students. In knee-length pants and a baggy undershirt, he looked more at place in a gym dressing room than responding to an emergency.

At the door of the school was a circle of villagers, standing supportively around one of their own. The man lay on the stone floor of the school's main foyer. He was dressed in the dyed-green leathers of the hunters. His smooth-soled boots were stained with blood. His blood. His left side was badly bleeding, but it was not the worst of his injuries. The right side of his face was blistering and already infected. His leathers around his shoulder were crisped and burned, as if they'd been thrown into an open flame.

Maestro Sara's face was a picture of horror. "What happened?!" she gasped. She rushed to the man's side and began to check his vitals. As she did, the foyer filled with students and instructors. All eyes fell on the badly wounded man.

"We were hunting in the northern woods," explained the lead hunter, a lithe man named Sebastian. He still carried his bow and quiver. "Keif here got separated from us." Sebastian shook his head. "We didn't see what happened. We only heard..."

"Heard what?" asked Def Alis, standing among the others. When he realized the students were amassed, he turned to them. "Return to your dormitories!" Few did much moving.

"Do as he says," Maestro Sara bellowed with a maternal command. The students hesitated but the other instructors turned and began to herd the curious out. Eyes remained fixed on the wounded man as the foyer was slowly emptied.

Def Alis knelt by Maestro Sara and the pair looked over his injuries. "What did this?" asked Def Alis, as much to the Maestro as of himself. He brushed the man's hair back and studied the blistering. "Did you fall into a fire?"

"No fire did this," said Maestro Sara. She stood and addressed the worried villagers. "Bring him into the main healing chamber. I shall see to this personally." She turned, removing the robe she had commandeered from Evein. "Go to my chambers. Bring me my angel robes."

"Y-yes ma'am," Evein said. He turned and rushed up the stairs.

As the villagers picked up their man, careful with his unconscious body, Def Alis rose and stepped near Maestro Sara. "What is this?" The head of the school was silent, until Def Alis asked, "...Sara?"

She looked at him, the boundaries of rank broken in the wake of something more terrifying. "I fear," she whispered to him. "I fear this was black magic." She stepped passed him, walking into the main healing chamber, leaving Def Alis to now share her worry.

The shuffle of feet accompanied the murmuring of the students. As a senior student, Evein acted as guide. He gestured the underclassmen through the doors that led to the balcony which overlooked the main chamber. Around the balchony, the student body filed in as the entire senior class helped maintain a semblance order. As Evein waved his junior classmates along the stadium seating, he spotted Def Abersoth and Alis. Both men were wearing their robes along with sullen looks as they approached. "Evein," said Def Alis as he neared. His cowl lowered, the robe looked more like the cape of a hero from some epic poem.

Def Abersoth took some note of the boy and remarked, "You're not aiding the Maestro?" He scoffed. "I thought that was an honor of the Premier student.

"He's not Premier," Def Alis said, simultaneously as Evein said the same thing.

Def Abersoth looked confused and more than a little disapproving. "Sure," he said with a shake of his head.

"Besides, this is a learning moment," said Def Alis, insisting with great certainty that which he was uncertain about. "The students will get to see the Great Crystal in use." Def Alis placed his hand on Evein's shoulder as he passed, walking into the balcony.

Def Abersoth lingered. "Really? You're not going to be Premier?" Evein could only shrug, just as lost as he. "There's no justice in this world," the big man griped as he headed in.

With the last of the students entering the balcony, Evein followed them in. While the others sat on the long benches, instructors and administrators sprinkled among them, Evein stood in the aisle along with other senior students. Def Alis was one of the few instructors who did as well.

The balcony was a long stone platform that wrapped around the wide circular chamber. Three rows of long benches created tight rings. Benches nearest to the edge were short and low to the ground, while the subsequent two were taller, allowing a good view for all. Said view focused down into the main healing chamber.

At the very center of the circular room was a large stone platform as if carved from the very living rock of the earth. It was seamless with the floor of the room itself, as though the castle had been built around that one platform. On the platform was Keif, the wounded hunter. Standing beside him was Maestro Sara, wrapped in the glowing majesty of the angel robes.

The robes of pristine white hummed like an angelic chorus and gave off a sovereign white light from within the very weave. The robe's style was identical to those worn by the students and faculty of the school. But while theirs were demarked with colors at the hem and cuffs, the angel robe was designated by sparkling diamonds of the purest cut.

Meastro Sara turned to the man and she waved her hand over his body, then looked up towards the ceiling. All eyes turned upward as the ceiling opened. Stone rescinded as easily as folded paper. Behind it, hidden by magics more ancient than the world itself, was the Great Crystal.

The size of a small wagon's wheel, the Great Crystal was a multi-faceted wonder. It lowered through subtle magics, floating effortlessly in the air and giving off gentle light from within. It hummed a tiny bit, the sound as comforting as the white light it gave to the world. A hush fell over the students and administrators alike as the crystal descended.

It lowered to Maestro Sara like a kindly friend coming to her aid. She reached to the crystal, her hand nearing it but never touching it. Aged fingers lowered and the Maestro looked at her broken reflection in a hundred tiny surfaces of the crystal. "We shall begin." Her words were low and her voice withdrawn but the statement carried in the room. It echoed off the stone floor and wall, rebounded along the balcony.

Maestro Sara turned to the man and waved her hand over him again. Knowing eyes searched the burns and the wounds, seeing the damage beyond the total and into the fragments. Before her was not an injured man but a host of interconnected systems that supported the life she needed to save.

The crystal began to glow brighter. The light took on a slight greenish hue and the humming changed its tone. The Maestro nodded, as thought they were conversing. She held her hand over the man and the crystal's glowing intensified. The man began to elevate. He floated off the stone platform, just as Maestro Sara lifted off the ground. She held her hands out to her sides and closed her eyes.

As the air throbbed with power emanating from the Great Crystal, the man upon the table began to shift. Light began to issue forth like a thick fog, billowing out from his wounds. The deeper, more serious the damage, the brighter the light. It shone like the day had never known, filling the great chamber with illumination. Evein tried to endure the light but it was too much. He had to avert his eyes, noting the instructors had to do the same.

The light persisted for only a moment, then it began to dim. The incandescent power grew dull and the light became manageable. Those with the strength to will themselves to face into the light cast their gaze down on the man. The light continued to issue forth from his wounds, but the most intense injuries were growing dimmer. As if the light was sealing the damage from within, the wounds were sealed up before their very eyes. Cuts and abrasions, deep gashes and infected nicks, all were repaired by the intense holy light summoned forth by the Maestro and the Great Crystal.

The light quickly dwindled, as did the humming, until once again the chamber had returned to the light of candles and torches. A hush passed over the chamber. The students and instructors alike were all in awe of what they had seen. Careful glances were passed around.

Evein waddled out of the water closet, still rubbing his rinsed hands together. In the late night, the stone floors of the dormitories were cold. He'd never invested in a pair of slippers as so many of his peers had done and every night, he reconsidered that frugality. His nightgown flapped lightly at his knees and his nightcap too dangled down around his neck. He yawned; his eyes refusing to fully open.

Whispered words caught his attention. After lights out, all the students were to be in bed. Parodically, some would sneak down and stay up late in the common room, but that was usually only for an hour or so. This late in the night was unusual. Evein snuck towards the steps that led down into the common room, discovering a light.

It was the flickering light of a candle, a single wick burning in the deep hours of the night. Around it, he discovered Def Alis and Abersoth. The pair were sitting in the couches of the dormitories. Def Alis had a bowl of peas that he was snapping open, munching on as he spoke. Eating like that, and at such an hour, worried Evein more than anything else.

"The burns..." said the instructor, staring into the middle distance of the dark as he thought and spoke.

"Lightning's the only thing I can think of," remarked Def Abersoth. He snapped open one of a few walnuts he had in his lap. The man of strength did so with his bare fingers. "Even if he fell into a fire, it wouldn't..."

"Lightning doesn't penetrate like that," whispered Def Alis. "He was punctured."

"Lightning rod?" guessed Def Abersoth. "Maybe he...he fell onto something..." Both instructors knew he was guessing and that only made it worse. A silence followed of fear and worry.

"Tomorrow, I'm going to propose to the Maestro that her fears are real. There's no alternative. We're..." Def Alis' voice caught. As certain as he was fearful, he whispered, "We're dealing with black magic." The solitary implication put a chill in Abersoth's gaze. He stiffened and looked away, as if the very thought of it was too much to grasp. Def Alis only nodded, agreeing at the reaction. He clapped his friend and colleague on the shoulder and they parted, neither sure what to say in the wake of such a statement.

The usual laughter was absent from the school yard as a village child cried out.

The young girl with blonde hair and half her face painted like a cat was pulling away from Evein, big lobs of tears rolling down her face. "It's okay, it's okay," he promised her as he held her wrist, keeping her from getting away from him. When she continued to struggle, he released her.

The young girl ran to the safety of the school marm. The older woman let the girl hug her knees fearfully, trying to keep from laughing. In the grassy field that was the children's play area, the other children were watching the exchange with a full range of reactions. A few kids had their left sleeves rolled up, their shoulders vibrant red from the magic.

"Candi," said the kindly school teacher, pulling the little girl off her skirt like she would pull a sticker from a prickly bush. "It's just a bit of medicine."

"It'll hurt!" the little girl sobbed.

"Not really," said the teacher. "It's more of a brisk cold." She laughed at the little girl's resistance. "Like being hit with a snowball." She scooped the girl up in her arms with surprising grace and carried her back to Evein.

The student mage rose, amused by the whole scene. Candi clung to the teacher's neck, still crying. Evein rolled up her sleeve, sympathetic to her terror. "It's only for a second," Evein promised the girl. He put his hand over her shoulder, cupping the joint with only a bit of space between his palm and her skin. His palm began to glow a gentle green and Candi yelped.

"And we're done," said Evein, pulling his hand away. The girl looked through the teacher's long hair at him, certain he was lying. "That's it," he promised. He looked to some of the other kids whom he'd treated, like he was hoping for their validation. "This will help protect you from coughs, and fevers, and feeling icky." He bopped her on the nose with a smile.

"All the icky things that keep you from coming to school," said the school teacher.

"But I like school," the little girl whimpered, still clutching to the teacher.

"And that's why we wanted to make sure you stay health—" The distant sound of neighing horses cut off Evein. A great commotion just out of sight rose up over the forests surrounding the village. Horses thundering and voices shouting. Worst of all were the screams of pain.

The teacher placed Candi quickly to the ground. "Children, get inside!" She urged them towards the small schoolhouse nestled in the adjacent grove. Evein helped her guide the panicked children through the wooden doors. Once the class of children were inside, Evein and the teacher shut the door.

As the woman set the heavy wooden beam across the door, Evein turned to the children. "Everything's alright," he told them. In their eyes, he could see they knew he was lying. He tried to smile, to dissuade their disbelief, then went for a window. He looked out at the woodlands south of the schoolhouse and could see nothing amiss. The din of chaos continued, the walls only muting the noise. "I've got to see what's going on," Evein said.

Meaning to speak only to himself, he was surprised when the teacher told him, "I'll see to the children. You go." Evein glanced back at her only for a second, then opened the window itself. He climbed rather ungainly out the window and fell rather than leapt to the ground below.

He righted himself and called back, "Make sure you—" The window was yanked shut, the wooden shutters sealed almost immediately. "Secure...the window..." he muttered. He turned and faced down the dirt road that led to the village. A horse's whiney and a man's scream of pain made him jump. He gathered his intention, however, and took an unsteady breath. With fearful strides, he began to rush down the path.

Dirt padded beneath his feet as he wound the familiar path through the village road. He arrived at the crest of one of the hills that overlooked the village to find several of the buildings ablaze. Fires burned atop several of the thatched roofs. A storehouse was rubble, wild flames burning amongst the remains. At least two people lay motionless on the ground. Blood pooled about them.

The sight of the dead nearly undid Evein right there. He let out a shriek and stumbled back. He tried to cover his mouth but lost control. Falling to his hands and knees, he vomited uncontrollably. He scampered back from his hysteria, shaking. He cried out again, only to learn it was a mistake.

"Here's one!" shouted a voice as rough as the hands that grabbed his collar. Evein shrieked as he was pulled to his feet by a large man who smelled of charcoal and whetstones. "Come on, young'n," said the man as he drug Evein towards the burning village.

Before Evein could even process his situation, he was thrown into the midst of the villagers. Corralled like cattle, they were wound in a tight clump at the heart of the village. A few others from the school were there in their white robes, trimmed in various colors and stained with mud and blood. Among them was Def Alis, who grabbed up Evein as soon as he hit the ground. The senior instructor pulled Evein to his feet and asked, "Are you alright?" Evein staggered a bit, his feet unsteady and his head swimming. He reached deliriously for Def Alis and realized blood was dribbling from his dark hair.

Before Evein could do anything more than stammer, a man stepped forward to the crowd. A half-cape of black leather flowed behind him while a sword with a blade for a pommel rested at his side. He looked as hard as the other men who had surrounded the villagers but with an intellect and astuteness that was even more terrifying. "This can be over very quickly," he said curtly. His words were short and his volume low. "There is an artifact of power. You know of what I speak." Eyes indifferent to violence searched the villagers' expressions. "Deliver it to me and, in exchange, the village will remain." He looked back over his shoulder as one of the nearby homes collapsed, the fiery damage too great for it to endure. "Well..." He turned to the people and squared his shoulders. "Where is it?"

Def Alis stepped forward. He was equal height to the man but lacked his physical presence. "I'm the head instructor of the academy of healing. Who gives you the right to do this?"

"I do," said the man, speaking crisply as though razing the village was but one of a dozen things he had to attend to that day. He studied Def Alis for a moment and recognition curled the corner of his lips. "Academy of healing, you say?" Smart eyes searched his memory. "And that makes you...?"

Def Alis hesitated but a second. "Maestro Alis."

The man nodded. "Well, I am Maestro Savali." Some of his men snickered.

"Maestro of what academy?" Def Alis demanded. When Savali didn't respond, Def Alis pushed. "I don't think you're really a maestro."

"I don't think you are either," he countered. His smile widened a bit. "Let me guess: Def Alis, correct?" No response, but also no refuting. "Def, meaning 'to defer'. A designation that means that anyone who interacts with you should recognize your tremendous education and hard work to be recognized as an expert." He paced a few steps, the eyes of the villagers going with him. "Or is it Def, meaning 'unable to hear'?" It was a challenge, and an insult.

Def Alis looked passed the bravado and the danger and at the man before him. "What is your hatred of the academy?"

Savali snickered, approving of Def Alis' intelligence. "Personal," he answered. "But this," he said with a gesture at the village. "This is business. Bring me the artifact." Def Alis didn't move to accommodate him, or even react. Savali studied his stone expression, drinking in every detail. "What is it?" he asked. "A staff? A scepter? A wand?" He giggled in spite of himself at that suggestion. "A crystal?" he guessed. Try as he might, Def Alis betrayed some clue and Savali noticed. "A crystal," he accepted. His eyes went wide and his smile wider. "THE crystal." He stepped back, nodding slowly. "Oh my, what treasure have we found."

He turned his back to Def Alis, his cape swaying at his waist. He walked a few steps away, several of the other men joining him. Their hushed words were lost to the din of fire and panic. Savali turned back to the village and announced to his men, "Forget the village. We take the academy. Move out!"

Just like that, the men abandoned the townsfolk they had rounded up like animals. They all went for their horses. Amidst cries of relief and lingering fear, the men mounted up and began to ride out.

Evein and the other students from the academy rushed to Def Alis' side "What do we do?" asked one of Evein's peers.

"We have to warn the others," Def Alis realized. He looked at those with him and said, "We have to buy them time. Go into the forest. They drove the village's horses loose. Grab us some and we will ride for the academy. If we cut through the forest, we might be able to get there first." Evein nodded and took off as Def Alis gave out similar orders to the others.

Evein leapt a fence connecting two homes, one of which was on fire. He slipped and fell in the mud of a pigsty but didn't let that phase him. He was up and running through the pit of mud. He vaulted the far side of the pen and landed in the soft grass that separated the village from the forest.

He spotted some hoof prints in the grass and chased after them. Evein was a poor tracker but the path left behind was obvious. Broken branches and ripped leaves filled the woods and neighing of a fearful pack horse echoed among the trees. He ran until his lungs burned and his feet gave out. He fell to his knees and panted, then pulled himself up, running again.

What he thought was a tree, however, grabbed his collar. Evein was yanked off his feet by his own momentum and fell flat on his back. He landed with a thud and groaned loudly, the air knocked out of his chest. A man with an eyepatch leaned over him and smiled, a cleft lip drawing attention to his missing front teeth. "What've we here?" he asked in a thick accent. He held up a wicked-looking knife, the rusted blade looking more terrifying than the jagged edge.

"Please," Evein panted, his voice a gasp. He wasn't sure if it was sweat or tears dribbling down the sides of his face.

"Don't think Savali would like you getting them horses," the man grinned. He reached down for Evein's throat and pushed hard. "One more body might dissuade such ill behavior," chuckled the man, readying the knife.

Whether it was ignorance of his dire reality or the lack of oxygen reaching his brain, all Evein could truly focus on was not the knife but the man's cleft lip. The parted skin exposing his mouth was easily fixed in youth and even older patients could have the deviation remedied. As the one-eyed man put the knife to Evein's chest, Evein reached for the man's face. His palm began to glow but his consciousness faded. Wild energies surged and the man yelped suddenly.

Oxygen came rushing back as Evein was freed. He coughed violently and rolled onto his side, his neck hurting as much as his throat. He managed to pull himself up onto his hands and knees and found the man with the eyepatch backing away, holding his face. Evein heard him shouting and had to stop himself from asking if he was okay.

With a growl of rage, the man's hands dropped from his pocket-marked face. His lip had torn entirely from his gums and his cleft lip now extended up to his nose. One nostril was torn open, blood flowing freely from the exposed tissues within. Evein looked down at his hands, the glow in his palm still fading out of sight. He saw only the magical surgery gone horribly wrong.

"I'll gut you," the man stammered, holding his knife forward. His words were warped by his new mouth. Evein looked again at his hands, then at the knife that threatened him. The man growled and then rushed at Evein, the knife ready to expose his innards.

Evein saw only systems of the body, tissues and organs. He thought of his attacker only as an invading ailment that needed to be neutralized. With his upheld hand, palm glowing, Evein numbed the remaining eye. As though preparing for cataract surgery, he simply deactivated the eye's ability to process and feel. And see.

The man went charging passed, stumbling and falling to the ground. The knife went skidding across the forest floor. "What did you do?!" screamed the man, grabbing at his face. He flailed violently as he crawled backwards across the underbrush. Again and again, he screamed, "What did you do?!"

Evein rushed to the man's side and put his hand on his head. The man of violence grabbed Evein's hand and yanked him to the ground. With skill born of experience, he rolled atop Evein and grabbed for his face. His thumbs found Evein's eyes and pushed into them. "See how YOU like it!" he slobbered.

Evein put his hand to the man's chest and his palm glowed. A quick shock caused his heart to pulse suddenly. The man grabbed his arm and yelped. In the second it bought the young magic wielder, Evein sat up and grabbed the man's face. He began to force oxygen from his head, forcing the man to sleep as though Evein was preparing him for an open surgery. The man flailed radically, fighting against the coming unconsciousness. He struck at Evein's arm and shoulder, blind strikes born of terror.

It took longer than Evein was used to. Much longer. And when the man fell away, he landed on the ground with a stillness and finality that chilled Evein to the bone. The boy crawled away from his patient, immediately able to tell something was very wrong. He'd seen patients go limp like that before, go still as a sheet on a line as the breeze died. Most terrifying of all, however, was the way the man's one eye stared vacantly upward. His eyes saw nothing, and never would again.

Long strides couldn't drive out the image of that one eye hung open. Staring into the heavens, its vacant, empty gaze was fixed on nothing. It was an absence of awareness that Evein had never seen. Lost patients, lost animals, couldn't compare to that absence. Evein was so distracted, so lost, that it fell to his horse to guide him. It raced along familiar paths towards the academy. Routes normally taken at a walk or a trot were now a race track, racing against time.

Evein smelled smoke and blood before he arrived. He knew the situation and the condition before he saw the academy. As he crested the hill and rode out of the woods, he saw the great stone fortress with black smoke trialing into the cloudy sky. He saw no flames but he could feel the heat on the late morning breeze. He saw the charred brick and ash where flames had devastated everything.

Only a handful of students were at the front of the academy, though they were all thankfully alive. More than a few were bleeding but had clearly been attended to. Maestro Sara sat on the front steps of the academy, a towel held against her neck. There was blood on the towel and it had dribbled down her left shoulder of her white robe.

Evein swung off his horse and his knees gave out. He fell onto the ground with a cough. He felt wet and touched his lips to find blood. He checked himself, using magic instinctively to feel a rupture in his stomach. "A stress ulcer," he groaned, like his mind was diagnosing someone else while he was distracted.

On the ground, he stared up at the sky. Rich textures of white clouds covered the sea of blue beyond. For a moment, Evein wanted to fall up. He wanted to fall into the endless sky. If he did, he hoped he might return to the world he knew. A world without the stench of blood. A world without vacant eyes, bereft of all function.

A body cursed with regret pulled itself up and Evein approached the academy. Several of the students looked at him, tears among their eyes. Evein could barely manage meeting their gaze. Instead, he fell into the habits of a student and went to the nearest instructor.

Maestro Sara's eyes rolled to Evein as he neared. He could see the trouble she had swallowing. "D-Def Alis..." Evein tried to report.

"He's here," said the Maestro, her voice weak with pain and injury. "Putting out the fire in the, the..." She gestured weakly at the rear of the academy. She looked at Evein and asked, "What happened?"

Evein's mouth dangled open as every word he knew failed to capture what he'd witnessed. He shook his head and stammered but nothing more than, "Raiders," came forth.

The maestro of the academy shook her head. "I know. I meant with you." Evein was surprised. "Something happened. You saw something else." She removed the towel and Evein saw the gaping hole in the side of her neck. The deep slash exposed arteries and the deep tissues. He could even see glimpses of bone. She held her hand to the wound and her palm began to glow. The tissues began to very slowly extend, the blood receding ever so slightly back inside.

Color drained from her face and her eyes drooped. She leaned back against the railing of the steps and returned the towel to her neck. "They saw violence," she whispered like a breeze through dead winter branches. She looked at the other students, prompting Evein to do the same. "They saw horrors." Maestro Sara's eyes turned to the young man before her. "What did YOU see? For it was something else."

Evein's eyes dropped and his mouth opened. "A man...in the woods, he...he attacked me." His jaw quaked. His eyes watered. "He's dead." The maestro didn't say anything, but looked with eyes heavy with empathy.

"Sara," called a familiar voice. Def Abersoth came around the far wall of the academy. The big man's right arm was in a sling, his fingers swollen and discolored. He was badly bruised, one eye swollen shut. When he saw Evein, he sighed with relief. "Evein, good to see you, boy. Def Alis was worried about you." He clapped the boy's shoulder, his heavy hand causing Evein to stagger. "Feared the worst."

"I-I'm fine," Evein whispered. "Is Def Alis...is he okay?"

"Fatalities are thankfully few," said Def Abersoth. "And injuries we can..." He clamped his mouth shut before he ranted unproductively.

"Who are they?" Evein asked. "Def Alis, he spoke with one. The leader. He said his name was Savali."

"We met," Maestro Sara assured Evein. She dropped her towel to reveal the wound. "He's the one who gave me this."

"Why?"

"Because I got between him and the Great Crystal," she told the student, like it should have been obvious. "That was what they were here for."

"The artifact," Evein gasped.

Maestro Sara nodded, then winced, clearly regretting the action. She leaned back and Evein could see her muscles relax when she set her head against the stone of the stairs. "I don't know what they want it for," she said, mostly passed Evein to Def Abersoth. "Perhaps they have no one purpose in mind. They seemed men who prized power. Perhaps that was all it was to them, and not a means towards an end."

"We can't let them take it," Evein insisted.

Maestro Sara laughed a sickly, weak laugh. "They've taken it." She gestured vainly at the academy and whatever had transpired. "It's gone, as are they, with the crystal."

"We have to get it back," said Evein. He could see only the caked, dried blood on her towel. Turning brown, the white towel was sopping with the maestro's life.

"We've no means to," Def Abersoth told him. "We might perhaps have them in numbers but we're no fighting force." He looked at the students in the field before the academy. "At our healthiest, we are mostly children."

His words were lost on Evein. The boy focused on the wound on the maestro's neck. He could see the skin and thought of how to purify it, to elicit a growth response. He thought of the muscles half-torn by some horrid blade. They'd have to be soothed to calm and then reattached. To get to the deeper muscles, he would put the maestro to sleep and then separate the superficial muscles so he could reach his attention to the deeper spaces.

In a delirious sadness, he thought about the vacant eye fixed upward. He thought about wishing he could separate that eye from the body. But then the head would still be there and he fantasized about separating the muscles. Not only muscles but soft tissue and nerves and bones, so that the whole head could be removed.

"Maybe we can fight," Evein realized with a sickening, empowering feeling of might.

"What do you mean?" asked Def Abersoth.

Maestro Sara noticed the grim expression on the boy's face and grew worried. She sat forward and warned, "Evein, whatever you're thinking, don't do it."

"We can't let them take the crystal," Evein breathed. His head felt too small, like his mind didn't fit inside his cranium. He turned and saw Def Abersoth. The man looked just as worried as the maestro. "We can't."

"It's not worth it," breathed Maestro Sara. Evein looked down at her, feeling strangely betrayed. He stared at her, unable to process how she could say such a thing. "It's a thing," she told him as he wrestled with his own thoughts.

"A thing with the power to split mountains," Evein told her with an exhausted but frantic gasp.

"But a thing still," she promised him, a vain attempt to sooth his worries.

In the distance, Def Alis called. "We've got more wounded!"

Maestro Sara and Def Abersoth both turned, the act causing the maestro to wince and freeze in pain. In the moment of distraction, Evein felt a terrifying, sinful clarity. He turned from them both and went back for the horse. He heard shouting, but whether it was to him or at him or for him or unrelated to him, he couldn't find the strength to notice.

Evein had to jump up onto the horse's back and land on his belly, then scramble to throw a leg over. Once he mounted the horse, rudimentary skills took over. As if sensing his focus, the horse began to trot away from the academy. It obeyed Evein's wild ambition and began to follow the path away from the rubble of the academy.

Evein was no tracker but the brigands made no effort to hide their path, nor did they make any haste. Through forested routes Evein had barely traveled, he rode. Leading towards the west, winding through leafy trees and open fields of the wildlands between the villages, Evein followed the path neither left nor obscured by the raiders. He rode in a daze, muscles doing the task the mind could only observe from a broken distance.

In less than half an hour, he caught up with them. The clop of his horse's hooves alerted them but they seemed unbothered by a singular rider. Two dozen men turned around, some drawing swords or readying other weapons. A few dismounted their rides and fanned out, but most waited to see the foolishness unfold. A few of the unkempt snickered, unsure if they witnessed humor or madness. All were armored. All were armed. All looked heady from the violence and destruction they had wrought and game to do a little more.

Evein rode right towards the group, inexperienced with conflict and having no thought except to go straight. "I recall you," said Savali from near the front. He grinned and dismounted. He left a heavy wool blanket tied to his saddle. "You were with Alis in the village. One of the healers."

Evein slid off the side of the horse, not falling but dismounting without any grace. The men laughed but their mirth was lost on him. He saw only that wool blanket hanging off to the great grey horse's side. "So are you a 'def' as well?" mocked Savali.

"Give me back the crystal," Evein said. It was his voice that spoke but not him. He didn't feel like he was there. He was witnessing, not doing. Something else was controlling him. Something that felt very right, and felt wrong for feeling right.

"And here I was thinking you were asking to join us," Savali said, getting some snickers from his men. Evein walked right between them, heading not to Savali but through him. The leader's smile faded with his good humor. "That's far enough, son."

"Give me back the crystal," Evein repeated.

Evein walked within arm's reach and Savali grabbed his collar. "I said—"

It was a simple blockage spell, one Evein had used a dozen times in the past year alone. It stymied blood flow and dulled nerves to allow for surgery. When he grabbed Savali's hand, Evein placed the spell just passed his elbow. Everything below it went not only numb but quickly pale. Worse, his head immediately began to throb because of the spiking blood pressure in the rest of his body.

Evein was calm and he wasn't sure why. He felt neither good nor bad, scared nor secure. He felt like a placid tree while dark clouds rolled passed. A delightful sickness was rolling around inside of him, his thoughts sloshing like a glass less than half full. The man in front of him shouted and stumbled back, grabbing his hand as he tried to force sensation back into his fingers. Savali dropped to one knee and screamed as his hand went terrifyingly, unnaturally white. His men were too stunned to move. Hard men of action, they were unprepared for the subtlety of what they were seeing.

Evein looked at Savali and thought of the dead bodies in the village, of the bodies in the academy. He thought of the bodies, of the corpses. He saw the blood on Def Alis' head. He saw the violent gash on the side of Maestro Sara's neck. His academic mind instinctively thought of every muscle, every vein, every artery, every lymph node, every bone, every ligament and tendon, every nerve. With unblinking eyes, he thought of the spells needed to part the tissues. It was so simple. With clinical detachment, Evein simply held forth his hand.

Savali's head went rolling away from his body.

Evein's detachment intensified. He watched the head of a man, the face of an enemy, go rolling away and all he could think of was the Great Crystal. He thought how similar in shape and size the head was to his objective. Thoughts of the crystal returned Evein to his task. He took a step towards the horse and took the wool blanket from the saddle. He tried to open the improvised pouch but couldn't undo it at first. "Does anybody have a..." he started to ask when he finally got the knot loosened.

Inside, the crystal glittered at him, as if it merely slumbered. Evein felt relief but not accomplishment. He felt like merely an important task was done. Little more. Keeping the crystal in the blanket, he stepped over Savali's body and left the party of stunned brigands where they were. He awkwardly climbed atop his horse, again having to lay on his belly and swing his leg over. Astride the animal, he clicked it casually into action and it was all too happy to be away from the thieves.

***

Evein sat alone in the library. It smelled of tinder and charcoal, with occasional whiffs of roasted bookbinding adhesives. The far side of the room was black from the flames, now silent and cold. The table his arm rested upon was charred but still standing. Barely. His seat was fine, the fire only just getting to that side of the room before it was put out. It was night through the windows. The black sky looked more colorful than the charred and scorched walls.

Evein's face was in his hand as he kept himself propped up. He had no energy to do anything, even sleep. The events of the morning replayed in his mind. It was a replay unlike any test he had taken, any quiz or trial he had undergone. He wasn't reviewing a grade but something far more fundamental. The books around him held no insights he could look to for guidance, not that too many of them were legible anymore.

Without a door on the library, he could hear Def Alis' footsteps well before he arrived. He didn't have the energy to sit up, however, even when the instructor took a seat opposite him. Opposite him, not next to him. Not near him.

There was nothing tangible Evein could put his finger on, but something potent told him this would not be like previous conversations. Instructor wasn't sitting across from pupil this time. Def Alis wasn't addressing a student when he told the young man, "Since the fires never reached your section of the dormitories, you'll be able to get your things." He used soft words and a soft tone, not quite a whisper. "I've prepared a letter to your parents. I can send it ahead of you, or you can take it."

Evein very weakly shook his head. His eyes were fixed on the charred and ruined tabletop. "They can't read it," he said. "They can't read." Now he sat up, only to sigh and lean back in his seat. "They can't read." Def Alis nodded sympathetically. Evein looked at the academy walls and shook his head, too stunned to do much of anything. "I can't...I can't imagine...imagine life without this place."

Def Alis nodded again. "I know."

The shout came from nowhere. "Then why are you kicking me out?" He gave a sob and then fell back against the chair again. His belly shook, then his chin, then he began to cry. "Why are you kicking me out? I-I got the crystal back." His crying subdued a bit. "Why are you kicking me out?"

Def Alis was sympathetic but not apologetic. "You killed that man," he told Evein. "You killed him. You...you killed."

Evein was at a loss. "We've all lost patients. You yourself, more than once in class, you said that you couldn't graduate to the upper ranks without seeing someone die."

Def Alis nodded, like he expected these accusations. "Very true. But there is a far difference from losing a patient – even committing some grievous error that costs a life – and killing someone."

"Is it because I used white magic?" Evein pled. "I'll never do it again, I-I swear!"

"I know," Def Alis told him, again like he anticipated the exchange, like it had been scripted. "It's not about the magic. It's not about the method you used to kill. It's that you killed. It isn't the techniques that make you a healer; it's the commitment to life." Def Alis leveled a hard look at Evein and told him, "And that is a commitment you can never swear full loyalty to. Not now."

He stayed and sat with Evein a bit longer, but neither had anything further to say.

Robert V Aldrich

Inequitable

-- Day One --

The house sat alone in a cluster of trees.

A private glade in the middle of a wide field, the trees were just taller than the three-story house. Faded white with grime and age, the house looked as forgotten as the fields that surrounded it. The horizon was dotted with similar trees, keeping their distance. Overhead, a blue sky held a few wisps of white clouds that traveled slowly above the brisk breeze that turned the tall grass in the fields. The sun was directly above, overseeing the pleasantly warm summer day.

Along the lonely stretch of two-lane highway that passed uninterrupted before the house, a moving truck slowed and turned awkwardly into the dirt driveway. It came almost to a halt as it navigated the narrow bridge across the drainage ditch, before finally righting itself and continuing towards the house.

Followed by two cars, the truck slowly idled its way down the earthen path. It reached the circle driveway before the house, turning around the simple stone fountain, and stopping just passed the steps to the front door. Inside the cab, the truck finally coming to a full and complete stop, Thomas Hastings turned the key and brought the truck to silence. He closed his eyes and listened to the leaves turning in the wind. He smiled with a sense of relief.

"Quit it," said his son.

Thomas opened the truck door and leaned out to see his youngest son, Wright, running ahead of Kirstie. The two youngest kids raced up onto the wrap-around porch of the house and peeked in through the windows. Thomas pulled his shoulders back to pop his sternum as the rest of the family piled out of the cars.

Alan and Ian, Thomas's older sons, were appraising the house with more muted consideration. The pair of teen boys had hair that was darkening with maturity, matching Thomas' hair. Their younger siblings on the porch still had bright blonde hair like their mother.

Last around the car came Susan, Thomas' wife. She looked at the house with unbridled reservation, almost sneering with disapproval. Thomas felt the urge to snap, to say something snide to her, but he pushed it down and instead smiled. With a clap of his hands, he did his absolute best to be optimistic and cheerful. "Well, here we are." He joined them at the back of the truck, looking up at the small mansion of a home. "The new Hastings Estate."

"Estate?" asked Ian with a smirk.

"Would you prefer manor?" Thomas asked the high school senior.

"He could use some manners," Alan teased his younger brother. Ian scowled at him in return.

"Guys," said their mother. She took from her pocket a key and handed it to Alan. "Go let Kirstie and Wright inside and check out the rooms. We'll start unloading in a minute." As their sons departed, Susan turned to Thomas and leaned in for a hug.

The two held each other, their eyes open as they stared in opposite directions. "This is gonna be good for us," Thomas told Susan.

"Yeah," she said coolly but committed. "Yeah, I know." She stepped back and looked up at him and gave him a weak smile. She sighed as she looked at a man she had once loved. She laid her hands on his chest and smiled again then turned for the house. "Let's get inside and claim the master bedroom before Kirstie does." Thomas snickered and followed.

Up the steps and through the front door, a large foyer room was waiting. Empty save for stale air and the smell of aged timber, it was the color of old. The white paint on the walls was faded with age and though it was chipped at edges and joints, it was enduring. Hardwood floors created an almost-steady pattern beneath their feet as well as subtle creaks with each step. Homely and adjacent to endearing, the sound of life seemed welcome by the old floor. A sitting room was to the right, with bookshelves built into the very walls. A dining room was off to the left, a modest chandelier hanging just a hair above head height. At the rear of the house was the kitchen and laundry, as well as a spare room meant for tasks and chores, not comfortable living.

Spacious stairs on either side of the foyer led up to the second floor. The stairs were devoid of much stylistic concern but weren't without aesthetic appeal. At the top of the stairs was a wide balcony that wound around the house and overlooked the foyer. The master bedroom took up the entire right side of the house at that level. The remaining three rooms were arranged at the opposite corners, with the third and smallest room next to the master suite. Each bedroom had a small balcony that looked out over the countryside and no room wanted for space. Between the two rooms at the apex of the stairs, a single stairwell led to the third floor. There, three smaller rooms waited as a tight cluster, as well as access to the mild attic.

Light fixtures and outlets were aged but copious. Wood runners and thick lips followed the floor and at waist height. The house was decorated by austere but pleasing carpentry, not paint or light. Windows were plentiful but most were smaller in size than felt common. Fixtures like door handles and joints were chipped of their paint, and their metallic finish beneath had lost all luster.

Thomas found Wright in a second-floor bedroom just as his son was opening the balcony door. The young boy rushed out into the open air and looked down, grinning in awe. "Can I tie a zipline to that tree?" he asked his dad. "That way, I can just swing down there to get to the school bus."

Thomas was stunned by the mere suggestion. "Uh...probably not. I know your mom won't go for it."

"How about we cut a hole in the floor and we set up a fire pole like they had in Ghostbusters?" Wright pushed, like it was a completely reasonable compromise. Thomas nearly caved just on the eagerness in his son's eyes.

Susan entered the vacant room to see her daughter at the window, looking out at the back fields of the property. The young girl was framed in the daylight against the old room. The floor creaked when Susan entered and Kirstie turned back to her. "You like the room?" her mother asked.

"I don't know," she ventured, a hint of a breeze stirring her hair. "The balconies are kind of cool." She turned to her mom and leaned against the windowsill. "The rooms are definitely bigger than our old house." Susan nodded as she entered the square room. Kirstie was about to say more but a loud bang echoed from upstairs. "What was that?" Kirstie asked with a suspicious glance at the roof.

Susan, though, sighed. Another bang came from above. "It's your brothers fighting again." She exited the room sharply and rushed for the stairwell, Thomas opposite her. The pair stopped abruptly at the entrance of the stairs and Thomas smiled curtly and gestured for her to go first. Susan tried not to be sarcastic in her smile back and she ran up the stairs. Behind her, Kirstie exited her bedroom and stood next to the closet by her door. She looked upwards at the fight she could almost see, it was such a common occurrence.

Onto the third floor, the two parents arrived right as Alan slammed Ian into the wall and pinned him against it. The older boy held his sibling against the wall and said angrily, "Stop it." Ian responded with a growl, a shout, and then he kicked his brother in the leg. The blow destabilized Alan and he dropped Ian, staggering back.

Thomas ran between the two boys and then had to physically restrain Ian for swinging at Alan. "What the HELL?!" he yelled, pushing Ian back. "What has gotten into you two?! Again!"

"This jackass thinks he can pick whichever room he wants!" Ian screamed.

"I didn't even pick a room yet, you little bastard," Alan yelled back.

"Guys!" Susan shouted, the voice of mom finally ending the confrontation but not the animosity. She joined Thomas between the two boys, her presence widening the gulf between them. "What IS this about?"

"He doesn't get the biggest room," Ian yelled, pointing at Alan.

"Biggest room?" Thomas asked of no one in particular.

"This is the biggest room on the third floor," Alan told his dad. "Eye-an thinks he should get it."

The use of the hard-I in his name made Ian sneer, ready to start throwing punches again. "Yeah, I should. Because I'm actually going to live here; not go back to college."

"You're going to live here for one year and then you'll go to college," Alan pointed out. "I mean, you know, assuming you can get into one."

"Alan," Susan snapped. He didn't persist. "Boys, we've got a lot of work to do."

"Those of us who will be here, yeah," Ian agreed with his mom while eyeballing his brother.

"Boys," Thomas said, exhausted from having to put out one fight already. "Let's...let's get to unloading." He turned and gestured for Alan to go first. "Come on." Alan glared at Ian, but then turned and started out. "You too," Thomas told Ian, urging him next.

The two boys exited, leaving father and mother to address the fight. They looked guiltily at each other, unsure what to say, where to even begin. Friction from the emotional tension was already building during the very event meant to give them some solidarity. Thomas finally just turned from his wife and departed. He stopped at the door. He looked back at her, wanting not to say something but feeling guilty for not speaking. Want for words couldn't take the place of words, however and he couldn't speak. He continued on, his chill lingering around Susan in the afternoon heat.

Dusk settled. A cool breeze rushed over the flat fields, twisting through the occasional tree branches and rustling the leaves. A few windows were lit in the giant house as Thomas and Ian pulled up. Huge bags of fast food in the backseat of the car, they stopped right before the house.

Thomas turned off the car, but stayed still. Ian, ready to get out, paused when he noticed his father lingering. He sat back in the front seat and waited.

"This is a chance for something new," Thomas said after a moment. He looked out through the windshield at the trees and the fields beyond. A shadow crept over the grass, a cloud between them and the distant sun.

"Look, me and Alan...I just got pissed off," Ian started to say.

Thomas smiled and admitted, "I was talking about me and your mom." He smiled at his son, then opened the car door. Feeling guilty, Ian got out as well.

The light from the lantern descended the stairs ahead of Kirstie and Wright. The pair looked cautiously down the stairs into the darkness, holding each other's hands. "Do you see anything?" Kirstie asked, unable to keep the light from shaking a bit.

"Keep it steady!" Wright squealed.

"I'm trying," Kirstie told him. She knelt and held the lamp forward rather than descend another step into the darkness. "I can't see anything."

"Me either," Wright said. He lowered as well, then suddenly jabbed his fingers into Kirstie's side and screamed.

Kirstie shrieked at the top of her lungs and threw the lamp into the air. She leapt half her height off the steps and tried to go eleven directions at once. The lamp hit the steps and went tumbling down to the bottom of the stairs while Kirstie turned and smacked her little brother repeatedly. "You DUFUS!" She kept hitting him on the shoulder as he laughed.

"Kirstie?" called their mom from elsewhere in the house. "Are you okay?"

"Yes!" Kirstie yelled. "Wright's not going to be." She smacked him again and descended the stairs to retrieve the lamp.

"Both of you, quit it," Susan called.

Kristie glared at Wright and he giggled. She smacked him again, then looked down into the darkness. The lantern sat at the base of the steps, illuminating the darkness but not dismissing it. The pair were quiet as they looked around at the giant basement before them. Thick pillars seemed as sturdy as the concrete floor beneath them. There were no lights in the basement, no electrical outlets, no sign of modernity of any kind. It was a giant space divided by the stairwell and the six pillars that ran down the middle.

"Wow," Wright said on the first step. "It's like some kind of dungeon or something." He beamed with absolute fixation.

"Yeah," said Kirstie. She shone the light around but saw no doors or crevices of any kind. "It's big," she said, listening for her echo. She turned around and smacked her brother again.

"Ow! What was that for?" he asked.

"Scaring me, dufus," she told him before she paddled him back up the stairs.

-- Day Two --

Kirstie slipped the microwave breakfast sandwich into the microwave and hit the auto-cook. She paced back away from the microwave, a comic book in her hand. She tapped her foot as she read until she heard steps at the stairs. She quickly pulled the comic behind her until Alan entered with a yawn. Relieved, she set the comic down. "Morning," he said, going for the fridge. He opened it, pushing some emptied cardboard boxes aside as he did. Just opening the antique caused the entire appliance to shake. "Geez, how old is this thing?" He took out a bottle of orange juice and drank it straight.

"Gross," Kirstie said before the microwave chimed. She got out her sandwich and tested the edges. "When do you go back to State?"

"Week after next," Alan said. He took another swig from the orange juice. "We're supposed to start doing ER rotations this semester. I need to study." He said 'study' with two syllables for emphasis.

"They have an emergency room for animals?" Kirstie asked.

"Yeah," Alan said, surprised she found the idea confusing. He gawked at her for a moment and she glared back at him. He went back to the orange juice for another swig before putting it back in the refrigerator. "Dog gets hit by a car; minutes matter." Kirstie nodded and read and ate at the same time, pacing in the kitchen.

Ian came inside with a sleepy "Good morning."

"Sup," said Alan. "How was the sleeping bag?"

"I got cold," Ian said, going for the orange juice. He unscrewed the lid, then looked at Alan. "Did you drink out of this?"

"No," he insisted. Ian put it back and got a bottle of water instead. Alan went over to the basement door and opened it. He stared into the pitch blackness waiting down the stairs. "You and Wright checked this out yesterday, right?" he asked. He looked around for a light switch but couldn't find one.

"Yeah," Kristie confirmed from behind her comic. "It's big but it's kind of cold."

"Maybe we can wire in some lights or something," Alan said, mostly to himself. He ran his hand over the smoothed wood, tapping a bit to discern its toughness.

"Maybe we'll put your room down there," Ian added as Alan left the door open. Kristie noticed. She started to protest but Alan and Ian both departed in a silent cloud of communal rancor. She got up and shut the basement door.

Mid-morning, Susan walked passed the open door into Wright's room, only to stop and backpedal. She stopped at the door and asked, "What are you doing?"

In the room, arranged on the wooden floor, were several dozen action figures. All in seated positions, they were aligned in careful rows and columns like an army of tiny plastic men. Wright turned to his mother and smiled brightly. "I'm unpacking."

"I told you to unpack your clothes," Susan laughed. "Not your toys."

"I wanted to get them all out. See how many I had," he told her. He looked over his collection with some pride. "I'm going to use one of the shelves and set them up."

Susan nodded and then looked expectantly at his stacks of boxes still waiting for his attention. "Clothes, honey," she reminded him and then walked on.

Once she was passed his door, she glanced back and her smile faded. She crossed the second floor all the way across to the master bedroom. Thomas was shifting the dresser to a space between two southward-facing windows. She waited until he'd straightened up from the effort and was appraising its positioning before she shared, "I'm worried Wright's stressed out."

"We're all stressed out," Thomas ground out as he resumed his struggle to get the heavy wooden dresser into just the right spot. The wooden floor creaked and he stopped, appraising his progress. "Why did your mom have to have such heavy stuff?" He pushed it some more.

"No, I mean..." She checked back at the door. "I'm afraid he's regressing. Or something. He's got his toys all out on the floor." She began to gather up the copious ropes and cords the family had used to secure their things in the moving truck, like a half-hearted effort to clean up.

"He's a kid, honey," Thomas said. With one final shove, he pushed the dresser into the wall. He stepped back and considered it, unsure if it was truly where he wanted. Deciding it was good enough, he turned to his wife. "What are you worried about?" Deciding he asked that too harshly, he rubbed her arm. "What's he done with them?"

"He's got them all out, on the floor, in lines," she conveyed, neither accepting or rejecting the physical affection. "It just seems..." She sighed and looked to Thomas. "He's in the eighth grade."

"Right, eighth grade. Rising eighth grader, too," Thomas said. "He's still a boy. He's still going to do kiddie things. Ian's a senior and he and Alan still fight like they did when they were in elementary school."

"That's different," Susan maintained with a shake of her head. She wrung her hands on the packing ropes.

"I know," he agreed. He drew her into another chilly hug. "But I just...between the move and the new house and the thought of a new school and all of that. I think it's a little too early to be worried that we've done some kind of irreparable damage. He's a boy."

Susan worked to accept the logic of it and nodded.

Kirstie ascended the steps to the second floor with a cardboard box. Behind her was a loud clatter and Ian yelling, "I'm okay." With only a roll of her eyes, Kirstie didn't even break stride. She took the box to the closet outside her bedroom door. She left it there on the balcony that wrapped around the second floor and overlooked the foyer. She went into her completely square room to retrieve a box opener from her desk, then returned to open the box. Full of fluffy towels still smelling of the detergent from their dryer at their old home, she then opened the closet and began to set the towels on the deep shelves.

Satisfied with her work, she sliced the box's base with the cutter and then tossed it down onto the foyer where the family was letting their discarded boxes fall. Wright collected the box and pushed it over onto the stack he was responsible for collecting. Bit by bit, one by one, the house was beginning to take shape.

Alan sat on the lip of the fountain in the front yard, his bare feet in the murky water. In his hand, he was turning over a pipe. He held it up towards the sky and tried to look through it. "What's that?" asked Ian, coming down the steps.

"Careful, those step-things are tricky," Alan teased.

"I was carrying boxes, man. My balance was thrown off," Ian defended yet again. He came over to the fountain and sat on the lip with Alan. He looked into the water and sneered. "Geez, man, that's gross."

"That's why we need to get it working," Alan said, digging his finger into the pipe. "Standing water means mosquitoes. Maybe worse." He popped a pebble out of the pipe with a laugh. "There we go." He waded back across the fountain's base, brackish waves kicked up with each step. He knelt into the water, all while Ian watched with increasing disgust.

Alan stuck his hand into an alcove, bending over until his shoulder was submerged in the soupy water. His face showed his effort as he worked, before he announced, "Got it." He pulled his hand and stood, looking at the top of the fountain. Sludge dribbled off his wrist as he waited. "That should have done it."

"Sure you didn't break it worse?" Ian challenged. Instead of answer, Alan flung water at Ian. "Ugh, dude!" Ian shrieked, scrambling up. "That's gross!"

"Don't I know it," Alan said as he waded through knee-deep water back to the edge. He stepped over with some effort, his soaked feet next to his sneakers and socks. On the solid ground, he turned back to the fountain and sighed, troubled. "I just can't figure it out. The motor should be working. It's a simple enough process, too." He turned back to the house. "Maybe there's a breaker we need to flip."

"Dad and me checked them when we first got here," Ian said. Alan didn't stop. "Dude, we already checked them." Ian grabbed Alan's arm and yanked him back. Alan spun and lost balance falling. He caught himself on his hands and groaned. He checked his palms and saw they'd scraped up from the ground. "Crap, I'm—" Ian began to apologize.

Alan shoved Ian away with a frustrated growl. "Hey, watch it!" Ian yelled. He moved in and shoved Alan in return. Alan responded with a heavy fist across the jaw. Ian crumpled to his knees and fell back as Alan got to his feet. "What's your problem?!" Ian yelled from the ground.

"You, you little ass!" Alan yelled back, shaking his hands. When he returned his attention to Ian, the high school senior tackled him to the ground. The brothers quickly scrambled against each other, striking and hitting at any opportunity.

"Boys! BOYS!" yelled Susan from the second floor. "Thomas!" she howled.

Out through the front door came bounding their father. Thomas grabbed Ian by the scruff of his shirt and yelled, "Stop it, STOP IT!" He pulled Ian to his feet and pushed him away, then stepped between the two boys. Ian rushed at Alan again but Thomas grabbed his son and yelled, "STOP IT!" again.

With the subtlest of reprieves in the violence, Thomas turned to Alan and demanded, "What happened? What's it about this time?" Alan didn't answer. He only rubbed his face, a bruise spreading across his cheek. He scowled at Ian, but said nothing. Thomas looked to the younger of the two but got a similar reaction; angry glares but no words. "Get inside, both of you."

Ian tried to make a plea. "Dad, we were—"

"Inside," he repeated fiercely. As the two boys rose and headed up onto the porch, Thomas looked into the fountain, as if it somehow represented all their woes. He turned and checked up, to the window on the second floor. He saw Susan looking down at him. Their mutual distrust was replaced with paired concern for their children. No words were said or were needed. She turned and slipped back through the window as his eyes fell to the door through which his sons waited.

Back in the foyer, Alan and Ian waited for the scolding they both knew was coming, and both knew they deserved. From the back of the house by the kitchen, Wright appeared. The two older boys hesitated when they saw him and his expression. He didn't seem surprised that they were fighting, only worried for how long the reprieve would last. Guilt and shame magnified in them both.

"Everyone!" called Thomas as he entered the house, shutting the front door behind him. "Susan, Kirstie, Wright," he called. Wright approached while Kirstie and Susan stepped out from opposite rooms on the second floor. Thomas looked up at his wife and sighed. His gaze fell to his daughter, then to his three boys. To them all, he said, "Look, we need to have a talk." He headed to the stairs and sat down, creaking not unlike the wooden step he set upon. He pushed the box by the stairs away with a little effort and exhaled. "I feel like, I don't know, maybe we've all been dancing around this for a while now." He wiped his mouth and exhaled. "Your mom and me...things have been stressful. We had that year where I was living in the apartment. We were in counseling. We..." He gave up recounting what they all knew so well. "It's been stressful."

"Honey," Susan warned quietly. Thomas looked up at her and she pled with only her eyes that she not make this about the two of them.

Thomas nodded, then looked at Ian and Alan. The two brothers stood together still, just inside the doorway. More alike than not, their similarities seemed magnified in the silhouette they created against the brightly lit doorway. Thomas told them, "You two have always been competitive but it's gotten a lot worse."

"Yeah, because he's been an ass since he went to college," Ian insisted. Alan said nothing.

"Honey," Susan reprimanded with nothing further needing to be said.

"We're all stressed," Thomas said. "And we're handling it in different ways. Some less constructive than others." He eyed his eldest sons. "But just like your mom and me, we all need to be more...more cognizant, more aware of what we're feeling and we need to express those feelings. Constructively," he added with a glower at the boys, "but we can't keep them bottled up inside of us."

"Okay," Alan said. He fixed a glare at his father, one Thomas wasn't expecting. "What are you wanting us to do?" It didn't seem like a question but an accusation.

Before Thomas could really even process the answer, Wright turned and ran.

Thomas rose from his seat, surprised by the sudden departure. Ian and Alan both turned as well, but it was Kirstie that took chase. She rumbled down the stairs without a thought and ran into the kitchen. She arrived just in time to see the door down into the basement fall shut. Kirstie grabbed a flashlight from the kitchen counter and clicked it on as she threw open the door.

Down the stairs she raced, coming to the bottom of the basement. She saw the empty floor of hard concrete and the pillars that lined the middle of the space. At the far end, in the distant corner, Kirstie saw Wright sitting atop a metal disc. Like a bowled manhole cover, the metal disc was set into the floor, just a step removed from either of the nearby walls.

Wright was crouched atop the disc, his face buried deep in his arms that he crossed over his knees. He wasn't crying; only sitting perfectly still in the darkness of the basement. Kirstie's light fell over him and she neared slowly. "Hey," she told her little brother. The clack of her wedge sandals echoed in the empty room, the sound rebounding back and forth.

Wright's head rose and he looked at her with huge, sorrowful eyes. "I hate it when they fight."

All Kristie could say was "I know." She came and sat next to him, the cold of the disc matching the chill of the room. She sat forward like her little brother, saying nothing. She shared the cold, the darkness, the bleakness.

"We gotta go back up, don't we?" Wright asked.

Kirstie thought for half a second and sneered. "Yeah," she admitted. She stood but she didn't step away. She held her hand out towards Wright. He looked up at her and, though the room was dark, her smile brightened it. Wright was slow in taking it, but take it he did. He rose off the disc in the corner of the room and followed her and the light out of the basement and up the stairs into the house.

-- Day Three --

Through the windows of the kitchen came the amber light of dawn. Twisting in through the branches of the distant trees, the light cast out the darkness. Long shadows still covered the world and stars twinkled in the dark sky overhead but the day was fast approaching.

Susan entered the kitchen with a heavy yawn. She shuffled over to the counter and felt around until her hand grasped a familiar-ish handle. She pulled, only to realize she'd grabbed the microwave. Nearly tugging the appliance off the counter, she shook herself a bit more awake and reoriented to the coffee maker. Filter, grounds, and water, she turned to the sky as it percolated.

The steps groaned in the front and Susan turned. Thomas descended, pulling on a flannel shirt over the heavy t-shirt he'd worn to bed. "Hey," she whispered as he joined her. He smiled and slipped in behind her. He wrapped his hands around her waist and hugged her. The gesture was awkward but the attempt was appreciated. The pair stared forward into the dawn, the act of intimacy more imitation than genuine.

"What's the plan for today?" Thomas asked, disengaging from the embrace. He went for the fridge.

"I'm going to start organizing the downstairs," Susan said. She was speaking a little more normally, waking up. She looked around the kitchen, trying to decide what needed to be done and realizing the space was more or less how she wanted it. For now, anyway. Realizing she'd just trailed off, she told Thomas, "I've got an interview with a research firm this afternoon. I'd like to have at least one room done by then."

"Phone interview, right?" Thomas asked. "Or do you need a car?"

"Depends," she joked. "It's a phone interview but if Alan and Ian don't quit acting out, I may have to drive into town to find some place."

"The library's nice," shared Thomas. He put some bread in the toaster. "I don't know what to do about the boys."

"I'm still worried about Wright," Susan said.

"That's what I mean," Thomas agreed. He stared vacantly as the toaster quietly hummed, the heat escaping the two slots. "I hope this wasn't a mistake." Susan averted her eyes, casting her gaze to the floor. She traced imaginary patterns between the wood. Her lack of response wasn't lost on Thomas.

"I think I'm going to get a shower first," Susan said, departing from the kitchen. She headed out, leaving Thomas behind with his worries. She headed up the stairs to the second floor, to the closet by Kirstie's room. She opened the spacious closet shelves and reached all the way to the back to grab a purple towel. Soft but with some texture to it, it was her favorite. She pulled it out, but heard shifting from inside Kirstie's room. The door ajar, Susan leaned inside.

Kirstie stood at the window, looking out into the backyard at the dawn. Susan smiled and knocked on the door very lightly, more to push it open. Her daughter turned and smiled. "Good morning, mom."

"Hey," Susan said with a genuine smile. She crossed the room to Kirstie and hugged her. The window ledge was wide enough for Kirstie to sit upon with ease. Hugging Kirstie, Susan felt a pang of regret for not being more supportive of Thomas. A look out at the farmland beauty of the sunrise made her question her own hesitations. The view was breathtaking.

Susan turned and started to leave when something caught her attention. She looked around Kirstie's room, not sure what but troubled by something. The square room was hardly filled. A map of the solar system – a beloved prize from a cereal competition years ago – was all that decorated the wall opposite the bed. A chest sat opposite the bed by the window and boxes littered the far corner. Most of the spacious room was empty, waiting to be filled with the personal belongings still in boxes downstairs.

Susan turned back to Kirstie, who could see her worry but didn't understand it. "What is it?" she asked as Susan stepped out of the room. "Mom?"

Susan stepped out onto the balcony that rounded the second floor, connecting the rooms. She turned and looked down into the first floor, then back to the second. She looked at her daughter's room through the door, then at the closet just a step away.

"Mom, what is it?" Kirstie asked.

Susan looked down at her towel. "I haven't had my coffee," she muttered. But her resolve wouldn't let her surrender. She opened the closet and looked inside, at the arm's length to the back. She reached inside and had to stand on her toes to reach over the linens to touch the back. The wall was solid.

Susan re-entered Kirstie's room and looked at the wall. The room was perfectly square, as it always had been. Susan turned and focused on the door itself. "Where's the closet?" she asked aloud, looking to where the wall should have indented. She knocked on the wall, the echo resounding loudly through the house. The knock was heavy and solid, the wall sturdy.

"Susan?" Thomas said up to her from the first floor as she exited Kirstie's room. "Was that you?"

"Yeah," Susan said, going back onto the balcony and checking in the closet. She reached inside and banged on the rear wall, getting a hollow sound, like there was a gap in the space. Susan stepped back from the hall closet and realized, "Something's very wrong."

Ian and Alan both met at the door into Kirstie's room, comparing their respective tape measures. "You're off by two inches," Alan told Ian.

"No I'm not," Ian argued caustically. "I measured exactly where you knocked."

"I knocked two feet, twenty-four inches, from the door frame," Alan corrected him.

"No, you didn't," Ian said.

"Boys," said Susan, leaning on the banister. "Something's up with the closet. You both may be right." The pair looked unprepared to accept that explanation.

"This isn't possible," said Thomas, standing with Ian and looking into the closet. He tilted his head to see up at the top of the closet. He leaned out and checked the height of the second-floor ceiling. "That's taller." He walked around his boys and checked into Kirstie's room. "Yeah, this is too."

All four entered Kirstie's room and took turns assessing it compared to the roof level of the second floor. "This looks like it's, I don't know, almost two feet higher," said Ian.

Alan leaned over the bannister near his mom and craned his neck to see up the small opening to the third floor. "That can't be right. The third floor isn't that much higher."

"I'm not making it up, Alan!" Ian snapped.

"I'm not—" Alan stopped himself and lowered his voice. "You're right," he told Ian very deliberately. "I'm not saying you're not; I'm saying it's another...thing."

"This is like something out of Dr Who," said Kirstie. She was chewing on her nails.

"Maybe we can charge tickets," Ian suggested. "Make it a tourist attraction." Alan actually nodded, though with a pained look.

Thomas exited Kirstie's room and said, "First we've got to figure this out. There's got to be something we're not seeing."

"We can measure every surface, dad, but..." Alan held both hands at the closet. "You can see it as plainly as I can, as any of us can. That closet SHOULDN'T be there. It can't be."

"We live in an MC Escher house," Ian proposed with a sick chuckle. To Alan, he chided, "Well, not you." Alan resisted responding.

Thomas turned and checked in Kirstie's room, then looked out onto the balcony. He looked across the house to the door to Wright's room and saw it open.

The toys were still arranged in perfect little rows. "Wright?" Thomas called. "Wright?" he called louder.

Susan turned and looked at the house, still listening. "He wouldn't go outside without saying something." She ran to the nearest window and pushed it open, straining against the friction of ancient paint. "Wright?!" she called into the air outside. No sound came from the outside world except the chirp of summer insects. She turned back around into the house, panic gripping her throat. "Wright, honey, where are you?"

The only answer was the dusty silence of the old house.

"He was right here a minute ago," Ian said, looking around. He dashed off, charging up the steps to the third floor. "Wright!" Alan and Thomas ran down to the first floor, calling the youngest's name as well. Susan began to search through the second floor.

Kirstie rushed down the stairs to the first floor. She rounded into the back towards the kitchen. Inside, she saw the single flashlight on the kitchen counter. Grabbing it, she threw open the door into the basement. The cone of light pierced into the darkness and she ran down, shouting, "Wright?"

Light waited for her. Kirstie stopped halfway down, expecting to see Wright with the flashlight. Instead, she found a circular opening at the far end of the room. "DAD!" Kirstie screamed. She scampered back up the steps, exiting just as Thomas and Alan ran in.

Kirstie pointed down the steps, her finger shaking. "There's a thing down there," she said as she clutched to her father. Taking her flashlight, Alan raced down the steps. His footfalls rattled the wooden planks but when he reached the bottom, he froze.

"What is it?" Thomas yelled.

"There's a, there's another level," Alan reported. He looked back up. "There's nothing below the basement, right?"

"There wasn't a basement that I recall," said Thomas, following Alan down. "Not when the realtor showed it to us."

Alan gestured at the far end of the basement and said, "You really need to talk to the realtor then."

A metal disc was open, revealing light coming from underneath. Thomas and Alan approached carefully. Roughly a meter in diameter, the lightly bowled disc had a handle and a latch. It leaned against the far wall and moved with surprising ease, given its obvious weight.

Through the hole was another floor. After a foot or more of solid concrete, the space opened up into what appeared to be a room. Soft light like candles or lamps came up through the hole. Thomas leaned down over the hole and tilted his head. He swallowed fearfully but called, "Wright?" He waited for a second then tried again. "Wright?!"

A distant call followed.

"Dad?"

Thomas nearly fell into tears that instant. He grabbed Alan's arm with relief and gasped for air. "Son, I need you to come back!" he yelled into the hole.

"I don't know how!" screamed Wright. "I don't know what's happening!"

Thomas and Alan looked confused. Thomas turned to Kirstie who stood at the base of the steps. "Honey, go get your mom." He turned back but Alan was already climbing down.

Beyond the concrete layer, wooden dowels were stretched from one side of the wall to the other. They groaned and creaked with his weight but Alan climbed down without too much trouble. He found himself in a hallway of paper walls. Like some sort of Japanese construction, the walls went from floor to ceiling, both of rough, uneven concrete. The frames were deeply stained but otherwise unstylistic. The paper was off-white, yellowed with age more than design. The walls all seemed to glow, like a candle waited just behind each sheet of paper.

"What do you see?" Thomas asked, leaning down into the hole.

Alan nodded towards the end of the hallway. "I think I see a junction," he said. He looked back at his father. "Something is seriously up, dad."

"Yeah, and we've got to get Wright out of there," Thomas agreed.

"Yeah, but how?" asked Alan.

Thomas thought for only a moment, then realized, "I've got an idea."

"Honey?" Susan called into the paper walls. "Wright, can you hear me?"

"Mom!"

"Stay where you are, honey!" she called to him. "We're on our way."

She turned around as Thomas began to explain, "This rope is tied off. Kirstie, I want you to hold this end. We'll go until the packing rope stretches, and then you hold this end of this rope." He put another long stretch of furniture cord in her other hand. "We keep going until this stretches and then Ian, you will hold it. We will stretch as far as possible and we'll find Wright. We just go systematically and clockwise and we will find him in no time."

"Yeah, this can't be that big," Ian agreed. His confidence wasn't absolute, nor was it shared by the others.

"And the hatch isn't going to close?" asked Kirstie, looking up the ladder wall at the entrance of the maze.

"It's propped open with a 2x4 and two of the bricks from the old garden," Susan promised her.

"And besides, that thing is heavy; it's not going to fall back against gravity," Alan added as well. She only fell silent, not even nodding.

"Come on, guys," Thomas told them. He tugged on the rope tied to the dowels, confirming it was solid. "Let's go." As he started down the hall, he called, "Wright! We're coming towards you. Can you hear me?"

"Yeah."

"He sounds farther away," Susan worried as she stayed close to Thomas.

"No he doesn't," Ian insisted. Alan glowered at him.

At the end of the hallway, they arrived at a T-intersection. Thomas glanced down both paths, seeing identical routes in either way. "Wright?" he called. "At the first intersection, do you remember if you went left or right?" This time, there was no answer. "Wright? Wright!"

"Oh god," Susan gasped, her hands tightening.

"Come on," Thomas insisted, focusing on moving proverbially and literally onward. They turned to the left and started down the waiting hallway. They only made it halfway to the end when Kirstie was brought to a stop. She said nothing, only looked guiltily at the rope now pulled partially taught. The five looked worriedly at each other, then Thomas urged them on.

At the next intersection, another T-route just like the first, Thomas called, "Wright?" He still got no response. He chose right this time instead of left. They kept going, moving carefully but with some urgency, until Ian came to a stop. "You okay, Kirstie?" called Susan.

"Yeah, mom," she yelled. "Just freaked out."

"Okay," Susan acknowledged. She touched her son's face, but then the remaining three continued on. They headed down the path until they arrived at another intersection. A T-intersection, just like the previous.

"This isn't possible," Alan reasoned, looking in all the possible directions. "We've already walked more than the house is wide."

"Don't think; just go," insisted Thomas. He chose right again and kept going. They didn't get far before Alan had to stop.

"Kirstie, you okay?" Thomas yelled.

"Yeah."

"Ian, how about you?" asked Susan.

"Fine," he called.

"Okay," Thomas concurred. "Wright?"

Still no response.

They made it through two more intersections before Susan had to stop. With terrified looks, she and Thomas said nothing. Thomas faced into the seemingly endless maze and took a deep breath. "Alan, you okay?" he called back behind them.

"Yeah," Alan said.

"Ian?"

Thomas already began to walk, his heart racing and his steps unsteady.

"I'm fine, dad," Ian yelled.

"Kirstie?"

Thomas stopped walking entirely. He spun around and yelled, "Kirstie?!" A hard, oppressive silence hung in the air. "KIRSTIE!" Thomas yelled. He turned and took one step back.

He was plunged into total darkness.

Thomas froze absolutely still, too stunned to even react, too startled to even scream.

In that pitch blackness, more absolute than any darkness or night he had ever experienced, he was aware of two things: the slightest turnings of a breeze within the second basement level of endless paper walls.

More terrifying, though, was that he had lost the rope.

When the light slowly returned, like an old lamp taking its time to gradually illuminate, Alan spun around, panic gripping his throat. A sheen of sweat had broken out across his brow as he looked frantically about the hallway. The light had returned but there was no sign of anyone. Only a seemingly endless hall in either direction. Despite the light, the distance was lost into darkness.

"Guys?!" Alan called. "Wright!" he yelled. He listened as his voice was lost inside the hallway itself, the wood and paper absorbing his echo. "Mom?!" he yelled again. His voice tripped out of his throat, cracking as it went tumbling into the darkness. He turned to his right, then his left, then back again, eyes trembling just as his voice had.

Susan ran down the hall. Eyes wide with hysteria, she screamed at the top of her lungs, "WRIGHT!!!" She skidded to a halt, terror clutching her. "Kirstie! Alan!" She spun around and around, but found nothing but endless hall in both directions. No sign of her family, no sign of the rope, no sign of the way out. In the dimly-lit darkness, she was alone.

Ian punched the paper wall.

Furious, he struck with his knuckles. The paper rapped and bulged inward but it didn't quite give.

Ian backed away from the paper wall and looked at it as a whole. He backed all the way to the adjacent wall and then screamed. He threw himself forward, kicking the wall. The paper bowed deeply but didn't give. Ian dropped his foot but kicked again, and again. He pounded on the paper wall with all his might, determined.

When the paper refused to give, Ian roared furiously and grabbed the wooden frame. He tried to tear the wooden pieces apart with his bare fingers but was unable to get a hold. He drew back as he had done a moment before and kicked the frame itself, determined to do damage. Kicks rattled the frame and shook the paper walls. Punches and slaps shook and rocked the post but the sturdy wood held no matter what.

Ian backed away from the paper for a moment, watching the light dance on the page like a candle on the far side. He looked down the endless hall in either direction, then looked at the paper again. An idea struck and Ian grabbed his belt buckle. He undid his belt and slid it off, then held the buckle in his right hand, the tooth between his index and ring finger.

With a wide swing, Ian swung his fist at the paper. The tooth of the belt punched through the heavy paper like he was punching through thin wood. But the damage done, Ian was able to peer through the tiny pinprick of a hole. He saw nothing but now he had a target. He began to punch at the paper wall and the tiny hole was torn open, bit by bit, until there was enough to fit his hand through.

With another feral growl, Ian ripped at the paper. Like tearing heavy cotton, he had to put his entire might behind the act but the wall finally gave and the paper tore. With all his strength, Ian ripped the thick paper down from the middle of the wall to the base, dropping to his knees as he did.

A blustery pulse of an invigorating breeze struck Ian but then the lukewarm air stagnanted again. Ian muscled his way through the paper, struggling to get through what moments ago had seemed fragile enough to tear with ease.

Like sliding through the membrane, the rough edge scratched Ian as he passed into the new territory. He fell out onto familiar concrete flooring. He scrambled quickly to his feet and turned around with a start. All that waited for him was an identical hallway. Ian looked in both directions, seeing nothing but the endless expanse of wooden slats of the paper wall.

Rage blunted by uncertainty, Ian turned again and again, until he forgot which way he had first found himself facing. "M-mom?" he called into the distance. No answer returned.

Kirstie slid to a halt, not stopping in time before she went sliding passed. She scampered back to the missing slat of wood in the wall. As innocuous as the rest of the hallway of wooden frames and paper walls, a single stretch was missing a pane. As if it had simply been overlooked, the gap was unremarkable.

Kirstie carefully stepped to the threshold and peeked her head into the adjacent hall. She saw more endlessness in both directions, with no distinction between this new expanse and the one she had been traveling. "Hello!" she yelled down the hall. "Is anyone there?!" she called in the other direction. No echo carried and no response came back.

Thomas ran along the hallway, trotting in the stagnant air that refused to move. He raced a dozen slats in the endless hall, then slowed and looked back. He rested his hands on his head as he tried to make some sense of what he was seeing, unable to handle the disorientating distances of the hallways he was passing through. He checked again the roof and saw only more concrete. For a brief instant, he felt vertigo, unable to remember floor from ceiling.

He turned back the way he'd been facing, about to start running when he heard a shout.

"Dad!"

It was distant and it was faint and it was Wright's voice.

Thomas turned and ran in the direction of the voice. "Wright?!" he yelled. "I'm coming!"

The loud grunts of effort were absorbed by the wooden slats and the paper walls.

Ian punched the paper wall again with the buckle of his belt, only to shriek in pain suddenly. He dropped his belt and leapt back from him, holding his hand. Blood pooled in his palm as he winced and growled in pain. He smacked the nearest paper wall in fury, then glared down at his belt. A small chunk of skin was stuck to the metal buckle.

Ian screamed and kicked his belt, then yelled again. He glowered at the wall he had been battering and kicked it. Doing so didn't tear the heavy paper but the light on the other side went out.

The sudden darkness stunned Ian, his jaw dropping open, eyes wide in surprise. "What the hell?" He spun around, certain he was about to be jumped from behind. He saw no one and nothing, only the short line of torn walls from one row of halls to the next.

It was in looking back that Ian realized the light hadn't disappeared. The previous wall he had stepped through, with a gaping hole torn and ripped through the middle, was still alight. Despite the lack of any candles or torches, despite the lack of any light source visible, the paper walls still glowed with the vibrant, textured light of flames just on the other side.

Even the torn walls.

Ian looked through the hole, at the previous walls he had torn his way through. Those walls were just as illuminated as the untattered walls. Every panel of paper gave off the same ambient, soft glow.

All except one.

Ian turned back to the single darkened pane of paper like it was the source of and solution to all of his problems. He snatched up his belt, the buckle still slick with his own blood. Holding it in his left hand, he went for the paper with all the determination he could muster.

Susan almost ran passed it.

Determined to find the next intersection, determined to find the route out, determined to find her children, determined to find some sign of hope in the dark endless hallway, she almost missed it.

A single pane of paper, one out of a hundred just like it, was completely dark. So focused on her family, on her children, Susan didn't process the anomaly until she was already running passed.

She skidded to a halt and turned. She ran to the sheet of fragile paper and put her hands to it. An icy cold came off the paper, like there was no heat to be found on the other side. A glance around and Susan realized all the other panes were still alight with soft firelight just behind. She backed away from the pane, looking at its inert darkness, unaware she was no longer alone.

The soft fall of sneaker footsteps on concrete proceeded Kirstie as she walked down the hall. She glanced over her shoulder, worried something or someone would come up behind her. Instead, each glance only showed her the same endless hallway extending behind her into the stagnant, endless darkness.

It was only by chance that she noticed the darkened spot. It was only because she was turning to face forward once again that she picked up on the pane in the hallway wall. The patch of paper walling was perfectly dark unlike its neighbors. Kirstie stopped before the pane, then looked up and down the hall, certain someone would blame her for the irregularity.

After a moment of stillness, she reached for the wall. Her fingertips touched the parchment-like paper, then she gasped when it fell forward. Kirstie shrieked in shock as the entire segment of the wall fell inward, collapsing onto the adjacent hallway.

The clatter sounded like an explosion. So used to the tense silence of the hallway, with only her breath and her feet to hear, the collapsing wall segment was almost too much din for her to process. Yet as the clatter subsided and the walls soaked up the noise, the silence resumed. With tentative, fearful steps, Kirstie approached the opening.

The wall had not fallen cleanly onto the far concrete floor. While the space beyond was identical to the previous hallway, another long row of endless wooden panels with seemingly thin paper lit from behind, the darkened panel that had fallen onto something.

Kirstie stepped over the threshold into the next hall and bent down to move the panel. She shifted the surprisingly light pane, with no more weight than a breezy screen door. She moved it with ease, only to discover beneath the pane the corpse of her own mother.

"Dad!"

Thomas ran as quickly as he could, desperate to make it to his son. Every step carried him preciously closer towards Wright, but not nearly as fast as needed.

Thomas thought nothing of the darkened pane as he ran passed it. It didn't register with him in the slightest as he ran passed the single solitary bit of wall that held no illumination. He just ran on, focused on his son's calls and nothing else.

Alan spotted the paper flap dangling in the stale air.

He slowed his jog, approaching the singular derivation with great caution. He checked over his shoulder, then looked ahead, but the dark hallway remained as ominous as ever. The closer he got, the more he could make out. A piece of the frail paper wall had been torn, a large flap bowing in. The flap was still illuminated, light coming off of it as if a candle hung just beyond. When Alan neared, his approach kicked up the paper material. The flap half-floated at him like a reed in a breeze. Both sides glowed brightly, the paper reaching for Alan.

He looked to the pane, the fragments of paper hanging loose where they had been torn. Waiting through the ripped pane was another hallway, seemingly identical to this one. The one exception was a figure laying in the middle of the concrete floor.

The instant he recognized it, the instant he placed the boy's face, he muttered in horror, "Ian?"

Before Alan could rush to the cold body of his brother, the panes across from him went dark. Three adjacent panes zapped of light, as if the candles beyond them were snuffed out. Alan looked at the darkness against those fragile bits of paper and felt a chill enter his soul. The very instant he realized he wasn't alone, he bolted.

Quick feet carried Alan down the hall, away from the torn paper, away from the darkened panes, away from the body of his brother. Quick, furtive glances back told Alan nothing of whoever or whatever had been near him. He didn't know how far away he was getting, only that his lead was mercifully increasing.

In the distance, something appeared in the darkness. Not an object or a person but a change in the featureless blackness. The endless distance faded, becoming another pane of paper wall. The end of the hallway was revealed.

Alan set his sights on it and tore for the edge of the hall. He looked back again, certain he wasn't alone. He ran faster and faster still, pushing himself until his lungs burned and his legs ached. The distant wall was looming, drawing closer with agonizing sloth.

The nearer and nearer Alan came, the more he realized the far path led to no mere wall. Not a dead-end or an intersection, but the exit itself. Somehow, through turn after turn, he'd found his way back to the exit. Against the wall, set against the paper pane identical to so many others, were a row of dowels. Wooden rods running horizontally, they went from floor to ceiling with roughly a foot between each. And just above them, through the concrete ceiling. Above them, through the circular opening that led back into the house, awaited freedom and safety of the world beyond. Escape.

Within sight and then within reach, Alan stretched out his hand. His fingers reached for the dowels, only to be brought short by crippling pain. Alan screamed in agony and fell to the floor, his legs giving out beneath him. Just a few inches from the ladder, he screamed frantically. He tried to crawl the last little bit, but a loud crunch of snapping bone drowned out his subsequent scream. His body rebelled against him, refusing to move. He shuddered in pain, his mind unable to grasp the agony he felt.

As he struggled, as he fought to retain some sanity in the face of the pain, sneakered footsteps passed over Alan. In terror, he looked up as Wright stepped passed him. Through his pain, Alan heard hysterical crying. He rolled onto his back and tried to lift his leg but what should have felt like an easy movement felt like dragging a sack of rocks. He sat up only enough to see his legs utterly misshapen from internal damage. The bones within were in fragmented disarray.

"Wr-Wright?" Alan stammered, turning to his littlest brother. "Wright! G-get out of here!"

Wright was crying. His face was twisted in sorrow, hysterical beyond all rational thought. His mouth was warped downward as tears streamed off his cheeks. He passed Alan, walking calmly and casually towards the dowel ladder, towards the escape. "Run!" Alan told his brother.

Wright climbed the rungs with a certainty of movement impossible for his emotional state. He moved with a grace Alan had never before seen in the young boy. He crawled up the ladder with great ease but not great hurry. Crying with every step, Wright ascended the ladder to the apex of the hole. There, as Alan watched, he shoved away the wooden beam blocking open the escape. Alan could hear the 2x4 go sliding across the floor of the basement. A second later, he heard the metal lid slam shut with terrifying finality.

Then, Alan felt it. He didn't hear it. He didn't even see it. He felt it. He felt a darkness encroaching. He managed through the pain to look down the long, endless hallway. The straight path for which there had seemed no end was now ending. The far distance that enveloped the hall was beginning to draw near. Pane after pane of paper wall was darkening. Rapidly, the end of the hall, the end of the light, was approaching.

"Wright...?" Alan whispered, turning back to the ladder out of the basement. From the hole dropped Wright. The little boy landed on the concrete floor, his left ankle twisting painfully. Wright screamed in pain but he didn't drop. Despite the crunch of bone, despite the warped and visibly broken joint, the boy remained standing. He even stepped on the foot, causing the crying boy to scream out.

"Wr-Wright..." stammered Alan as the boy approached.

"I CAN'T STOP!" Wright sobbed as he neared his eldest brother.

Alan looked back as the darkness drew near. The closest panes were going out, one by one, leaving only absolute blackness beyond them. The subterranean realm was growing dark. Alan looked to his brother as the boy knelt. A single hand reached out for him, fingers Alan knew touching his arm. The instant contact was made, Alan howled in agony. His own arm snapped against itself, forearm and elbow both twisting violently against their own form. Alan screamed again and fell onto his back as Wright moved closer and the darkness swallowed them.

The sun directly overhead oversaw the pleasantly warm summer day. A blue sky held a few wisps of white clouds that traveled slowly above the brisk breeze that turned the tall grass in the fields. The horizon was dotted with green trees. They stood in the distance, as though they refused to have any part of a solitary cluster in the middle of the fields. That cluster stood alone in the feral farmland through which ran a single, two-lane road.

In that private glade, that small cluster of trees, sitting alone was the house.

Robert V Aldrich

Music as Life, part 03

Steve Borden pinched the bridge of his nose as electronic dance music battered his ears. At the bar of the dance club, he stirred his soda and considered the purpose of existence, both for himself and the tiny straw he used to create bubbles in his drink. The dark brown refreshment seemed to absorb the light coming off the neon runners of the bar as well as the blacklight bulbs lighting the vibrant wall's graffiti-like decorations.

Steve checked to his left and saw a line of club goers. Ravers. Technogoths. EDM fans. Vinyl and leather. Chains and piercings. He checked to his right and saw more of the same. Small gaggles of people, clustered together. Drinking. Talking. Half-dancing, like they were warming up for the dance floor at the far end of the club.

Steve checked on the bartender. A woman in a surprisingly subdued black tank top and jeans, she had hearing-protecting ear plugs hidden by her partial afro. She was dumping ice into the chiller, an intense look on her face like she was juggling a to-do list well over a dozen items long. Steve turned back and looked into the club as a whole, listening to the throbbing pulse of the dance music. A cacophony of beats and hisses, he tried to find some rhythm or melody to it and could find only repetition.

A woman walked passed and Steve smiled at her, giving her a bit of a nod. She smiled very uncomfortably back and didn't even break stride as she rushed on, like she was desperate to make it from one conclave of people to the next, all in-crowds, all plugged into their own scene in the crowded club. It wasn't a party; it was a collection of private affairs all sharing the same space. And between it all was Steve, leaning against the bar.

"Dull," said Steve. He sat in the padded seat, a sneer on his face and the memory in his mind. In the warm attic, he clicked his tongue and shook his head. "That...that doesn't feel like it's enough, though."

"What doesn't?" asked Morgan Brandywyne, sitting across from him. Significantly taller than Steve, Morgan looked less like a therapist and more like a quarterback. He sat to one side, his head resting against his left hand. The chair was the same as Steve's, the two facing each other in an attic space absolutely full of music: CDs, cassettes, records, and a stereo system better than some radio stations.

"It wasn't just dull, at the club," Steve tried to consider. He was dressed from work, in jeans and a button-up shirt beneath an office jacket. "It was, like...it was like it was a let-down. Like it was disappointing. Like..." he laughed. "I've got to stop saying like." Morgan gave a singular smirk but otherwise didn't move.

Steve sat forward, his hands clasped together and hanging between his knees. "Like, I can handle - there, I did it again - I can handle not liking something. That's fine. Taste is subjective or personal or whatever. But this was, like, personal. You know? This was like going to a comedy show and the comedian making fun of something you legit like, or...or..." He finally just shrugged. "It was...I was offended to be so bored, I guess? Maybe?"

Morgan nodded. "What kind of music do you like?"

Steve shrugged. "I like a little bit of everything, I guess."

"Everyone says that," Morgan groaned.

"Well, I mean, it's true," Steve defended. "I listen to some country, some hip-hop. My boyfriend's big into metal so I've got some punk and some thrash. I own a couple of classical albums. I've got some Mannheim Steamroller, and not just the Christmas albums. I got Hamilton and Godspell. I even got some reggae that's not Bob Marley."

"But no EDM," Morgan observed.

"No, I've got some electronic dance music," Steve said. "I've got some Darude, some Jesse Felice, Traci Lords. I even have Psyche Rock by whats-his-name. The dude that did the Futurama theme."

"Pierre Henry," said Morgan. "And the song pre-dated Futurama by thirty years."

"Right," said Steve. "So I'm not the biggest EDM fan in the world but I'm not ignorant of it either."

"Okay," Morgan allowed, switching from his head leaning on his hand to leaning on three fingers. "Could it have just been a bad DJ? Bad club? Bad night?"

"No, because this has been happening," Steve pondered aloud. "It's been, I don't know, a few years since I went to a club and was, like, yeah! This is the new hotness, you know? It's been a while since I heard a song that really blew my hair off." He sat back and laid his hands on the armrests of the square-shaped chair. "I love music. Always have. Or at least as much as any non-musician. And I don't have this kind of set-up at home." He gestured at the floor-to-ceiling stereo system to his immediate right. "But I...but..." He gestured at the whole situation. "I know music. I like music. I love music. But I can't..." His words trailed as his enthusiasm deflated. He gave a giggle. "Maybe I'm just getting old, you know? Maybe I'm just too set in my ways."

Morgan surprised him when he said, "It happens."

Steve was a bit taken aback by that. "Well, I mean..." He wasn't sure how to defend himself. "I'm not THAT old. I got another two years until I turn thirty."

"Being old and a specific age are not the same thing," Morgan told him. "I've met teenage old women. I've met scrappy young octogenarians."

"Hmm," said Steve. He looked around the room. He saw milkcrates full of records and spotted a few titles he knew immediately. "I just...I don't know. I feel like everything that's being made now isn't as good as music that—"

"Let me just stop you right there," Morgan insisted. "Don't give me 'new music isn't as good as old music'. That tired old gripe is patently untrue. I can prove it a bunch of different ways, so let's not even go down that road."

"Then why can't I find anything that registers with me?" asked Steve.

"If a key doesn't open a lock, you don't say the key's defective: you recognize the key goes to a different lock," Morgan said. "As for your inability to find music you like, part of it is probably what you're getting exposed to. How do you find new music?"

"Well, I go to clubs," Steve said, as if that were the obvious choice. "Clubs are the ideal way to find new music."

Morgan stared for a second. He finally blinked then rubbed his eyes. "You're going to have to explain that one."

"Clubs thrive on popularity and hotness, the new hotness," Steve explained. "Clubs don't last long, either. Most clubs have, like, a two-to-four year life-cycle. Clubs provide you with a good snapshot of the good music, of what's popular. Popular and good don't always overlap but there's still surprising carryover. You find a good club and you go to it regularly and you keep your finger on the pulse of the music scene. When the club's attendance starts to drop, you move to somewhere else."

Morgan nodded thoughtfully. "That...almost makes sense, in an awful, superficial sort of way."

"I mean, it's not a flawless way to find music, but it beats a Youtube random generator," Steve said. "Algorithms are overrated. Besides, clubs have drinks. And people."

"You started going to clubs for the people?" Morgan asked.

Again, Steve shrugged without commitment. "I mean, I started going for the people, yeah. Clubs used to be more about picking up girls than the music, but the music is a part of it. Used to be, anyway."

"Okay," Morgan nodded. "What else? How else do you get introduced to new music?"

"I found it." James said, handing two concert tickets to Steven. "This band plays some songs that the older bands used to."

In the after-work hotspot downtown, Steve accepted the tickets between their two pilsner glasses. "And?" Steven said, looking at the tickets. As suits and ties unwound around him and well-paid waitstaff moved between the plush seats, Steve read off the tickets, "Beef Kittens?"

"Yeah, but they do it with electric guitars." James explained.

"They do what with electric guitars?" Steve asked. "Cover Journey?"

"No, not old like that; like Rosetta Tharpe-older stuff," he explained. "They do some Beethoven stuff too that's really good. It's all across the musical spectrum, but done as hardcore rock."

"I'm sure there's a moral to this story." Steven said, still staring at the tickets. He lifted his sunglasses, staring at the tickets closely. "Are these scalped?"

"You and me are going," James informed Steve.

"Says you. The last CD you gave me I had to fight my growing urge to kill you."

"See, you don't listen to enough metal," James said as he took the tickets back. "If you listened to metal, you'd know how to handle this kind of rage."

"Nothing about that sounds healthy," Steve told him. He sipped his beer and looked around at the restaurant. An expression not unlike the one he'd worn at the club came to his face. Resolved to not fall into complacency, he gave James an exaggerated smile. "Okay, honey, I'd love to be your date."

"Beef Kittens?" Morgan said with a quizzical look on his face. He thought for a second, his eyes darting about as he tried to process the name. "Yeah, they did the Dr. Seuss stuff, didn't they?"

"Yeah, that was them," Steve nodded. "Green Eggs and Ham to heavy metal. It was fun." He again shrugged. "It was more interesting to see which stories they did. The covers were..." He shrugged. "They closed the show with How the Grinch Stole Christmas, which was honestly a little underwhelming. Like, it was clear they were trying to avoid doing a Boris Karloff parody but it was like, just own it dudes."

Morgan turned in his chair. "Have I got one of their albums?" His eyes searched a seemingly random corner of the attic-turned-counseling-space. "I think I have just a couple of their MP3s."

"I mean, yeah, it was...it was fun," Steve went on. He got a cup of lemonade from the small shin-high table between and his therapist. "It was fine, but it wasn't like, mind-blowing. First concert I went to it, it was Billy Joel with my mom. It was...it was amazing. I didn't even know the words to Piano Man and I was singing along like a thousand other people or however many were there. And it was like that, all through my teens and college and after college. I loved going to see bands and musicals and stuff. I knew every piano bar in town. Karaoke was my jam. I'd go to indie book stores just to hear whatever weird mom-and-pop jam band was playing that afternoon."

Steve's eyes grew a little dark. "And then it was like, I stopped doing it. Not all at once, but...but I started listening to more classic stations than the new stuff. Wanting to hear covers rather than original works, you know? Before I know it, I can't name a single song more than three years old. Except maybe with derision. And it costs money, too. I used to buy albums just for one song, partially so I could discover all the other songs on there. Now...I take back almost every album I buy because they just don't do anything for me." He shook his head, growing just slightly angry. "I want some new music."

Morgan began to offer. "If you're looking for some recommendations, I'm sure—"

"No, that's not it," Steve lamented. "I want...not like music-music, but like the music I had. I want something that blows me away again." He snickered cynically. "Maybe the problem is me."

"More than likely," Morgan agreed too quickly for Steve's comfort.

"What the hell, man?" Steve balked. "I thought you were a therapist."

"Yeah, but I'm not a good one," Morgan retorted. Steve couldn't tell if he was joking sardonically or being apathetic. "This is a very vague class," Morgan told him. "It's built around self-exploration. In order for self-exploration to be valid, it must be honest. My role is to provide honesty. And, honestly, your problem is probably you." His tone wasn't brutal or even caustic, merely unpoetic. "You've got a simple equation: you and music. The music hasn't changed. Maybe it's a little better, maybe it's a little worse, but it's mostly as good as its always been. So if that variable remains constant, then we have to look at the other variable. That's you."

Steve weighed the response and accepted it but didn't quite know how to process it. Instead, he just sighed. "I just, maybe I've...maybe I'm full of music," he suggested. "Like, I've got a song for every emotion, every situation, you know? I've got my fast driving song, my heart broken song, all of that. Maybe there are only so many song-related needs in life and I've got a song for everything." Steve pondered that statement and admitted, "That's not a very comforting thought."

Morgan smiled. "Fortunately, music doesn't work that way."

"So you just go and...and what? Just talk about music?" asked James. He flipped the burger on the grill, juices sizzling. "That's therapy?" He took a swig from his longneck. "Is it, like...do you listen to music or something?"

"He offered but nah," said Steve. He tore open a bag of chips and fished out a handful. "Dude's got an amazing music collection. Like, his whole attic is just like this giant warehouse of CDs and records and stuff. It's amazing."

"Cool, but I don't get how it's therapy," James said. He sat on the deck railing that looked out over the freshly mowed lawn in the summertime dusk.

Steven moved to sit down on the nearby wicker seat, only to find a gray and white cat on the pad. He padded the cat to move but the animal didn't shift in the slightest. It only let out a deep-seated growl and remained perfectly motionless. Steve reconsidered his plan, leaning against the siding of the house instead. "It's talking through music, and why it's important and stuff." He ate a few of the chips out of his hand.

"Is this about the Beef Kittens concert again?" James groaned.

"No, man, it's..." Steve fell silent as he looked off. "You know, I'm not sure what it's about. It's just...it's about...something."

James nodded. "Yeah, that's worth paying for therapy over."

Steve gave him a look. "Dude, come on. I'm not feeling something that I should."

"And what's that?" asked James.

Steve only shrugged. He ate more chips, still shaking his head as he tried to reason his way towards expressing his own issues. "I've got an MP3 player that holds over a thousand songs. I used to buy a new album every week. But now...it's like music just isn't working. It's like music just isn't what it used to be, isn't what it should be."

James snickered as he closed the lid of the grill. "Yeah, that's because modern music sucks." The accusation didn't sit well with Steve but he didn't refute it.

The sliding glass door of the patio opened and James's daughter Denise came out into the twilight. "Are the burgers ready yet?" she asked in her bratty tween voice. It contrasted with the chirp of crickets in the manicured lawn.

"Not yet, honey," said James. Steve offered her some chips and she accepted a few before returning to the house. "You should try heavy metal again," James suggested after the sliding glass door shut.

"Yeah, no," Steve waved off. "That stuff's nothing but a bottled up bad day in one go."

James laughed. "What?" He checked the burgers, turning them again. "Almost ready," he told himself, savoring the anticipation.

"Metal," Steve restated. "Look, I mean, I've got a few Black Sabbath songs." James laughed at that. "I dug hard rock and stuff back when I was younger too. But no, man, these days...it just seems unhealthy. It's just...it's just so angry. All it does, all that music makes you feel is violent and pisses you off."

"Yeah," James said. "Your blues stuff makes you feel depressed and terminally sad. And man, some of that stuff, I do mean 'terminal'."

"But violent, Jim," Steve argued. "That's not healthy."

"Neither is being depressed," said James.

It took Steve several minutes to say anything else.

In the interim, James loaded the plate with the burgers cooking on the grill. He replaced them with new paddies of meat and handed the plate over to Steve. "Go take these in to the kids, will you?"

"Sure," said Steve. He collected the plate and started to head inside when he was goosed on the backside. Steve spun around and stared at James, who was playing innocent, drinking from his beer. Steve blushed terribly and headed in through the sliding glass door.

Denise was in the living room, on her phone, while her two younger brothers were paddling away on the controls of a Star Wars game on the big screen TV. The instant Steve entered, though, all three smelled the burgers and turned to the plate. "Ooh, I want a cheese burger," said Franklin, the youngest boy.

"Me too!" squealed Elliot, both of them jumping up.

"Just hold on, okay," Steve told them as he set the plate on the table at the back of the room. "Your dad's got more cooking too." He got out of the way as the three kids attacked the plate of burgers like piranhas.

He turned when he heard the door opening. James was slipping inside. "Hey, have we got..." He saw the ruckus. "Denise, watch the burgers, will you?"

"'Kay," she said, phone in one hand and a burger with a bite missing already in the other. She surrendered neither hand to open the sliding glass door. She pushed it narrowly apart with her elbow and slipped backwards outside, her eyes not leaving her screen.

Steve watched her go and asked, "Who eats JUST a burger? No condiments or anything."

"She's going through this weird 'pesticides-are-bad-so-vegetables-are-bad' phase," James waved off. "Come here," he told Steve. He led the way down the hall to the far room at the opposite end of the house.

"Ah, the man-cave," Steve teased.

James flicked on the light to reveal a modest but respectable entertainment center. On the wall were dozens of gothic posters from underground heavy metal bands. James turned on the stereo and cued up a song on his player. Almost immediately, driving guitars and drums came barreling through the speakers.

"Feel that?" James asked Steve. "Feel that, in your gut?"

"I feel it in my inner ear," Steve said with a grimace.

"Feel the anger, feel the emotion," James pushed. He pointed at a werewolf's poster on the far wall. "Fix on that. That's what you hate."

"What I hate?" snickered Steve. "Like mange?"

"Shut up," James insisted. "That's when the waiter got your order wrong. That's when the remote didn't work. That's when you dialed the wrong number and the person was a dick. That's everything you hate." He jammed his finger at the poster. "Look at it!" James yelled, pointing at the metal post as music made of rage and aggression blasted out the speakers. "That's everything you hate. That's everything that's ever held you back. That's everything that has ever made your life hard, difficult, miserable, and otherwise unbearable. Look at it. Stare it. Yell at it!"

Steve glared at the poster. He balled his anger around the werewolf like it was a fist closing on the monster's throat. As the music drove, he began to nod, breathing harder. Reaching inside, he let out a loud groan. What was disappointing though gave him momentum. He followed it with a shout that came from his chest. That was followed with a final, torrential scream. Like something had truly broken within him, he let fly all his anger and roared at the top of his lungs.

The door of the room opened and Elliot peaked inside, looking not so much worried as confused and inconvenienced. "Are you two making out again?"

Steve laughed, blushing terribly. "I'm teaching your future stepdad to appreciate music," James told his son.

"Can you do it without drowning out the game?" his eldest son asked, shutting the door as he departed.

"Ugh," Steve groaned, covering his face. He looked at James and asked, "Well? How was that?"

"Not bad for a geriatric scream," said James, patting Steve on the back.

"You listen to music that makes you feel like doing this all the time?" Steve asked. "Seems crazy to me. And I'd lose my voice in an instant."

"Yeah, but you get used to it," said James. "So, do you feel any better?"

Steve looked at the poster, then at James. "Yeah. I mean, I guess so."

"See, the thing is, you can't listen to too much of this stuff," James explained as they exited the room. "You listen to it until you get the feelings out, then you, I don't know, go listen to something about making out."

"Now, that I can understand," Steve nodded before he goosed James in return.

"Huh," Morgan said as Steve finished recounting the exchange. He nodded and decided, "Yeah, that...yeah." He shifted in the seat and sat his head against his right hand. "I mean, he's definitely on to something. Lemmy Kilmeister said 'Heavy Metal was rebellion for the sake of rebellion', so that makes sense in a weird way."

"In a juvenile way," Steve said with a giggle of reminiscing.

"Music is emotional, not necessarily mature," Morgan defended.

"I guess," was all Steve had to suggest. He looked at the wall of CDs to his left. His eyes drew over a few titles he remembered like fingers sliding along the texture of a chain-link fence.

Morgan noted the dropped conversation and changed subjects. He shifted in his seat and asked, "You keep coming back to this need to find something new. You keep wanting to find something else, something that catches your attention like music used to." Steve nodded. "That hasn't been addressed. You are focusing on the solution: new music. Where is this need coming from?"

Steve seemed astonished. "What do you mean? Why's it so weird to want something new?"

"It's kind of counter to a lot of what others want," postulated Morgan. "Most people don't want new; they want the same-old."

"No, the new hotness is always what sells," Steve asserted.

"No," Morgan corrected. "People want the old repackaged as the new. Sequels. Prequels. Follow-ups. Covers. New versions of old phones. They want what they know."

Steve gave it some thought. He decided if it wasn't true, it was certainly compelling. "I wonder why," he speculated.

"It's comforting," explained Morgan. "It's why kids like to watch the same TV show again and again. Same for older folks watching reruns of shows they grew up with. It's comforting to know what's going to happen. In a chaotic and hectic world, knowing the outcome brings us some solace, some sense of control. New stuff can be scary, even if it's just the uncertainty of knowing whether or not it will be quality."

Steve rolled that idea around in his head. "Makes sense, I guess," he said distantly. "When I was young, my uncle came to live with us. He was a lot older than my mom. Like, a decade and a half older or something. He had had a stroke and...you know, she was the only one in the family with a college degree, much less a masters. She was the only one with, like, a real job. So the whole family was kind of just, 'unload Uncle Davie on her'." He sighed. "He spent all day watching westerns. Old westerns. And, like, the same stuff. He watched all of Rawhide in one week or something. I guess it was for the comfort. He was scared, either because of the partial paralysis or because he knew he was going to die."

The specter of the dark thoughts passed like the shadow of a cloud crossing over the sun. "But that's what I mean. Back then, I got Rawhide stuck in my head. The theme to the show?"

"Frankie Laine," Morgan attributed.

"Yeah," Steve said, having no idea if that was correct. "That's what I mean. That song..." Words dribbled off as thoughts slowed to a stop. "That song meant something to me back then. It was unique and fresh and...and good!" He asked Morgan, "Why can't I find stuff like that now?"

The elevator parted and Steve was standing in the very middle of the doors. Laptop slung on his side, he bopped his head a bit as he exited. In high-top sneakers, he headed across the office floor, well aware of the eyes of all the suit-clad workers watching him go. The office was an open layout, with tall cubicle walls over which was a frosted skylight. Some music lightly played from a few cubicles as offices and conference rooms lined the perimeter.

He crossed to the far side of the elevators, towards the only office with double doors. He knocked on the frosted glass of the central office, then opened and peeked inside. "You called?"

In the very center of the spacious office, the company president turned. She exhaled with relief. "Oh thank god," she said with elation. The silver-haired woman waved frantic hands at her desk, urging Steve at her workspace. "I don't know what happened," she summed up as she surrendered her seat.

Steve went sliding right behind her desk and dropped into the seat. He looked at the screen full of report data. He moved the mouse, then tapped a few keys, the screen totally unresponsive. "It just froze?"

"Just like that," she said with a nod at the screen. She stood on the receiving end of the desk, between the two comfortable office chairs.

Steve clicked a couple of buttons and his brow furrowed. "And you—"

"I tried turning it off and on again but that didn't do anything. The screen came back on, just like that," she said. "I thought about unplugging it but I wasn't sure if I should." The worried uncertainty didn't match her normal, quietly commanding charisma.

Steve tried a few more button combinations. "Did you download the new patch for WoW?"

"I stopped playing World of Warcraft," the corporate matron insisted. Steve leveled a disapproving glare at her. "At work," she insisted. The look from Steve didn't change. "What?!" she exclaimed. "I switched to Final Fantasy."

Willing to believe that, Steve leaned back in her chair. "Did you delete WoW?" She nodded. "Maybe that's the problem. Something got crossed up in the..." He took out his laptop and opened it, then fished through the bag to find some wires. "If the deletion didn't take, or if you deleted while the patch was downloading or something..." He began connecting the two computers.

"Just please tell me I didn't lose my computer," said the president.

"You are backing your stuff up on the network, right?" he asked her. The older woman blushed apologetically. "Becky! That's why you wanted us to set up the backup server to begin with! Specifically for this! Specifically!" He flailed at the frozen computer monitor.

"I know!" She paced away for a moment. She tapped nervously at her thigh, a quirk from her smoking days never quite purged. "I just, I can't get into the habit. All my spreadsheets are on the local drive."

Steve half-covered his face as he waited for the auto-diagnostics to run on his laptop. He watched the progress bar travel across the screen, then numbers began to dribble forth. Becky came up behind him and looked at the screen. "What does that mean?" she asked, pointing at a red set of numbers.

"That the flux capacitor is going critical unless I can reverse the polarity," he told her before glowering up at her. "You run the business. I'll..." He derisively waved his hand at the computer.

Becky went to the shelf of glass and light near the front of her office. "I can't do much running with my computer down," she complained.

"Yeah, well, if only the company had a huge and expensive computer system you could back up your data on," Steve said as he clicked on his laptop.

"Yeah, yeah," she ignored. She pulled from the shelf a glass bottle of brandy and filled a small glass a third of the way. "Want some?"

He shook his head. He realized what he'd been offered and asked, "You keep your booze that far from your desk?"

"Otherwise I drink it all by noon," she answered as she returned. "Why, where do you keep your wine coolers?"

"In a shoe box under Dave's desk," said Steve.

Becky lost it, giggling. "I knew there was a reason I never fire you."

"My boyish charm?" guessed Steve sarcastically. Becky just made a sour face. "Having a gay IT guy gets you some kind of diversity credit?" She shrugged, halfway accepting that as not a bad reason. "My stellar record collection? Or my embarrassingly comprehensive knowledge of American gas station chains?"

"I think it is your clever and high-brow manner of framing your coworkers," she said. She set down her brandy and opened a drawer on her desk. She took out a pack of peanutbutter crackers.

"What, have you got an entire snack bar down here?" Steve asked, looking in the shelf. "Cripes, the vending machine isn't that well-stocked."

"I have Jorge stock it with various goodies," she said as she opened the pack. "Keeps my taste buds on my toes." She flipped him a cracker like it was a coin. "After The Change, I figure I'm eating whatever I damn-well please."

"Makes sense to me," Steve said as his laptop beeped. "Okay, there we go," he said with a relieved sigh. "Okay, yeah. WoW and Final Fantasy XIV aren't playing nice. Who knew two MMOs would be so problematic?"

"I deleted it," Becky insisted, leaning over Steve so she could look at his diagnostic screen.

"Sometimes, it doesn't take," he assured her as he clicked his keyboard. "They make programs hard to get rid of." He was momentarily distracted. "And then if a patch gets released and they..." More distraction. "Yeah," he finished.

Becky had some more brandy and paced a bit. Unused to, and uncomfortable with, even a moment of inactivity, she asked blindly, "Are you still doing your music thing?"

Steve snickered, a delayed response as he worked. "My music thing?"

"You got on that kick a few months ago about asking for suggestions for new music," Becky recalled. "Takara gave you that whole CD collection of classical music."

Steve nodded, his attention mostly on the computer. "Yeah, that was awkward."

"He doesn't know how to give gifts," she reasoned. "Anyway, are you still looking for suggestions?"

Steve was focused on the code. "Sure," he said a little absently. He leaned forward, like doing so would magically make the letters and numbers make more sense. A few more keyboard strokes and the program made no more sense. He undid what he'd just done and kept working.

"I was thinking about this band my granddaughter likes," Becky waxed. "We went to go see them last weekend. It's some K-Pop band."

"K-pop?" asked Steve.

"Korean Pop music," Becky explained. "They did some shows here in the United States. A few conventions and some full concerts."

"Cool," was all the thought process Steve could spare.

"But yeah, it was good stuff," said Becky. She strolled around the chair on the opposite side of the desk and sat down. She had another cracker and said, "Boys were cute too."

"I'll bet," Steve said. He ducked under the desk for a moment and could be heard fiddling with the computer tower.

"Not a pop music fan?" Becky asked.

"Not really," he said. He pulled out and checked his laptop screen. He smiled and nodded, pleased with himself, then sat back and began to type. "I mean, I like some of it and it's good popcorn stuff, I guess, but I prefer music by people who actually write it themselves."

Becky scoffed. "Not a fan of Backstreet Boys then? Not a fan of Nick or Jonas?"

"Nick was in N'Sync; Jonas was...I'm going to guess the Jonas brothers?" He kept typing, scowling now. "And, again, it's okay ear popcorn, but they don't write their own music."

"Neither did Frank Sinatra," Becky countered. "And who's to say that N'Step or whoever didn't help write some of their songs. Sounds to me like you just aren't willing to give it a chance, just because you don't want to."

Steve gave it some thought and then grudgingly admitted, "You've got a point."

Becky opened her purse and fished around for a bit. "Here," she said, handing over a CD. "I got this at one of the shows. My granddaughter already got the songs, so I don't need it." She handed Steve the disc. "You can see how talented they are," she teased, referring to the gorgeous Asian models on the cover of the CD.

"Yeah, you can really see their...I say goddamn," Steve gawked, accepting the CD.

Korean music was humming out of Steve's speakers as he puttered along the freeway. His sunroof was open, as though letting the music out. The music wasn't bad by any stretch, nor was it particularly different. It was pop music: nigh identical to what he knew of domestic pop. Only the words were a different language, but he was confident he could infer from context in the music as to what was being sung. The melody was catchy but it didn't even manage to inspire a toe-tap.

Steve pondered this as he checked his blind spot, sitting forward to see out his rearview mirror. He scarcely had time to confirm that his way was clear to merge when he heard a squeal of brakes and the terrifying crunch of metal. He swerved out of the way just before he would have rammed into the car in front of him, instead diving to the side of the right-most lane. The car that had come to such an abrupt stop had plowed straight into the car before it, as it had done with the car before it. The three-car pile-up brought traffic to a complete stop as the three cars were condensed into the space of narrowly more than one car.

Steve idled passed the crash, the ridges of the shoulder slowing him quickly. Coming to a stop, he threw off his seatbelt. Not even uncranking his car, he leapt out and started to jog back towards the crash. Already several car lengths passed, he ran with increasing worry and bewilderment. Several other onlookers were already responding.

The front-most driver had already gotten out. The car sandwiched in the middle of the collision was crumpled badly but the driver seemed awake, aware, and moving. Most importantly, he seemed calm.

The rear-most car was the terrifying issue. The driver inside appeared to be panicking, or flailing in pain. He was kicking and beating at the door. Steve and several others rushed to help him but the door was slammed shut, the metal crumpled over repeatedly.

Steve beat on the roof and shouted, "Are you okay?" What followed was a string of profanities. Before Steve could process it, the man kicked out the door. Steve and several other responders backed away as the driver leapt out. He saw the car before him and yelled. He started stalking right for the driver's door. "Whoa, whoa!" Steve yelled. He and the others moved to intercept the road raged driver, not physically stopping him but getting between him and the door.

Steve backed out of the fray and surveyed the situation. The angry driver was stopping, though still furious and not without reason. Likewise, traffic in the far two lanes was beginning to move, albeit slowly. Steve pulled out his cell phone, backing up farther into the curb. He dialed 911 and tried to grapple with the sight of the crash. He looked for some sign of where they were on the interstate.

"911, What's your emergency?" came the woman on the other end of the phone.

"Yeah, hey," said Steve. He realized he was out of breath. "I'm, uh, I'm Steve." He balked, not sure what to say. "Uh, there was a, an accident. With cars."

"Okay, Steve, are you on the interstate?" she asked.

For a moment, Steve panicked and was afraid he was in trouble. "....yeah?"

"Okay, we're already getting a million calls," she explained. "Responders are already on their way. Is anyone hurt?"

Steve watched the handful of guys still trying to keep Road-rager from losing his cool all over again. "Not yet," he said. "The dude in the rear-most car is kind of pissed."

The 911 Operator scoffed. "You kidding? I would be too. His rates 'bout to go through the roof."

Steve nodded. "Well, yeah."

"Sir, if nobody's hurt, please return to your vehicle," she advised. "Responders are on their way. The best thing to do is clear the area as much as possible so that they can get to the scene quicker."

"Okay," Steve said. He was still out of breath. "Bye," he said by habit alone. He hung up and stared at his cell phone for a moment, trying to understand why the screen was red. He looked again at the crash scene, as if wanting a second opinion that he should leave. Road-rage was still getting talked down by a few others, but otherwise, the situation seemed as calm as a three-car pile-up could be. He returned to his car.

Steve got back in behind the wheel and put on his seat belt. He cranked his car, only to startle himself by realizing it had been running the whole time. He still felt out of breath. He closed the sunroof instinctively and the insulated, sealed nature of his car weighed against him. In the car, he felt silence but didn't hear it. Instead, he heard the K-pop band playing along. The song, upbeat and lively, was totally the opposite of the chaos outside. Steve checked his mirrors, confirmed he had space, and carefully pulled back onto the road.

Once he was on the highway, he resumed speed. With the accident behind him, traffic was thin. He felt like he could finally breathe again and he set his cruise control. It was then that he realized he was humming to the music. He glanced in the passenger's seat and saw the CD jewel case and the model-looking band of five looking dramatically back at him.

"I mean, I'm not saying I suddenly know Korean but I know the refrain to Snow Dive," Steve told Morgan. In the attic space, he wore a huge smile, one that was every bit as relieved as it was enigmatic. "It's just so weird," he lamented happily. "Like, I didn't like this stuff. And now, it's all in my head."

"I think you found the missing piece," Morgan said as he sat across from Steve. "Context," he said more solidly when Steve remained confused. "Without context to the art – its creation, its consumption, maybe even both – without context, it's really just noise. Maybe pretty noise, but noise. The music you've been listening to, that so failed to move you, it isn't that it lacked quality; it lacked context."

"How do you give music context?" asked Steve.

"Context isn't given; it's found," Morgan explained. "Context is found by doing. And in order to do that, to find context, you have to put yourself into a chance for context to occur. As we get older, it gets a bit harder to find context because context can be so tricky. Context needs some gravity to it, and as we get older, we have so much more to compare it to. But a three-car pile-up is pretty dramatic, and thus the song has a context to it."

Steve nodded slowly. "Put myself in the chance for context to occur."

Morgan gave a slightly sarcastic wince. "There's probably a better way to phrase that."

"Probably," agreed Steve. "But still, I get it."

"Then go get it," Morgan encouraged him.

Steve Borden pinched the bridge of his nose as electronic dance music battered his ears. At the bar of the dance club, he stirred his soda and considered the purpose of existence, both for himself and the tiny straw he used to create bubbles in his drink. The dark brown refreshment seemed to absorb the light coming off the neon runners of the bar and the black light bulbs lighting the vibrant wall's graffiti-like decorations.

Steve checked to his left and saw a line of club goers. Ravers. Techno-goths. EDM fans. Vinyl and leather. Chains and piercings. He checked to his right and saw more of the same. Small gaggles of people, clustered together. Drinking. Talking. Half-dancing, like they were warming up for the dance floor at the far end of the club.

Steve checked on the bartender. A woman in a surprisingly subdued black tank top and jeans, she had hearing-protecting ear plugs hidden by her partial afro. She was dumping ice into the chiller, an intense look on her face like she was juggling a to-do list well over a dozen items long.

Steve turned back and looked into the club as a whole, listening to the throbbing pulse of the dance music. He focused on the beats, finding the rhythm to it. Letting it be noise, he let its energy drive him to his feet and then towards the dance floor. If only his dancing, he would find something to make this music unique in his life.

Made in the USA
Columbia, SC
29 December 2018